W9-BRW-790

Jericho: Dreams, Ruins, Phantoms

Jericho

Dreams, Ruins, Phantoms

Robert Ruby

Henry Holt and Company
New York

Henry Holt and Company, Inc.
Publishers since 1866
115 West 18th Street
New York, New York 10011

Henry Holt® is a registered
trademark of Henry Holt and Company, Inc.

Published in Canada by Fitzhenry & Whiteside Ltd.,
195 Allstate Parkway, Markham, Ontario L3R 4T8.

Library of Congress Cataloging-in-Publication Data
Ruby, Robert (Robert Steven)
Jericho: dreams, ruins, phantoms/by Robert Ruby.—1st ed.
p. cm.
Includes bibliographical references and index.
1. Jericho—Description and travel. 2. Jericho—Antiquities.
3. Excavations (Archaeology)—West Bank—Jericho.
4. Warren, Charles, Sir, 1840–1927—Journeys—West Bank—Jericho.
5. Ruby, Robert (Robert Steven)—Journeys—West Bank—Jericho.
I. Title.
DS110.J4R83 1995 94–33933
933—dc20 CIP

ISBN 0-8050-2799-8

Henry Holt books are available for special promotions
and premiums. For details contact: Director, Special Markets.

First Edition—1995

Designed by Betty Lew
Maps by Ann Rebecca Feild

Printed in the United States of America
All first editions are printed on acid-free paper. ∞

1 3 5 7 9 10 8 6 4 2

To Holly

Contents

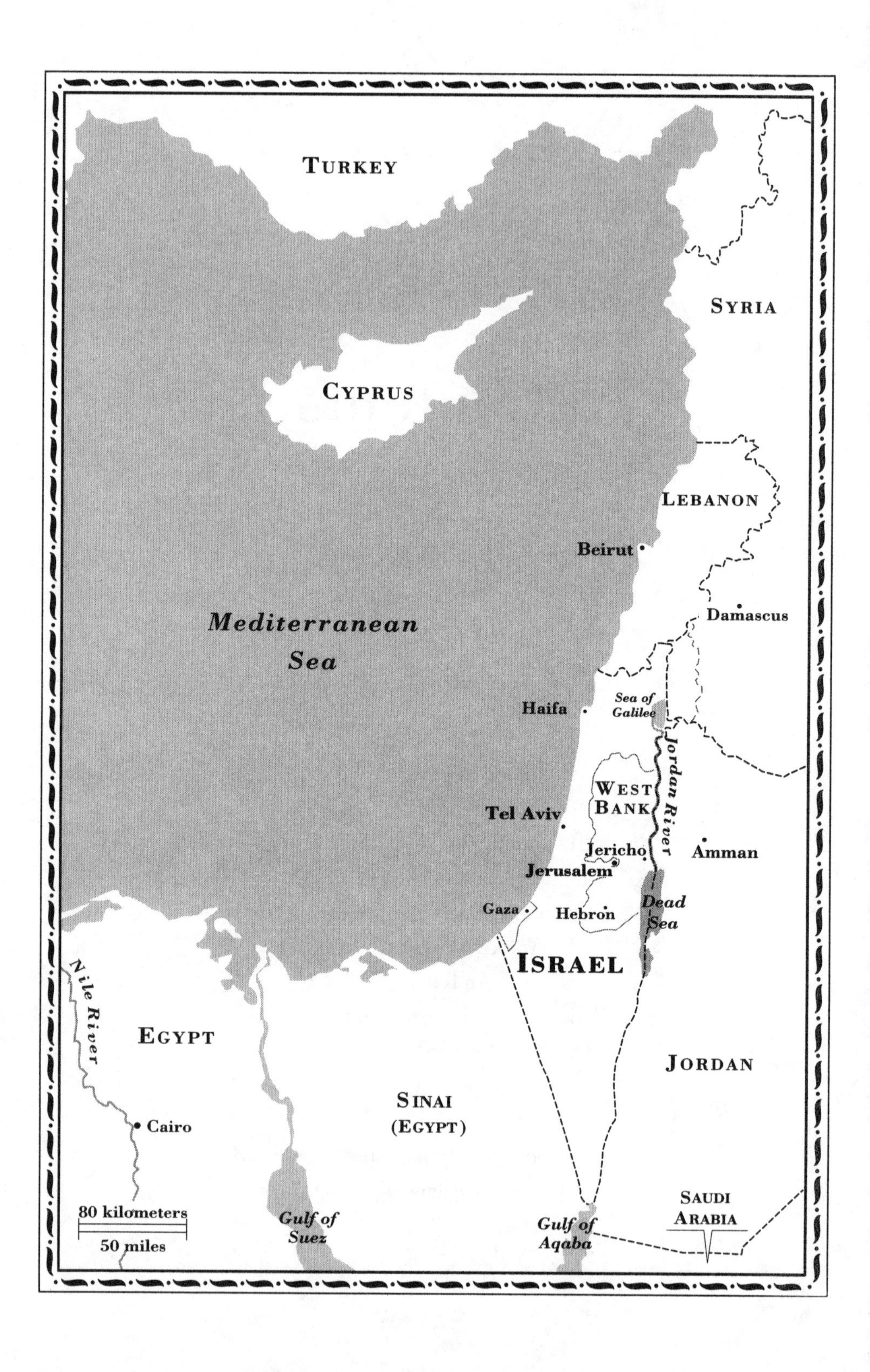
TURKEY
SYRIA
CYPRUS
LEBANON
Beirut
Damascus
Mediterranean
Sea
Haifa
Sea of
Galilee
Jordan River
WEST
BANK
Tel Aviv
Jericho
Amman
Jerusalem
Gaza
Hebron
Dead
Sea
ISRAEL
Nile River
EGYPT
JORDAN
SINAI
(EGYPT)
Cairo
SAUDI
ARABIA
80 kilometers
50 miles
Gulf of
Suez
Gulf of
Aqaba

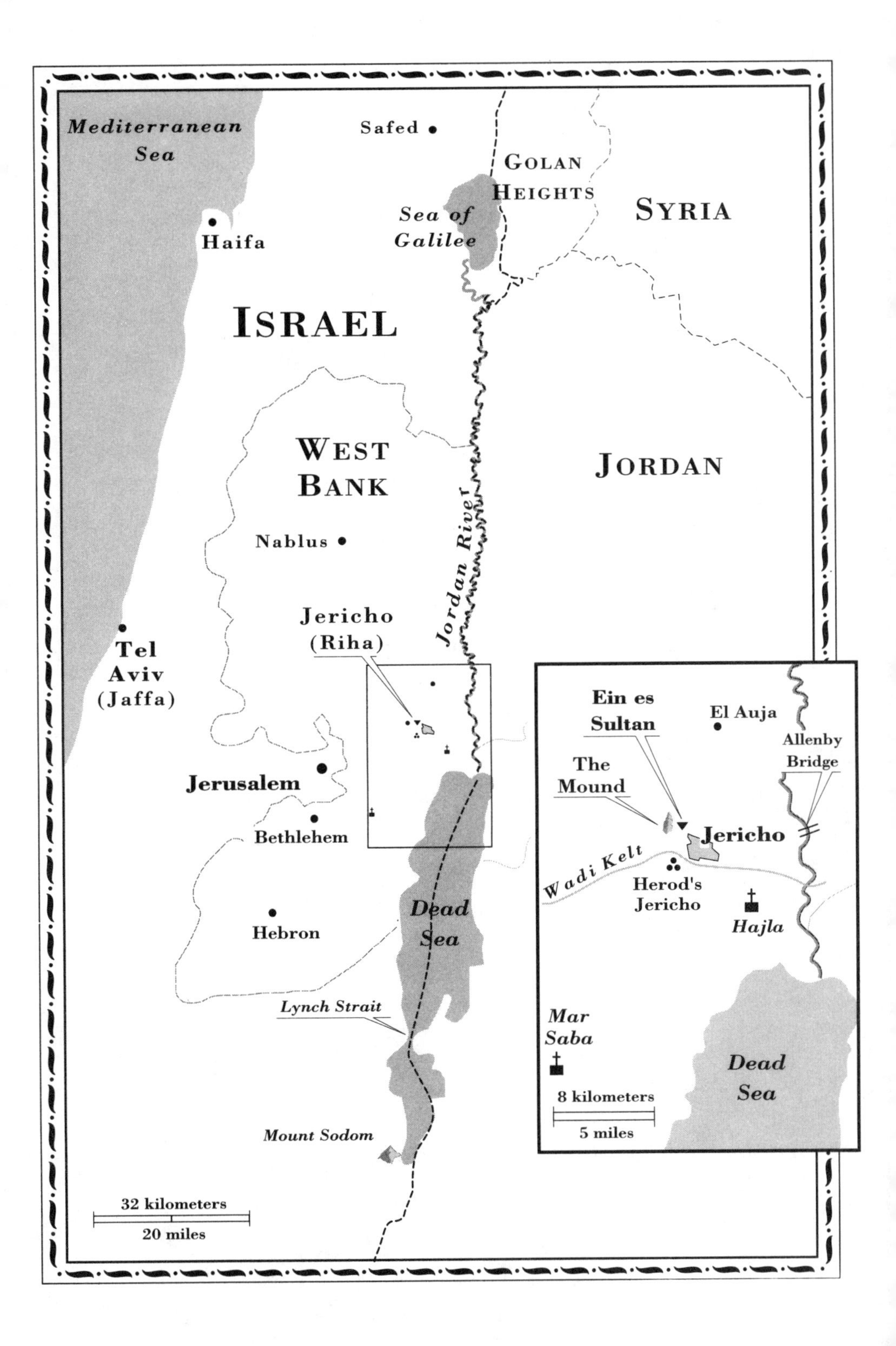
Mediterranean Sea
Safed
Golan Heights
Syria
Sea of Galilee
Haifa
Israel
West Bank
Jordan
Jordan River
Nablus
Jericho (Riha)
Tel Aviv (Jaffa)
Jerusalem
Bethlehem
Hebron
Dead Sea
Lynch Strait
Mount Sodom
32 kilometers
20 miles
Ein es Sultan
El Auja
Allenby Bridge
The Mound
Jericho
Wadi Kelt
Herod's Jericho
Hajla
Mar Saba
Dead Sea
8 kilometers
5 miles

Jericho: Dreams, Ruins, Phantoms

Are you not dreaming of the unknown beautiful world that exists up there;—beautiful, as heaven is beautiful, because you know nothing of the reality? If you make your way up there and back to-morrow, and find out all about it, do you mean to say that it will be as beautiful to you when you come back?

Anthony Trollope, *Can You Forgive Her?*

Stony mountains & stony plains; stony torrents & stony roads; stony walls & stony fields, stony houses & stony tombs; stony eyes & stony hearts.

Herman Melville, *Journals*

I

Winter Castle

Almost everything was low and small-scale and the color of the sandy landscape, and remains so. There were irrigated pockets of green—palm trees and thorn bush—but Jericho was mostly flat bare earth, like migrant land from an African drought. In the extreme dryness, even the vegetation appeared to be a species of dust.

Charles Warren was new to Jericho and to Palestine; and Palestine was a land famous, revered, and unkempt. Lieutenant Warren, of Her Britannic Majesty's Royal Engineers, had arrived in February 1867 on a mission that seemed noble—to explore the city of Jerusalem foot by foot, above and below ground, to find traces of it from the days of the Bible. Disputes with authorities consumed much of his time, and he wanted a respite from the wintry rain. By April he was sufficiently frustrated to give up on Jerusalem, at least temporarily, and organize a trip to Jericho.

It lay at the bottom of a malarial valley about to turn suffocatingly hot. Nothing had the energy to rise above the dun-colored flatness except a lumpy earthen mound—a stunted mountain like half-baked bread, long and brown.

Everyone of course had heard of Jericho. Not many people had willingly traveled there, whether Arab or Westerner. Still fewer of the Westerners could reconcile their expectations, all that they had imagined, with what they found upon arriving. Magic name, but a dismal settlement. In Charles Warren's day it was the most benighted place in a backwater slice of the Ottoman Empire. The village was isolated and it had nothing but the ramshackle, the small, the coarse: a scattering of hovels, a place always hot. The inhabitants were said to be mentally dull, a characteristic travelers attributed to the great heat, and also leering and uncontrollably licentious. There was nothing else to remark upon except the lumpen mound—that long, brown loaf—rising next to a freshwater spring. One of Warren's fellow officers had recently determined the valley in which Jericho lay to be the lowest place on the surface of the earth. You could sink no lower than Jericho or the Dead Sea. Odorous, obscured by haze, the Dead Sea was six miles to the south; at the edge of that lake, the Jordan River valley was 1,346 feet below sea level.

Warren was a draftsman, gunnery expert, tunneler par excellence, and anxious to work. On a bright April morning he stood near that large rounded mound. He was gifted with a sense of the practical and was not without ambition. Pick raised in the air, he was about to find another, older Jericho. A connection between the distant human past and the odd, stunted mountain was about to be made.

Warren prided himself on being an officer, not an archaeologist. In 1867 archaeology was known, to the extent it was known at all, as an endeavor largely indistinguishable from digging a pit. It had little to do with the orderly or precise. But Warren uncovered some of the secrets of the mound and some of the general principles of the semi-science that did not yet exist—which is remarkable. He correctly guessed that the remains of another settlement were in the mound. He suggested they were recoverable.

His conclusions were less obvious in the mid–nineteenth century than they sound at the end of the twentieth. Warren had a limited understanding of what he saw and was unsure how the actual work should be performed. If his field had been medicine, his suggestion would have been that important diagnostic uses might be found for a penetrating ray; his advice would be that someone more learned and less pressed conduct the search for it. Nonetheless, he realized he had found a promising place to look: there, next to the freshwater spring.

Jericho was both a place and a hieroglyph, the deus ex machina of an action-filled story in the Bible. In Warren's day the village consisted of perhaps a dozen huts. The mound was where villagers went to obtain stones for repair of the huts or the making of a fence. A century-plus later, archaeologists are still attempting to reconstruct the history imperfectly preserved there. There is no shortage of contradictory theories. You can read the flat hot land in different ways. An oasis, a pocket hell, crossroads, route to nowhere. But freeze Warren there, pick suspended in the air. The digging is yet to begin. For Warren, Jericho was a spare-time excursion. Jerusalem was the site of the work he was assigned to do and also the source of his early fame. He wandered to Jericho as an escape, and I begin with him because he led me to make the same trip to the overheated, earthen basement of the world.

Like everyone else, I had heard of Jericho. The city is part of the basic curriculum of every Sunday school. My mother was the Sunday school principal when I was growing up, so I was fated to have nearly perfect attendance year after year. I heard the story at least once in every grade. I never tired of it. Clever, heroic Joshua, leader of the wandering Israelites, sending spies across the Jordan River to the city; Joshua leading his men around and around the city walls; the blare of trumpets on the seventh lap; the walls tumbling down. It was a conquest a child could understand. Even a child could have led it, for surmounting the walls had required no weapons or feats of athleticism. All the many books purporting to show the city as Joshua found it seemed to be inspired by a child's mind.

A friend once found for me a nineteenth-century biblical picture book: it was a handsome, rare volume that had as its centerfold a hand-colored drawing of the Jordan Valley. The panorama obeyed all the conventions. In that book Jericho was a metropolis of castles protected by crenellated walls sprouting towers and following a perfectly circular course—Jericho as Mont-Saint-Michel. To the east the Jordan River flowed as a thin blue line that was perfectly straight. To the north a small puddle of blue represented the Sea of Galilee. Jerusalem was a larger hill of fairy-tale castles, lying across a mountain range to the west. The Dead Sea spilled off the southern edge of the page, and the hills leading up to its shore were a rich, fertile green.

No one warned me about the heat. The temperature was more than a hundred degrees when I went for a first visit. Summer was not for another month. Jeff was a newspaper correspondent writing about the Middle East and living in Jerusalem. I was a correspondent living in Paris and relying on his hospitality for part of a vacation.

We left Jerusalem in a tired Renault and drove down steep hills and past a sign marking sea level. The road continued downhill. Everyone's ears popped, so sudden and large was the change in altitude, as voluptuous hills gave way to desiccated plain. The car was packed with children and all the accessories for a day at what was grandly called the "winter house." Jeff and his wife, Anne, talked of it being heaven.

My view was partially obscured by having a bouncy five-year-old girl on my lap, and a thick layer of insects was smeared across the windshield. But we had arrived in Jericho. I saw weedy yards that surrounded flat-roofed houses made of stucco, and every house stood at a different angle to the road. The road was lined by low, crumbly walls, where a few dark-skinned men sat in small corners of shade. The cloudless sky was bleached to a flattening white; everything looked as if it had been frozen in the painful brightness of a camera flash. We saw donkeys nibbling at weeds and passed a line of fruit stands selling oranges and tomatoes. It was not the picture I remembered from Sunday school.

Nothing seemed to move, or to be capable of it. Jericho looked heatstroked and in deep sleep.

Jeff drove the car onto a gravelly path that had a steep drop to the left, where an irrigation pond was ringed by palm trees. A wall of white hills stood as a backdrop. He turned again, and we were on a narrow ledge between the pond and the craggy hills. The house, a small box of mud-brick covered by stucco, stood at the far end of the ledge. It overlooked the irrigation pond and a banana grove lower down the slope. The most important feature, as shown by where the children headed, was a big concrete tub adjoining the house and shaded by a pomelo tree. Part of the neighborhood's irrigation system, the tub was the estate's swimming pool—algae-filled but cool, and long enough to accommodate a half-dozen strokes by a child.

There was a long iron key that unlocked one of the three doors. A firm shove would always open the others. The house—the trim painted bright blue—ruled over the ledge like a castle. It was sunny in the front rooms, and in back were a dark kitchen, a toilet in need of fresh air, and a small loft. We sat outside with a view of the palms. Jericho was hot, buggy, lush.

When Jeff left the Middle East, his tour as a correspondent over, I was his successor. A fringe benefit was inheritance of the little stucco house. My castle, my buggy overheated kingdom.

I made the trip from Jerusalem to Jericho as often as I could. I lived in the area for five years during the sporadic violence that the Palestinians called the intifada. For most of that time, Jericho was a shelter from the turmoil. Most of the time, it was the town where almost nothing happened. It seemed becalmed. Or apolitical, addled by heat—no one could ever fully explain the quiet.

But then the changes began. Jericho became a headquarters for political experiments, and at least for a time a Palestinian capital. It was busier, though by no means a metropolis. By then I had learned of social experiments that had occurred there in the past. They were no less significant than those I was watching. They had begun in approximately 9000 B.C. and continued for a long, long time.

I kept driving into the valley, a thirty-minute trip from Jerusalem. On the outskirts of East Jerusalem, the Palestinian half of town, one or another young man would sometimes stand on the shoulder of one or another road, and gaze at me for what felt like a very long time, and throw a stone, shattering a window of the car. Except for the stones, the trip was always a comfort. I had never seen more beautiful desolation.

From the edge of East Jerusalem, the bare hills of the Judean desert were laid out for inspection like a fine carpet with a sensual pattern. A green coat of vegetation, as thin as a varnish, always appeared after the first winter rains. The sheep and goats consumed it by midspring. Their trails etched the hills, gave them the wrinkles of someone wise from great age. Closer to Jericho, the only danger in the trip came from herds of sheep idling in the road.

At first, all my attention was concentrated on the heat. I used the "winter house" mostly in summer, though no one really wanted to be in the valley then. But it was the time I had. Jericho would be fully awake by 7:00 A.M. but after midmorning would go back to sleep. The insects thrived. At the house I relied on the shade of the pomelo tree.

I learned of Charles Warren by reading about nineteenth-century explorers. They were my escape, like the trips to Jericho, from the calamitous news of the moment, and their stories were as stirring as the one of Joshua leading the Israelites. I found Warren's book *Underground Jerusalem,* which was published in 1876 and was the frankest and most entertaining of the several accounts he wrote about his travails. In *Underground Jerusalem* he almost never bragged and since by then the work was finished he made everything sound a jaunt. When I began to retrace his steps, they led me back to Jericho.

Warren set off into the relative unknown, demonstrated great resourcefulness, and sometimes acted bravely. He did not always realize he was in every sense breaking new ground. At this early point in his career, he was an imperialist of the least offensive sort. There was no planting of foreign flags or energetic pillaging. He was in Palestine in part for the glory of Great Britain but mainly for himself, to have more fun than he could foresee having as an officer stationed at home. He wanted the luxury of working on his own; in Palestine he had it.

He introduced me, so to speak, to Charles Tyrwhitt Drake and to Claude Conder, both of whom he inspired. They were several years younger and would prove no less adventuresome. When I left Warren, I wandered through the Jordan Valley with Drake and Conder. Conder was joined later by Horatio Herbert Kitchener, who was at the beginning of a career that would make him Britain's most famous officer, though perhaps not its most likable. The lives of these men crossed and recrossed: for a generation, the explorers were held to be *the* experts on Arabs and Jews, and on what might become of Palestine. I came to understand them better through the letters they sent to their families and to the organization that had dispatched them to the Middle

East. While in their twenties, they were obsessed by money or terribly anxious about love or wanted at any cost to make a "name." When they reached Jericho and the Dead Sea, they became desperately afraid of falling ill.

They traveled together for years at a time. They were not saintly and, I suspect, not easy companions. They were ferociously ambitious. What they wanted most was fame. They traveled to Palestine for the sake of their careers and shared an enormous capacity for jealousy, especially when any one of them seemed a step ahead of the rest. But unlike the white men who explored Africa, or those who traversed the remotest parts of Afghanistan or Persia, they expected no commercial reward and received none. And though this was not necessarily what they wished, no territory changed hands.

Charles Warren and his successors explored territory with which every reader of the Bible could claim general familiarity. But the actual country was largely unknown. Palestine was only slightly less foreign than the remotest African river basin; no one had yet closely examined the landscape or fully mapped it. Warren's sponsors hoped he would find artifacts to confirm the words of the Bible and in that way show the land and the book to be perfect reflections of each other. The explorers had the mission of finding ancient roads, the battlefields known from Scripture, inscriptions, and ancient cities—like the castled Jericho of the picture book.

My inherited estate was a fifteen-minute walk from Warren's old campsite. He had camped at the freshwater spring alongside the odd earthen mound. Many people had come there before him, during more centuries than Warren might have believed. After his time, people searched again for remnants of the city described by Joshua, sought fame there, in some cases encountered disaster, occasionally solved mysteries about the long history of Jericho and the valley, in the process discovered others, and made Jericho something more than the subject of a hand-colored panorama or the topic of a Sunday school class. They made this ancient place modern and real.

Gradually, I expanded my horizon beyond my little stucco house. I could see Warren's campsite and, straight ahead of me, the high mound baking on the rocky plain.

Charles Warren had recently turned twenty-seven. He was the son of an army general who had gained fame by fighting hand to hand in China with a bayonet and living to tell the story. The younger Warren was a survivor of Britain's Royal Military Academy at Woolwich. One braved Woolwich because it was the only gateway for would-be officers of the Royal Engineers. They were the logistical experts for empire building. Royal Engineers mapped territory that was either conquered or about to be; had fought at Bunker Hill in Massachusetts in 1775; and in 1814 had set fire to the White House and the Capitol. They designed fortifications, erected bridges, and supervised the building of whatever else an officer demanded. Part of their motto was *Ubique*—Everywhere.

But Woolwich was a place of notorious difficulty, both academic and social. Combine young men, officially approved hazing, and a rigid sense of class, and you have Woolwich. You have young men and mean-spirited games. The unofficial curriculum gave seniors the right to strike the junior cadets with belts and bats. So they did. A few years after Warren graduated, the cadets mutinied against conditions, then mutinied a second time.

In his mid-twenties, Warren was bearded and reedy and had a large squarish face. He had spent seven years in the British colony of Gibraltar surveying the territory, supervising the construction of artillery batteries, and becoming all too familiar with the great rock. Now, with his wife, he was returning to Britain to take up a new assignment of the sort to break an adventuresome man's heart. The Royal Engineers were to make him an assistant instructor in surveying.

Then came a request for a volunteer.

It was made by an organization barely out of diapers, a child noisily proclaiming its existence but largely helpless. Its only real asset in 1867 was an impressive-sounding name: the Palestine Exploration Fund.

Behind the name was, at first, the enthusiasm of an English merchant who had enriched himself through an indigo factory in India. He was James Fergusson. He had retired at a young age thanks to his wealth, and wrote at great length about architecture, and seemed not particularly bothered by the poor response to his books. It was certain that he didn't need the income, and he had well-armored pride. Fergusson said, perhaps not apocryphally, that four copies were sold of the book he considered his best.

He helped make exploration of Palestine a fashionable topic. In articles and in drawing rooms, Fergusson promoted unconventional theories—*eccentric* is not too strong a word—about the geography of biblical Jerusalem. A pet theory was that the tomb of Jesus was to be found under the Dome of the Rock, one of the mosques on the Temple Mount, which was the enormous stone platform where the Jewish Temple had stood. He had no less distinctive ideas about the past course of the walls that surrounded the city.

George Grove shared Fergusson's enthusiasm. As friends, they encouraged each other to believe they were on the side of intellectual and social improvement. Grove's career had taken him from avocation to avocation, and most recently to an intense fascination with Palestine. Trained as an engineer, he had designed lighthouses; was an amateur scholar of the Bible; and wrote the weekly program notes for music concerts performed at London's Crystal Palace, where he was the administrator. He would become best known as the progenitor of the bible for musicologists, the *Grove Dictionary of Music and Musicians.*

Other friends were consulted—financiers, members of Parliament, eminent clergymen. Then came the exploits in Palestine by an officer of the Royal Engineers.

Captain Charles Wilson was the officer. He surveyed the city of Jerusalem, a job the War Office had offered in 1864 after a private benefactress volunteered to pay the cost. Miss Angela Burdett-Coutts had been distressed to learn of the terrible state of Jerusalem's water supply, which was delivered via an infamously bad network of open pools and never-cleaned cisterns. Infested with worms, polluted by centuries' worth of offal, it contributed mightily to the abysmal health of the city's inhabitants. Miss Burdett-Coutts was informed that the first step toward making improvements was a municipal survey made to the high standards used for London or Manchester. She pledged five hundred pounds.

"I was generally considered to be going on a fool's errand," Charles Wilson reflected later, knowing that some of his colleagues had rejected the assignment. The War Office had stipulated that the officer in charge would have to pay his own expenses.

Wilson made the first accurate map of the city—a work of startling precision. It is clear, finely detailed, in its own severe way as beautiful as the monuments he painstakingly measured and sketched.

"I find much less difficulty than I expected in getting about to different places," he reported when the mission was under way, "and from working quietly at first, have established a sort of right to go wherever I like, and the inhabitants are now quite accustomed to seeing my head suddenly appearing out of wells and cisterns." At the request of his superiors, he found time to calculate a precise figure for the elevation of the Dead Sea.

In London, George Grove was sufficiently excited to address a letter to the *Times* suggesting additional subjects for Wilson to investigate. And showed his own great skill at gathering backers for his latest avocation. What Britain needed, Grove told each of his contacts, was an organization devoted to the exploration of the Holy Land. A clearinghouse for information. Information gathered scientifically. Thus, in May 1865, the birth of the Palestine Exploration Fund.

Its first expedition was led by Wilson. In November 1865, he took a small party to Beirut and began a four-month journey to the Sea of Galilee, to Nazareth, and from there along the rocky spine of the country between Nablus and Jerusalem, to map the countryside. Progress was slowed when villagers stole a tent; on another occasion they attempted to loot the camp. Since Bedouin were firing at each other from opposite banks of the Jordan, Wilson avoided the area near Jericho. When the PEF ran out of money, he returned home.

George Grove drew encouragement from the results, incomplete though they were. For the Palestine Exploration Fund had made itself known. Now, his friend James Fergusson wanted someone to dig up parts of Jerusalem to prove his odd theories right about the city's topography. Being rich, he was indulged rather than regarded as a crank. The PEF sought a volunteer.

Charles Warren stepped forward from the Royal Engineers.

His mission was not the usual nineteenth-century search for trade routes or for new colonies, though it was no less imperial. The Palestine

Exploration Fund wanted geographic knowledge that might have spiritual uses. The War Office approved of this—geographic findings might also prove useful in politics and for an army. Search the Holy Land for physical remains of the places and events described in the Bible—so went the thinking in London—and you prove your devotion to all things godly. You could also ready a claim to that territory should the weakness of the Ottoman Empire ever prove fatal. You might also embarrass other God-fearing, imperial powers for failing to show devotion equal to your own. To lend her prestige to the new enterprise, Queen Victoria gave the PEF a contribution of one hundred fifty pounds.

The night before Charles Warren was to leave for Palestine, Grove met with him in London at the Charing Cross Hotel. Warren received a check for three hundred pounds. He was told to go forth and prosper. His benefactor neglected to tell him that the money just handed over had emptied the PEF's treasury.

Warren sailed into the port of Jaffa in February 1867. Three corporals had joined him. His charge was to excavate as much of Jerusalem as Ottoman authorities could be wheedled to allow. No one in London doubted that Jerusalem was the best place for him to explore. In the Old Testament, it was the city God considered holiest. "To us of the Palestine Fund," George Grove liked to tell the organization's supporters, "Jerusalem is really and strictly what it was believed to be in the Middle Ages—the center of the world."

The customs officers in Jaffa waved through Warren's boxes of picks and crowbars but were suspicious of other items. A sextant was initially determined to be a weapon. Assurances were given that a sextant could not be loaded or fired. Approved. A box containing barometers went missing somewhere between England and Palestine. Warren's telegram inquiring as to the whereabouts of the box was garbled to say "Boy not arrived, make inquiries." So more time lost.

Warren and the three corporals loaded the boxes of tools onto hired mules and horses. The expeditionary force rode to Jerusalem against a gale that kept blowing the mules off their feet.

In Jerusalem, Warren subjected himself to rounds of meetings with the many dignitaries. There were sheikhs, pashas, effendis; he visited patriarchs, bishops and rabbis, and the foreign consuls. All were assured of his good intentions. He wanted to offend no one's religion, he said, and no one's authority.

The meetings served to fill the time while he waited for a firman—the imperial letter from Constantinople granting him permission to begin work. Warren was inexperienced in dealings with Turkish officialdom and, in these circumstances, his innocence was a blessing.

The Ottoman Empire was a Great Power visibly losing strength. Judged by the maps, the domain of the sultans was impressively vast: at the beginning of the nineteenth century it took in the Balkans, including Greece; Egypt, with most of the rest of North Africa; a large portion of the Caucasus; Syria; Lebanon; Palestine; and, of course, Turkey. But the empire was undergoing something akin to radioactive decay. Parts were breaking away from an unstable center and heading off onto independent paths.

For Westerners the empire seemed wholly foreign. It was Muslim, not Christian. Not even Western. And for that reason was found exotic, sensual, an attractive stranger, one regarded as half-undressed. The image conveyed by painters (Delacroix, Ingres) and writers (Flaubert, du Camp) was of a voluptuous woman desiring seduction—beckoning and defenseless, wanting to be rescued.

Other Great Powers, tempted by the image, invited themselves into Ottoman territories to ransack them. You attacked the Ottomans because they were presumed to be weak, and they became the surrogate for some other enemy you dared not attack directly. So it was with Napoleon. In 1798, about seventy years before the adventures of Charles Warren, he sailed to Egypt with fifty-five thousand soldiers and sailors, to challenge Britain by challenging the sultan. You win Egypt, then you strangle trade routes to British India.

Napoleon overthrew the authorities in Egypt and led part of his army into Palestine. But he had no further luck. A British fleet destroyed the French battleships anchored off the Egyptian coast, and a combined British-Turkish force defeated Napoleon's land army at Acre, on the coast of Palestine. Britain became involved less as a show of respect for the sultan than in acknowledgment of the sultan's inability to safeguard British interests. Plus, common sense called for Britain to prevent a rival from gorging itself on territory that might be parceled out later for everyone. Every foreign minister in Europe half hoped, half feared the fruit of the Ottoman Empire would just fall off the rotting tree. Hoped the tastiest bits would fall toward his own hand. Feared, of course, a rival would make the catch.

Some of the turmoil was internal. After Napoleon's forced departure, the sultans still lacked real control over Egypt or Palestine. Bedouin ruled the desert, and the appointed governors in the towns exercised less authority than the leaders of local clans. There was, for example, the violent career of Abd al-Rahman in the city of Hebron. In 1834, he murdered the Ottoman governor. Authorities responded by naming al-Rahman tax collector, for lack of any other means to control him. It gave him license to pillage, and he did so. Later, he intimidated two other governors into resigning. The Ottomans then promoted al-Rahman to the post of Inspector.

In Egypt, control passed into the hands of an Albanian named Muhammad Ali. He professed loyalty to the sultan but ran the country as he liked and eventually threatened the government in Constantinople. In the meantime, he installed an adopted son, Ibrahim Pasha, as ruler of Palestine and Syria.

Ibrahim Pasha was a reformer and was ruthless. The judicial branch of his government in Palestine was a buffalo-hide whip. He sent an army to fight the Bedouin marauding in the desert until the power of the Bedouin was crushed. Farmers throughout the area were taxed; men were drafted; the traditional leadership, composed of landowning families and religious judges, was ignored. Each of these groups had reason to wish Ibrahim Pasha harm.

A revolt broke out against him in 1840. It was winter. Ibrahim Pasha, leading an army of forty thousand men, marched from Damascus into the mountains east of the Jordan. He was in Bedouin country, and the Bedouin took their revenge. Half the army died in three days. Snow and cold winds killed many of those who managed to survive the Bedouin. Others drowned in the swollen Jordan while trying to reach Jericho. Rather than wait for the pillaging to begin, everyone in Jericho fled. Ibrahim Pasha, finding no food, razed the village. After several more disasters, the remnants of his army escaped into Egypt. And once again the sultan ruled Palestine.

A list of the empire's wars is a little ditty of place-names. Revolts sprang up in Serbia, in Greece, again in Serbia, in the deserts of Arabia. The nucleus was decaying and everyone watched the disintegration. But no one in the West wished for a total, immediate collapse. Britain and France looked pleadingly to the Ottoman Empire to block another rival, Russia—to prevent Russia from expanding toward the Mediterranean, and to keep it out of the Balkans.

That was the Eastern Question: How does one control the Russians? It had the same dull, crushing weight as the next century's identical question about the Soviets. And in the endless parliamentary debates the answer to the question never changed. If one sought a buffer against the Russians, the Ottoman Empire was the only candidate.

For the Turks that was not a great honor. The Sublime Porte, as the government was known, found itself with bewildering problems not of its making. The outsiders meddled. Adjusted the buffer just so, weakened it to accommodate their own interests. In 1853 France and Russia, each claiming to be the protector of the empire's Christians, argued over control of Christian shrines in Jerusalem and, through no real fault of the sultan, failed to reach a compromise. So began the Crimean War. France, Britain, and the Ottoman Empire fought Russia, and the Ottoman side won. But having borrowed enormous sums to field its army, the empire had impoverished itself.

By the time Charles Warren arrived, Palestine was notably poor. It was not lawless, and the Sublime Porte had recently instituted significant reforms, but no one—not even the sultan's ministers—considered the territory well governed. Almost everything outside of Jerusalem was regarded as barren, as after a sandstorm. No one felt at peace: Muslims and Christians feared each other, with reason. In the countryside, there was no contact with authority except when the tax collector arrived to confiscate crops or when soldiers impressed a son to fight in one of the empire's distant wars. The Jordan Valley was even poorer, hostage to the raiding Bedouin.

One of the few powers left to the Sublime Porte was an exquisitely refined policy of delay. There was no safer, surer form of control to exercise over a Westerner than to make him wait—for an audience, for a firman. Not unrelated to the delays was the breathtaking corruption.

At about this time, the word *baksheesh* entered the English language. The word had made its way from Persian into Arabic and Turkish like a virus and whoever controlled Palestine became infected. *Baksheesh* was tip. Bribe. Foreign travelers regarded the term with the alarm ordinarily reserved for a serious illness. It had a foul odor; it evoked everything that was in some way irregular, especially when hissed by a guide persistently tugging at your sleeve. It always carried a hint of the underhanded, the dark. Baksheesh is what every servant—the peasant renting you a mule, the governor presiding in his citadel—expected from a stranger.

The practice became strictly reflex, like a carnivorous flower. Delicately place a bribe in a hand, and the hand closed. After time for digestion and recomposure, the requested service—delivery of a firman, the release of a prisoner—might be forthcoming.

Landowners bribed tax collectors for tax relief. Tax collectors bribed pashas for the lucrative right to collect the taxes. Pashas, to obtain and keep their governorships, generously bribed their patrons in Constantinople. The worst off were inhabitants of isolated villages, like Jericho. A tax collector would legally take up to half the year's crop but then, for baksheesh, demand more. Soldiers arrived to demand payment for themselves. Bedouin arrived to demand feed for their animals. If the farmer were lucky, he could meet the needs of his family until the next harvest.

In the eyes of George Grove, Charles Warren was thus engaged in a rescue mission. He was to find and closely examine sites of biblical interest in Jerusalem to save them from venal misuse by the Muslim Turks. The PEF wanted him to focus his work on the structures atop the Temple Mount.

Warren was warmly received in his rounds of meetings. The authorities generally prohibited excavations. But since the Crimean War the rules had been eased, a measure of thanks to the empire's Christian allies. The local governor generously gave him permission to begin his explorations, though the firman from the Sublime Porte was still unseen. Warren accepted a restriction that he stay away from the Temple Mount at least temporarily. The Royal Engineers began to dig near the city walls, and the honeymoon lasted three days.

On the fourth day soldiers demanded Warren stop his strange work. The governor was this time less accommodating. He suggested Warren do nothing more until the firman arrived. When it did, it carried bad news. The firman was vague in promising cooperation but precise in prohibiting work at any site holy to Muslims or Christians. That included almost everything of interest to Warren.

To console him, a Turkish officer confided that Muslim traditions already offered a full description of everything to be discovered underground. Everyone knew, the officer said, that the stones of the Temple Mount lay atop the leaves of a giant subterranean palm tree. The roots of the tree were the source of the world's rivers. So any attempt to excavate risked calamity.

"Extremely civil," Warren said of him.

I found Warren unflappable in every trying situation, and he always cast whatever he wanted as the world's natural order. Diplomatic, seemingly calm, he also was intimidating and very stubborn. *Difficult* was the word his critics used. He never abandoned the idea that he knew best, an energetic adult forever disciplining a childish world. Yet he was imaginative, never less than confident. Of all the Royal Engineers to work for the PEF, Warren was the one whose company a person in grave danger would want most.

Warren had a talent for bending rules. For doing so, he usually won praise. When he volunteered to excavate in Jerusalem, he was relatively young, flexible, and expectant that the world would be no less bendable. When the disappointing firman arrived from Constantinople, he seemed instinctively to know what to do. He served his employers by drawing on hitherto unrevealed resources of deceit.

As written, the firman prohibited Warren from performing his assigned tasks. Nothing in the firman, though, required him to show the document to anyone else. His rules of conduct were adjusted accordingly. Have firman, resume work. Radiate confidence. If challenged, calmly reply that the firman has arrived. However, don't let anyone read it.

Warren hired workmen. The excavations resumed. He and the corporals supervised the digging of vertical shafts that began a respectful distance from the walls surrounding the Temple Mount. Some feet down, the shafts changed orientation from the vertical to the horizontal. Without entering the tunnels, who would know? No one bothered to look. Out of sight of authorities the workmen tunneled to the Temple Mount.

Warren was at the same time making excursions out of the city. There was a whole country he had never seen. With several companions he traveled in the hill country between Jerusalem and Bethlehem to observe the Bedouin. It was a countryside of stones and improbably steep paths. When a mixup left Warren on his own, he invited himself into a Bedouin camp to spend the night.

Theirs was a different culture, as foreign to Jerusalem's as the ways of that city were foreign to London's. Warren received the overwhelming hospitality that Bedouin reserved for total strangers. He communicated he was far too hungry to wait for the butchering of a goat in his honor. Instead there would be the junior feast. Sign language was the lingua franca. The lieutenant equipped himself with three pancakes of bread to serve as napkin, plate, and spoon. To signal his readiness to begin, he rolled up his sleeves. A goat milk aperitif preceded an omelette. A caloric series of goat milk entrées followed. He dined on sour goat milk, curdled milk, pressed curds, sour butter, curd cheese, a dessert of goat junket (sweetened milk served in goat intestines), and coffee heated in a goat-dung fire. He retired to the goatskin tent reserved for guests and lay under a goat-hair quilt. Sharing it were many fleas. Their feast that night was Warren.

A trip to Jericho was always a risky undertaking. The Bedouin could be unwelcoming. You might be stripped of literally everything, to wander home dazed and naked. The descent from Jerusalem (and the more difficult return) became associated with misadventure, a tradition never captured better than in the travelogue written by Felix Fabri, a Dominican priest from the German city of Ulm.

Fabri visited Palestine twice during the 1480s. It was the era of the Marmelukes, who had captured the last stronghold of the Crusaders at the end of the thirteenth century; thirty years after Fabri's journeys, the Marmelukes would be swept away by the Ottomans.

Until Fabri, pilgrim literature is a dreary genre in which the travelers are interested more in promoting religious feeling than in describing what they see. They traveled from shrine to shrine, it has been said of them, "with their eyes closed." They rarely offered a word about the countryside. One holy site was "of wondrous beauty" and so was the next, leaving much to the imagination. Fabri was a daring innovator because he discarded the usual tone of censorious piety. For him there was faith and there was also what you could see for yourself. He found some of his priestly companions to be rogues. To his fellow travelers' reports of miracles, he expressed a polite skepticism. His response to hard-to-believe claims was always the same: "A sensible man must decide for himself."

On the first of his two trips, Fabri sailed on a Venetian vessel with a party of Frenchmen. Having reached Palestine, the captain accompanied his passengers to Jerusalem, where they argued for a full day over whether to travel into the Jordan Valley. The captain was opposed on grounds of safety. The pilgrims threatened to persuade France to declare war against Venice. The captain compromised by staying in Jerusalem and letting the pilgrims make the trip at their own risk.

Some surely wondered if they had made a terrible mistake. A pilgrim was excommunicated by a priest over the nonecclesiastical matter of who got to ride a particular ass. (Later, the excommunication was reversed.) Guides were found stealing the pilgrims' food. At the Jordan, pilgrims realized they could not swim. Some swore that one hour of bathing in the river would make a pilgrim one hour younger. A sensible man would have to decide for himself. There were hikes along vertiginous trails in the Judean hills; Fabri feared he would fall to his death. By the time they reached Jericho, the pilgrims were hungry and tired.

They did not so much as stop but made a forced march straight through the village. Instead of bread and water for refreshment, they found, Fabri wrote, "the bread of anguish and the water of tribulation." Guides tried to hurry everyone in order to avoid having to pay a toll. The villagers did everything possible to collect it. While women and children threw stones at the pilgrims, the local menfolk rushed to block the road and sought to pull the guards off their horses.

> There was such a disturbance that by the running to and fro of men and beasts the dust was stirred up from the

> ground so thickly that it seemed as though Jericho were wrapped in a dark cloud. . . . So we came forth from Jericho not only empty but also beaten and disordered whereat many of the knights were moved to wrath, and wished that fire might come down from heaven and consume Jericho and all who dwelt therein.

The Jordan, too, inspired a voluminous literature of disappointment.

One or two miles east of the village you came to the water, a deep wound in white bare land. The river made a curiously long passage through its own short valley. From the Sea of Galilee to the Dead Sea, in a straight line, was sixty-five miles; by river, the distance was approximately 135 miles, but rowing that length of the river was an undertaking that killed most of the people who tried it. The Jordan twisted and was shallow so that a boat bounced from shore to rock. There was also the heat and the Bedouin.

In its last miles the river was not easy even to see unless you were actually in it. The valley had the form of a staircase, the river as the bottommost step and almost hidden by the steps above it. The plain on which Jericho stood was, in Arabic, the *ghor* (the depression). About a hundred feet lower was the *zhor* (the thicket). In the *zhor* were tangles of reeds and thorns and the turnings of the river. Early in the twentieth century leopards and wild boar still lived among the reeds.

In the Old Testament, the Jordan is the last physical barrier separating the Israelites from the Promised Land. In the New Testament, the water is said to purify. The Jordan was held to separate the godly from the profane and to be a zone of the miraculous. To go beyond the Jordan, metaphorically, is to enter another existence. That is weighty symbolism to keep afloat in a river that in winter and spring is small and muddy and during the rainless summer and autumn is still muddy and smaller.

"I should never advise any pilgrims, whose life hath any value in his own eyes, to visit the Jordan, no matter how strong he may be," Felix Fabri counseled, "because in both my pilgrimages, I have seen many nobles and strong men fall sick and perish." A Russian Orthodox priest leading a flock of pilgrims to the shore issued this warning: "Don't expect the Volga." François René de Chateaubriand—revered in France as an essayist, diplomat, politician—touring the Holy Land in 1806, wrote enthusiastically and at exhausting length about almost everything but could not hide his disappointment about the Jordan. When his guides brought him to the shore, he could not discern the water. Chateaubriand found the Jordan "a sort of moving sand."

He drank some river water from a leather canteen, recalling a pious missionary's assurance the water would have the sweetness of sugar. "I found it, on the contrary, rather brackish," said Chateaubriand.

In Arabic, the settlement was called Riha. Jericho, or Riha, in the nineteenth century was nothing more than a few hovels. A tangle of thorny bushes surrounded them, and a squarish tower used by Ottoman soldiers as a fort stood nearby. In 1838, Edward Robinson, an American who was the greatest biblical scholar of his day, methodically toured the countryside of Palestine for six weeks. Of all the villages he examined, he declared Riha to be "the most miserable and filthy." It was associated with wretchedness, primitiveness, isolation.

Riha was the settlement closest to Ein es Sultan—Spring of the Sultan. It was the most copious source of freshwater in the southern half of the valley. Ein es Sultan gushed cool water into a small pool from a source that seemed hidden underneath the high lumpen mound. The mound seemed mostly dirt, had stones poking out from it, was in winter covered with grass like the rest of the plain. Every visitor assumed the mound to be another natural oddity of the valley.

Edward Robinson applied every expression of horribleness to Jericho. Its inhabitants were "a mongrel race," he said. Everyone, including the local governor, was "shabby and filthy." For reasons the governor never offered to explain, two Christians were in his tent in chains. When Robinson was ready to travel on to the Jordan, his guides claimed the risk of attack was too great. Such was the normal way guides demanded baksheesh. When it failed, their leader offered a sort of reassurance. "Let come who will," he said, "we will all die together."

Something about the villagers deeply upset Westerners. They would wring their hands over the impoverishment of the Holy Land but become venomous when describing Jericho. "It is said," a traveler reported, "that morally Jericho is the most debased and degraded place in Palestine." The villagers were described as ugly, so low as to be subhuman, and women were singled out for special abuse. They were "degraded looking." "All very filthy." "Most repulsive in feature." They sometimes left their faces unveiled and walked to the travelers' tents to dance with the expectation of receiving a few coins, which the travelers found unacceptably immodest, perhaps erotic, so all the more disturbing.

"I never saw such vacant, sensual, and debased features in any group of human beings of the type and form of whites."

And travelers found the heat intolerable. They complained about the mosquitoes. People who slept in the huts were driven out by fleas; sleep outside, you had to kick away the large population of dogs. A Dutch officer, a Lieutenant C. W. M. Van de Velde, visiting in the 1850s, camped on a plateau of donkey manure and pronounced the locale "wretched." How painful the disappointment: to risk one's life to reach a place of such miserableness. You looked for a Jericho that was Eden but found Riha. Ein es Sultan was found more tolerable since it offered cool water and the shade of a giant fig tree. Looming above was the steep-sided mound.

Looked like a rubbish heap, Edward Robinson said of it. He commended the view from the top.

Rubbish and sand, said Van de Velde.

Many remarked on the mound's great bulk. On its strangeness: one small mountain in the middle of a plain. But religious piety justified only one day in or near miserable Riha. Then you hurried away, to avoid the Bedouin or the fleas. The mound—it might contain relics of something, might justify some digging, said Van de Velde. But he too was in a hurry to leave.

Like everyone, Charles Warren hired guards to lead the way into the valley. Bedouin handled the selling of protection as a franchised business. Between Jerusalem and Jericho, protection was the affair of the

Arabs living in the encampment called Abu Dis, named after a sheikh from the distant past. Their relatives included the Ghawarneh, the Bedouin of the *ghor,* who claimed the area between Jericho and the northern end of the Dead Sea. Cooperation was such that the men of Abu Dis offered a package deal; a traveler leaving their territory would be handed over peacefully to the Ghawarneh. Another tribe, the Jehallin, controlled the desert hills south of the Ghawarneh's territory. But agreements involving the Jehallin had a way of ending in disputes over baksheesh.

Warren duly consulted a sheikh named Salah, the person in charge of such matters in Abu Dis. Salah assigned himself and ten other men as Warren's escort, and there was no choice but to hire them. Warren suspected, correctly, that his guards were the same individuals who would organize an attack if he dared to travel alone. Who knew better than the men of Abu Dis about ambushes? Who knew whether a stray shot would produce a tragedy? So Warren always traveled with at least one guard from Abu Dis.

In case of real threat the escorts were likely to run away. It was the most sensible action to take, given the culture. The Bedouin rigorously upheld the principle that all attacks had to be avenged in kind: if someone were killed, the required vengeance was another death. The second killing might not occur for a year or a generation. But for honor's sake it would happen, eventually.

It was better to leave the foreigner. He was not likely to be seriously harmed, unless he were foolish enough to resist. If he were robbed, an attempt would be made later to recover whatever was stolen. Better that than staying with the foreigner and risking someone being killed and dragging the entire clan into a murderous feud without end. "When they see a hostile party approaching to attack," Warren said of his guards, "they note the tribe to which it belongs, and then bolt to give information; the party then comes up and robs you if you don't resist, but is afraid to do you much harm, because the tribe is known."

The situation occurred often enough to justify an aphorism of warning: *El-badawi akh'ath be-tharo ba'ed arbain sanah, wo qall, ba'karet.* The Bedouin took his revenge after forty years and said, *ba'karet*—I was a bit early.

A few years before Warren's time, a Mr. and Mrs. Corsbie and their friends decided to make a trip into the valley. They hired the usual Bedouin guards, and the Bedouin were astounded to see enough luggage to burden sixteen donkeys. The Corsbies then violated a cardinal rule of Middle Eastern travel by failing to keep their luggage in sight at all times. When the party reached Jericho the donkey train had disappeared.

Back in Jerusalem the Corsbies complained to the British consul; he visited the sheikh of Abu Dis to remind him that the Corsbies were due the respect Bedouin accorded to guests.

The sheikh set off into the desert. He traveled to the southern end of the Dead Sea. He rode another nine days, into the deserts of Arabia.

Some weeks later, sixteen laden donkeys appeared outside the consul's door.

Whenever he ate a late dinner that was drenched in olive oil, Warren had vivid dreams of mayhem in his sleep. He considered the dreams important since in *Underground Jerusalem* he wrote about them at great length. If he slept in a tent, the dream was always the same and invariably left him elated. He would be attacked—he never identified or otherwise described the attackers—and in the dream be forced to battle hand to hand as his father had done in China. In the dream young Warren never missed a shot with his revolver and his club never failed to smash the skulls of his enemies. He was dreaming of a traditional soldier's conventional success. After masterfully bludgeoning his way to victory, he would awake for a brief time, feel satisfied that he had properly digested his dinner, and then sleep soundly until morning. To be on the safe side, in Palestine, he buckled a revolver around his nightshirt.

But he suffered through nightmares whenever he slept in a building. Attacked once again, his revolver would not fire and his club became useless in his hand. He was killed and killed again. On his first night at Jericho, however, he was unsettled by an altogether different dream.

His party spent most of an April day riding from Jerusalem into the valley. They reached Jericho during the afternoon and pitched the tents at Ein es Sultan, the well-known spring. The mound beside it was as knobby and irregular as a gnarled hand. It rested on a plain otherwise as flat as a tabletop, tilted a few degrees toward the river. It was more interesting than the classroom an assistant instructor of surveying would see in Britain. And that night Warren dreamed about success without the pyrotechnics of battle. He was excited both asleep and awake. He dreamed "fame was before me." Touch the mound—in the dream a touch was sufficient effort—"and the sculptures of old Jericho would spring forth." In the dream, Charles Warren, twenty-seven years old, was about to rediscover the famous city and find glory.

In the brightness of morning, a first close look at the mound dissipated the dream. Instead of seeing the scattered remains of a city he found naked mammarian hills. He rode to the Jordan, then returned to the camp. He was an unwilling audience when villagers from Riha came to perform a dance; "and the only sentiment it inspired us with," Warren complained, "was disgust." It is likely he considered returning to Jerusalem. But he was at a well-watered place, had already spent the Palestine Exploration Fund's money on useless guards, and the Ghawarneh—the Bedouin living near Riha—were peaceful enough in their tents and miserable shacks. It was a convenient place to explore. Some of the workmen tunneling with Warren in Jerusalem had been sent for and were ordered to the mound.

Initially there were ten workmen. In early April temperatures could be ninety degrees, and it was the beginning of the season for the *khamsin,* the sandstorms and overheated winds that turn the sky putrid yellow and suck out every drop of moisture. The landscape inspired sloth. Everything beyond the spring was rocks and scrub.

The workmen stood on the mound, their picks raised in the air.

Now: Unfreeze them.

Let the picks tear a gash in the mound, then deepen the cut. The digging has begun.

In the heat the men stripped nearly naked and sang as they worked.

Proto-archaeology began at Jericho without Warren paying close attention.

According to Warren's account, he rode south that first day. The day after, a Saturday, he sent one of the corporals to Jerusalem for more picks and mattocks. Warren gave the workmen Sunday off, led the prayer service for the party of Englishmen, and climbed a steep trail to see a cave-dwelling monk, who was friendly but mentally a little worse for wear from the rigors of living as a hermit.

Work resumed, and what Warren observed at the mound was confusing to everyone. There were neatly laid courses of bricks and mortar, which at the slightest touch crumbled into fine powder, as if they were only part of another dream. "We were groping in a land of shadows and phantoms," Warren said. Dust bricks were separated by phantom mortar in phantom walls.

Warren's generation had trained itself to think in terms of stone. Antiquity consisted of the stone temples of Greece, the Forum in Rome, Roman aqueducts in Britain, sturdily built amphitheaters, the enormously thick stone walls surrounding the Temple Mount. And everyone searched accordingly. In 1838 Edward Robinson had climbed atop the mound the better to examine the plain surrounding Ein es Sultan, which he judged the most likely site of ancient Jericho. He searched for ruins he felt appropriate to a great city—"a circus, palaces, and other edifices"—and in that expanse of flatness saw nothing of the kind.

In most situations, Edward Robinson showed himself to be unconstrained by scholarly convention and was a gifted, highly original researcher. With an Arabic-speaking colleague, Eli Smith (a fellow American), Robinson had seized upon the idea of using Arabic place-names to help pinpoint geographical features described in the Bible. In their brief travels, Robinson and Smith rediscovered more than two hundred biblical sites—more than the total previously known. "We just pursued our own course; went where we would, and undertook what we pleased; asked no leave of the government or others, whenever it could be avoided; and thus encountered no opposition," Robinson said, as if there had been no hardships.

When published in the United States and Europe, his nearly two-thousand-page account created a sensation. He was to biblical studies what the discoverer of a dozen natural elements would be to physics, the discoverer of a hitherto invisible reality. One of his many admirers anointed him "the greatest master of measuring tape in the world."

But at the mound above Ein es Sultan, Robinson made an error, though an understandable one. Looking for stone, he was not predisposed to search for mud-brick or to recognize it. Neither was anyone else at the time. Mud-brick speaks of a different kind of settlement than what people were looking for, and recognizing it seems to require a different sensibility. Surveying the plain from atop the mound and deciding little or nothing was to be found of the ancient city, Robinson unknowingly stood on its remains. A city could be crumbly dirt.

Charles Warren spent a month camping up and down the valley. In the spring of 1868 he returned to dig on a larger scale. This time the workmen numbered 175. They opened long trenches and sank shafts down thirty feet. Warren uncovered fragments of charred wood, two stone mortars, flints, bits of pottery, and an earthen pot that disintegrated into dust. No one could doubt the objects were man-made.

Warren concluded the mound was artificial. Ever the military man, he believed it was a platform on which had stood a fort or palace, whose ruins he was uncovering.

The general theory was nearly correct. The mound was in fact a human artifact top to bottom, all of it the accumulated debris of settlement. No one would know that with certainty until the 1950s. Charles Warren was the first to grasp the principle that the melted-looking hills were evidence of something both human-made and old. He advanced as well the understanding of mud-bricks, which sound terribly mundane but are no more so than the wheel. As a building material, mud-bricks make for social revolution. They hint of people living in one place rather than wandering. Make mud-bricks and you can move out of your tent. Create permanent shelters and you change relations within and between clans. Support a large settled community, and there must be agriculture and the revolution that comes with it.

At the mound, the digging party eventually understood the mud-bricks to be a building material, but the structures the bricks formed went mostly unrecognized. Without anyone realizing it, one of the workmen's shafts bore through a mud-brick wall, a wall that had surrounded the city during one of its many incarnations. To Charles Warren and the workmen, it was just more dirt.

Warren had found remains of (he thought) a fort or palace, and unfortunately for him they were not in a form that could be taken to Britain.

At the Palestine Exploration Fund, George Grove would undoubtedly be disappointed: there was nothing suitable to place on display. In Warren's dream, one touch had uncovered great sculptures—correct principles, mistaken details. But it was a dream that had come at least partly true.

> It may be said for a certainty that these mounds are artificial throughout, and that they probably are the remains of ancient castles. . . . If this be so, I have to suggest whether it would not be worth while shifting the whole mound with the prospect of finding among the remains some record of the past; this could be executed for 400 £.

Warren left the valley to return to Jerusalem when a new governor forced the exploration party into a trying game of hopscotch. Wherever the Royal Engineers dug in the city, the governor ordered them to stop. Moving to another location brought the same result. They would feign forgetfulness and skip back to the original square. To charm the new man, Warren demonstrated the workings of a sewing machine, as one might try to entertain a child, which left the governor "intensely delighted" but still unwilling to change the rules. His orders prohibited digging within forty feet of the Temple Mount.

So Warren expanded his clandestine tunneling. The locals nicknamed him the Mole. He kept a large lizard as a pet, and to Warren's good fortune, the lizard was eaten by the fearsome guards on the Temple Mount. Lizard, grilled, was a delicacy, and the guards became friendlier after their meal. Warren hinted that if the guards averted their eyes while he worked, more lizard would be forthcoming. He thereby continued exploring the Temple Mount.

In the war against petty authority, the second front was George Grove of the PEF. For eight months, not a word from Grove. Also no money. Grove was having little luck as a fund-raiser. The expedition had long ago spent the PEF's three hundred pounds, and Warren advanced one thousand pounds of his own—even for the aristocratic, an enormous sum. He unwillingly became the organization's chief patron. James Fergusson, the retired indigo merchant, turned miserly when the diggings failed to produce support for his pet theories about biblical geography. Since George Grove had no money to send, his standing in Warren's eyes plummeted farther once contact was reestablished.

"Give us results and we will send you money!" Grove wrote.

"Give me tools, materials, money, food, and I will get results," Warren replied.

"Results furnished, and you shall have the money!"

Grove, so desperate was he for artifacts with which to impress contributors, and so unrealistic were his expectations, went on to urge Warren to find the tomb of King David—"or we shall be bankrupt."

Warren's needs were mundane. He needed to buy planking to cover the ceilings of the tunnels, and he wanted more ladders. One of the shafts was by then nearly a hundred feet deep. "The anxiety of mind caused lately, by having to keep the workmen going without adequate means for their protection, is more than I can put up willingly with any longer; we must have plenty of money for the excavations or stop them altogether," he informed Grove.

But the explorations continued. With one of the corporals and a workman, Warren crawled through the tunnel King Hezekiah had ordered built sometime before 701 B.C. to supply water to Jerusalem in case of siege. Warren measured the passageway to be 1,708 feet long. At the entrance it was four feet, four inches high. Then, two and a half feet. Then, less than two feet, including one foot of water; "and here our troubles began." In one hand he held a compass, pencil, and notebook. A candle was in his mouth except when his mouth was under water. He was in the tunnel nearly four hours but emerged with nothing worse than a case of the shivers.

With his wallet at stake and perhaps also his career, Warren rescued the expedition with a display of charm and an adeptness at public relations. He invited Western tourists to be lowered into the shafts for candlelit tours, ladies cordially included. For a time his financial support consisted solely of contributions from the tourists. Then, George Grove bestirred himself in London with articles and public meetings in which he painted Warren's efforts in patriotic colors. To deprive Charles Warren of the means to finish his work would embarrass Britain in the eyes of the world and give the Muslim Turks an easy victory over Christendom, or so Grove suggested.

Money began to trickle into the PEF, and Grove could slowly repay his man in Jerusalem. But the conflicts between them continued. Warren—ill and feeling unappreciated—traveled to Britain to pour out his frustrations. Within a short time he had won the power struggle within the PEF. Grove surrendered most of his authority.

There was really no such thing as finishing the excavations. Warren, presumably more confident of his position, had returned, but the squabbles with authorities never stopped. Cave-ins occurred in the tunnels; every member of the party repeatedly fell ill—already one of the corporals had died of fever.

All the uncertainties about how to proceed were resolved by the arrival of a revised firman. This time there could be no appeal: the new firman expressly prohibited any work involving the Temple Mount. So in 1870 Charles Warren, after two and a half years work, came home again.

In contrast to his quiet send-off from the Charing Cross Hotel, he was hailed upon his return as "Jerusalem Warren," a figure well-known to an enthusiastic public, which was reading in newspapers about his feats of tunneling and the battle of wits against the Turks. Editorialists lauded his pluck. And admired the patriotism of the Palestine Exploration Fund.

Warren, in his stressful alliance with George Grove, helped interest his countrymen in the prospect that Palestine contained treasures waiting to be discovered. More than that: they were awaiting rescue from the presumed negligence of the Muslim Turks. Britain versus the Ottomans. Christendom facing the heathens. Who could resist? Who would want to stay aloof? Glory was surely waiting.

Grove and his friends had tapped a rich lode of patriotism. Unlike any other foreign land, Palestine had a history that, in some sense, Europeans (and Americans) considered their own. India promised raw materials and markets, and Victorian Britain and the other Great Powers hoped that the vast new colonies in Africa would offer the same. But only Palestine might soothe the imperial soul.

The Archbishop of York, William Thompson, belonged to a large cast of prominent persons Grove had coaxed into serving on his board of directors, and the cleric proudly confessed to these proprietary feelings about Palestine and congratulated Warren for strengthening them. "We look on Jerusalem now—we English people—as a city that in some measures belongs to us," the archbishop said at one of Grove's fund-raising meetings. "It is with the history of that country, and with what was done upon its soil, that our hopes of salvation have been knit up." And the audience cheered.

In the glow of patriotism, George Grove's struggling infant, the Palestine Exploration Fund (Warren wrote derisively of its "scarce breathing body"), had seemingly come to the rescue of the Holy Land. Grove was luckier than he realized in having Charles Warren lead the charge. As a young adventurer Warren wore the white hat of civility and common sense. In *Underground Jerusalem,* his problems melt away to become part of the higher education of Charles Warren. Salah the Bedouin is a respectful, well-meaning fellow; Jericho supports an unsavory population, but a dose of baksheesh can resolve any conflict; disputes with Ottoman governors are reduced to part of an endless boys' game, a continuation of good sport as indulged in by upperclassmen at Woolwich with their bats. Warren was a tireless advocate of bluff. Design an artillery battery, draw a map, dig through forbidden Jerusalem—ask the Royal Engineers. Ask Charles Warren.

Ask the Palestine Exploration Fund. For whatever his shortcomings as a manager, George Grove was sowing enthusiasm. By the time Warren returned home, the roll call of PEF members included two former prime ministers; the Speaker of the House of Commons; eight other members of Parliament; the deans of Westminster, Christchurch, Canterbury, and Chester; Sir Moses Montefiore, who was the most prominent Jewish philanthropist of the day; and, as chairman, the Archbishop of York. Queen Victoria gave her consent to be awarded the honorary title of Patron. "The proudest muster-roll of this country," said one immodest member. Another who was attending one of the organization's first meetings told his colleagues they were to be geographers, archaeologists, and more. Since the transcript of the meeting italicizes these remarks, I assume the speaker at this point raised his voice: "*We are to be the illustrators of the Bible.*" More cheers.

Grove already had a new project in mind. Instead of concentrating on Jerusalem, Grove suggested, a team of men should be dispatched to survey all the territory west of the Jordan. The land of the Bible could be mapped to the highest standards of the Royal Engineers. Whatever degree of detail the Royal Engineers included in the best maps of Great Britain ought to be matched in this new map of Palestine—from Mount Hermon in the north to the bottom of the Jordan Valley in the south, from the Dead Sea across the desert and hills to Beersheba and the Mediterranean. A team representing the Palestine Exploration Fund should be charged with tracing every road and locating every ruin and, among other tasks, trying to discover the origins of the Dead Sea and explaining the great depth of the Jordan Valley.

Grove and his eminent colleagues assured themselves the survey would be a simple task. Whatever the problems in Jerusalem, Grove promised there would be fewer in the countryside. "People are fewer and simpler," he said. "The villages are friendly, and the country contains prominent points which will make it all the more easy for surveying, and there can be no reason why it should not be begun and gone on with and finished without interruption." Like British Victorians who read the Bible for moral and religious instruction, the PEF proposed to "read" the biblical landscape.

During my time in Jericho I tried to understand how a presumably learned group could be so wrong.

I read minutes of the PEF's meetings and the organization's many volumes of published reports, and I learned that members of the PEF were all too right in bemoaning the lack of up-to-date knowledge about Palestine. They were convinced all would go reasonably well with a new survey party because much of what they knew about the country was what they had learned from the Bible. Several members, including George Grove, had traveled to Palestine and ventured into the countryside. But, like so many imperialists, they refused to take seriously the climate, the local authorities, or the people living there.

At one of the meetings at which the survey project was discussed, an enthusiastic supporter noted that Palestine was no larger than two English counties. This, of course, was intended to inspire confidence. The audience was reminded that all of Jerusalem would fit into London's Hyde Park. On the back of tickets to the meeting, the PEF had helpfully superimposed onto a map of London the area covered by Jerusalem. You saw Jerusalem as a little village that fit within Piccadilly, Charing Cross, and the Houses of Parliament. The Mount of Olives, the speaker pointed out, would coincide with Regent Circus, Mount Zion with the Foreign Office.

Europeans had designed and built the Suez Canal, and in America, a railroad spanned the continent. In comparison, what was the making of a map? Members convinced themselves that a few energetic members of the Royal Engineers could survey the whole country as easily as they could design a bridge. They would be the new pilgrims but also conquerors of the terrain. Knowing the Bible, advocates of the project cited the lists of villages in the Book of Joshua as among the obvious guides for the survey party. And the Old Testament account made entering the country sound easy. It suggested a first place of special interest. "And Joshua the son of Nun sent two men secretly from Shittim as spies, saying, 'Go, view the land, especially Jericho.'"

II
In a Postcard

The old man with the camel at the pillar marking sea level was Jericho's ornery welcoming committee. I never learned his name. He was a member of the Jehallin tribe and earned the cash part of his income, such as it was, selling photo opportunities next to the camel. He camped almost every morning on a narrow shelf of rock overlooking a dry riverbed, and standing on the shelf was the pillar marked "Sea Level," like a large white tombstone. Whether sea level was to be found precisely there, or at the bottom of the wadi, remained a mystery. The old man was dependent on the goodwill of bus drivers; they had to brake to a stop where the descent from Jerusalem was at its steepest, and find somewhere to park on the Bedouin's sliver of theme park. Out of the buses emerged tourists with cameras and a few coins to be exchanged for a picture of the camel next to the pillar. You stood at or near elevation zero and looked down into the small gorge.

He was very suspicious, the man with the camel. I might be the tax collector. I might covet this place alongside the road, however implausible that seemed. He had given up the tent life a few years before and built a small house in Jericho, where he kept a herd of goats. He wore a Bedouin's traditional long cloak, a white keffiya, sandals, and a watch with a wide silvery bezel. He was very dark and slight and kept most of his face obscured by the keffiya. He could have been a weathered sixty or a limber eighty. At 5:00 A.M. he rode out of Jericho on the camel and two hours later reached the sea-level marker and set up his office, which was a small bench of stones around a fire fed with twigs. From a burlap sack emerged a plastic jug of water for coffee, and bread, and grimy jars with the ground coffee and sugar. "All I do is have my camel and I work," he said.

He had been coming to the sea-level marker for fifteen years, he said. After reflection he amended the figure to twenty-five years—then again, maybe longer. We talked many times, but the conversation was always brief. He avoided looking directly at me and made no move to share the coffee. In the habit of selling small favors, he hinted that his name and other courtesies might be available for a price. He showed no disappointment when I walked away.

From sea level, the topography accelerates downward. You glide down on the road, fast, to a plain as flat as a landing strip. Every time the sensation was of falling. Approaching the plain was to approach an exotic foreign place after a long disorienting voyage. Every time, though the trip for me was less than twenty miles.

The plain is seabed. It is not old. Most of the valley was under water until, in geologic time, the last blink of the eye—about 14,000 years ago. Its history until then was a cycle of oceanic inundations and gradual recessions, depending largely on changes in climate. The valley alternated between being a fjord of what became the Mediterranean Sea and shrinking to become a long deep lake. Its last appearance 14,000 years ago is called Lake Lisan. The Sea of Galilee and the Dead Sea are its remains—the deepest puddles and so the last to evaporate.

In every sense the valley is a place apart, which does much to explain the apartness of Jericho, as isolated as the old man with his camel. In the valley you are in a deep cleft in the earth, the deepest that is not submerged by the oceans. How it came to be is a story of great geologic drama.

The valley is an open-air theater of rocks tilted, faulted, and folded to extremes, as if the earth had no greater resistance than dough. Much of the action is recent. Underground pressures, less than a million years ago, squeezed out a plug of salt along the western shore of the inland sea, like crystalline toothpaste from a leaky tube. On the way up, the salt pushed through more than a thousand feet of marl, sandstone, and conglomerate and dragged some of the material along for the ride. The salt pulled the rock upright until fractured parts stood like a lower jaw of teeth. They have eroded into brittle incisors and a large menagerie of animal forms. The salt mountain is roughly seven miles long, a quarter mile across, and rises seven hundred feet to a serrated edge above the plain. Geologists have drilled down ten thousand feet, salt all the way.

From certain angles, one fractured chunk resembles a woman, if a woman can be the height of a four-story townhouse. People call it—or her—Lot's wife. In Genesis she is the cautionary character in a story about obedience and faith, and is turned into a pillar of salt. Her fate was punishment for ignoring an angel's warning not to look back at the sinful cities of Sodom and Gomorrah as they were being destroyed by a rain of fire. In a more modern explanation for the pillar, Lot's wife is a freak of salt, limestone, and erosion, and some of the pressures that created her will eventually cause her to come unglued and fall. Every few months a car-size chunk of salt tumbles from the mountain. The salt plug is called Mount Sodom.

The local dramas are a testimony to the theory of plate tectonics, according to which the earth's crust is broken into large mobile rafts. Continent-size plates are said to collide, or to grind against each other, or to yaw apart, or to lie indefinitely at rest. The plates are able to change direction, though over long time spans. The land masses we know as Africa and Europe are said to have been one, to have separated, kissed, and reseparated, and to have done so more than once. A relationship no less complicated formed the Jordan Valley and made it deep.

One of the earth's seams is along the valley floor. It follows a course that is roughly north-south and is the boundary between two plates, the African and the Arabian. On the African plate lies the western half of the valley, plus Israel and the Sinai Peninsula. The Arabian plate carries the valley's other half, with Jordan and other lands to the east.

Both plates are moving, but in different directions. As the African plate heads west, the Arabian plate travels north. The most widely accepted theory is that they have been enacting their divorce for ten million to twenty million years. Their movement, which is apolitical, is termed "leftist." A person standing on one side of the seam sees the other side moving leftward.

As they move the plates leave a gap, which is the Jordan Valley; the larger entity of which it is a part is the Dead Sea Rift.

Several kinks lie within the rift. It is more nearly a jagged lightning bolt than a straight line. As the plates shear apart, the crust thins and twists at the kinks, and the twisting deepens the valley. A French geologist named Lartet was the first to speculate about this being a region of slowly moving rafts. In 1869, he looked at the outlines of Africa and Arabia and saw them as pieces of a jigsaw puzzle that could be fitted together. One had merely to close the water-filled gap known as the Red Sea.

What became the classic works on the subject appeared in the late 1960s and early 1970s and were written by Raphael Freund, an Israeli, along with several colleagues. Freund elevated one highly technical paper into narrative eloquence by reminding his audience of the words of the Old Testament prophet Zechariah. Describing a future battle in which God will defend the people of Jerusalem, Zechariah refers to the Mount of Olives, the high ridge at the eastern edge of the city, and makes an eerie prediction: "one half of the Mount shall withdraw northward, and the other half southward." So it has come to pass on the two sides of the Jordan Valley. The mountains have moved.

Most of the scholarly literature (there is some dissent) concludes that the Arabian plate has moved 105 kilometers north, from the starting line with the African side. Its trip has been a generally slow one, over those ten million to twenty million years. Three-dimensional play with the jigsaw puzzle provides the most convincing proof that the trip has occurred. Push the eastern (Arabian) side of the valley south by 105 kilometers. In the strata twenty million years old on each side of the valley, the rocks will match.

Avihu Ginzberg, another Israeli, suggests with mild impatience that the theory is beyond the reach of controversy. He is chairman of the department of geophysics and planetary sciences at Tel Aviv University. Professor Ginzberg is a trim, handsome man looking to be in his mid-fifties with the coolness of a slender pillar of highly polished granite. I went to see him on what was a warm end-of-winter day, and students were littered on the lawns for sunbathing. He led me from his office into a cluttered side room to stand by a poster-size satellite photo showing Israel, the West Bank, and Jordan. The Dead Sea looked like an inky blue kidney, the Jordan River a tangled blue vein.

As a specialist's present to a layman, he offered the easy way to calculate how fast the plates move. "You take 105, 110 kilometers and divide by ten million years," Professor Ginzberg said. Every year, 1.1 centimeters of movement.

The matter is more interesting and more complicated, since the plates have moved at varying rates. For long periods, they apparently did not move at all. The plates sometimes are truly at rest. At other times they are stuck, pressing hard. When they become unstuck, the sudden movement is an earthquake. Over the last 25,000 years (roughly), the hills on the Jordan side have jogged 150 yards. In four million years (or perhaps somewhat longer), the Jordan side has traveled about 25 miles. If the Jordanian side is pushed 26.6 miles south, the riverbeds on each side of the valley connect, like severed arteries neatly sutured. Geologists call the rift a geosuture.

In the planetary scheme of things, the Dead Sea Rift is a provincial highway linked to a crustal interstate, the East African Rift system. Including its many side fissures, the East African Rift stretches 3,400 miles, beginning in Mozambique, in southern Africa. Its northernmost extension adds another 500 miles, passing Jericho and continuing into Syria and Turkey. Look for a north-south chain of lakes or a deep north-south valley on land or under water—you find the rift roughly there. Nowhere deeper than at the Dead Sea.

Three plates intersect at the southern tip of the Red Sea, where the Arabian Peninsula comes close to the Horn of Africa. The plate junction is the Afar Triangle. The intersection is temporarily busy with traffic, all outward-bound. Arabia is traveling north. Most of Africa is moving west. A plate carrying Somalia is drifting east. Given time and no major change of traffic pattern, Somalia will be carried into islandhood.

As the plates veer apart, water fills most of the widening gaps: the Red Sea, between Africa and Arabia; the Gulf of Aden, between the plates bearing Arabia and Somalia; the Gulf of Suez, where Africa and a miniplate holding the Sinai follow their slightly different paths. Geologists predict that the future will probably bring more of the same. Wider gaps, larger seas. The Red Sea will grow as Arabia continues its drift north and east.

"Eventually you'll have the same thing here," Avihu Ginzberg said, after a walk from the satellite map back to his desk. The Dead Sea Rift will continue rifting. "The eastern side of the valley will move away, and there'll be an opening." The Jordan Valley will widen and, as the crust stretches, deepen and admit water. In most of the foreseeable scenarios, water will eventually cover much of the valley. Again.

"It will get here, eventually," Professor Ginzberg said.

He smiled at my predictable "When?"

"Oh, I would say ten million years. Not very long."

My experience of the valley was slightly skewed by one of the wettest winters in decades. For several Technicolor weeks the plain bloomed into red poppies growing in fields of green felt, a Pissarro desert. Even the sand sprouted green. One wet winter allowed who knows how many years' worth of seeds to seize their single chance to germinate. People driving to see the wildflowers created traffic jams.

Descending from the hills, you could hardly get lost going to Jericho. There was only one obvious track. When the road from Jerusalem bottomed in the valley, you could continue eastward, toward the gray mists hovering over the Dead Sea, or turn north in the direction of the greenery, toward Jericho. In the hot months the white sky always seemed low, an unadorned bowl of china overhead, and cast a flat light that made everything look no more than an inch high. The traffic mixed sheep, trucks loaded with vegetables, and the tourist buses.

The town always looked a more orderly place on a map than it was on the ground. I could never relate the two. There were said to be 12,000 people, but many of them lived on distant farms. No one ever spoke of Jericho as a city, nor did it feel like one. In less than twenty minutes you could walk from end to end. The road plan was simplicity itself, but the town sprawled along small dirt paths and climbed partway up some of the hills. Nonetheless, it never ventured far from a leaky network of canals carrying irrigation water from Ein es Sultan, or from the other springs.

Coming from Jerusalem, you entered on Jerusalem Road. To reach Ein es Sultan and the mound, you veered left and turned onto Ein es Sultan Street—and within a mile or two found yourself back in desert.

Traffic going in the direction of the river stayed on Jerusalem Road. It was the valley's Champs Élysée, Piccadilly Circus, Broadway. The resemblance was sociological, not physical. Jerusalem Road led past the concrete dome of a new mosque—which if it were ever completed would be the largest building in town—and the entrance to the wholesale vegetable market. In early morning the area was choked with fumes from farmers' trucks. The average truck in Jericho entered middle age after twenty or twenty-five years, with a long wheezing life still to be lived. At the vegetable market the drivers parked under a metal roof, which was crinkled like old foil, and between two rows of little offices that decades of fumes had painted sooty gray. Each office was furnished with a wooden desk and a half-dozen plastic chairs and an old adding machine and the latest Arabic newspapers from Jerusalem and scowling, chain-smoking men drinking cups of coffee and glancing at the arriving trucks. A nod of the head invited a farmer inside to begin negotiations. "I say two shekels, the farmer says three," one of the scowling men said. "I say two and a half, it goes on." And past the entrance to the market, traffic came to a curving strip of one- and two-story buildings that constituted the business district.

The buildings all followed the same plan. They were narrow but deep. On street level was a stone-faced money changer sitting behind a counter, a one-chair barber in the building alongside, a cramped food store, a small restaurant saturated with the odor of hot cooking oil, or a shoe store (in three small buildings was a tightly packed line of six). In the grander buildings, a staircase off to one side led to an upper level with an office of some sort. City Hall, with a total of three levels, was the grandest of all. Some of the older buildings had roofs of baked mud sprouting high weeds. Every storefront had a metal shutter, an eyelid pulled down by early afternoon. You had to dodge the bicycle riders, who themselves were swerving around double-parked taxis, most of them black Mercedeses stretched like metallic rubber to bus-length. They were the *services,* making regular runs to Jerusalem and the major towns of the West Bank. They were cheap though not very comfortable except in the seat up front with the driver. No matter how long it took, the drivers waited until they collected enough passengers to fill all ten seats.

For a long time the place to go for quiet was the town square. It was overlooked at one end by the police station. City Hall stood on the opposite side, where people were always to be found. But the police end was Antarctica, cold and isolated. Traffic routed itself away from there and pedestrians did not linger. During the early days of the intifada, Israeli police regularly ventured into that end of the square to double- and triple-check identity papers, or to tell a driver he owed an enormous fine or had a previously unknown tax bill. Sometimes the bill was calculated on the spot. The alternative to immediate payment was usually to hand over the car. Impounded cars filled a large sandy field to overflowing. The police became sufficiently hated that, for their own protection, a fence almost as high as the station was erected midway into the street to create a protective moat. The fence became the jail, the police the inmates. Soldiers were usually on the roof. Then the Israelis ceded authority to the Palestinians; children climbed the fence, decorated it with palm fronds, and pulled it down.

Cars traveling in the direction of the river either went slowly past the police station or went through the congestion on Jerusalem Road, and after several more slow curves returned to a world of severe orderliness. This was Amman Street, a straight line. It went past stores selling farm tools and seeds. It narrowed when it reached a flat countryside of small vegetable farms and after a mile or so narrowed further and turned to dirt at an army checkpoint. It was one of several hurdles, physical and bureaucratic, on the way to the river and the main crossing point to Jordan, for those allowed to travel past it.

In town, men jostled each other on the sidewalks and carried on shouted conversations with friends on the opposite side of the street. Or they idled at small metal carts, where the cook would work at a frantic pace frying falafel or cooking lamb or bits of chicken and sliding them with tomatoes into pockets of bread. Or they visited the restaurants hosting day-long card games and visited a second time and drank more coffee. Every man seemed to have at least an acquaintanceship with every other, which made a walk along Jerusalem Road necessarily slow. There were days when the only observable activity in Jericho was the act of lingering.

Women, most of them with their heads covered, waited silently in lines. I occasionally joined the lines at butcher shops where women would choose a live chicken from a caged défilé. The butcher grabbed the bird. He would bend back its head to make the neck taut and draw a long slow cut with a knife. Three men who almost never smiled worked in the butcher shop across from the old mosque, and they must have been brothers since all three had the same long face and puffy mouth, as if they had mumps or had been in a fight. On hot mornings, parts of downtown smelled faintly of chicken shit and fresh blood.

The main Christian area was one long block of downtown. A Russian Orthodox compound was there, and a Greek Orthodox Church, set back from the street and mostly hidden behind a high wall. From the street one could usually only peek at the church through a metal gate, or look up and see the church's small gray cupola, a ribbed bulb topped by a cross. Two Christian schools, one for girls, the other for boys, were across the road.

There wasn't a sleepier part of town. Then the calendar brought Christmas or another important date on the Christian calendar, and the neighborhood experienced manic transfiguration. I witnessed it one Easter.

About a dozen buses had arrived outside the church with pilgrims from Greece. Before the visitors could reach the church, they were set upon by merchants loudly hawking fruit and vegetables from wooden carts that donkeys had pulled from the market. The pilgrims were mostly elderly women, wearing long black dresses and heavy shoes. The women looked to have arrived as exhausted as Felix Fabri, the fifteenth-century priest from Ulm, and had the same unrealistic hope for quietude.

They arrived bearing Greek drachmas. The merchants demanded dollars, Israeli shekels, or Jordanian dinars, and performed remarkable feats of mathematics and imagination by minting a different exchange rate for each customer. It was fascinating to observe, in the way it is fascinating to watch a cat bat around a bird not quite dead. Prices for oranges began in the stratosphere, dropped precipitously, drifted upward whenever another bus arrived, and eventually stabilized at a price in shekels approximately triple the normal price at the market, two blocks distant.

For a long time my feelings when I was in town alternated between a sense of claustrophobia and a sense of isolation. They were the physical characteristics I associated with the valley. Only after many months did I begin to take pleasure, finally, from the landscape. Certainly, the landscape in the valley was dramatic. But its sole purpose seemed to be to give tangible expression to the word *desolation.* To think of Jericho as an oasis—a famous one, no less—was a fatuous idea, until you looked at the town from a hill high enough to place it in the context of the desert. Or until you saw the states of the Arabian Peninsula or North Africa. From a distance Jericho was a postcard of greenery. Entering it always caused the colors to fade. I tried keeping one foot in town, one outside, shifting weight from one leg to the other, to be able both to look at the postcard and to be in it. And that was the real fatuousness. No matter how long I stayed, I could not be *in* the postcard; I was always outside. I could only be foreign. I had light-colored skin and laughably limited Arabic, not to mention a reporter's habit of betraying a sense of being in a hurry. Those were handicaps in a society organized along clan lines, one that insisted on taking its time. People were reconciled to the idea, true or not, that their lives were unlikely to change, or that change could not be rushed. I began to find pleasure only when I began to do things more slowly. And still, the other men crowded on the sidewalk were walking slower than I was; the old Mercedes taxis, despite their drivers' feats of daring, moved through town at a stroll.

Over the years I heard many people talk dispiritedly about a golden age. No one ever said it was the present. It was always some other time. Never very distant, but always past.

In the form that most people knew it, local history began with the Ottoman Empire's inglorious end in World War I. What was striking was that right up to the Ottoman's collapse the valley remained in the same semi-lawless state that Charles Warren had seen in the 1860s. Describing a ride from Jericho to the Dead Sea in 1910, a British physician named Gurney Masterman approvingly mentioned the construction of a stone bridge on Jericho's outskirts, but added that conditions were "very unsettled and there had been a robbery of a number of donkeys, loaded with wood, in this part a few weeks before."

Dr. Masterman made periodic visits from Jerusalem on behalf of the Palestine Exploration Fund to measure the water level in the Dead Sea. His reports usually included mention of general conditions. The reports are bland and tedious, but cumulatively have the impact of a biblical list of divine punishments. Life in the valley was a series of tribal wars and droughts. In early 1911 Masterman warned that "no European would be safe here for more than a few hours at most." Several months later his small party watched the approach of six Bedouin on horseback and feared the worst, though the Bedouin veered away once the Englishman made a show of bringing out a rifle.

The Ottomans entered World War I on what became the losing side and were ultimately among the fatalities. In 1917, a British army commanded by General Edmund Allenby captured Beersheba with the help of deception and surprise, took Gaza, and quickly cleared the way to Jerusalem. Before the bulk of Allenby's army had time to arrive, the Turkish garrison fled the city. It was left to the mayor to go out from one of the city gates with a white sheet in search of someone to accept Jerusalem's surrender. Two British scouts were the only soldiers he could find. They sufficed, and Allenby entered the city a few days later, on December 11, 1917. About the political maneuverings that followed—for the number of secret pledges made and broken, the negotiations fully deserve the label "Ottoman-like"—it is enough to say the British gained control of Palestine and did not relinquish it until 1948.

The younger the person, the more that era sounded like the golden age. My poll was unscientific but the findings were consistent over time. I talked with people I encountered by chance and with those I was directed to by others. It was my excavation of Jericho, but I dreamed of no special artifacts. I was looking for present and past, and for a sense of the process of change. For some of this exploration my guide was Hakam Fahoum. A Palestinian, he was a figure foreign journalists relied on as a translator, fixer, and éminence grise, despite his being in his early thirties and younger than most of his clients. He lived in East Jerusalem, but his family owned a farm in a village north of Jericho and a comfortable, well-shaded house between the business district and the mound at Ein es Sultan. Hakam spoke English fluently, expertly juggled assignments from a dozen reporters and, probably without anyone ever explicitly demanding it, appreciated that the way to keep every customer happy was to plead ignorance when one of us inquired with false innocence about the activities of a competitor. He was determinedly entrepreneurial in ways I was happier not knowing in full; he had the ability to make all things possible. When a television crew needed scenes of a Palestinian feast, Hakam bought the sheep required for the main course.

Being with a Fahoum in Jericho carried a certain weight. A lot of people knew the family. No one wanted to offend the son of a well-to-do, property-owning father. In Hakam's company, I could count on total strangers becoming solicitous or at least being curious once they heard his name. If people did not know that Hakam and his father were often on less than sterling terms with each other, I was not going to tell them.

One spring, I wanted to find people who had lived in Jericho during British times. People directed us to a one-lane road about a half mile from the business district and said to look for the concrete hut belonging to Abu Ali.

He was a tiny, frail man confined most of the time to bed. The bed was the only furniture in the front room of the house, and in the back was a rudimentary kitchen and a wheelchair whose seat was piled with neatly folded laundry. An unshaded lightbulb was the only electrical appliance in sight.

A son and daughter-in-law helped Abu Ali sit up and shifted his legs, as thin as canes. Abu Ali had long unwrinkled fingers but arthritis made it difficult for him to shake hands. As soon as I sat down on the plastic stool that was brought in from the back, the daughter-in-law disappeared into the kitchen. Eight people—Abu Ali, his son, his daughter-in-law, and five grandchildren—lived in the four rooms of the house. Its floors were bare concrete and the windows were without glass or frames, but the house was spotless. Wear and tear had uncovered several layers of blue paint beneath the latest coating of white. Abu Ali was in his mid-seventies but looked just on the young side of one hundred.

"When I opened my eyes, I found the British here," he said. All he saw around him when he was young was terrible poverty. His father and the other farmers in the valley often found it difficult to obtain enough food for their families. Many meals consisted of rotten tomatoes dipped in olive oil. Because the Ottomans had done nothing to develop Ein es Sultan or any other water supply, the wheat crop failed repeatedly for lack of irrigation. In times of real desperation, people needing flour for bread resorted to looking for grains of wheat in camel dung.

The daughter-in-law returned with coffee in cups just large enough to accommodate the small end of an egg. No one became unduly upset when Abu Ali, his hands affected by a tremor, spilled most of his coffee onto his clothes and the mattress; his family showed its affection by not making a fuss or interrupting his raspy soliloquy. With unmistakable pride he recounted the important local occasions, the once- or twice-yearly official visits by the British High Commissioner from Jerusalem. Herbert Samuel was the first person to fill the position, and he built a winter cottage on the southern edge of town. Later, his cottage became the public works department. What used to be the living room was storage space for road signs. One of the bedrooms served as an office for two municipal employees. (They were happy to receive a guest, listened to the story of the house, and said somewhat apologetically they had never heard of Herbert Samuel.) Later still, the grim-faced chief of the Palestinian police took the cottage as his headquarters.

Jericho's elders, including Abu Ali's father, formally received the commissioner on each official visit, undoubtedly greeting him with the same effusive deference previously reserved for the Ottoman governors. These occasions made a lasting impression. No matter how poor the household, at least one person in every family told me at one time or another that a grandfather or great-grandfather was the person the commissioner respected the most, called upon the most, depended upon more than anyone else. Jericho's mayor, a rotund, charmingly vain man, bragged that the British called his father "the dictionary of the Jericho Valley," so great was his ability to answer their questions.

Friendly relations came to an end by 1936, the year Arabs throughout Palestine began a revolt against British rule and the accelerating pace of Jewish immigration. In sleepy Jericho a mob burned down the military headquarters on Jerusalem Road, and the British replaced it with an imposing concrete fort across the way from Herbert Samuel's cottage. The fort is still there. It has been a military headquarters for the British, after 1948 for the Jordanians, after 1967 for the Israelis. Now it belongs to the Palestinians.

Whenever I asked for descriptions of Jericho of the 1920s or '30s, or inquired if relatives had photographs or some other mementos from those days, anyone older than about fifty would shake his head and with excessive politeness ask me to repeat the question. The question was naive. "What was Jericho? There was never any Jericho," Abu Ali said from his bed. "It was just where farmers lived. There were just tents." One might just as well have asked to be shown the opera house.

A threesome of men in their late teens or early twenties took upon themselves the task of leading me to more people who had lived in the valley many years; young men in Jericho always had time to spare. They crowded into the car and directed me along a dirt road to reach the home of Salim Hajah. He belonged to the same generation as Abu Ali. With a banana grove and a sizable herd of sheep, he was well-to-do, but his memories were mostly of poverty. Hajah seated me on a couch on his porch with a view of the banana grove and a patch of withered tomato plants. It was an April day with a dry wind blowing an advance of summer.

"People here didn't know civilization at all," Salim Hajah said. He said he had clear memories of everything that happened after 1925. Hajah was sixty-nine and had a long, handsomely proportioned face, and he wore a light blue *galabiyah,* the body-length shirt styled like a dressing gown, and a white keffiya. His family was part of a large seminomadic clan that had lived in tents until the mid-1950s. In a single momentous step that Hajah never fully explained, the family went from pastoral to bourgeois, dividing its time between a house on the outskirts of Jerusalem and the one in which we were talking.

Traditional agricultural societies are usually poor in upward mobility. Living in an area chronically prey to raiding parties, drought, and great heat, a family hoped to grow enough food to feed itself and to get in the harvest and hide it before a visit by a corrupt tax collector or hostile Bedouin. A settled person in the valley did not build with permanence in mind. He lacked reason to believe that improving what already existed was worthwhile, since the Bedouin could return at any time or the winter rains could fail. When that happened, families moved west into the hills, for a season or forever. The Bedouin labored in their own manner and rode away with their flocks once they consumed the local vegetation. The more a farmer worked, the more there was to be taken by the lawless. Old-timers refer to those conditions as "the tribal way of life." None of the men who had fully left it sounded nostalgic. Even now, few real luxuries were to be found around Jerusalem Road, but well within living memory it was a rural slum of earthen hovels entirely open on one side, shared with animals. At night the inhabitants lit smoky fires of bamboo to keep away the snakes. And those few people were at least settled; the bulk of the population, through the 1940s, remained in tents. Jericho's most striking feature was its primitiveness. Self-improvement meant leaving the valley or selling whatever land one owned to a wealthy family in the hills. At most, a permanent resident could add another room of mud-brick.

"There were no rich people," Salim Hajah said after passing around a single glass and a pitcher of water. He stepped into the house for a moment to tell one of the women inside to begin preparing coffee. "The only rich people were from Jerusalem who would buy land." He was immune to mild irony, since he immediately began telling how little he used to pay the young men who worked in his vegetable garden. "I would employ somebody that age," he said, looking at one of my silent escorts, "and paid two and a half dinars a month"—about five dollars. That was in the 1960s and 1970s. In earlier decades conditions were worse. "People would change their clothes once a year," he said, tugging on his *galabiyah* and making a show of peering down at his chest. "I remember a man looking inside his clothes and picking out insects."

The wealthy of the time regarded Jericho as a playground. For well-to-do Arabs coming of age between the 1920s and the mid-'60s, Jericho was the winter destination of choice. A house in Jericho was to the land-rich what a beach house on the Costa del Sol became for the oil-rich. The well-off living in the hills on either side of the river began an annual winter migration into the valley as vacationers instead of herders. Members of the landowning aristocracy from Jerusalem mingled with relatives of Emir Abdullah, ruler of Transjordan. Those who did not build houses in the vicinity lived at one of the hotels. The Winter Palace was the most prestigious.

A special endorsement of sorts came in the 1930s from the former Khedive of Egypt, Abbas Hilmi, who commissioned the construction of a winter home. Abbas Hilmi had been unceremoniously deposed in 1914 as Egypt's ruler but maintained a Khedive-size appetite for luxury. He intended to lend a touch of royalty to the valley. Jericho's mayor still kept atop a cabinet beside his desk the architect's drawings for Abbas Hilmi's palace, the papers brown and crumbly. But construction never went beyond the foundations—money ran out, or Abbas Hilmi's interest waned, perhaps the weather was too hot.

"They all used to come," the mayor said with a wide sweep of his arm, as if to summon back the comfort. "All the big shots."

The Erakat family had long held a rank of importance. When I telephoned one day from Jerusalem, Rashid Erakat began his instructions for finding his house with a question. Did I know his nephew, Saeb? I answered, of course I knew Saeb. It was nearly impossible for a journalist not to know Saeb Erakat given his involvement at the time in political negotiations with Israel. Saeb had given me the telephone number. Then go to Saeb's house, I was told, and ask whomever I happened to see in the neighborhood. Anyone there could direct me the rest of the way.

Jericho maintained the gossipy intimacy of an extended family and a family's sense of hierarchy. Everyone was imprinted at an early age with a sense of who were the chiefs, and rarely failed to show deference. So the two men laboring over the engine of a Volkswagen pondered my question. We talked in the middle of a narrow paved road. An irrigated field of corn was on one side and on the other side was dry scrub. One of the men jogged a few steps to repeat the question to a slender young woman, a striking apparition emerging from the field. She was tightly wrapped in a long bright blue gown intended to confer modesty but accomplishing quite the opposite. The woman twisted her hand to illustrate the turnings in the road, and slipped back into the field. On my behalf the man condensed her instructions into the simplest Arabic—right, left, stop. There was the house of Rashid Erakat. Anyone there could have told me.

He was waiting in a front room. A bright mountain of bougainvillea lit the front yard. Rashid Erakat presented himself with the comportment of a diplomat years beyond any risk of appearing ruffled. Everything he said, and much of what other people said about him, supported the idea that Rashid Erakat considered his large family the closest approximation to valley aristocracy. This reflected self-confidence and reality.

Once we took our places in the room he began, "We were one of the families that used to come here."

That was intended to answer the important questions about the Erakats. Winters in the valley, summers in the hills. Not in tents since long ago. His orange grove was visible beyond the bougainvillea.

He was an utterly charming host, offering many hours of conversation and insights about local society and how it had changed, though many of the changes displeased him. Move him to a Delta county in Mississippi, and he could be mistaken for a gentleman farmer, one of those powerfully built men who is a generation removed from having to do the labor himself, but who owns vast tracts of prime farmland and serves as president of the Rotary.

Erakat worked for more than thirty years for the United Nations agency that was created to take responsibility for refugee camps housing Palestinians. The camps were born in 1948 as huge tent cities on the outskirts of Jericho. Erakat's first job carried no great prestige; he was only one of many dozens of people hired to determine if individuals in the camps met the agency's technical definition of *refugee.* Association with the UN, though, permitted him to confer on himself a diplomat's sense of immunity from various indignities. He was an Erakat, and he was at least tangentially of the UN.

The prestige of the family was traceable to Charles Warren's time. I was in the graciously civilized company of a grandson of the sheikhs of Abu Dis, the tribesmen who either sold a traveler protection for heading into the valley or threatened to make the trip a misery.

Rashid Erakat, in fact, was a grandson of the last of the sheikhs to have a guaranteed monopoly in the protection business. Grandfather Erakat (first name, Rashid) had found the last decades of the Ottomans a grand, enriching time. The governors in Jerusalem had given up the pretense of keeping order in the valley with soldiers, who had proven to be both brutal and ineffectual. Sending soldiers there was not how the governors wanted to spend what little money they had. Deputizing the men of Abu Dis was cheaper. Semiretired brigands became police. With government blessing, the tribesmen were to ensure travelers suffered no mishaps in the desert. They did so in honorable fashion and, in cash and privileges, were well paid for their efforts. Grandfather Erakat became a distinguished elder statesman awarded medals by church patriarchs and governors. When Kaiser Wilhelm of Germany visited Jerusalem in 1898 (accompanied by a two-hundred-member retinue), he presented Sheikh Rashid with a sword.

(Kaiser Wilhelm's visit was the event that shamed the Ottomans into beginning a frantic program of modernization. In advance of his arrival, the port at Haifa gained a new pier; the road between Haifa and Jaffa was widened to ensure the kaiser's carriage could pass safely; the same was done for the roads connecting Jerusalem to Jaffa and Bethlehem. Beggars in Jerusalem were escorted into the hinterlands. Jericho's role in the celebrations was consistent with the town's reputation as a backwater. On the chance that the emperor would visit, a telegraph line was extended from Jerusalem to the hamlet to allow him to remain in contact with advisers in Berlin. He decided against the excursion. Worse, someone cut the telegraph line.)

During the conversation Rashid Erakat excused himself several times to disappear into another part of the house, each time returning with what grew into a small pile of family mementos, including photographs of his illustrious grandfather. They were postcards for tourists presumably wanting to take home an image of the most fearsome-looking man they were ever likely to see. The grandfather was superbly cast. Along the bottom of the postcards was printed the legend "Sheikh

Rasheed Jordan Escort," or "*Chef des Arakats.*" In the photographs was an unsmiling, trim, dark-featured man wearing a long dark cloak, the *d'mmayah,* over a striped gown, the *qummbaz,* and on his head a white keffiya. Hanging from his left side was a long sword with a terror-inducing curve. "An Arab sword," said the admiring grandson. A field marshal's worth of medals was pinned to his chest, while one of his hands rested on the bridle of a horse. The animal stood between the chief of the Erakats and a smaller, much younger man. His expression suggested fear of either the camera or the sheikh.

"He got married to his third wife—the second one died—when he was eighty-five," Rashid Erakat said of his namesake. "He used to get on his horse when he was 104." Returning again from another room of the house, he brought the kaiser's sword. Another expedition produced a scroll, covered with Arabic calligraphy as fine as the veins of a leaf, showing the family tree. Males only. Starting from the bottom I counted forty-five generations up the trunk before reaching Grandfather Erakat.

Ottomans tottered, fell, and disappeared. The Erakats prosperously continued. The British, finding no reason to tinker with old arrangements, commissioned Rashid Erakat's father and uncles as captains, put them into uniform, and made Rashid's father police commander responsible for territory along the river. No Arab in the valley held greater authority. The stack of family photos included one showing him posed with a round-faced man visiting Jerusalem in his capacity as Britain's colonial secretary, in 1921. The secretary was there to meet with Emir Abdullah and create a country for him. Transjordan was the country, Winston Churchill the colonial secretary. He towers over Abdullah in the photos. Their meeting was among the last at which a British minister could draw a line on a map of the Middle East and declare the line a border and have it be so. And so it was. Erakat senior posed for the photo because his clan was the closest approximation to a local government. Every winter he moved his family to Jericho, into the house where now his son presided. An uncle built a house next door. Hearing the family's story, one realized Rashid Erakat's air of mild formality was not pretense, or coolness toward an inquisitive stranger. The family was at one time the stablest authority in this part of the valley. Its rule had been far from selfless, though no worse than the model provided by the Ottomans. The family prospered during the British Mandate; if there was a golden age for the clan, perhaps it was during the British-ruled 1920s and early '30s. Even without his grandfather's sword and groom, Rashid Erakat was imprinted as a chief.

Then the world as it had been known ended.

In 1948 the British left; Israel established itself as a state. One of the immediate results was the first of the Arab-Israeli wars.

Any elaboration is, at best, contentious. The field remains dangerously mined with national mythologies, none entirely false. For Israelis, the conflict was the War of Independence and one of their most heroic hours. For Rashid Erakat and the generation of Palestinians to which he belongs, that chapter of history is called "The Disaster," and the label does not allow qualification.

It refers to events his generation found humiliating, both at the time and nearly fifty years later. Hundreds of villages emptied themselves while others were emptied forcibly, and Arab society, albeit economically poor before the war, became catastrophically poorer. Beginning in 1947, more than 700,000 Palestinians left their homes. When the weather cooled, tens of thousands of the refugees camping in the hills began making their way to the warmth of Jericho. They walked, rode donkey-back, or clambered aboard trucks of the Transjordanian army, heirs to the British in the territory between Israel and the river. That territory is the West Bank. Promoted from emir to king, Abdullah became its ruler.

There was no shortage of rivalry for leadership, especially among the old landowning families; but it is enough to say that not everyone admired King Abdullah.

"Our family was the last to pay loyalty to His Majesty," Rashid Erakat said. He pronounced "His Majesty" in a tone appropriate for addressing a goat.

"We Erakats opposed the 'other occupation,' as we used to call it."

King Abdullah organized a political convention at the Winter Palace Hotel. Landowners and other notables—more than a thousand of them—were invited on the understanding they would proclaim support for the king, and they dutifully fulfilled their assigned role. Later, Abdullah cited this less than spontaneous expression of the public will as a basis for formally annexing the West Bank, in 1950, the year Transjordan renamed itself Jordan.

Rashid Erakat was in his late teens at the end of the war. Because of the family's prominence, the Jordanians awarded him the job of go-between for the UN and the several Arab armies that had arrived during the fighting but that were proving slow to leave. His job placed him in frequent contact with the flood of refugees.

It was winter. Little Jericho—crossroads for farmers, rough-hewn resort—was flooded with tens of thousands of the newly landless. Some people in the valley dealt with the new situation by deciding the resort life should continue. One night Erakat and two of his cousins took offense at an especially loud celebration in a hotel near Jerusalem Road; they complained to the revelers about the disregard for the refugees living in the open air.

As Erakat told this part of the story, the change in atmosphere could not have been sharper had he moved his chair to put more distance between us. He averted his eyes and his voice became nearly inaudible. In Erakat's version of events, he and his cousins had a brief, polite conversation with people at the hotel.

It's not difficult to imagine something different, beginning with the din of a feast, the arrival of the three uninvited guests, followed by a loud, frank exchange of opinions. A crowd had accompanied the Erakats part of the way and was waiting in the street. Meanwhile the party continued. Some of the people outside stormed the hotel, and when the riot was over two officers from the party were dead, a Jordanian and an Iraqi. Rashid Erakat had come to the hotel with a gun but, he said, never fired it. He added somewhat blandly, "I don't know if my cousins killed anyone."

All three Erakats were jailed at the imposing concrete fort. Given the family's connections with local police, Rashid made a less than miraculous escape and hid in Abu Dis. King Abdullah let it be known he wanted the three hanged. In those days it was always easy to incite a mob to act. Fortunately, members of the clan dissuaded the king from taking rash steps, and he was persuaded to refer the matter to a civilian court. The three were acquitted of every charge related to the murders—for lack of evidence, lack of guilt, or because of clan loyalty. All was forgiven between the Erakats and the king.

Rashid Erakat, like several dozen of his relatives, became an officer in the Jordanian army, but a year or two in uniform prompted him to look for another career. A chance encounter with an official from the UN led to a first job with the agency running the refugee camps. He did not change employers for more than thirty years.

One of course was loyal to a king or a president, though one ruler would always be succeeded by another; and loyal to an employer, though the employer too might change. Above all else, loyal to one's home, which was always Jericho.

One of the refugee camps was in the sand on Jericho's southern outskirts, like a listless foreign country. A sister camp no less parched or dulled lay to the north across the road from Ein es Sultan, the perennial spring. These small, harsh places have barely changed in more than twenty years. One never saw there the types of deprivations associated with the poorest parts of the Third World. That kind of deficit living did not exist in the valley, not in a gross form—the acute tragedies requiring immediate infusions of food, doctors, and money. And to find conditions worse than those at the camps required no great search. Parts of Cairo would do. But the hemmed-in desert with its baked, dull emptiness implied a daily terribleness; it always hinted at something even worse than what there was.

Jerusalem Road and the little business district were simple and none too polished; but they were recognizably of this century, since most of the area (not all) was swept, had plumbing, was electrically lit. The camps stood as outposts of a different civilization. They were in every respect premodern. In his book *The Yellow Wind*, the Israeli author David Grossman called them "ruins of ruins."

The larger camp, Aqbat Jabar, looked to be a transplant from an African disaster—Mali, Ethiopia during the drought years. It was a mile-long strip of mud-brick huts scattered behind a high fence and was the first manifestation of Jericho one saw on the drive from Jerusalem: an exotic blur of mud-brick scenery from the car. Early on during the intifada, all the windows in the camp school closest to the highway were destroyed—whether by young men from the camp or soldiers or both, everyone had forgotten. Seven years later no one had yet replaced the windows. Soldiers had commandeered the building and established a lookout post on the roof. The high fence appeared at the orders of the soldiers when all seemed quiet. "One day," a UN officer in Jerusalem shrugged, "we found them putting up a fence. Who knows?"

The second camp took the name of the spring, Ein es Sultan. A third was bulldozed when its residents fled across the river to Jordan in 1967, two wars after the refugees arrived. Ein es Sultan camp adjoined the mound, the two separated by a wire fence. One side could be mistaken for the other because the camp and the mound shared a tannic dustiness. I collected various UN publications listing several decades' worth of improvements—a school, a center for distributing rice and other staples, two mosques, three small stores. All those improvements existed but were rendered invisible by the sameness of sky, buildings, and the sandy earth. A mud-brick house would be patched, would collapse, be picked over for reusable furnishings, be raked smooth, and replaced by another mud-brick house. The adjoining mound had grown by the same process—one layer atop another.

About seven hundred people lived in the camp. Before the war in 1967 that brought about the mass exodus across to Jordan, the camp population was twenty thousand. (At the other camp, Aqbat Jabar, the population dropped no less dramatically.) Hakam Fahoum and I spent one morning walking about in search of someone who had arrived in Jericho as a refugee in 1948 and never left, which is how we came to visit Khamis Ibrahim.

He lived with his wife and one of their sons in a house as fine, by camp standards, as anything contemplated by the Khedive of Egypt. It was cinder block, not mud-brick. It had two doorways and two rooms and stood on land slightly elevated above most of the camp, and so afforded the luxury of privacy. Khamis Ibrahim was a fit compact man in his mid-seventies, clear-minded, but with an air of permanent distraction. He wore a prayer cap and the T-shirt and loose faded trousers that were the uniform of a manual laborer. He showed no surprise or curiosity at seeing us.

When we arrived he was in the midst of a loud argument with his son and two laborers over the cost of adding a room to the house. Ein es Sultan was not a place he expected to leave.

"It was in 'fifty or 'fifty-one, we started to realize we would never go back," he said. His version of family history was without second thoughts. He expressed none about having left his village in 1948; at the time people believed they had no choice. To say you should have taken more time to weigh your decisions or to foresee where they would lead—well, events in wartime had a way of outrunning your thoughts. He also sounded untroubled by the decision in 1967 to stay put in the camp even as others scrambled to Jordan. "I had a roof over my head and my little spread."

"They took everything from us!" interrupted his wife, Alizza. She refused to listen to an account in which the family, in terrible fear, had done as many others had in 1948, by half walking, half running away from a house in a village near Ramleh, in what became Israel, and never being able to reclaim it.

"The Jews have taken everything from us! The bracelets! The necklaces!" Her husband stared her into silence. Whether anyone literally took jewelry from her was for her irrelevant. She once possessed luxuries and no longer did. She did not knowingly choose to be a refugee. She turned away to busy herself with laundry.

Khamis Ibrahim's family, forty-five people in all, left the village at a time when people had wildly differing convictions. That a massacre at the hands of the Israelis was imminent; that the Israelis were about to be crushed by Arab armies. That everyone would be able to return to his village within a few days, or at worst within a month. After the war. Most of the family walked to Ramallah in the West Bank, camped there in an olive grove, and when the weather began to turn cool, rode in the back of a truck to the Aqbat Jabar camp. For housing, Khamis Ibrahim and his wife made do with burlap sacks and then a real tent and, after two years, a mud-brick hut. They stayed in Aqbat Jabar fifteen years. By 1967 Khamis Ibrahim cultivated a small orchard and owned several sheep. "I couldn't take them, and I couldn't leave them," he said. Eventually the family moved the short distance to the camp at Ein es Sultan.

Some in the camps were bitter, some were resigned. And the camps themselves, already older than most of the buildings in town, seemed as permanent as the plain.

In 1967, Jericho belonged to the front line. I spent a long time reading about the 1967 war because I was usually writing about the aftershocks. I studied the conflict and The Conflict. Each side—Arab, Israeli—cited reasons why it was entirely in the right. There were claims of perfect rectitude based on religion, on who inhabited a place first, and on the use of force. I pored over maps that had arrows to show the movements of large armies, thin broken lines to show where a cease-fire had held. I could just as well have ignored 1967 and ignored the intifada. Some of the parties wanted to readjudicate 1948, others to include in the balance sheet riots that occurred in 1929. It took no special effort to find people willing to argue passionately about the British, the Ottomans, the Crusaders. Occasionally I witnessed battles as they were fought for a second or a hundredth time.

From this I learned to listen without forcing myself to decide who was right. The Conflict would not be resolved by adding up examples of heroism or brutality and awarding the prize to whoever had the better score. Everyone had points. The best an outsider could do was hope the parties involved would hear each other out. There was a chance each party would feel better for having been heard and realize the other side had a case to make. That seemed to be the process that led Israel in 1994 to cede to the Palestine Liberation Organization control over the Gaza Strip and Jericho. Almost everyone agreed that the land, in some way, would have to be shared. Deciding a final, stable division of it is going to take a very long time.

I once heard an Israeli politician, a figure of the left, propose an analogy for relations between Israelis and Palestinians; he cited as his model ties between Germany and France. The model had its roots in the terrible battles Germany and France fought during the nineteenth and twentieth centuries over the border provinces, Alsace and Lorraine. "They killed each other over Alsace-Lorraine for, what, a hundred years? Three, four major, horrible wars.

"Now everything's peaceful, and there's an open border and tourism. The French and the Germans can't stand each other, and it's paradise." For Israelis and Palestinians, it was something to hope for.

Rashid Erakat kept a sort of diary during the 1967 fighting. They were notes he started writing as just one more report to his superiors at the UN office in Jerusalem. The first entry told of radio bulletins about air strikes in Egypt. In the second entry, Erakat matter-of-factly told of seeing a bombing raid against a Jordanian military camp close to Ein es Sultan. He wrote, "We thought Egypt would be strong enough to stop another catastrophe."

He was in his front room and read aloud from the diary. Sometimes he paced as he read, and wiped his eyes. The notes gradually abandon their somewhat officious reporting in favor of shorthand accounts of enormous pathos. During the second day of fighting, air raids struck closer to the camps, and the refugees frantically made preparations to leave. "Everybody was in a great panic and horror." People from Jerusalem and the hill villages jammed the road through Jericho as they headed toward the river and into Jordan. On the third day, Jordanian soldiers did the same in a disorganized mob. Jericho became filled with retreating soldiers and then emptied. The sight "was intolerable and unbelievable and affected greatly the morale of the people." On his way to the river, a Jordanian major stopped his car at Rashid Erakat's house to say he had seen Erakat's mother making her way down the road from Jerusalem. The major, who had crammed eleven members of his family into the car, apologized for not having stopped for her. Erakat commandeered a UN truck to search for his mother. Hearing airplanes overhead, he swerved onto the shoulder, nearly overturned the truck, and gashed his head in the wreck. He went to one of the UN clinics to be bandaged, and returned to his house. A hundred people from Abu Dis, the Erakats' home village, camped in the yard and orange grove. Panic overwhelmed the refugee camps.

"Horrible conditions took place. Mothers left their children behind. Husbands left their wives and children. Children left their parents. They lost their minds and everybody was trying to save his own life only."

At the end of the third day Rashid Erakat attached a white sheet outside the house.

He wrote at the time, "I had never believed in my life that such a thing could happen. I was disappointed, feeling desperate and bitter, and I felt that something had blocked my throat and I started crying like a baby who was not fed for days, or has lost the most valuable thing he possesses.

"At 8:00 P.M. there was a quietness as if everyone in the town was dead."

I arrived outside the fort a few minutes early for my appointment with the Israeli military governor, and the soldier at the gate left to make the necessary telephone call. He walked back to say that the governor and the officer who was to do the translating were running late. The governor was at the river seeing off Muslim pilgrims on their way to Mecca, for the haj. Like his Ottoman predecessors, the governor oversaw the arrangements and accepted orchestrated thanks.

The guard allowed me into the compound, and I stood in the shade of an enormous sycamore tree. It was very warm and still, and the wildflowers from the winter rains had become dry stubble. A major who walked by promoted me into an air-conditioned office in an annex to the fort; while the major attended to the papers on his desk, I sat at a table with a view of the air conditioner and a large safe. That was where the translator, Major Elise Shazar, found me.

From occasional meetings and many phone conversations, I knew her simply as Elise. She worked as the spokesperson for the military government, and she passed the test for professionalism by never giving much hint as to what she thought of all the military's doings. Elise soldiered on by answering questions and arranging interviews.

Twenty or so women soldiers were chattering near the entrance of the fort, on break. In the 1930s, when violence was increasing between Arabs and Jews, the British had embarked on a crash security program that included a chain of new forts. For economy's sake, all of the buildings followed a single set of blueprints, cookie-cutter style. Each fort was concrete and stucco the color of wet sand, stood two stories high, and was a demonstration project for long straight lines. No frills. Sir Charles Tegart, who had made his name suppressing anti-British violence in India, was the force behind the building program. He allowed for a prim veranda along the upper level of the fort and kept the interior ceilings high. The identicalness of the buildings made for disorienting moments: you saw, or thought you saw, the Jericho fort in Ramallah and Nablus. Fort by Tegart, during the British heyday, was no less evocative than Church by Wren, as clear a symbol of empire as the Union Jack.

We took seats in a rather austere waiting area on the second floor. When the governor arrived, he exhaled in a long sigh and shook his head. It was hot, and the pilgrims had taken too much of his time.

Lieutenant Colonel Avi Ilouz was in his early forties. He was nearly the last of the line of Israeli governors of Jericho, though neither he nor I knew it at the time we spoke. He would look powerful even without benefit of his rank. He was very fit. His hair was black, graying at the fringes, and he wore a pistol on his right hip as a backup weapon to a hard sharp stare. He was in charge of a military government that had an ironically deceptive name: Civil Administration. It was the military's administration of what ordinarily would be civil affairs.

His district was the most nearly quiescent in the West Bank. Most of the people lived in Jericho or the clusters of farms that were nearby. For twenty-six years the military governors administered the schools, hospitals, police, every office that issued (or denied) permits. What made the Jericho governorship unlike any other were the two bridges at the Jordan River, which took most of a governor's time.

They were short narrow spans that supported heavy loads—human, vehicular, political. Since 1967, the bridges worked as sluiceways between Israel and Jordan; politics determined the direction of traffic and the rate of flow. Trucks carried West Bank farm crops across the river into Jordan, and Palestinians and foreigners (but not Israelis) could travel, with some bureaucratic difficulty, in either direction. Most trucks used the bridge called Damiya; individuals used the bridge named for General Edmund Allenby, the conqueror of Palestine.

Allenby was memorialized by a structure that epitomized engineering modesty. The Allenby Bridge (the King Hussein Bridge, Jordanians said) was erected to a World War II design for spans that had to be assembled in a hurry, aesthetics be damned. An earlier, more substantial version collapsed into the river during the 1967 war. The existing bridge is homely and monumentally small. It has foot-thick wooden planks patched with steel plates, the whole assemblage being prone to Saint Vitus' dance. When a truck crossed, the planks clattered and jumped.

It was a mapmaker's oxymoron at the bridge—a one-sided border. Jordan for many years refused to fly its flag on its side, to do its symbolic best not to recognize Israel's occupation of the West Bank. A moonscape of fantastical buttes added to the sense of unreality. There were ravenous flies, the heat of the bottom of the valley, and intimidating border checks.

You had to take a *service.* The driver needed a special permit, and some tension always rode with you. We always left from Jerusalem in the early morning. Compared to the hill country, Jericho would feel hot; the time of year didn't matter. The *service* would make its way to the head of a long line of cars to reach a checkpoint on the road east from town. Ahead of us the ground was bare and white, the East Bank hills close but never more than a hazy outline. Beyond the checkpoint the road became a bumpy trail of hard-packed dirt, and thick layers of barbed wire were on both sides. The real deterrent to waywardness was a series of small yellow signs attached to the fencing. On some of them, the sun had partially erased the important message. *D nger! Mi es!*

The landscape had not one butte but fifty—cones, pyramids—and zigzags of dry streambeds. It was the bottom of old Lake Lisan, everything made of marl. Everything was white except for a narrow tangle of reeds at the very edge of the river, which was a trickle concealed in the *zhor.*

All that Westerners really needed at the bridge was patience. Crossing into Jordan, you could tell the British had been there and had taught the etiquette of Whitehall. The officer who laboriously filled out the forms that had to be taken to Amman—he was a Jordanian and worked in that same job for years and years—believed in the purity and goodness of pins. Papers must be *pinned,* never stapled, never clipped. I thought of other officers, in uniforms no less fine, learning the same lesson in Cape Town and Delhi.

Going in the other direction, you found the same dry heat, different uniforms. A soldier examined your luggage and wished you a pleasant stay in Israel.

For Palestinians the procedures were much more trying, until Israel and the PLO agreed to share authority. Until then, almost everyone had to endure several hours of humiliation. An officer from the Civil Administration had let me watch the procedures, which took place in a cavernous building separate from the one used by Westerners. With exceptions for several categories of VIPs, everyone had to strip down to his or her underwear and be searched. A soldier would take away a person's shoes to be x-rayed. Another soldier examined the contents of each suitcase item by item, and the empty suitcases were x-rayed too. Anything folded was unfolded; what was wrapped was unwrapped. Everything was returned, several hours later, so that the new arrival could repack and leave the building in search of a *service* to take him to his destination. The agreement between Israel and the PLO promised less onerous procedures, though the document outlining the arrangements was memorable for its precise details—the type of glass to be used in passageways, the number of personnel to be at each desk.

"In comparison to other districts, I have no problems," the governor said, addressing himself to Elise.

"Was the locale's reputation for sleepiness deserved?"

"Of course. It's an agricultural area, not urban. This is a population mostly interested in tilling the land."

He drove an hour every morning from his house in Tel Aviv. If there was time he quickly toured Jericho in the company of a driver who doubled as a guard. On the street he took long quick strides, so people wanting to add a last detail to a plea for some kind of help ended up in a jog, trying to keep pace. They asked for permits to cross the Allenby Bridge or the governor's intervention to cancel a ban on travel to Jerusalem or relief from a tax bill. An elderly woman needed medical treatment for her eyes; the governor called the local health department to arrange for her operation to take place at a hospital—a good one—in Jerusalem.

"Sometimes I invite people here to discuss their problems," the colonel said. "Sometimes we deal with things in the field."

That was disingenuous. An invitation was almost invariably an order. Usually it was delivered in a brief phone call in which a person was told when to be at the fort. One was never too busy. I had watched the mayor pick up a ringing telephone in his office, mumble to his guests he really must go—an important matter, a thousand apologies, urgent, his job—and hurry out of the room. A factotum would serve another round of coffee to those of us left behind and say, "The governor's office."

Colonel Ilouz sat at a standard-issue desk with a view of two walls of charts dense with numbers. Rotation schedules for army units. A count of trucks crossing at the bridges. A census of teachers and schools. "I like being outside, not in the office. The part I like is the contact with the population."

I had spent the first part of the day in one of the livelier restaurants just off Jerusalem Road, with Khaled Ammar. The restaurant had one large, dark room plus several counters set up along the sidewalk for the sale—no hour was too early—of falafel and roasted chicken. Most of the liveliness was in the decor, since a goodly proportion of the customers whiled away their time reading and rereading slim newspapers and drinking coffee. A plastic Mickey Mouse beamed from the wall opposite the entrance and was surrounded by posters of Arabic singers. There was also a modestly framed verse from the Koran. Prices depended on who you were—discounts for a familiar face—and the mood of the young man in charge of the cashbox. Khaled and I plus a foursome of unsmiling men were the only customers.

Khaled Ammar almost always had something interesting to report about the local goings-on. But nothing he offered about other people was as striking as his own adventures with the Civil Administration. Khaled wrote occasionally for two Arabic papers in Jerusalem. He lived in Jericho, maintained a storefront office a block from Jerusalem Road that was a meeting place for the idle, and was one of the men familiar around town. Whenever he took a walk people on the street formed a reception line for a handshake. Exactly how he supported himself was never clear to me, since the newspapers paid very little and he seemed to have all the time in the world. He was about thirty, unmarried, and lived in his mother's house.

His dealings with the Civil Administration had to do with renewing his driver's license. In Israel a person could obtain a new license by mail. Under the military government, Palestinians in the Gaza Strip and the West Bank were required to make a round of office visits. Khaled Ammar went to the police to have them certify he was not sought for a crime, and he went to the office for property taxes, where everything was found to be in order. The problem arose at the office for income tax. After checking the records, a clerk said Khaled's father owed back taxes on a store.

Khaled explained that his father had never owned a store and had been dead for five years.

The clerk was unpersuaded.

Khaled returned with the death certificate and collared a family friend and marched him over to the clerk to explain that the father had in any case worked as a school office clerk, not a merchant. "I started thinking maybe the clerk knows more than me and my father's alive," Khaled said. "I told him that if he proved I owned a store, I would give him half of it."

The standoff continued for a week until Khaled complained to the mayor, who made a telephone call to the fort. Khaled received his license. When one of his brothers applied, the problem repeated itself. This time the family resolved the matter by slipping two hundred shekels (at the time about eighty dollars) to one of the Palestinians who often loitered outside the tax office. They were part of the landscape. They acted as go-betweens, informers, solicitors of bribes and, presumably, conveyers of information to the intelligence officers working at the fort. In exchange for two hundred shekels, Khaled's brother promptly obtained his driver's license.

In her very professional way, Elise expressed no surprise about Khaled's misadventures. The rules required "all this running around" from office to office as a reminder that the military government was in charge. She talked about the need of "assuring some contact day-to-day with the population." The governor too talked later about the importance of "contact." Khaled had had contact, so in a sense all was in order.

Colonel Iluoz usually returned from his inspection tour by 10:00 A.M. For the rest of the day, every day, he commanded meetings. When I visited him, he handed over a typed summary of a session he had held with school principals. While Elise translated the text, he busied himself with phone calls. One principal had asked the Civil Administration to pave a road; the governor referred the matter to the mayor. Another wanted four more classrooms; referred up the chain of command to an officer in another district. Four principals asked for telephones. The session had lasted three hours.

Phone calls done, the governor told Elise he was late for his next meeting, an indoctrination session for newly arrived soldiers assigned to the Allenby Bridge.

Some months later the files and furniture were carted out of the fort as part of the preparations for giving it to the Palestinians. Almost until the end it was possible to argue convincingly that an Israeli military governor having authority over day-to-day affairs was part of the natural order of things in Jericho. That it would match in duration the four-hundred-year chapter of the Ottomans, and then exceed it.

"I feel that I'm welcomed," the colonel said of his forays into town. "They invite me for coffee. *They* invite *me*, and we sit in public places. Everybody can see us when we talk.

"They don't have to do that; I'm not the one making the invitation."

This is behavior familiar from earlier centuries. Claude Conder, on assignment for the Palestine Exploration Fund, had observed the government as it had existed during the 1870s. His descriptions of an Ottoman governor could pass for one of Colonel Ilouz.

In every sense Conder was a successor to Charles Warren, and interest in travel and Palestine was almost in Conder's blood. His paternal grandfather, Josiah, had earned a small degree of fame for writing all thirty volumes of a series called *Modern Traveller*, though Josiah had never traveled outside Britain. Conder's father, a civil engineer, would write about both Palestine and the Bible. Conder himself, like Warren, graduated from the Royal Military Academy at Woolwich and was commissioned as a lieutenant in the Royal Engineers. He was one of the men the PEF sent to survey all of western Palestine, the project made possible by the public enthusiasm generated by Warren's work in

Jerusalem. Compared to Warren, Conder was less experienced and more impressionable. So Ottoman rule left him aghast.

"The system of government is simple," Conder wrote. "The duties are to collect taxes, and to put down riots, which constantly occur." A governor would be both fawned upon and reviled. He was given obsequious greetings. The elaborate show of politesse meant only that he was powerful. To be admired was something altogether different.

III

Downtown

I made my rounds, the stucco house to the mound to the spring to the little downtown. In early mornings the traffic was shepherds and sheep walking toward patchy greenness. A few hours later a gleaming train of tourist buses descending from Jerusalem steamed into the parking lot at the mound, the same time the first taxis from the Allenby Bridge—the cars dusty, crowded, top-heavy like camels with luggage strapped on their roofs—plodded to a stop near the municipality building, downtown. By then the mayor had made his own rounds. For a long time he would wave me a greeting but otherwise stayed out of reach.

He kept unpredictable hours at the municipality building, the local skyscraper at three stories tall. It was a product of the local boom during Jordanian times. For about a decade when the town belonged to the Hashemite Kingdom of Jordan, the vegetable farmers in the valley fed all of Jordan, fed Saudi Arabia, and fed the rest of the Arabian Peninsula, and landowners for the first time had a bumper crop of cash. Jericho was, briefly, puffed up with self-importance. Some of the mud-brick huts on Jerusalem Road were replaced with buildings faced with white stone, one of them becoming the town hall. The city gained a look of permanency. Modernity was not an unrealistic hope. But then came the wars that froze everything, as if in a snapshot. Except for the cars on the streets, the little business district was circa 1967 for twenty-five years, and everything showed the effects of having been a long time in the sun.

A butcher shop and two cramped grocery stores occupied the ground floor of the town hall, and a staircase in the center led up to the offices. A half-dozen men made themselves at home in the upstairs hallway and busied themselves with idleness. They nodded a greeting at everyone cresting the steps. One or another of the men always knew your purpose, or guessed at it, and the tilt of his nod directed you in the right direction. The mayor's gatekeeper held court in a large room on the left, a holding pen furnished with threadbare chairs. His windows overlooked a mud-brick house with a grassy yard populated by roosters and a tethered goat.

"Ah! Ah! So good to see you again!" We clucked and preened. When he put his hand near his heart I did likewise as part of the formula of pleasantries between men feigning great pleasure, two more roosters in the pen. Our small talk—the wet winter, a photograph showing Jericho in the '30s—did not camouflage the absence of the mayor, Jamil Khalif. No one knew when he might appear to deal with the growing crowd of supplicants. But I was welcome—"*most* welcomed, Mr. Robert!"—to spend the day waiting. An elderly man entered bearing a tray with coffee. Tell a stranger in his home he is a thief, call his children louts, and you send the same message given by waving away coffee. My heartfelt distaste for it was a social handicap. Rather than insult the host I always accepted the little china cup.

Jamil Khalif was late again when we met a few days later, though he apologized. A good mayor, he explained immodestly, is always stopping to inspect a sidewalk. A worthy chief executive offers a cigarette to the man sweeping the street, or asks in a fatherly way if a truck driver has remembered his morning cup of tea. Always busy. "That's the kind of man I am," he said.

Jamil Khalif was stubby and had a thin mustache gone to gray. He wore open-necked shirts and, heat permitting, a blue blazer. He had a friendly face wider at jaw than forehead, a fez in flesh and bone. His father had been mayor under the British and, briefly, the Jordanians. The son inherited respectability guaranteed by large tracts of land planted with bananas and orange trees. His ample girth radiated prosperity.

The office slavishly followed the rules of decor for Middle Eastern potentates. Chairs lined the sides of the room while the center was left empty, a wide aisle for the ruler to make his way through an adoring crowd. The chairs were plush and uncomfortable. Your derriere slowly sank into a netherworld of soft foam. The princeling at his desk had a view of smiling faces craning in his direction even as the bodies struggled to remain afloat.

Visitors with appointments confidently took seats close to Khalif. People arriving unannounced went through a reception line of clucks and handshakes and placed themselves in the rear. Across the hall the gatekeeper monitored the social mix and the numbers and steered the overflow into another room. Each person—it made no difference if you arrived immediately after a party of ten, and if the prayer leader of the mosque and his retinue were climbing the stairs—was warmly assured he was next.

On the street Khalif could be rather engaging, a teller of anecdotes, relaxed, and enjoyable company. But the office stiffened him. Even if we had spoken the day before, he opened every talk there the same way. Seated at his desk and facing that vast audience of seats, he was all rote. "Jericho you can explain very easily," he always began.

"Jericho is a famous city. Jericho is a holy place."

He was not easily deflected.

"Jericho is famous for its vegetables," he said, as if his farm were the main draw. He declared that the local oranges had an especially appealing fragrance. He bragged about the lightness and taste of the water. "Very rich land, very lovely oranges."

Khalif enjoyed his title more than his work. As mayor his duties were to cooperate with the military governor, but not so well as to risk being branded a collaborator by other Palestinians; and to cooperate with the several Palestinian factions emerging from long years in the underground, but not so well with one group as to enrage another group. He was in constant search for the middle ground. It moved unpredictably and sometimes melted away, like an ice floe. So he stepped carefully.

Hanging on the wall behind the desk was a picture taken on the Allenby Bridge showing Khalif with Jimmy Carter when Carter was the American president. Khalif had met Yasser Arafat of the PLO and Jordan's King Hussein. He called that "high politics" but did not aspire to work at such heights. He cared mainly about his family and his properties, and also about the town's prosperity since it affected his own.

Like others the mayor both took comfort from the town's reputation for quiet and felt embarrassed by it. At the time, perfect calm was unpolitic. There was nostalgia for the years when Communists and Baathists were active in the refugee camps, even though the Baathists had no followers and the Communists only a few, and for the era of the *fedayeen*, when they recruited for guerrilla raids, even though the raids left no mark. The wishful gossip was that firebombings against the Israelis occurred every week. Because the gossip was comforting it was repeated as being true. People wanted to believe their community offered more than dry heat and an annual surplus of bananas. Khalif was not the person to challenge a satisfying story. I was familiar but not really known, so for the mayor it was better to steer away from politics.

"Jericho is a famous city," the mayor repeated. Jericho was old. Jericho was below sea level. Several sites had been known by this same name. The newest was the town also called Riha, where we talked. Depending on the pronunciation, the word meant "small" (REE-hah) or (RAH-hah) "rest." To the north of the business district was the oldest Jericho. (This was the mound picked over by Charles Warren, though I found no one in town aware of his work or name.) To the south, behind the concrete fort and nearly in the shadow of the hills, were the ruins of Roman Jericho, the sumptuous palace of King Herod. The Jews had come here. Jesus, baptized in the Jordan, walked through Jericho on his last trip to Jerusalem. Lovely oranges.

All familiar stories, and in Sunday school the familiarity was so comforting and even cheering that I never noticed the mayhem at the stories' heart. In the potted history, the town is the setting for unavenged calamities. One population is wiped out by newcomers destined to fall victim to some other communal disaster. Sometimes warnings of doom are sounded but go ignored. God delivers cautionary messages through prophets. Then catastrophe befalls people who have done little wrong other than to be in that particular place.

The mythic history of the town begins of course with Joshua of the Old Testament. His story about the Israelites' capture of the city includes the suspense of espionage and the drama of a bloodbath. After bringing the Israelites to the eastern shore of the Jordan, Joshua sends two spies across the river to enter the walled town. They find their way to the house of Rahab the prostitute, who realizes that the Israelites' invasion is destined to succeed. After the city gates are closed, she masterminds the spies' escape. They promise to spare everyone in her house during the battle to come.

When it is time for all the Israelites to cross the Jordan, Joshua orders twelve priests to lead the way. Exactly as God has promised, the river stops to allow everyone to reach the opposite bank. To commemorate the event, the Israelites carry twelve stones from the riverbed to a new camp, called Gilgal. Several days pass before the newcomers launch their attack. Following God's instructions, the army marches around the city walls once each day for six days; each day seven priests blow rams' horns. On the seventh day, the Israelites circle the city seven times, the priests again sound their trumpets, and on that cue all the Israelites raise a great shout. The city walls collapse; the Israelites enter Jericho.

> Then they utterly destroyed all in the city, both men and women, young and old, oxen, sheep, and asses, with the edge of the sword . . . And they burned the city with fire, and all within it.

Only Rahab and her family are saved.

Joshua placed a curse on the destroyed city to ensure it would remain desolate. Nowhere in the Old Testament is another city singled out in that grim way. Anyone repairing the city's foundations would lose his firstborn son, the Israelites were told; anyone who persisted and went so far as to rebuild Jericho's gates would suffer the loss of his youngest-born son too.

As recounted in the Book of Joshua, the pillaging at Jericho became the grisly standard for the military campaign that followed. "And you shall do to Ai"—the city that became the Israelites' next target—"and its king as you did to Jericho and its king." The Book of Joshua says it was done at Ai, at Bethel, at Libnah, Lachish, Debir, Makkedah, at Eglon. "He left none remaining, but utterly destroyed all that breathed."

The accounts of violence have not gone unnoticed, which is to understate several millennia of intellectual endeavor. Parsing the actions of the Israelites as they announce themselves in Canaan is part of the seminarian's basic heavy industry, his foundry. The essays and books—there are thousands—are by theologians who are Jewish, Roman Catholic, Orthodox, Protestant; scholars who are none of the above; professors of literature; scholars who maintain that the story of the conquest was recorded by Joshua himself; others who suggest the person called Joshua is best thought of in the same light as Oedipus or Moby Dick, an illuminating symbol of powerful forces but something other than actual flesh. There are learned commentators whose starting point is a belief that the story is in every detail the literal truth. There are others who regard the text as the product of many hands working over a long period, producing narratives that are neither wholly factual accounts of observed events nor tales entirely divorced from what people experienced or found inspiring. This last view has come to be the scholarly mainstream, though its course has been a long time in the making and has included many turnings. For the sake of full disclosure I should say that I am most at home in that current. The scholars exploring those waters are not of one mind or one theory. They offer varying ideas, in many more thousands of essays, about whose hands were at work in Bible writing, when they worked, where, and what purposes the lengthy editing process served. The current meanders. There are also the archaeologists, promoters of a different set of ideas about what to analyze and how to do so. But their story is for later.

The story in the Book of Joshua was more than a tale of adventure. It distinguished God's character from man's. God promised Canaan to the Israelites, and with their arrival at Jericho—buildings about to be destroyed, its population about to be slaughtered—the Israelites began to take possession in their messily human way. Being human their behavior was inevitable. They repeated the bloodbath more than once, at other Canaanite towns. Righteousness, in this story, was God's monopoly. God offered instructions at Jericho only up to the point of the walls' collapse. The rest was left to the soldiers. Joshua's army did the killing and burning. God remained the untainted master strategist. He is the offstage hero powerless to make the chosen people better than the humans they are.

Later, we are told by the Old Testament, a man named Hiel ignored the curse announced by Joshua and rebuilt Jericho and thereby lost his eldest and youngest sons. Later still, Jericho was a populated city once again, but the curse lingered in the form of unhealthful water at the spring. We are told that people blamed the water for miscarriages and poor harvests. In those days, the prophet Elijah walked with his disciple Elisha from Jericho to the western bank of the Jordan. When Elijah struck the water with his cloak, the river parted to let them continue their walk, until a chariot drawn by horses of fire came between them, making way for a whirlwind that swooped Elijah into heaven. Elisha, left alone, returned to the town; there he heard the many complaints about the water. We are told Elisha threw salt into the water and made it forever wholesome. And in that way the curse on Jericho was removed, and in that way the water became known as Elisha's Spring—the spring also called Ein es Sultan.

This era of miracles eventually ends. No one ever again glimpses horses of fire or the like. But the later history of the town, and of the valley as a whole, when they are divorced from the holy and the magical, is no less fantastical. Certainly no less violent.

In the second century B.C. the valley hosts the fratricidal dramas of the Hasmoneans, Judea's last independent dynasty of Jewish kings. The Hasmonean named Simon was invited to a banquet at a fortress overlooking Jericho. Its commander, Ptolemy, made murder the main course. Ptolemy killed Simon and kidnapped Simon's wife and two of his sons. A generation later two Hasmonean brothers—Aristobulus and Hyrcanus—battled each other in a civil war, their armies fighting at Jericho until stalemate. Later, the Romans entered on the side of Hyrcanus and helped breach the walls of Jerusalem to attack Aristobulus—Jews fighting Jews. A historian from that time writes with no particular emphasis that the fighting in Jerusalem caused twelve thousand deaths. Aristobulus was captured, then escaped. Several dramas later, he was poisoned. One of his sons was beheaded. Another son resumed the battle against Hyrcanus, captured him, and bit off his ears. And the military commander allied with Hyrcanus slipped out of the country and made his way to Rome.

Herod was that commander.

No other individual has had as large an impact on the valley. In Rome, the emperor Octavian declared him king of Judea, though at that time control remained in the hands of the Hasmoneans. Herod returned to Judea to prepare an assault on them. Jericho became his supply depot. Not for the last time, people living there fled into the hills, the better to avoid the plundering soldiers. After capturing the town and enjoying a rest, he marched toward Jerusalem to begin a siege.

By one account the siege lasted fifty-five days; according to another, five months. Whichever was the case, his army was enraged by the length of the campaign. Finally breaking into the city, in 37 B.C., they slaughtered much of the population and beheaded the Hasmonean king. And Herod became Judea's ruler in fact as well as name.

He kept Judea free of invaders; rebuilt the Jewish temple in Jerusalem, something that had been left undone for centuries; erected new cities on the Mediterranean coast and in the hills. He built an impressive chain of fortresses. But better to be Herod's pig, it was said, than his son.

Herod assumed many of the people around him were treasonous. With ten wives over the course of his life and fifteen children, his household was never short of intrigues. His favorite wife was Mariamne, a Hasmonean. Unable to bear the thought that she might remarry in case of his death, he gave orders for her to be killed if he failed to return from trips abroad. Mariamne was unappreciative of such devotion. They fought. Disagreement was more than the king could tolerate since it suggested Mariamne had less than perfect love for him. Herod executed Mariamne.

Whether his behavior was exceptionally cruel is hard to judge, for lack of benchmarks. He is the only Roman governor saddled with a written biography, and that has been to the lasting cost of his reputation. Most of his peers, when they are known at all, are only entries on a list of names. The surviving reports about Herod are detailed enough to disclose his finances and some of the laws of his administration and to tell of his moods. In Christian legend, he also is saddled with the Massacre of the Innocents, an attempt to have Jesus killed. In the imagined portraits painted during the Renaissance, that is the most common image of him: Herod as murderer of children.

Emperors in Rome were themselves not strangers to intrigue or murder. Closer to home, there was the cruelty of the Hasmoneans. A generation before Herod, the Hasmonean Alexander Jannaeus killed six thousand of his subjects in retaliation for his being pelted by lemons. During subsequent troubles, Alexander Jannaeus dined with his concubines while his army, in the midst of the king's banquet, crucified eight hundred men and slaughtered their families.

Herod ordered the deaths of one of Mariamne's brothers (drowned in a swimming pool at Jericho) and her Hasmonean grandfather (strangled). He executed three of his own sons. He incited a crowd in Jericho to stone to death two of his bodyguards. Once, he heard out a retired army officer named Tiro, who loyally told the king of disaffection within the military, thereby prompting Herod to convene another crowd to stone to death three hundred officers. Tiro was killed too—anyone sufficiently courageous to bring the king unflattering news was brave enough to become a plotter—as was Tiro's son. One of the king's barbers was another victim, for maligning Tiro.

For the king, Jericho was meanwhile a private sunroom. He had inherited from the Hasmoneans a royal estate about a mile from the spring. Everything the Hasmoneans had built, Herod rebuilt. He had inherited a mud-brick palace alongside a wadi and a second, fortified palace atop an artificial hill; there were plantations of palm trees, a system of aqueducts, and a network of swimming pools. He added a pool large enough to be used for boating, and enlarged some of the others. In what had been desert were trees whose resins were made into perfume and medicines.

Cleopatra, queen of Egypt, was for a time the estate's owner of record. Therein lies another story of social pathology. The kindest phrase offered by her contemporaries was that she was "prone to covetousness." She increased her wealth by arranging for the deaths of relatives; relatives murdered, she relied on the seduction of friends. Mark Antony tumbled in love with her, when he was part of the triumvirate governing the Roman Empire. In love "to the degree of slavery," even "bewitched," a chronicler relates, he offered her Jericho and the plantations as a gift. Herod became Cleopatra's rent-paying tenant.

She toured Judea and was said to have shown great passion for him. Visit over, she sought to obtain the rest of his kingdom by scheming, unsuccessfully, to have him killed. She and Mark Antony would later find themselves on the losing side of a war against the rest of Rome; the lovers committed suicide, Cleopatra famously so by the bite of an asp.

A fine resort Jericho surely was. When an earthquake damaged the original Hasmonean palace, Herod erected a new one, then another, this last one so large it occupied both banks of the wadi. Two forts provided security from atop the cliffs. The reception hall at the main palace was ninety-five feet long and sixty feet wide and was paved with imported marble. Frescoes decorated the walls. The grounds were landscaped with fountains and elaborate gardens. Sole proprietor after Cleopatra's death, King Herod. There were enormous baths arranged according to an appealing logic, like an exotic taxonomy. A tepidarium for warming up, leading to a caldarium for more thorough heating. Another caldarium led to a round frigidarium for cooling. The winter climate was another luxury: while the rest of the kingdom was snowbound, people in Jericho dressed comfortably in linen. Summers were less than wonderful—hot, the landscape a burning desolation—and Herod and his guests adjourned to palaces elsewhere in Judea.

In old age he was in great misery. Worms infected sores on his genitals and he was afflicted with painful bowels and intolerable itching. His breath became horribly foul, and he gasped constantly. Twentieth-century physicians extrapolating from that information have offered diagnostic guesses: pancreatic cancer, advanced diabetes, cirrhosis of the liver, kidney failure, gangrene of the scrotum, or hardening of the arteries, in some hard-to-determine combination.

He wanted guarantees he would be mourned, even if only vicariously. One of his last orders was for soldiers to bring the kingdom's most prominent Jews to Jericho and imprison them in one of his vast public works projects, a combination hippodrome-amphitheater. He asked his sister to have the prisoners killed immediately after his own death. He would die, all the prisoners would be murdered, so families throughout the kingdom would be bereft and go into mourning. Knowing his subjects would be distraught, the king could die happy.

I began walking to the palaces from Elisha's Spring, which was Charles Warren's old campsite, and turned off from the highway onto a gravelly road that soon narrowed into a footpath. The path skirted a banana grove that was filled mostly with woody stumps, and slipped between thorny hedges of nubk. Farmers cultivated nubk or tolerated it, in lieu of erecting a fence. The waist-high hedges were impenetrable even by a goat. Walking on his own one day, Charles Warren became snagged in one such hedge, the thorns catching him by his coat. Thrashing about, he entangled his arms and legs, predictably, until the only movement left to him was that of one hand. He used it to draw his revolver. Warren pointed it at a passing Bedouin. The Bedouin was persuaded to help untangle him. "I was very much tickled with the idea," Warren said.

The trail passed a crumbly dome of earth at the head of a banana grove, the dome like a large mud pie stranded by low tide from an evaporated sea. It was early morning, before every shadow disappeared into white glare. So I saw courses of mud-brick in the dome, the bricks uneven and thick. It was what remained of Herod's hippodrome and amphitheater. On one face had been the stadium where the audience sat in curved rows cut into the bricks. On the top now were deep pits dug by archaeologists looking, in vain as it turned out, for enough debris to recover a sense of the building that had stood there. But it had disappeared. The excavators, working during the 1970s, uncovered enough stone embedded in the ground to trace the probable path of the racetrack. It had sent the jockeys and the chariot drivers on a course like a drag strip, arrow-straight for 1,100 feet through the banana grove and on into a vegetable patch. Most of the remaining stones that marked the perimeter were concealed by nubk. I wondered how often the farmers here had struck something hard with a hoe and cursed the stones; and what explanations were given, once the mud-brick structure lost its purpose and form, for the straightness of the borders of this field. From the top of the stadium, you saw the valley obeisant at your feet.

Beyond the hippodrome the trail wound past fields of vegetables covered with plastic sheeting, and several abandoned huts, and headed toward the banks of Wadi Kelt. I was within about a mile of where the wadi emerged from a steep-sided canyon that was of the wadi's own slow making. Water's sharp knife had sliced through the limestone hills; where the hills gave way to the plain, the wadi widened and traveled along the floor of the valley the last two or three miles to the Jordan. Wadi Kelt was bone dry at least ten months of the year but a torrent at the end of winter. You could never predict exactly when the tap would open. The most lethal combination was an end-of-winter downpour in Jerusalem on a day when Jericho was baking in sunshine. Leave Jericho for a hike into Wadi Kelt, and fight for your life in a flash flood while the sun shone at your back.

Two children climbing one of the wadi's banks showed the way under a fence, and waved as they walked the rest of the way home to a long flat-roofed shed. A family of goat herders there was supposed to keep watch over Herod's palaces. No living creature except a dog tending the goats paid the slightest attention to comings and goings.

Everything of transportable value had disappeared a long time ago. Herod's palaces now were low courses of stone, and several dozen deep pits set into coarse reddish sand, less building than played-out quarry. Following the stones, I could trace rooms and entire buildings. But the sense of grandeur that remained was in the scale. Herod had made the banks of the wadi a grand royal stage, built up with earth dredged from the wadi. The platform offered enough room for Buckingham Palace and the House of Parliament. But other than the dog and goats, it had no actors. Beyond the fence in the direction of the hippodrome was the dense dark greenness of a palm grove, the trees a restless audience rustling in a hot wind.

A mound, steep-sided like a cone, was the remains of probably the first Hasmonean palace. Herod or the Hasmoneans had dumped earth on top to create a platform for another, presumably finer building, but nothing remained of it. At Herod's main reception hall, which was several hundred feet away, the ground was embossed with the pattern of the marble flooring, an intricate fossil of closely fitted octagons and squares. But the flooring itself was gone.

I stumbled across Wadi Kelt, a dry river of sand and boulders. On the opposite bank was another high cone. Its lip was irregular and cracked, like the crater of an eroded volcano. In Herod's time a building stood atop it—a guesthouse, perhaps another set of baths. From the top, the real luxury was the view of oasis, desert, and mountains.

If Herod's palaces were lost in jungle, I would have seen them as somehow less dead. On a tour of the Holy Land in 1857, when his spirits were already low, Herman Melville traveled from Jerusalem into the Judean desert and in that way inspired and further depressed himself. He traveled through Wadi Kelt and by the crumbled cones, and in his journal he described the countryside. "Whitish mildew pervading whole tracts of landscape—bleached—leprosy—encrustration of curses—old cheese—bones of rocks." At the time only one road went from Jerusalem to Jericho; it would have brought him within a few feet of the ruins. "You see the anatomy—compares with ordinary regions as skeleton with living & rosy man.—No moss as in other ruins—no grace of decay."

Vines growing out of a fetid mulch would be evidence that life, in some form, continued. Instead there was a bare sandy platform. Not even a weed was growing.

From the palaces, it was an hour's climb to the mountain fort called Cypros. I had to stop when I reached a ridge about fifty feet below the summit; the last zigzags were blocked by a mothballed army post built by Israel after the '67 war. There was a modern battlefield-in-waiting, below Herod's fort. The mountain face was honeycombed with a network of trenches, a sealed-up supply depot of some kind, and firing positions, and tunnels presumably leading to more trenches. At your feet were the valley and the roads laid out by the Romans. You could pick out buildings on the other side of the river or see the horses of your enemy, or your enemy's tanks and trucks, until the haze from evaporation appeared in midmorning, or until the sun overheated the air into crazy shimmers. To one side was the northern edge of the Dead Sea, the color and weight of stainless steel milled flat and thin.

Cypros caught every breeze, so there was no reason to leave. I idly scuffed my shoes in the dirt. Then dug more industriously, because there were bits of colored stone—small well-cut squares in white, blue, and black.

By the time I uncovered a short strip of mosaic I knew to stop. "Yes," Avner, an archaeologist back in Jerusalem, sighed into the phone much later. "Yes . . . mosaics on Cypros." They had been examined in the past, the pattern damaged long before it was scuffed by a shoe. Yes, everything was covered by dirt or was supposed to be since for the moment that was the best way to protect it. In any case how many people walked up the slope? What were you doing there? It was an army place.

Sometime around the year 500, which was five hundred years after Herod, Christian monks seeking seclusion had lived there, probably no more than one or two at a time, given the limited space. They had a deep cistern and a roughly rectangular room whose floor was the mosaic; the pattern was no longer discernible. On the summit on the opposite side of the wadi were the ruins of a monastery, where another Herodian fort had stood. Reaching them required a difficult climb I never made. But from Cypros I gazed down on the palaces and the herders' shed and small black forms that were goats; and I heard, or so I imagined, the barking dog.

Excavators found the Jewish burial ground from Herod's time in the 1970s, by chance. In Jericho's little downtown someone noticed a limestone chest in the shop of an antiquities dealer. Other chests like it had been found in Jerusalem. They were taller than they were wide, stood on stubby legs, and were in some cases decorated with well-carved rosettes; all included well-fitted lids. The chests were ossuaries—boxes for bones.

As should be expected the dealer said his information was of course only thirdhand but that someone—of course, he did not know who—had found the chest near town. Of course, he did not know precisely where.

Rachel Hachlili, an Israeli, was the archaeologist assigned the task of searching for the original burial place of the Jericho chest. "I had a feeling," she said, "there was more than one tomb." She found more than a hundred, all of them square, well-made chambers carved into the shoulder of the limestone hills west of Herod's palaces.

Wooden coffins were in the oldest graves. But for reasons that remain a mystery, Jericho's residents abruptly altered their burial practices, beginning about 10 A.D. Given the radicalness of the change you can reasonably conclude that people changed their beliefs about either life or what awaited them after death. The living no longer sealed the remains of someone newly deceased into a wooden coffin but made a temporary burial to allow the flesh to decay from the bones. The skeleton then was exhumed. It was disassembled to allow the bones to be fitted into one of the limestone chests.

Hachlili is confident more graves remain to be discovered, "hundreds and hundreds."

The aqueducts—built by the Hasmoneans, improved by Herod—were still in use, snaking down the hillsides onto the plain. They brought water from springs in Wadi Kelt and from other springs closer to Jericho, to irrigate the westernmost part of the valley. The system had fed Herod's gardens and the several swimming pools, then gradually fell into disrepair. Motivated by profit, wealthy families in Jerusalem revived the system near the end of the nineteenth century. They had acquired vast tracts that included the palaces, though except for the two high cones everything of Herod's was deeply buried in sand and by a jungle of nubk. Herders called the area Tulul Abu el-Alayiq, Hills of the Father of the Bramble Bush. The landowners, who knew nothing of buried palaces, knew farming and knew the valley's winter climate. After repairing the aqueducts, fieldhands planted vegetables and winter wheat. The crops and the owners thrived.

The swimming pools were uncovered about the same time as the cemetery, in the 1970s. Their existence was known thanks to the writings, then roughly 1,900 years old, of the historian Flavius Josephus.

His is a remarkable life. He was born in Judea in 37 A.D. Josephus became priest, military leader for the Jews, adviser to the Romans, and prolific historian; and above all else, consummate survivor. In his most ambitious project as a writer, *Jewish Antiquities,* Josephus sought to tell the history of the Jews from creation to his own time. He is the best chronicler of the Hasmoneans, the de facto biographer of Herod, and a valuable witness to the phenomenon that became known as Christianity. Most important, his is the only eyewitness account of the Jews' calamitous revolt against Rome. He is an actor in many of the events he describes, and when he is not a participant he is reasonably nearby in time or place.

Josephus mentioned the swimming pools in a matter-of-fact description of Herod's murderousness. In this instance it was directed against Herod's eighteen-year-old brother-in-law, named Aristobulus. The young man was extraordinarily handsome, a Hasmonean, and recently appointed as high priest. He was much admired by the public and thereby judged by Herod to be a threat. Josephus writes that Herod invited Aristobulus to visit Jericho and relax in the company of the king's friends.

> But as the place was naturally very hot, they soon went out in a group for a stroll, and stood beside the swimming pools, of which there were several large ones around the palace, and cooled themselves off from the excessive heat of noon. At first they watched some of the servants and friends [of Herod] as they swam, and then, at Herod's urging, the youth was induced [to join them]. But with darkness coming on while he swam, some of the friends, who had been given orders to do so, kept pressing him down and holding him under water as if in sport, and they did not let up until they had quite suffocated him. In this manner was Aristobulus done away with when he was at most eighteen years old and had held the high priesthood for a year.

Finally, in 4 B.C., Herod died.

His prisoners were still at the hippodrome in Jericho, but his sister balked at his plan to have them killed. After his death, she falsely told the prisoners the king had changed his mind and wanted them released.

The royal succession did not go smoothly. In Jericho one of Herod's servants crowned himself the new king and looted the palaces, until soldiers beheaded him. After much squabbling among Herod's three surviving sons, the emperor in Rome divided Judea among them.

Reading Josephus, one could mistake the story for a fiendishly clever invention, so appalling are the events in his chronicle of the last decades of the Jews' small measure of self-rule under Rome and then their revolt. He presents a huge cast whose behavior becomes steadily more reprehensible. In the city of Caesarea, non-Jews killed twenty thousand Jews in an hour. Jews destroyed Gaza. At Cypros, Jewish mutineers cut the throats of soldiers and destroyed the fortifications. When civilians fled toward Jericho and beyond to the Jordan, they found their way blocked by the river. A Roman army killed fifteen thousand people along the banks, Josephus writes; and as the river current did its work, the Dead Sea filled with corpses.

Josephus became the Jews' commander in the Galilee but surrendered to the Romans, an event he described at great length in an attempt to justify his actions. He served the Romans until the end of the war as a translator and spokesman for their cause.

Knowing the outcome of the story—the Romans win the war; they capture Jerusalem in the year 70 and Masada, the last desert outpost, in 73—does not make his tale less horrific. Josephus claimed that more than a million persons perished in the fighting. "It was then common," he writes, "to see cities filled with dead bodies, still lying unburied."

After the war Jericho boomed with Christianity. For other than Joshua, Jesus was the personage to give the town its greatest fame. John the Baptist had baptized him in the Jordan, and despite several improbabilities, the traditionally honored site was the fording place closest to town. In the Gospel of Luke, Jesus had performed a miracle as he approached the town. In Mark and in Matthew, the event occurred as Jesus was leaving. But in or near Jericho, Jesus cures a man of blindness. Or cures two men. On the same journey Jesus encounters Zacchaeus, the tax collector in Jericho, who had climbed a sycamore tree to see over the crowd waiting to glimpse the renowned visitor.

By 325 Jericho had a bishop. This was a different, "new" Jericho, its center shifting away from Wadi Kelt and closer again to Elisha's Spring. The "new" Jericho would experience destructions, rebuildings, long periods of neglect. Romans would be succeeded by Persians, Muslim Arabs, Crusaders, Marmelukes, and by the Ottomans, whose preoccupations allowed the Bedouin to overrun the valley. But the direct descendant of that Jericho, sharing more or less the same site, is today's Riha, the Jericho of tourist buses and the PLO.

An otherwise anonymous Christian traveler from Gaul, the Bordeaux Pilgrim, wrote of an arduous journey made in 333, and his is the earliest firsthand account of the new town. Unfortunately he was content merely to name what he saw without otherwise describing it. The convention endured until the late 1400s and the arrival of Felix Fabri.

But this first rendering still has considerable power. The Bordeaux Pilgrim's laconic notes about day-to-day logistics reveal his own quite extraordinary devotion. His travel from Bordeaux to Constantinople had required roughly fourteen weeks. He needed another eight weeks or perhaps somewhat longer to cover the additional twelve hundred miles between Constantinople and Jerusalem. He most likely walked or, for part of the distance, rode a donkey. The return home was still ahead.

He visited Nablus, Jerusalem, and Bethany. At Jericho he reported seeing the sycamore tree Zacchaeus the tax collector had climbed three centuries earlier. He was shown a house said to be the dwelling of the prostitute Rahab, the house Joshua's conquering army had promised to spare. The authenticity of the sites went unquestioned. The improbable was evidence of the miraculous. Belief became credulity.

In the sixth century a pilgrim from Piacenza, near Milan, examined in Nazareth the school bench used by Jesus, or so the pilgrim said. Christians could lift the bench without difficulty but, the pilgrim said, Jews found it unmovable. He experienced Jericho as "a paradise," a city "full of remarkable things." Rahab's quarters were a guesthouse in which the bedroom where she had hidden the Israelite spies was set aside as a chapel. He visited Gilgal and saw there in a church the twelve great stones carried by Israelites from the bed of the Jordan. Elisha's

Spring watered the whole of the town. Dates grew to weigh a pound. The pilgrim remarked at length on a forty-pound lemon. A chapel surrounded the tree climbed so long ago by Zacchaeus, though the tree was "now dried up."

A French bishop called Arculf was the last pilgrim to make mention of Rahab's house, sometime near the end of the seventh century after the Persians had taken Jerusalem. Rahab's house was roofless, Arculf said. He found Jericho uninhabited yet fertile: everything was covered by vineyards and cornfields.

Five hundred years later the Crusaders used water from the springs to cultivate sugarcane on the plain. Then exit the Crusaders with their defeat by Saladin, in 1187. Exit the farmers. Enter the Bedouin.

Herod's Jericho seems long before to have entirely disappeared from view. The Bordeaux Pilgrim, in 333, explicitly mentioned seeing it but was the last visitor to do so. A small number of people may have lived along the banks of the wadi and depended on the water that collected in the old baths and on whatever building materials were left to be stripped. But mostly there was sand and nubk. Occasionally a traveler took note of the steep-sided cones along the old Roman road where Wadi Kelt opened onto the plain. Certainly, Charles Warren found them most curious.

Warren assigned some of his workmen to Wadi Kelt during his second spring in the valley, in 1868. They dug trenches eight feet deep into the two high cones, mounds "No. 1" and "No. 2." At the first Warren saw colorful flakes of glass and found a large amphora. He described the second as a heap of stones. "There can be no doubt that the whole of it is artificial," he wrote, "and there are signs of human art of great antiquity within, but everything crumbled away when exposed." The trench cut into the southern cone remains visible as a long gash, an almost-healed scar in the mound's face. Warren's tools and curiosity took him no farther. He advanced no other speculations about the history of the mounds.

Claude Conder retraced some of Warren's footsteps and went well beyond them. Though Conder had his eccentricities, as I was to learn, and held pet theories that were to do his reputation lasting harm, he was admirably deductive at Wadi Kelt. For inspiration he had only a burned-up wilderness and the descriptions of Herod's estate by Josephus. Conder was always self-consciously working to match ground with text, was willing to imagine the Herodian city, so also was prepared to recognize it. In 1873, while surveying the territory for the Palestine Exploration Fund, he saw in the desert the remains of aqueducts. In the wadi not far from the two great cones were large pieces of an intricately worked concrete, its surface built up into a netlike pattern. Other explorers had taken note of the aqueducts and the remains of old foundations and guessed that the site might be Herod's Jericho. But the evidence seemed slim. Conder recognized the patterned concrete as *opus reticulatum,* a speciality of Roman builders.

In a brief remark included in one of his regular letters to the PEF in London, Conder said he had found the probable site of Herod's Jericho. And this time the evidence was clear.

"More coffee? Water? Our water is, you know, very light."

Jamil Khalif, the mayor, realized he had told the potted history before, now that his retelling was nearly done. We were back to Jericho's water—"very famous"—and Khalif was praising a Mr. Shepherd, an English engineer who in the 1930s built a new network of canals from Elisha's Spring, Ein es Sultan. Shepherd's additions to the aqueducts were the first since Herod's time. Sixty years later Shepherd remained the mayor's hero. "Very fine man." Khalif had held onto Shepherd's drawings, browning in an overheated office.

Ein es Sultan was a small humid bowl of grass and palm trees. Mahmoud, the custodian, appeared overjoyed to have a visitor. We shook hands, and I connected his joy to one of our earlier meetings. Desperate to escape his demands for baksheesh, I had handed over a few shekels to buy quiet. The next time I stopped at the spring I had happened to come with Hakam Fahoum. Hakam had told Mahmoud at high volume he was a pest, he would get nothing, he did nothing, did he understand? Now, Mahmoud was delighted to see me, alone.

He smilingly asked the whereabouts of "your friend." Dear friend Hakam.

"In Jerusalem."

"Welcome! Welcome!"

He was a thin, short, loose-jointed man who never moved very fast. Mahmoud's job was to oversee the pump house at the head of the canals, and to mind some of the locks, which were metal gates that could block the water. The precisely scheduled openings and closings of the locks directed the water from canal to canal, customer to customer. You could buy land in Jericho without water, and water rights without land, which meant buying access to one of the canals. Water was sold by the hour, though for reasons no one remembered, a water-hour in Jericho was twenty-four minutes long. An hour's worth of water was the amount the aqueducts delivered to your property in twenty-four minutes according to a schedule dating back to Shepherd's time. People speculated in land, speculated in water like Texans gambling on oil, and endured booms and busts.

During his shift Mahmoud stood at the headwaters of all that flowed. His domain was a grassy island, surrounded by the canals and a crisscross of leaky pipes from the stucco pump house. The smell of ozone and hot grease from the electric pumps usually overpowered the perfume of the water. The pump house badly sagged, as if weakened by the odors and the labor of constantly pumping. It vibrated with the turning of the electric motors inside. The bulkiest of them was a remnant of Empire: manufacturer, "Ruston & Horn (India)." On the floor was a bucket of thick oil for lubricating the pumps, and seeps of grease and water, an exhibit on the early industrial age.

Everything was unimpressively small, as if this were only a model for the real thing. Since my last visit the pipes outside had been painted a gaudy blue, and someone had painted on a wall verses from the Koran in the same color. The pipes still leaked.

Mahmoud led the way to the spring. We went by the side of the pump house and into dense reeds, to a small pool made of concrete. It backed up against the bank that supported the main north-south highway, eight or so feet above us. The road had been built in the 1930s and came like a fence between the spring and the bulk of the mound. In the '30s no one had fully appreciated that the bank was part of the mound, albeit badly eroded. In the 1950s the remains of a building roughly four thousand years old were uncovered at the edge of the road. But anything else that might have been there was lost to the many gradings and layers of asphalt.

Ein es Sultan's magic was this: a steady stream of water emerging without drama from under the bank, and then filling the small pool. Another stream flowing out from a tunnel of rocks. A third appearing from an otherwise invisible vent in the midst of high grasses.

No gushers. Lots of mosquitoes, though. Ein es Sultan discredited every desirable stereotype of a spring except for the most important, which has to do with consistency.

The flow is one thousand gallons every minute of every day of every year. Millennium after millennium. A wet winter or a decade of drought produces no change. Ein es Sultan is an ideally small, restricting tap on a large underground reservoir. If the opening were substantially larger, the spring would show variations in flow. Substantially smaller, there would have been insufficient water to support a permanent settlement. Some of the mystery has been dispelled by hydrologists having calculated the spring's hidden source to be (approximately) 480 feet underground, and roughly a dozen miles from the outlet. The specialists do not declare, scoutlike, this natural reservoir to be under a given hillside; but they point in the general direction of Jerusalem.

"Baksheesh for me?" asked Mahmoud, my unsought guide. I waved him away and returned alone to the pump house. Vines of black cords descended from a window to a black telephone kept outside. A hefty padlock gripped the dial. Mahmoud had for company only an occasional incoming call from the municipality. He wanted to repeat the grand tour. I demurred but handed him some money. He thanked me and then quickly turned and began to urinate.

Every traveler knew in some detail about the spring, thanks to Josephus. Some who claimed to have visited quoted him at suspiciously great length or remarked only that Elisha's Spring was exactly as he had said. Or like the pilgrim from Piacenza they contributed embellishments consistent with the Bible though not with the landscape. The Piacenza pilgrim advised that a traveler, as he left Ein es Sultan and Jericho, would see the ashes of Sodom and Gomorrah.

Josephus had rhapsodized about waters sweeter than any others and bountiful gardens. Edward Robinson, the American biblical scholar who found Riha so irredeemably miserable in 1838, saw at the spring only one tree, everything else either marsh, because of the lack of drainage, or desert. So no gardens.

For a representative account of travelers' experiences, there is the description written in the mid-1850s by William Allen. A captain in the Royal Navy, he had assigned himself the task of searching for shorter trade routes to the East. Allen was especially tired from riding through these "sad regions," he said, when his party arrived at Ein es Sultan one winter evening. He captured all the frustrations.

> Here we pitched our tents, and passed a very cold and uncomfortable night; which was not improved by the incessant talking of our [guides], discussing their peculiar politics with their friends; the crying of more babies than I could have calculated on meeting in such a small village; the barking of dogs; the confusion caused by our horses breaking loose, for the pleasure of kicking and biting each other; so that we were not sorry to resume our journey long before daylight.

But one could create a more pleasant reality through sheer force of personality. An Anglican clergyman, the Reverend Henry Baker Tristram, in the 1860s proved this. He was a person of large enthusiasms. God's creatures fascinated him no less than God's book; he avidly hunted game of all kinds, and his scholarly writings on zoology and botany rightfully earned him great respect as a naturalist. Enlisted as a contributor for a new dictionary of the Bible, Tristram had been assigned the task of writing an entry on the fish of the Sea of Galilee. He searched museums for specimens. Finding none, he left Britain in 1861 for a six-week tour of Palestine to collect specimens himself.

Reverend Tristram wrote of pleasurably gathering plants there and shooting birds—"three or four"—and beginning in late 1863, he made a second visit that lasted nearly a year. The number of birds in his collection reached twenty thousand. One cannot determine from his writings whether the greater satisfaction was in the cataloging or the hunting.

From those writings emerges a patrician figure with an unshakable conviction that Palestine belonged as much to the British as to the Ottoman Turks or to the country's inhabitants. He believed the territory offered pleasures that were meant to be savored. A traveler should no more ignore them, he strongly suggested, than should a gentleman refuse to partake of a banquet laid before him by his friends.

So at Ein es Sultan he feasted. Tristram arrived with a parade of thirty-two horses and mules, various companions from Britain, and fourteen Bedouin armed with long spears. Everyone camped near the spring. Wood was plentiful enough to keep three watch fires burning every night, where now there are barely enough trees to provide kindling. "In zoology Jericho surpassed our most sanguine expectations," he wrote. "It added twenty-five species to our list of birds collected in the tour, and nearly every one of them rare and valuable kinds." Already he had discovered *Amydrus tristrami*, an orange-wing blackbird to become better known as Tristram's grackle. Nightingales swarmed near the spring. He saw a blue kingfisher by the water and turtledoves in the trees. A member of the party trapped a lynx. Tristram ventured from his tent to hunt wild boar, shot many more birds than could be preserved in the heat, and ate exceedingly well. He praised the nightingale soup. Sunday dinner included fish from the spring, boar, partridge, and plum pudding. Everything was grand except the inhabitants.

A delegation of women had come to the spring and began to sing. "There was no trace of mind in the expression of any one of these poor creatures, who scarcely know they have a soul, and have not an idea beyond the day," Tristram complained. They had intruded on his day, and the women had arrived unveiled. Tristram joked about their ugliness; his remarks were kinder toward animals. A liberal amount of baksheesh restored quiet. Only later did the foreigners realize the women composed a wedding party. The childlike girl who was the bride was given a silver coin.

When the Reverend Tristram returned home he talked with his friend, George Grove, about these experiences. For Grove, the conversations of course were more encouragement for creating the Palestine Exploration Fund. Grove had learned Hebrew, twice visited Palestine, and, along with his wife, compiled an index that listed in Hebrew, Greek, and Latin every mention of every name in the Bible. He could hardly have been more serious in his enthusiasm, which was part of a national infatuation with all things Oriental.

The Orient was broadly defined. Every square mile of territory, terrestrial or marine, that lay between Britain and India was held deserving of the nation's attention. Now, Grove wanted to make an intellectual capture of the Holy Land. Much as Napoleon had intellectually captured Egypt.

Napoleon's brief occupation of Egypt, beginning in 1798, had been a military disaster. The series of battles, and bubonic plague, killed more than 40 percent of the soldiers and sailors and left many of the survivors as invalids. But Napoleon had also brought a remarkable army of savants: twenty-one mathematicians, sixteen surveyors and cartographers, thirteen naturalists, ten men of letters, four architects, and three astronomers, among others. They were given the task of measuring, drawing, cataloging, and in every other possible way capturing in tangible form the wonders of the country. The men of learning were to take history and culture as prisoners, for the glory of France. Wherever the soldiers went, the scientists accompanied them and sketched the ancient statuary and temples, supervised haphazard excavations, and chose antiquities to be shipped to France.

The British, having defeated the French army, took many of the antiquities. But the savants found a way to transport to France much of what they had observed but had been unable to carry away physically. They worked for the next two decades writing and illustrating *Description de l'Egypte:* ten volumes of text plus fourteen volumes of plates (the second edition was even more imposing) presenting Egypt as an open-air theater where the present was as romantically exotic as antiquity.

George Grove convinced his friend James Fergusson, and convinced the Reverend Tristram, and other prominent figures in public life, of the *necessity* for the Palestine Exploration Fund, and in that way led them to that first public meeting of the Fund, in 1865. The Archbishop of York, presiding, announced the organization's three high-minded principles: the PEF would carry out its work "on scientific principles"; as a body it would take no sides in controversies; it was not to be conducted as a religious society. The founding members assumed science and Scripture would be each other's faithful servant.

The founders knew of the havoc already wrought in the name of science. Charles Lyell's *Principles of Geology,* the first volume of which appeared in 1830, and Charles Darwin's *Origin of the Species,* published in 1859, had reordered geologic and human time, extending them millions of years into a past that was seemingly unacknowledged by the Bible. Lyell argued that geologic change had taken place through processes working at a constant rate over extremely long periods of time, while Darwin allowed for never-ending changes in organic life over similarly long time spans. They were processes about which the Bible, again, was silent.

There were also the Bible's well-known inconsistencies. Moses is credited with writing down the names of thirty-six Edomite kings who reigned after his death. In one chapter of the Book of Joshua are three accounts of where the Israelites permanently set up the twelve stones taken from the Jordan River: in the middle of the river, on the river's western shore, or at Gilgal. The absurdities seemed undeniable. For the liberal-minded in Britain, the Bible was not divine revelation and thus not infallible, but it was thought to render an accurate history that a truly modern inquiry would confirm.

"We are about to apply the rules of science," the Archbishop of York declared at the inaugural meeting. But there were subtle limits. Members of the PEF confidently forecast that the work would unfailingly support the Bible, perhaps even undo some of the damage inflicted by the new sciences.

"The Scriptures of the Old and New Testament will be found exactly to adapt themselves to the facts and requirements of the case," a supportive clergyman predicted when the PEF was already several years old. "We have no fear whatsoever of exposing them to this crucial test . . . and if our faith needed a firmer basis on which to rest, we should find it in these investigations." The explorer's task was thus to buttress the implicit accuracy of the Bible with physical finds. Neither the PEF nor the first men it sent into the field seriously considered the prospect of discovering contradictions—something not built or not destroyed as Scripture said. Disagreement of that sort was assumed to be either impossible or temporary; it would mean only that the physical findings were incomplete or had been misinterpreted.

So at the end of 1865 Charles Wilson led the first survey sponsored by the PEF into the countryside. He reported that every hilltop appeared to have a ruin worthy of study. And everything he mapped, he said, compared to what remained to be done "as the seam of the coat to the whole garment." Then, Charles Warren's tunneling in Jerusalem—the ultimately successful gamble by George Grove to garner attention and money.

Every few years the PEF changed addresses, the newer offices in some instances less grand than the offices just vacated. The original members of its board gave way to newcomers. But neither the Reverend Tristram nor George Grove ever lost interest, even though Grove was pushed aside because of his squabbles with Charles Warren over money. The PEF was "feeble and imperfectly organised," confined by "its swaddling clothes," Warren complained. But it never collapsed. The person who kept it running, and who for more than thirty years was its one constant, was the figure named Walter Besant.

He was thirty-two, unemployed, and an aspiring novelist when he was hired to manage the Fund's operations. What attracted him was the job's moderate demands, not the middling salary of two hundred pounds a year. What initially made him attractive to the PEF is harder to fathom: Besant had briefly studied theology but had earned a living teaching mathematics. He was given the title of Secretary. Efficient, methodical to the point of brusqueness, he hoped the post would leave him time to write. He proceeded to write nine novels with a coauthor and then twenty-five novels on his own at the steady rate of one a year.

Besant and a clerk sat all day in the office preparing the PEF's quarterly journal and tended the accounts and corresponded with the querulous prideful men in the field, and fended off the occasional crank drawn by the vast promise and mystery in that name: Palestine Exploration Fund. One office visitor declared himself to be possessed by Nimrod. Another gentleman arrived wanting to dispute the existence of Jews.

In 1871 the Fund announced formally its plans for surveying all of Palestine. The proposal, as formulated by Charles Wilson, called for sending a new survey party to search for biblical place-names and, based on that work, to draft a detailed map. As long as the Ottoman Empire survived, knowledge of the Holy Land's names and places seemed to be the only available substitute for physical possession. The mapping would capture the Holy Land for Britain.

An extra spur came from the United States. A group of academics and mostly conservative churchmen had recently announced the establishment of a new organization in New York, the Palestine Exploration Society. The PEF welcomed the Americans as partners. It proposed a division of labor: the Americans would survey the territory east of the Jordan; the British, the lands to the west.

In June 1871, every speaker at the PEF's annual meeting favored the making of the great map of Palestine. There was an implicit promise that a small party of Royal Engineers could recover biblical history. Supporters were told the expedition would require four years to conduct its surveys and deliver the finished drawings and photographs. The annual cost would be three thousand pounds, to be raised through contributions from the public. George Grove was the first speaker after the Archbishop of York addressed the meeting as chairman. Grove set the optimistic tone for all the speakers to follow.

"We should make a clean sweep of what has been done before," he said, "and there is no doubt that we ought to produce, and can produce, in a definite time and for a certain definite expense, a complete map, which once done will be done for ever."

The optimism would last until the survey party began the work.

IV

Digging Down

The waters in the valley rose. Receded, rose. In the area of the Dead Sea, the accumulated sediments are more than four miles thick and weighty enough to have helped deepen the rift. *Homo erectus* stood 1.4 million years ago by a freshwater lake that was in the northern part of the valley. Ubeidiya, as the site is known, has yielded stone tools and testifies that conditions in the valley have changed. There are bones of elephant, rhinoceros, and hippopotamus.

Ofer Bar-Yosef was one of the excavators of Ubeidiya. He is a professor of anthropology at Harvard, an Israeli, and enviably prolific in his research; his knowledge of early human settlements is Levant-wide, rift-deep. His interests are second-generation since his father too studied archaeology. The elder Bar-Yosef was offered a job as draftsman with a prestigious team excavating the site of ancient Megiddo, but this being the 1930s he chose instead a position with the Mandate Treasury Department and stayed when it became the Treasury Department of Israel. His son the professor calls it the tenure track.

In the 1950s Ofer Bar-Yosef entered the Israeli army, as required, but volunteered to spend part of his tour as a laborer at Kebara Cave, an archaeological site near the city of Haifa. The cave is richer in prehistoric artifacts than any other place yet discovered in the Middle East. During the thirty-minute coffee breaks, Professor Moshe Stekelis offered the volunteer workers lectures on Paleolithic archaeology.

Bar-Yosef, army tour completed, studied at Hebrew University in Jerusalem and with Stekelis in the field. With zoologist Eitan Tchernov and other colleagues, Bar-Yosef also began excavations of his own. The younger generation quickly impressed its elders by introducing new techniques. When Stekelis died, in 1967, Bar-Yosef and Tchernov were chosen to direct the fieldwork at Ubeidiya.

For *Homo erectus*, it was a stopping place on his way out of Africa and into Europe. The site, two miles south of the Sea of Galilee, was discovered in modern times because the tectonic movement within the Dead Sea Rift had folded and raised some of the underlying rock, and because that movement had exposed to erosion the several hundred feet of earth that, over millennia, had collected on top of the human and animal artifacts. A farmer in 1959 happened to notice some bones in the earth as members of his kibbutz planted a vineyard.

What has been preserved of the early counterpoint between man and Middle East are a couple of random notes—Ubeidiya and a scattering of other sites. The chances of finding another are exceedingly small. A million years is ample time for water to have washed away most of the early human camps or buried them in alluvium. There is at one site a partial skull with a molar and an incisor; at another, several broken femurs—the two separated by hundreds of thousands of years.

Hunting and gathering were the only professions. The hunter-gatherers are known, to the extent they are, by how and into what forms they shaped stone into tools. Sometimes the term is "tools"; the quotation marks are a reminder not to expect implements in their modern form. You come across a sliver of flint, small enough to disappear in your pocket, with a face that has been smoothed or in some other way shaped; or you find the small flakes left behind from the shaping. A paleoarchaeologist's flints are an entomologist's *Lepidoptera,* a subspeciality that is almost infinitely large. The broad categories of forms are finite in number but contain an infinite number of variants, like fingerprints.

The working face of a flint tool may be oval, chisel-like, amygdaloid, trapezoidal, resharpened once, more than once, polished, left unpolished. It may have a tang that is shouldered, triangular, tonguelike. If the butt—the area below the point—is wide and flat-topped, it is *chapeau de gendarme;* a point's profile can be Concorde, arched like the aircraft. Through such characteristics extinct cultures are discovered, named, and followed from camp to camp. An edge may display a sheen typical of the cutting of grains, marks from woodworking, wear from butchery. When resharpened, the new working edge may be the right, left, or both, may be convex, straight, wavy, toothed (with one or many teeth). A "tool" will show whether it was separated from a larger rock with blows struck on one face in a single direction. Or in several directions. Or on two faces, or more. Blows convergent, divergent, or radial. Working again in Kebara Cave in the 1980s and early 1990s, Bar-Yosef and his colleagues, restricting themselves to examples one inch or longer, collected 25,000 "tools."

They tell you something, though not everyone is certain what. Did Neanderthals make tools using the methods that have been retrospectively worked out by tribes of graduate students? With the same respect for pattern? It is only a small step from there, a serious-minded critic has pointed out, to assuming the Neanderthals could also read French, so knew of the Concorde. Another critic, tongue in cheek, has suggested that a small group of paleoarchaeologists live indefinitely in a cave. They could thereby more closely study "the accretion of materials."

Tools say the Archelu-Yabrudian culture (180,000 years ago) was succeeded by the Mousterian, the Ahmarian, and the Kebaran. Named after the cave, the Kebaran culture appears twenty thousand years ago, when the region's climate becomes drier and cooler. Lake Lisan recedes to become the Dead Sea and the Sea of Galilee. Jericho thus becomes dry land.

Dry conditions then give way to wet. Kebarans give way to Geometric Kebarans (the shape of the tools explains the peculiar name), who find a cornucopia. This better climate—wetter, warmer—made food more easily obtainable, according to one theory, and the Geometric Kebarans could stay longer in each camp. Staying put longer, they had more children. Camps became larger, thus harder to move. And by staying put longer, people could observe close-up a larger portion of the annual cycle of the local flora and fauna. Over the generations people observed, perhaps, the conditions in which legumes and wild grains thrived.

Climate worldwide then abruptly turned cooler, in a final frost of the last Ice Age. For this population that had grown larger, the change brought an unavoidable crisis. People now faced starvation or the need to exploit more productively whatever vegetation remained. Out of necessity would emerge a new culture of experimenters. The Natufians—named for Wadi el Natuf, the desert site at which their remains were first found—are the people whose experiments succeeded.

Just enough light shines on this period to say that it does not lie in total darkness. But it is a close call. Roughly twelve thousand years ago, the Natufians become the first people to cross the fine line between nomadic and more sedentary life. They are the first to stay, most of the time, on the side of sedentism. Natufians do not live in one place year-round. They acted, though, like property owners. They returned year after year to the same camps during whatever season favored the given location. And they made improvements. The rooms partially dug into the earth were rounded, like tents. Natufians built hearths, dug pits or created containers of some other kind for storing food, and had well-ordered cemeteries.

Significantly, the Natufians had mice. It is mice, not men, who arbitrate disputes over who is sedentary. They favor whoever has reliable food stores, and given a dependable food source wild mice gradually domesticate themselves. Eitan Tchernov, Bar-Yosef's collaborator, identified some of the remains from Natufian sites as *Mus musculus domesticus*. Domestic mice, therefore domestic hosts.

A change from nomadic to sedentary life has consequences as epochal as those our ancestors inaugurated when they changed posture from four legged to two legged. Chasing resources from setting to setting and holding little in reserve, society develops few skills except those needed for shuttling the extended family to the next campsite. Staying longer at one site requires different social arrangements and it produces different tensions. People redivide their labors. Time devoted to the logistics of moving is reapplied to food gathering and the making of objects, beginning with housing.

Hidden somewhere in the region was a large complicated machine churning out change, and working overtime in about 10,000 B.C., or so I like to imagine. Compared to the more distant past, the pace of change in human behavior was breathtakingly rapid. Whatever the real nature of the mechanism, the mix of climate and population that led to the beginning of sedentism existed for only an instant—about two thousand years.

It does not mean people became immediately bound to one location. "You don't need to be settled year-round," Ofer Bar-Yosef said, while we were sitting in his spacious, bright office atop the Peabody Museum in Cambridge. "You have to ask yourself, what *is* sedentism?" To remain at one place six months? Longer?

Bar-Yosef is in his fifties. He has a round unlined face set off by a mustache worthy of a frisky young walrus; his energy level is no less worthy. After his family, his interests are the paleoclimatic, the archaeozoological, the paleobotanical. For him "mice" is another name for the bioarchaeological.

He suggested thinking about the fellahin, the peasants, of nineteenth-century Palestine to understand the sedentism of the Natufians. The fellahin lived in their villages for nine or so months, moved to another encampment to avoid the rigors of winter (or summer), and then returned. "In this sense, Natufians were sedentary."

They camped at sites straddling plains and hills, in order to have access to the species of both. Presumably the Natufians sought rich, reliably watered soil—land that could support wild grains—and a water supply that could attract game in the dry months and provide water for themselves.

So Natufians came to Ein es Sultan.

Theirs is the earliest-known human habitation at the spring. The date, based on small pieces of charcoal, has been fixed at roughly 9000 B.C. The Natufians left behind flint tools and tools made of animal bone and mortars made of limestone. But if Natufian communities made the large step from hunting-gathering to farming, here or elsewhere, the evidence for it is yet to be found.

Kathleen Mary Kenyon, the grande dame of archaeology for a generation, unearthed the flints. Excavating the great mound at Ein es Sultan for eight seasons in the 1950s, deeper than anyone there before or since, she piled up a nearly unscalable mountain of shards and notes.

Hers was not an unambitious project. And Kenyon's was not an easygoing personality. The Palestinians, who performed most of the labor at Jericho, called her the Great *Sitt,* the Great Madam. She was proudly British. To stand atop some high place, be it the great mound at Jericho or elsewhere, seemed to suit her nature. Distinctly imperial, seemingly also 100 percent sure of herself—that was Kenyon. She was always kneeling to look more closely at something in the ground and lighting another cigarette. At Jericho she paid meticulous, even obsessive, attention to detail while moving vast amounts of earth. In the process some comforting theories about the past were buried. Kenyon added rigor to archaeology in the Middle East and new (though not entirely successful) methods of excavation. She was autocratic, inefficient in damaging ways, inspired in much of her fieldwork, and wrong in some of her conclusions. Her career, as I was to learn, was a humbling example of how almost everything in archaeology, and perhaps in a life, can be done to the best of one's ability and still go seriously awry.

Of course, the Natufians saw no mound. When they were there, they were laying its bottommost layer. They had come to a perennial spring on a gently sloping plain. Over a long period they returned for lengthy, repeated stays or, perhaps, began to live there year-round. Eventually there was agriculture, and after agriculture, cities. All that would appear centuries after the last Natufians. At the spring they were responding to climate and the ways it affected the availability of food. Trying to look back we may think everything the Natufians did was inevitable and that each step was clearly forward. It is just as likely each change occurred by mere chance, by a whim of climate, or by a whim of human experiment, and probably with little opportunity for planning, almost as if by the random churnings of a complex unknown machine.

In thinking about change, Kathleen Kenyon was an optimistic determinist. "Once man is settled in one spot," she said with admirable economy, "the rest follows."

Archaeology has its deities, though none is universally revered; and has fundamental laws, none immutable; and has holy sites, all of them subject to reinterpretation. Sir William Matthew Flinders Petrie is the founding deity of modern archaeology, wrote several of the laws, and discovered some of the holy sites.

Being organized was in his genes. He was born in Britain in 1853, the great-grandson of the officer in charge of supplies during the battles against Napoleon and the grandson of the navigator who mapped the coast of Australia. Flinders Petrie was sickly as a child and was twenty-four when he enrolled for his first and only classroom studies, a course in algebra and trigonometry. At home he had read and reread a book on Egyptian hieroglyphics and immersed himself in studying fossils and old coins. As a young man, he spent much of his time wandering through the galleries of the British Museum. He wrote a book that endorsed the newly fashionable claims for the symbolic importance of the dimensions of the Great Pyramid. To conduct his own survey of the famous monuments, he sailed in 1880 to Egypt.

In Egypt, the norm for archaeologists was not so much to excavate as to quarry, and they were as carelessly destructive as the fellahin. The fellahin looked upon the ancient monuments as a source of building materials and as a cash crop, which they called *antikas.* The typical excavator regarded blasting powder as one of his favorite tools and was as likely to record his observations in a systematic way as to wake a mummy. Antiquities were carted off. An archaeologist was the person who sought the largest of anything, or the most exotic, for a museum in Europe, for the marketplace, or for his parlor.

Flinders Petrie changed how excavations were carried out and, in a sense, changed their purpose. He introduced the rigors of cataloging, by looking at every object excavated and recording details about where every object was found. Directing large numbers of hired laborers, he supervised the workforce more closely and, it is said, more humanely than did his colleagues. He was rewarded by the laborers bringing more of their finds directly to him instead of selling them clandestinely to dealers. And he worked with remarkable efficiency: he excavated during winter, usually at more than one site, and his reports were ready for publication by the end of summer. His colleagues required years, if they published at all. Soon there were flattering reports in the British press and well-attended exhibitions, displaying ancient pottery and inscriptions. Petrie was to work in Egypt for forty-two years, in the course of which he uncovered more than any single pharoah ever built.

By the end of the 1880s Petrie seemed to be admired by everyone, except his original sponsors. He had broken with them, agreed to a reconciliation, then angrily decided on a second divorce, and thereby earned a reputation as a difficult character. The Palestine Exploration Fund, however, was willing to overlook this. It was more impressed with his efficiency, since this suggested frugality. In any case, Petrie was obviously experienced in the ways of the Middle East. In 1890, the PEF hired him to travel to Palestine to begin excavations at any site he chose.

Petrie had memorable habits and strong prejudices. At mealtimes in the field, he would complaisantly ingest the contents of cans already opened for a week and encrusted with green mold. Then he would bring out sterling silver spoons for eating dessert. T. E. Lawrence, before his transformation into Lawrence of Arabia, worked several weeks as one of Petrie's assistants and marveled at his employer's ways. "Why hasn't he died of ptomaine poisoning?" Lawrence wondered. Striking too was Petrie's theory of history. In lectures and books, he argued that history was driven by racial differences and that the races could be organized into hierarchies. Some races were held to be naturally superior to others. He was not alone in propounding these ideas. People were "bad stock" or "good stock," to be culled like ancient pottery. "Weeding" was one of his pet ideas—improving the world by offering rewards to encourage "good stock" to breed.

Traveling on his mission for the PEF, in March 1890 Petrie arrived seasick in Jaffa. Then he endured a three-week wait for the necessary firman from the Ottomans. Firman secured, he needed only two days to examine six potential sites for excavation. The one he chose was amid the sand dunes northeast of Gaza at a scorpion-infested hill—Tell el-Hesi.

"A very fine site," he wrote the PEF. Certainly, it looked promising. A wadi sliced through the hill, exposing some of the innards, and scattered on the surface and visible in the exposed face, like pockmarks, were bits of pottery.

During the next six weeks his workers dug trenches, and in some areas tunnels, into the exposed face. Bedouin men handled the picks as the womenfolk carried away the dirt in baskets. Petrie examined the pottery and flints, marking them according to the level where they were found. For exploration in Palestine this was new. Heinrich Schliemann, twenty years earlier in Asia Minor, had pioneered the practice of dissecting a site layer by layer when he uncovered Troy. Petrie had worked along the same lines at sites in Egypt. But until the digging at Tell el-Hesi, no one in Palestine had paid close attention to the relationship between objects and strata.

Petrie helped make classification as important as digging. He classified by comparing the contents of one layer to those of another, and artifacts from Tell el-Hesi to those he had already found in Egypt. That is, layer to layer, culture to culture. Calibrate artifacts with strata, and you can create a chronology of styles. For logically, whatever is discovered at the bottom of a mound will be older than the objects found in the middle or on top. Logically, but, as it happens, not always.

Consider this scenario: You discover three objects at bottom, middle, top. You date them as Early, Middle, Late. Label them style A, style B, style C. Now you can calculate relative dates for similar objects found elsewhere. The pottery from another site is Early—*probably* is Early—because it is style A. Or *like* style A.

"In future all the tells and ruins of the country will at once reveal their age by the potsherds which cover them," Petrie bragged to the PEF in an excess of optimism. He was sufficiently confident of his findings to believe that stratigraphy was already a fine-tuned science, offering certainties. By later standards, the information he recorded about each artifact was hopelessly imprecise. But he could calibrate the objects from Palestine with finds from Egypt. The cross-dating filled gaps in the chronology of both. It seemed safe to assume that any object he held in his hands would not keep secrets for long. "Pottery is now pretty completely known, and we shall be able in future to date the ages of towns at a glance, as I can in Egypt." He assumed the leap would be made from intuition and approximation to exactitude. Archaeology, however, has yet to make the leap successfully. Petrie did not foresee his colleagues' inability to agree on the calibrations between styles and time. Or even to agree on the styles' names.

The archaeologists fought a war of labels. One excavator's "Amorite" was another's "Canaanite." A third would call seemingly similar artifacts "Pre-Israelite." In 1922, a truce of sorts was arranged when, meeting in Jerusalem, the leading archaeologists of the day signed an agreement on nomenclature. It was a much-needed scheme. John Garstang, an Englishman, brokered the agreement with the heads of scholarly institutions representing Britain, the United States, and France. The expression "It lasted only until the ink was dry" is in this case the literal truth. The agreement lasted until the ink was dry. When each party published the list of newly agreed-upon terms, the list released by the French included several changes. The problem has never been solved and is something of an embarrassment in the profession to this date. Skirmishes are fought over the labels assigned to particular chapters of human history and over the division of artifacts among the chapters. There are disagreements about the dates at which the chapters begin and end. Depending on whom you read, "Middle Bronze I" describes the period 2000 B.C. to 1775 B.C., or 2100 B.C. to 1800 B.C., or 2250 B.C. to 1950 B.C. It is as if in physics each physicist insisted on a somewhat different periodic table.

Archaeologists were eager to apply Petrie's methods at more sites. Germans and Austrians, on their own, were developing methods similar to his. In 1899, an Old Testament scholar from Vienna visited Palestine to search for places suitable for excavation. Ernst Sellin thus came to stand for more than an hour on the great mound overlooking Ein es Sultan.

Sellin had one major advantage when he arrived. The Vienna Academy of Sciences was sponsoring him. It relieved him of most anxieties about money. He was conservative in theological matters but dashingly avant-garde in archaeology, in part because he had the money required to work without hurry. Standing on the mound, he knew of Charles Warren's efforts there thirty years past. Sellin could see the Englishman's old trenches and saw fragments of pottery. Warren's trenches were judged "not at all deep enough." He concluded that Warren had given up much too soon. "It was clear to me," he wrote, ". . . the Canaanite city of Jericho must have stood right at this site . . . and that given the history of this place all indications for a worthwhile excavation were present."

But first he worked elsewhere, perhaps influenced by a desire to excavate a site that remained untouched. He chose the high mound he would identify as Taanach, in northern Palestine, and arrived with a firman. In a relatively short time his team unearthed a Canaanite temple and forty cuneiform tablets, discoveries far more spectacular to the public than Petrie's at Tell el-Hesi. Sellin abandoned plans for a second project in the north because of problems with a local pasha—the pasha was demanding an impossibly large amount of money. He turned his attention back to the mound adjoining Ein es Sultan.

Sellin was cautious about beginning a project so large. "I did not want to stake everything on one card," he wrote. A modest sum was invested in some preliminary digging. The results pleased him. "After only a few days, certainty was already achieved that our expectations would be fulfilled."

With Carl Watzinger, a German archaeologist, Ernst Sellin supervised about two hundred laborers during three winters of work, beginning in 1908. It was the first truly expert excavation of ancient Jericho. Sellin brought along his foreman from Taanach; a master architect arrived from Dresden. Tourists came from Jerusalem to gawk at the digging and at an improvised one-track railroad, used to haul away dirt. The laborers dug a trench ten yards wide through the center of the mound plus shorter trenches elsewhere, which uncovered several layers of what clearly had once been buildings and town walls, some of which were still standing. A photograph made during the work shows the mound like a beached whale, long and humpbacked, slabs of earth torn away to expose the skeleton. Given the many layers, and given the differences in the various structures, Sellin and Watzinger realized they were seeing the remains of a succession of cities and worked to discern their differences. This, actually, was the expected result. For the Old Testament recounted destructions and rebuildings, and in the mound was unmistakable evidence of both.

Sellin and Watzinger published their findings in a volume sumptuously illustrated with photographs and fold-out diagrams. The oldest structures were classified as Canaanite and marked in blue; a later city was colored red; the remains assumed to be from the time of Israel and Judea were in green. Sellin and Watzinger concluded the walls they designated "red" were from the time of Joshua.

Determining when Joshua and the Israelites had arrived, though, was not an easy matter. Theologians suggested a date that was sometime after 1500 B.C. Calculating the year was (and remains) a lower science, more respectable than numerology but no less elusive. To calculate the Israelite arrival time you made a backward reckoning from some better-fixed biblical event. The Israelites, for example, had left Egypt, said the Old Testament, 480 years before the fourth year of the reign of Solomon; but biblical clues as to a date for Solomon were ambiguous. Or, you tried to count generations forward from the Hebrew patriarchs. Or tried to establish a synchrony with events in Egypt, which also required a science of approximation.

Tradition held that Joshua arrived and that the city fell. Arithmetic assigned the Israelites an entry date between 1500 B.C. and 1250 B.C.

There were partially collapsed walls, designated "red," and Sellin declared them to be from Joshua's time. They were much as Scripture said. There the matter rested, troubling only Sellin's partner Carl Watzinger and a small number of his colleagues.

In 1926 Watzinger conscientiously reviewed the archaeological finds from other sites in Palestine to compare them to what he and Sellin had observed nearly twenty years earlier at Ein es Sultan. Then Watzinger revised his conclusions about the walls. The "red" walls as well as the pottery, buildings, and everything else associated with them were hundreds of years older, he decided. In their design, the town walls were like those that had by then been excavated elsewhere and that were known to be from an earlier time. Like Flinders Petrie, Watzinger was comparing artifacts from Jericho to those found elsewhere, to calibrate their ages. A French scholar had reached the same conclusion as

Watzinger, that the red walls had collapsed earlier than first believed. An eminent American agreed. If the collapse should be dated somewhat earlier, most of the experts said, then so should the arrival of Joshua.

Watzinger's ideas were more radical. He freed the archaeological finds from the constraints imposed by the Old Testament. Associating the walls to the coming of the Israelites was an error, he concluded. Everything at Ein es Sultan had either collapsed or been abandoned long before the time that any of the painstakingly worked-out chronologies assigned to Joshua. According to Watzinger, Jericho had by then been *"eine Trummerstatte."* A heap of ruins. "In Joshua's time, Jericho was a heap of ruins on which stood perhaps a few isolated huts."

The response to this was unforgiving. That the new theory was propounded by a German was found, in Great Britain, at least as offensive as the theory's content. A well-to-do businessman forthrightly addressed the Palestine Exploration Fund about the gap between "our race" and "German theories." He announced his willingness to pay for new excavations to prove the Germans wrong and the Bible right. John Garstang was chosen to lead the work.

Garstang had negotiated the short-lived agreement on nomenclature, a failure that was not really his own. He was an organizer, a fine bureaucrat, and that is not to criticize him. In Palestine, he was the founding director of the British Mandate's Department of Antiquities, a position that made him, in effect, His Majesty's Royal Archaeologist. He had studied to be a mathematician, worked productively with Petrie in Egypt, and, before coming to Palestine, excavated in the Sudan. Much later he would leave Palestine in favor of excavations in Turkey—a change in orientation nearly as large as the jump out of mathematics. But nothing in his work makes him seem at all colorful; he was efficient, dutiful, but perhaps not inspiring. No one seems to have bragged about being his follower, or a member of the "Garstang School."

To John Garstang, the latest theories about Jericho sounded improbable—queer second thoughts about old fieldwork. His suggestion to the PEF was for "less theory and more research." Interpretations must demonstrate common sense, he lectured. In his remarks was the tone of professor having to teach a particularly dim-witted class, and he sought to impart the lesson that Scripture should be assumed correct. John Garstang wanted to find the Jericho of the Bible.

"The trouble is that there's nothing much to find but brick," Thomas Hodgkin complained after several weeks of work, "and brick looks very much like any other sort of earth." Hodgkin, twenty-two years old, was Garstang's unpaid assistant. Believing his interests lay in the Middle East, Hodgkin had turned down a government position in colonial Africa and volunteered for the work in the Jordan Valley. In letters to his parents, he wondered if he had made the correct choice. "Not that it's not a pleasant life, but a stupefying one—saps thought—and the standing and worrying round all day is tiring without being exercise."

Garstang's first impression was that Sellin and Watzinger had made a terrible mess. He found a mound that covered six acres; in places it was seventy feet high. Sellin's trenches had been left open and exposed to twenty years of weathering and pilferage. The mound seemed like the tipple of a carelessly abandoned mine already picked over for the best lumps—"a sorry spectacle for an archaeologist."

He excavated during six winters beginning in 1930. He examined 150,000 artifacts, moved several thousand tons of earth inconveniently dumped by Sellin, and devoted a large amount of time to a search for ancient tombs. Progress seemed slow, as if addled by the heat. "I may be wronging old Garstang," Thomas Hodgkin wrote home, "but he seems so far to think that the only part of archaeology that can be taught is patience." There were occasional visitors to break the monotony but mostly there was the hot sun. Emir Abdullah, ruler of the Transjordanian emptiness, crossed the river with some of his wives to watch the work during part of a winter afternoon. Always digging, the workmen consumed all of Hodgkin's aspirin plus the five hundred aspirin brought by Garstang. "Lovely shining weather," said Hodgkin, "—hard not to fall asleep after lunch."

The search for graves continued without success until a nearly desperate Garstang stood his workmen in two lines, stationed three miles apart like opposing armies. Their armaments were picks. The lines were to approach each other by digging up the intervening three miles of ground. On the tenth day, the men discovered an ancient cemetery; Garstang arrived just in time to stop them from using the picks to smash the contents.

His work established that the site had been occupied before the invention of pottery, and he uncovered the detritus of millennia of daily life—dress fasteners made of bronze, a stone wheel used to grind paint, bone inlay from wooden boxes that had decayed into nothing.

The best finds went to Jerusalem, into the Rockefeller Museum, itself a sort of artifact. It is a limestone fortress standing atop a rise opposite one of the gates of the Old City and is a tasteful example of Empire architecture, built to preside. A blunt tower rises from the roof, and turrets stand guard at the front corners. Carved into two courses of stone is this legend: Government Of Palestine, Department Of Antiquities. In the basement are most of the Dead Sea Scrolls. A visitor requesting a guidebook to the main galleries is loaned a sheaf of typed papers that has been softened by occasional use to the consistency, and legibility, of crumbled Kleenex. On the first page is the date they were typed, 1937. I never encountered a crowd.

Garstang's artifacts are scattered among the glass-fronted cases in an unintentional re-creation of stratigraphic confusion. In one of the cases was the bottom of a straw basket, or rather, its outline. It was dated to the Late Bronze Age, the several centuries before 1200 B.C. It is "basket" reduced to the platonic idea—an imprint in hardened earth of a strand wound in tight concentric circles. You could see the braiding, feel the tug that tightened it. It was nothing more than oxidized pattern, had no volume and certainly no carrying capacity. But it unmistakably expressed "basket." Another case displayed the pitcherlike cup that is Garstang's most famous find, because an anonymous potter shaped the vessel to look like a human head and gave it a distinctive face. A heavy brow sits above incised circles for eyes, a long straight nose, a not unfriendly looking mouth with pursed lips, and a long bearded chin. The handles are elephant ears. On the back the maker carved a distinct hairline. You drank from the crown of the head. I wanted to believe the face showed bemusement, in the willfully naive way I wanted to believe penguins wore tuxedos. Whether it represented a deity or a figure of entertainment, or something altogether different, no one knew.

During the excavations, Garstang became convinced his predecessors had been wrong about dates. He judged one set of town walls to be from the Late Bronze Age, the presumed arrival time of the Israelites. One did not need special training to see that those walls—somewhat charred—had collapsed. They fit the Old Testament story or at least didn't contradict it. In a subtle way, the Joshua story seemed to become as authoritative for Garstang as the physical reality of the mound itself. He used each freely as a guide to the other, as if they were one. But that could never be. The Old Testament described a people's faith, offered explanations for it, and located that faith in history. Whatever the authorship of the stories, no one could doubt they served to teach their audience and to inspire it. No particular intention, though, could be attributed to the mound. Artifacts had not crumbled away or been buried according to a plan or a purpose—not unless you were convinced too that Pompeii had existed for the purposes of being buried by lava and rediscovered. What you found were artifacts preserved at random and which could not interpret themselves. They speak to history but not to faith. The only connection between the mound at Ein es Sultan and faith was the one you chose to make.

Garstang speculated about the number of soldiers in Joshua's army and the population of Jericho at the time the Israelites arrived. He believed he had found the remains of a seige ramp from an earlier time and a well-built ledge from which the city's defenders had hurled their weapons—everything that would give Jericho the appearance of a medieval city, as in the storybooks. It was, he concluded, much as the Old Testament said: a once imposing city with charred walls from the Late Bronze Age, which was when the Israelites had first made themselves known.

John Garstang had intended to revise his reports but never found the time. In 1949, when he was seventy-three, he extended an invitation to an archaeologist a generation younger to review his voluminous records. It was thus that Kathleen Kenyon came to her work at Jericho and to the greatest success of her long career and much of its considerable pathos.

She was in every sense a large, domineering figure. As a young woman she had been undeniably attractive. Her brow was high and broad and her features strong, the look of someone at ease in the outdoors and with physical adventure. Field hockey was her sport, played agressively. Part of the family inheritance was a great fascination with detail and an insistence on order. Her father, Frederick Kenyon, was for more than twenty years director of the British Museum, was highly regarded as a translator of Greek papyri, and wrote popularized accounts of biblical scholarship.

By even the austere standards of Edwardian times, Frederick Kenyon was exceptionally reserved. Searching for compliments, friends commended him as "an admirable chairman of committees." He was praised for his imperturbability. His demeanor was that of a judge—remote, intimidating. The aloofness was another part of Kathleen Kenyon's inheritance. She was brusque and aggressive, as if always on the hockey field. Her friends say her off-putting manner was an expression of shyness. At Oxford came dabblings in archaeological fieldwork and studies in history. A woman could work as an archaeologist, of course, but the path to that career, for a woman, in the 1920s as earlier, usually included marriage—marrying a man in that profession, to gain acceptance. Kenyon, however, never married. In 1929, with the aid of some well-placed words from her father, she joined a professional excavation being undertaken in Southern Rhodesia by a former assistant of Petrie's. The new Oxford graduate, age twenty-three, was photographer and girl Friday.

By the time John Garstang singled her out, Kathleen Kenyon had worked at Roman sites in Britain, at the biblical city of Samaria in Palestine, and in Libya; she was lecturing regularly at the new Institute of Archaeology in London, was one of its administrators, and curator of the large collection of artifacts left by Petrie. Without intending it as praise, colleagues called her "formidable."

Kenyon found much to question as she reviewed Garstang's records from Jericho. In the fifteen or so years since his excavations, as she gently pointed out, many more sites had been explored. Calibrations between artifacts and time periods, she said, were now finer. Attention paid to where an object was found—its precise place of discovery and its position relative to other artifacts—was one of the two available guides to the object's age, the object's use, and the identity of its maker. Comparing objects from different sites was the second guide. You could hope to discover an ancient kingdom's archives, whose tablets would supply a legible account of long-ago events, but you would be foolish to believe you actually would. You relied on comparison and context. It was through them that the chronologies of pottery and architecture were slowly (and imperfectly) worked out and history gradually (and imperfectly) recovered.

There were fewer certainties than John Garstang had proffered. A drinking cup discovered at a depth of eight feet in a mound was not in every case older than the pitcher found three feet above it. At one time they could have been in the same building. When it collapsed—because of storm or earthquake, abandonment or attack—the contents were liable to be scrambled. One homebuilder would dig into the house foundations of his predecessors and scramble the contents again. Erosion moved debris selectively. With great deference, Kenyon made those points in a paper. Praise was offered for Garstang having gathered so much information. But Kenyon added that his reconstruction of history required "modifications." More work was needed—more pottery would have to be found and examined—to know precisely what had existed at Ein es Sultan at the time of the Israelites and what had occurred. To "settle the doubtful questions," she proposed to undertake a new set of excavations at the mound.

She began in 1952 and had trained a small army of colleagues by the time the work was done, a younger generation of archaeologists now nearing retirement.

Gus Van Beek is curator of Old World archaeology at the Smithsonian Institution in Washington, D.C. In 1952 he was a graduate student at Johns Hopkins, in Baltimore. A professor told him, as if in passing, that Miss Kenyon was about to begin excavations. Someone having dropped out, she could take on one more assistant. Interested?

The *Queen Mary* carried Van Beek to Southampton. He took airplanes to Brussels, Istanbul, Beirut, and a last hop to the alarmingly short airstrip at Kalandia in the hilly outskirts of Jerusalem. At about

9:00 in the morning, a taxi delivered him to Jericho. Kenyon said she was happy to make his acquaintance. She was busy, she said, and the suggestion was made that he spend his first hours observing the work atop the mound.

It was his first glimpse of the excavation method Kenyon had imported from Britain. She was refining techniques pioneered there by Mortimer Wheeler, one of her teachers, and applied them on a giant scale. She excavated in squares. Each square was five meters on a side and the mound was her checkerboard. An area one meter wide was left untouched between the squares and became a catwalk as the workmen dug. The digging in each square went down one soil layer at a time, guided by the differences in soil color and texture as they appeared on the sides of the catwalks. The catwalks—"baulks" was Kenyon's term—became a record of each layer's depth and contours. This constantly expanding record, though, had to be read and sketched into a notebook in the short time before the sun dried everything into a gray-brown sameness.

Seeing the layers was somewhat easier than describing them. In one small vertical section of one square were layers recorded as, top down, "rubbly grey," "grey stones and bricks," "grey brown," "tightly packed brown soil," "dark brown," "soft brown," "dark fallen brick," "small rubbly," "crumbly," "crumbly bricky." Unless you were there when the light and the moisture were just so, everything was just dirt, and disputable.

Before Kenyon, standard archaeological practice was, in effect, to skin a site. Excavators dug wide rather than deep and were not terribly discriminating in how they stripped away earth. They took off a layer several inches thick—no one paid attention to the natural contours—and then another. Kenyon introduced a surgical operation. She incised narrowly and very deep. She chose her squares on the checkerboard and aimed to dig until she reached bedrock. A hired workman with a pick was at each square. A second workman was in charge of the baskets containing dirt, and three or four younger men passed each basket up and out of the square, like buckets of water traveling through the hands of a fire brigade. The lines of young men grew longer as the squares became deeper. From the bottom it looked as if the men on top were building pyramids, the piles of dirt growing higher. Every few minutes a supervisor was supposed to stop the man with the pick and have a look. Kathleen Kenyon made doctor's rounds at least twice a day to examine the innards of her large recumbent patient. Her reliance on the baulks remains sufficiently distinctive for archaeologists to speak of similar excavations as "Kenyonesque."

Gus Van Beek had already worked at a dig conducted the traditional way. Soil was peeled off a site; a bulldozer might have produced the same results. His first ascent of the mound at Jericho showed him something different.

"It was like a religious experience," said Van Beek, and he was an immediate convert. "I came down absolutely euphoric."

Kenyon had some twenty assistants each digging season—usually January until mid-April—and she would hire a hundred or so laborers from a large jostling crowd of townspeople and refugees. She was, at times, Jericho's largest employer. The era when students did the work and paid for the privilege was still in the future. Two old millhouses at Ein es Sultan became the cramped headquarters. For lack of room, the men that first season slept in tents pitched in a banana grove. Kenyon haggled over rent and other matters with Awni Khalil Dajani, the local Inspector of Antiquities for the Hashemite Kingdom of Jordan, whose extended family owned considerable land and dabbled profitably in the antiquities trade.

Everyone at the millhouses was supposed to be awake for breakfast by six-thirty. The hired workmen were due at the mound by seven. Kenyon made her rounds. At four-thirty in the afternoon the head foreman sounded the whistle signaling the end of the digging and the start of the race to the spring, where everyone cleaned, in competition with women from the refugee camp, who were collecting water for an evening meal. The assistants then observed the rituals of afternoon tea before sorting the day's pottery for Kenyon's predinner inspection.

In the mess hall everyone noticed the forest of bottles first. On a hot day, when he was still new to the camp, Gus Van Beek saw a tall glass of clear liquid, so drank deep and fast. It was arak. "I coughed and I cried, and they roared with laughter, and I knew I was in a good place." At dinner Kathleen Kenyon always sat at the head of the long table decorated with bottles of vermouth, under bare lightbulbs hanging between the wooden rafters: professor with high-spirited drama club. They celebrated George Washington's birthday, followed by a party honoring King George III. Awni Dajani invited everyone to the family plantation for camel rides. Oxford battled Cambridge during a tipsy boat race on the Dead Sea. The best-preserved skeletons found in tombs at the mound became Freddie, Mimi, Agnes, and Fritz.

By the end of the first season, everyone at the dig knew that John Garstang had probably been wrong about dates. And that Carl Watzinger had probably been right. Late Bronze Age, Garstang had said of some of the town walls. The evidence necessary for assigning dates was in the pottery. Pottery styles were the clock. You read the shape of rims and handles, examined the decoration, and felt the burnish, and no two pots were going to be identical. (Except almost all were going to be found broken.) You had to speculate, though, on what a change in style meant. The existence of an odd-shaped mixing bowl could signal the passing of a century or the local potter—bored—having indulged himself with an experiment. Was that bowl produced by a hitherto unknown people? Did a cold snap affect the clay and the operation of the kiln? Did the potter have an off day?

No matter what technology was applied to the remains, the date was in any case only going to be approximate. At best, to within fifty years. The excavator had to remember that error was in everything. Consistency between two pots found at different places would not guarantee that the pots had been made at the same time—even likeness could be a potter's accident, not intention. From approximate dates, and an approximate typology, you could recover only a general history of a place or culture.

The archaeologist has few certainties. For a physicist, characteristics of the rarest, more ephemeral elements are ultimately knowable, quantifiable, and not subject to frequent amendment. An atom with twenty-two protons will be titanium, every time. As for the mixing bowl, if it is widemouthed and densely decorated by friezes painted red and black, the friezes divided by triglyphs, and if it depicts birds or an antelope, it probably dates from the Late Bronze Age. But it could be Middle Bronze. The archaeologist is left to make a judgment call.

"Even as a grad student I saw it right off," Gus Van Beek said. When Kenyon and her assistants examined the pottery that went with Garstang's walls, everyone was confident enough to assign it a label clear enough for a museum. "It was absolutely Early Bronze Age." Early Bronze, not Late.

At their closest, the two periods are separated by five hundred years. The differences in material culture are as large as those distinguishing 1400 A.D. from 1900 A.D., the world of Cosimo di Medici from Teddy Roosevelt's. In Early Bronze, small settlements grow into walled city-states that carry on trade with Egypt, Syria, and Asia Minor. It is likely that people had animal-drawn plows, certain they had the pottery wheel. They energetically cut the forests to obtain lumber for the building boom and to clear fields for agriculture. At Jericho, the houses come to be built in orderly rows. I never thought to wonder in Sunday school who was in Palestine just before the Canaanites; that there was a "before" escaped me. These peoples, who are otherwise nameless, are the answer to the unasked question and have a long reign. Including all of its many chapters, Early Bronze lasts (approximately) fourteen hundred years. It includes long periods of turbulence, large migrations of people, an economic boom, and then social and economic problems that grow out of problems in agriculture. The culture's final collapse is brought about by some unknown combination of crises: the possibilities include disruptions in trade with Egypt, overpopulation, a decline in rainfall, and further catastrophes in agriculture due to the erosion that follows the overcutting of the forests. During a hundred-year period, most of the large cities are abandoned or destroyed, and city dwellers become part-time herders. At Jericho, a fire deposits several feet of ash atop charred walls. For the next several centuries that site, which even then rose above the surrounding plain in the valley, was uninhabited.

Palestine thereafter became a scattering of small settlements, most of the population farming when conditions allowed but otherwise wandering with their sheeps and goats. Newcomers slowly drift in, probably from the north. Middle Bronze had begun. The word *Canaan* makes its first known appearance, on a cuneiform tablet at the city-state of Mari; the tablet would be found in the ruins of Mari, in Syria, during the twentieth century A.D. From Syria or Mesopotamia arrives knowledge of a new metal, called bronze, made when nine parts copper are heated with one part tin. Its impact on Palestine rivals gold's on California. When bronze replaces copper, tools and weapons become sharper edged. With bronze, people have sharper, more valuable products to trade, and with more trade, obtain greater wealth. Cities are rebuilt. They are larger, richer, and apparently prey to violence on a larger scale. The Canaanites devote their greatest ingenuity to fortifications as their cities become caught up in a missile race in which the antimissile is a higher, thicker wall. The anti–battering ram is a high embankment with a steep slope, coated with plaster for extra slipperiness—a genuine slippery slope. There are city gates protected by guard stations in high towers, and by walls swollen into obesity.

On spiritual matters people as always hedged their bets. At Jericho, the people of Middle Bronze show an endearingly modern streak of doubt as to whether the dead would go on to something better or were just lifeless meat. Their tombs are chambers hollowed out at the end of long vertical shafts cut into the soft rock. Families outfitted the dead with drinks and platters of roasted sheep laid on wood tables. Some of the dead were given wooden beds. Yet the show of respect had limits. Standard practice was to bury one person, wait for partial decay of the corpse, and then unseal the shaft. The bones would be pushed to the back in a jumble to make room for another corpse with another meal. Kenyon found the remains with serendipitous help from the Palestinian refugees living adjacent to the mound, as they dug latrines or mined ingredients for making plaster. Middle Bronze people had done the same thing in the same place. And now someone would half hear, half feel with his pick a hollowness in the ground, then trot the dusty way to the mound to announce the latest development. As soon as Kenyon made a modest offer of baksheesh, permission would be forthcoming for the foreigners to dig deeper.

The bones of roasted sheep were easily identified. The condition of the wood furniture, despite the passage of three thousand years, at first seemed excellent. But as fresh air reached the wood, it went limp. It oozed. It had a hard rind and a soft interior, like fresh Gouda cheese.

After five hundred years, Middle Bronze ended violently, though the exact chain of causes can still only be guessed at. At Jericho, some of the tombs contain children alongside adults. Contrary to custom, all the family members were buried on a single occasion and were never disturbed—a hint of something in the city being terribly amiss. Kenyon wondered if an epidemic had killed off entire households; if not an epidemic, some other catastrophe.

Eventually, violence spilled over from Egypt. A new dynasty of pharoahs sought to expel foreigners who had ruled the kingdom, and the Egyptian armies pursued them into Palestine. Cities are beseiged—by Egyptians, rival city-states, or both—the fortifications overwhelmed. Buildings are looted, then demolished. As an extra measure of intimidation, corpses are left in the streets. Once again, the largest settlements become ruins. Thus began Late Bronze.

During Late Bronze, it is believed, the area had only half as many settlements, most of them notably poor. Egypt administered it as an Egyptian province and the rulers of city-states were vassals of the pharoah. They had querulous relationships. The pharoahs chided vassals like errant sons, and those same vassals swore perpetual loyalty while plotting treacheries.

All this is known thanks to an Egyptian peasant who was digging for fertilizer in the local fields, in 1887. She was one of the *sebakheen*, whose life work was the mining of *sebakh*—dried mud-brick. She lived in Hagg Qandil, a Nile village 190 miles south of Cairo and a short distance from a flat-topped hill known to everyone in the district as a hidden sprawl of ruins. The hill was called Amarna, the name of the local Bedouin.

She uncovered clay tablets inscribed with cuneiform. It is said that the woman sold her interest in the matter to someone else for pocket change. Even in the years immediately after these events occurred, no one writing of them makes mention of the woman's name. The digging continued until the number of tablets was more than three hundred. In these matters the fellahin acted according to the lesson learned from every European visitor, beginning with Napoleon's savants. Elders passed this lesson on to their children: the Westerner had an appetite for the old and would pay to acquire it.

Someone dumped the tablets into sacks and took them by donkey to likely buyers. A part-time agent for the Louvre sent one tablet to Paris and was told it was a forgery; other experts failed to recognize cuneiform as an ancient system of writing. The tablets were carried again by donkey and camel. Some turned to powder during the trip. Within a year, most of the tablets that survived were in national museums in Europe.

The woman digging *sebakh* had discovered archives of the pharoah Amenophis III and of his son, the pharoah Akhenaton. The tablets were letters (and copies of letters) sent by pharoahs and foreign rulers during thirty or so years of the Late Bronze Age. In their correspondence, the kings of the day accuse each other of bad faith, reveal their grudges, and offer or demand gifts. Subandu—ruler of a city-state, presumably—writes of his sending the pharoah twenty girls and five hundred oxen. Pharoah Amenophis III tells Milkili, ruler of Gezer, in Palestine, that the pharoah's representative will arrive with sufficient silver to buy forty women. "Very beautiful women," he requests; he also asks that none be slanderers. The king of Babylon reports without discernible rancor that the pharoah's promised gift of twenty minas of gold was melted in a kiln and came out weighting less than five minas. He requests that the pharoah send an animal sculpture and pledges that once the sculpture arrives he will give the pharoah's daughter a necklace with 1,048 pieces of lapis lazuli, shaped like crickets.

There is talk of misdeeds by a brother and attacks by neighbors. There are desperate-sounding pleas for military help. The most striking feature in the messages from rulers of the city-states, though, is the wondrous degree of servility.

"To the king, my lord, my god, my Sun, the Sun from the sky," Yidya, ruler of Ashkelon, begins his letter to the pharoah. "Message of Yidya, the ruler of Ashkelon, your servant, the dirt at your feet, the groom of your horses. I indeed prostrate myself, on the stomach and on the back, at the feet of the king, my lord, seven times and seven times." Since he is at his master's feet Yidya likens himself to a dog.

The pharoah is cool and direct in his responses. In the Amarna letters the pharoahs begin, simply, "Thus says the king." Their letters end by reporting that the pharoah, like the sun in heaven, is well.

Rebellions occur in Palestine and are suppressed. A royal sculptor will brag in stone about the army of Tuthmosis III winning a great victory against 119 city-states of Canaan. He will list those cities and thereby create a partial inventory of the Canaanite kinglets in the Late Bronze Age. Jericho goes unmentioned in his list; Jericho also is unmentioned in the letters from Amarna. Later, a stele is erected to celebrate conquests by the pharoah Merneptah over Canaanite cities and a tribe called Israel.

Desolate is Tehenu; Hati is pacified;
Plundered is Canaan with every evil;
Carried off is Ashkelon; seized upon is Gezer;
Yanoam is made as that which does not exist;
Israel is laid waste, his seed is not.

It is believed that there were several years of drought, causing famine. It is believed that the pastoralists inhabiting Canaan's sandy fringes intensified their raids against the cities. The drought put large populations on the move in search of food. In their letters to the pharoah, the local kings confess to defeats at the hands of people they call the Apiru, who apparently were marauders and mercenaries. "The Apiru has plundered all the lands of the king," Abdi-Heba, king of Jerusalem, informed the pharoah. "If there are archers this year, the lands of the king, my lord, will remain. But if there are no archers, lost are the lands of the king, my lord." Turmoil was everywhere. The Hittite empire in Asia Minor was tottering; Ugarit, in Syria, would soon fall. Egypt meanwhile was beset by vast numbers of migrants coming with their arms from the west, where drought was even worse, and by the faltering city-states of Canaan, whose kings lament the devastation wrought by the Apiru. It is believed that as crops failed so did trade, and then authority. Once again, armies and the wanderers sacked the cities. And the physical demolition of this old order was the end of the Late Bronze Age.

Sometimes but not always, Jericho had town walls. From Early Bronze to Late Bronze, the town walls collapse during earthquakes, are weakened by weather, are destroyed by fire or battering ram, are rebuilt, patched, eroded, and are buried. Tear a wall down after fifty years. Rebuild it on the same foundations after a gap of a century. Was it one wall or two? Can you tell? Does a patch make three? They were Kathleen Kenyon's questions and had been John Garstang's. In one of the excavated squares there are, for instance, the walls Kenyon judged to be from Early Bronze. The oldest of them is wall I, made of white bricks and gray mortar. It is rebuilt to become I-a—brown bricks, gray-brown mortar. Built near the inner face is wall II, later, II-a. Wall III becomes, finally, III-f, its own great-great-great-great-grandson. Its replacement is Wall IV. All are Early Bronze. In other squares the number of identifiable Early Bronze walls and rebuildings reaches seventeen.

Invited to speak in London, Kenyon made a valiant effort to spare John Garstang's feelings. People noticed his coming into the lecture hall; a small elderly slow-moving figure who made Kenyon appear all the larger. Authority was changing hands as clearly as if Garstang were taking off a sparkling crown. Kenyon showed much grace in the way she reached for it. It was 1952, and she had worked at Jericho only one season. Not every foot of the walls had been uncovered, she said generously, and surely more pottery was going to be found and might change her conclusions. But there was no doubt at all about everything examined so far. *Early* Bronze, not Late. Garstang's walls were Early Bronze and had been deeply buried centuries before there could have been a Joshua.

"She looked really nice that evening," someone remembers. And after a celebratory dinner, Kathleen Kenyon went to an amusement park.

Progress in archaeology is to head downward, not upward. The excavator begins at the end of the story and travels toward the beginning. One recovers artifacts from a newly uncovered stratum—bones, seeds sifted from the dirt, pottery, the bricks that formed walls. A "house" might be only a small corner of plastered earth, which would be what had survived of a floor. Using Kenyon's methods, one sees only those parts of the structures that happen to intersect with her excavated squares. The view was narrow. The past was blurry. One saw not a whole building but a corner of it, like something torn at random from blueprints. Then, that building and that floor are necessarily destroyed, in order to reach the strata beneath them.

After two seasons Kenyon's workmen had dug their way to Early

Bronze and headed lower, earlier. They worked in the squares and also in three large trenches that Kenyon cut through the mound's perimeter. One was on the north side, one on the south, the longest on the west. On the east was the highway and the spring. In photographs, the western trench is a deep, wide gash, the sides straight enough to have been cut by a terrifyingly large knife. The workmen at the bottom are so far away their only distinct feature is the whiteness of their keffiyas.

Twenty feet down in the southern trench, the workmen found a mud-brick wall dated to Early Bronze with a squarish hole punched through it. Even stranger, the hole appeared to have been recently filled.

Records were checked. The name of Charles Warren was invoked.

In 1867 and again in 1868, as we know, Charles Warren had come into the valley and cataloged the odd-shaped formations he thought worthy of investigation. In the great mound looming above Ein es Sultan he had seen three peaks, which he labeled as numbers four, five, and six, south to north. He had already seen three others, perhaps a mile distant, alongside Wadi Kelt.

Warren is straightforward but frustratingly terse describing his own work, a lieutenant barking orders. An officer of the Royal Engineers would find nothing to say about digging into lumpen earth except that it was dull simplicity, requiring muscle. "No. 4 mound," Warren recorded when the labor was finished. "Two shafts were sunk to south." At a depth of ten feet he saw charred wood, and at twenty feet a mixture of gravel, clay, pottery fragments, and black lumps. Kathleen Kenyon's trench had happened upon Charles Warren's. At ten feet, Kenyon saw the same charred timbers, and at twenty, Warren's unsteady first steps as an archaeologist. Warren had reached one of Jericho's walls but unknowingly dug through it. Thus the hole. During the next eighty-odd years the vagaries of weathering had plugged it and filled in the trench.

In some of the squares Kenyon's workmen had already reached bedrock. They discovered the whole of the mound to be a human creation. It was self-cemented debris seventy feet thick.

When the waters receded from the valley, long ago, they uncovered a plain nearly as flat as nature allows and lower than any other. Alluvium had made it fertile. The seemingly unquenchable spring had supported plant life, attracted animals, and then attracted human beings.

The immediate successors of the Natufians at Ein es Sultan left modest remains. This people either lived at several camps in the course of a typical year or was struggling to invent housing suitable for year-round occupation. People relied on shelters made, probably, of animal skins, and the walls seemed to have been fastened down by balls of clay, which are protobricks. In one of Kenyon's squares, the remains were thin earthen layers accumulated to a height of thirteen feet—debris like corrugated cardboard compressed into a dry mush. Each layer represented another set of shelters, so another season of settlement; within the thirteen feet were hundreds of seasons.

What came next is one of the many gaps. A people would arrive at Ein es Sultan from places unknown and disappear for reasons of which there is no trace. You find deep underneath the surface of the mound a layer of silt, or a slope that has the fingerprint of erosion, and it is a place holder that says the site was unoccupied. The periods of abandonment last for centuries at a time. They hint at some unknowable turmoil. On occasion the next inhabitants are less, not more advanced than their predecessors. It was not unknown for a culture of housebuilders to be succeeded by a people who dwelled in pits. The archaeological record testifies that change was not steady or slow but came in unpredictable spurts, could reverse itself, and was deflected by catastrophes in unforeseeable ways. The catastrophes make archaeology easier—doable, in fact. An earthquake collapses walls flat or slices through a staircase like a knife. After a great fire, artifacts are buried in ash and charred. An attacking army leaves behind arrowheads, and the corpses of fighters show signs of having been buried in a hurry. But if everything is found well ordered and seemingly whole? Overlain by a thick layer of undisturbed soil? Then the question is why that people disappeared without protest, and why the next people was so long in arriving.

The climate had become warmer, and it was wetter than today, with rainfall spread more evenly during the year. When the rains were heaviest, the wadis channeled water and silt into the valley. The time was 8500 B.C., and newcomers were at Ein es Sultan. Like their predecessors they hunted gazelle and wild boar and gathered fruits and seeds. They also conducted experiments. First, the newcomers sowed chick-peas and lentils near the mouth of the wadis or in soil watered by the spring. Since the inhabitants stayed put, it is safe to say the experiments were a success. Within several centuries, the experiments extended to barley and wheat.

Kathleen Kenyon named the culture Pre-Pottery Neolithic A. Its largest known settlement, and its most sophisticated one, was at Ein es Sultan.

The people of PPNA lived in one place all year long and were the builders of the first permanent housing. Their houses were rounded with walls that leaned in toward the center, a tent expressed in mud-brick. The bricks are shaped like loaves of sandwich bread: flat on the bottom, swelled into a curve on top, well-fitted to the palm of a laborer. Plano-convex bricks (as they are called) lend themselves to inelegant, fast work that requires little training. No need to strive for close-fitting courses because, given irregularly curved bricks, perfection is impossible: you slather mortar into the inevitable gaps.

Sometime around 8000 B.C. the inhabitants busied themselves with public works projects. The population was organized to collect stones from the surrounding territory for a town wall. The wall did not merely happen; it was not an accident. It was designed. New, it was about six feet wide at its base and narrowed as it rose. Some of the many rebuildings increased the height to keep up with new houses being built atop old ones, and to keep up with the rising level of garbage. Each generation lived higher, building on top of refuse. So the topography changed. The whole settlement was going up on garbage, silt, whatever was brought by the wadis. When Kenyon uncovered the PPNA town wall, the best-preserved sections were twelve feet high and had been standing for ten thousand years. She declared the wall was surely for military defense.

The archaeologist Peter Dorrell calculated how much labor had been required to build it. One of Kenyon's most devoted assistants, Dorrell estimated the wall's original height, thickness, and circumference, and he assumed maximum ambitiousness by the PPNA people. The wall might not have existed on the eastern side, by the spring. But Dorrell allowed for a structure around the whole of the settlement.

He postulated a wall twelve feet high, six feet thick, about two thousand feet in circumference. Altogether, twelve thousand metric tons of stone.

A thoughtful coal miner could probably have guessed the required amount of labor. Until Dorrell, no one had thought to do the arithmetic: pounds of stone, divided by pounds transportable by one person in one day, times the number of workers. To assemble a twelve-thousand-ton wall, two hundred laborers would need about a week. Seventy-five people would need three weeks.

"This is a surprisingly modest requirement," Dorrell concluded with understatement.

The real accomplishment was for a people to have stayed at one location long enough to consider it a permanent home. Thus, worthy of a protective wall. Only if you have decided to stay do you decide upon a program of major physical improvement, plan it, develop the technical skills necessary to build it, organize the labor, and see the project as a worthwhile investment, which requires having confidence your household will survive long enough to enjoy the benefits. No one planned to leave. So the improvement program expanded.

On the west side, just inside the town wall, the PPNA people built a stone tower. It is round though tending toward ovoid, gently tapered, and the height of a modern three-story building. If another structure of this size and complexity was built during that era anywhere else in the world, that structure has yet to be discovered. The stone pyramids in Egypt are many times larger and much greater feats of engineering, but the first of them does not appear for another five thousand years. At the bottom of the tower a short passageway led to a staircase climbing to an opening on top. The crown is round when seen from above, flat when seen in cross section. It has a small opening on top yet looks incomplete—a platform for something else, a structure that has disappeared. Eventually the expansion of the PPNA settlement blocked the entrance at the tower's base. Another layer of stone was built around the core like a thick new skin. Now one can stand at the edge of a trench dug by Kathleen Kenyon and see the flat top of the tower fifteen feet below; the opening on the roof is covered by a grate. At the end of a wet winter, silt washed onto the crown supports a thick crop of grass.

In the top two feet of the tower's interior stairway, Kenyon found twelve human skeletons. The rest of the staircase was filled with dirt. Most of the PPNA graves were underneath PPNA houses, but the inhabitants might not have planned the arrangement or been aware of it. Originally, the corpses may have been buried in unsettled areas. As the settlement grew, open space became suburbs. A grave became your home's unknown basement.

On the west side, debris reached the height of the town wall, then buried it. Houses were built above it. On the north side, water washed away part of the wall and carved a deep channel. The upper courses of the town wall finally collapsed everywhere. By roughly 7200 B.C., a thousand years after they arrived, the PPNA people disappeared. You cannot say that they moved, since that presumes they traveled and arrived somewhere else. All that is known is that they were no longer at Ein es Sultan. Sediment accumulated on top of the town walls and buried the walls and the tower and formed a mound, a platform twenty feet high.

Kenyon discovered PPNA's successor before discovering PPNA; the later the inhabitants, the higher (usually) in the mound. Above PPNA was PPNB. It had a new town wall and its own, different architecture. Houses were rectangular instead of rounded and bricks were flatter, no longer similar to loaves of bread. In the houses, the floors and walls were coated with plaster. It bespoke organization and authority. The plaster was made of limestone that was crushed, placed in a fire, then mixed with water, and then mixed with ash or sand. A division of labor was the other necessary ingredient. To make plaster on a large scale you must quarry stone and find wood for the fire. You need a hearth, perhaps a kiln. You need a manager who can assign tasks not only within his own family.

At the end of the digging season in 1953, a young assistant named Peter Parr approached Kathleen Kenyon with the results of his day's work. Except for the final cleaning up, this was supposed to be the last day of digging until the following year. Most of the laborers, including the cooks, were already dismissed. Kenyon had packed her belongings.

Peter Parr handed over a skull he had seen for some weeks embedded in the side of one of the squares but which he had steadfastly ignored. Everyone knew the Great *Sitt* required the squares to be kept exactly that: perfectly, tidily square. During those weeks, he could see only the topmost part of the head. Now, the season finished, Kenyon had reluctantly given him permission to dig it out. The skull was not as he had expected. It was covered with plaster in which someone had shaped cheeks and a prominent nose, added a vestigial ear, painted on eyebrows, and implanted seashell eyes, which seemed to stare. The plaster was rendered realistically enough to be mistaken for flesh.

Kenyon canceled plans for leaving.

At the back of the hole he had dug, Parr saw two more skulls, and when those were removed, he found four others. Working them free required nearly a week. The *New York Times* saw fit to print news of the discovery on the front page. According to Kenyon, the decorated skulls were the earliest naturalistic renderings of distinct individuals. If not the earliest, then surely the best, since they were as distinct as the living—none could be mistaken for another. During the subsequent forty years, other decorated skulls would be found at various sites in Syria, Jordan, and Israel, as well as small plaster statues of humans, all of them a product of the same homogeneous PPNB culture. The claims, though, about "earliest" and "best" remain true; the change is that they apply now to, approximately, thirty objects from those several sites.

Kenyon distributed her finds among various institutions and sponsors. In that way two of the decorated PPNB skulls and one "plain" skull from PPNB came to the Archaeological Museum in Amman.

It is one large dusty room. On a wintry day the museum was none too brightly lit. The "plain" skull rested between the two decorated with plaster, all on the same shelf. You could see what should have been obvious but was not: the decorated skulls were small, unnaturally squat. They lacked a lower jaw. During PPNA and PPNB, skulls were severed from the corpses (usually, not always), and the jaw (usually, not always) wrenched off. The molding of the plaster gave the illusion of a jaw still being present. On that shelf the decorated skulls unpleasantly appeared as if they were only partially decayed, because of the realism of the details rendered in plaster. Each eye was two cowrie shells—small white crescents—and the gap between the shells made for a natural-looking pupil. One skull had chipmunk cheeks. Cracks in the plaster could be mistaken for the wrinkles of age.

The skulls are eerily lifelike, cool, affecting; they have the ability to redefine the natural. They look primitive until compared to a skull left plain, and "plain" becomes more frightening, intolerable. The mottled bone, the unpleasant toothiness of an "ordinary" skull say very clearly that it is real, but it is the object that seems unnatural, fantastical, a bizarrely complex sculpture. The decorated skulls are the more comforting, more believably human. They push away death.

They all were found stuffed with dirt. All were smoothly finished on the bottom, so evidently had never been displayed as parts of statues. Peter Parr had found them under a PPNB house, which seemed to include debris of an earlier house, under which were found some thirty skeletons, most of them without heads. A decorated skull memorialized a relative or was believed to offer protection, or both. The skull—the body part that best represented the personality of the deceased—would be kept on the floor or maybe on a built-up platform, in plain view. No one has yet proposed a more logical explanation for the care taken by people of circa 7000 B.C. in decorating skulls with plaster and seashell eyes. People of PPNB revered the dead to safeguard the present and the future; they would not be the last to do so. It was a "cult of the heroes," according to anthropologists, or a "cult of the ancestors." It is what we know as religion.

By the end of the second season of work, Kathleen Kenyon was manager, accountant, and star performer of an unwieldy conglomerate. To pay for the excavations, she had support of various kinds from nineteen universities, eleven museums, the Palestine Exploration Fund, the British School of Archaeology in Jerusalem (of which she was Honorary Director), and several private foundations, these supporters scattered in eight countries. The only name on the organization chart was Kenyon's.

She was not one to delegate authority. For the daughter of Sir Frederick Kenyon, sharing responsibilities was tantamount to admitting you were not up to the job—a shameful surrender. She had gone to Jericho believing the project was not especially large. She was, she believed, on a brief goodwill mission for the British School of Archaeology. As Honorary Director, she had partial responsibility for the institution, which was without money, without a building, and, because of Britain's inelegant exit from Palestine in 1948, with few admirers. Its first chairman had been Sir Frederick. His daughter was coming to wave the flag. Best to plant it at a place known to every household and to every newspaper editor. So Jericho it would be for one season, maybe two. She could tidy up the loose ends left by Garstang.

"That we miscalculated," one of her colleagues reflected many years later, "is, as everybody knows, an understatement."

Including the universities and museums, the number of sponsors reached forty-seven. Kenyon presented slide shows, wrote for popular magazines in Britain and the United States, spoke wherever she was invited; the magazine payments and her lecture fees went into the budget. And there was always more fieldwork. Her assistants at Jericho found she slept only four hours a night. In the evenings, after she examined the latest pottery, she was writing, slowly, a paper on her old excavations in Britain. Dig season over, she began another season of public lectures and taught her courses at the Institute of Archaeology. Meanwhile the artifacts from Jericho and sketches that were black with a thousand small details—the record of everything observed in the baulks—were awaiting her attention. She had seven *tons* of artifacts from one season's work in Libya, work done in '47; she was needing to write that report too.

And archaeology was poor, dirt poor, in a way "hard" sciences would never be. Archaeology was always going to be the old. It had no effect on the price of eggs. PPNA was not a weapon, useful household gadget, disease, or cure. Kenyon, though, did know how to tantalize. She made her name familiar. There were occasional progress reports in the *Times* by "Kathleen Kenyon, Director of the British School of Archaeology in Jerusalem," who could stretch the truth for the sake of improving her story. No, she had not yet found walls from Joshua's time. She *did* find a small jug—"perhaps abandoned when the housewife fled before the approaching Israelites." This was not demonstrably false, not demonstrably true. It was a masterful "perhaps"; perhaps the Old Testament account would be confirmed.

In 1956 the BBC broadcast a television program on the excavations. A year later Kenyon described her preliminary findings in a 267-page book entitled *Digging Up Jericho.* It is earnest, dry, occasionally wry, and was intended for a mass audience. The book appeared when the excavations were still under way. But for some years it was her best attempt to synthesize her findings, as other projects began to consume greater amounts of her time and the volume of the Jericho materials became overwhelming. She alone worked on the big picture, plus the trenches and squares. She assigned the bulk of the analytical work to herself.

In *Digging Up Jericho* are tales of supplies arriving annoyingly late from London, as in the era of Charles Warren; of a temperamental electric generator prone to short circuits; of the frantic search each year for boxes and old newspapers for shipping pottery shards to Britain. There are hints of the excitement at finding the PPNA wall and tower. In 1957 no comparable site was known. The PPNA community at Ein es Sultan had crossed the threshold from settlement to town and seemed to have come into existence three thousand years in advance of any other. In the concluding sentence of her book Kenyon repeated what the newspapers had reported many times at her prompting: "Jericho can make the proud claim to be the oldest known town in the world."

Since then the known world of PPNA has become larger, its scattered parts found one by one. It includes Qermez Dere and Nemrik 9 in Iraq; Mureybet and Tell Aswad in Syria; Nahal Oren in Israel; Gesher and Netiv Hagdud in the Jordan Valley. By 7500 B.C. all of them, like Jericho, had round or oval houses, and as at Jericho, some of the dead—usually headless—were buried under the earth floors. Of these several "oldest" towns, Jericho remains the most sophisticated and largest.

Ofer Bar-Yosef, paleo-anthro-bio-archaeologist, discovered Netiv Hagdud in the 1970s, eight miles to the north of Ein es Sultan. Still another PPNA settlement lay between them. Netiv Hagdud was a small fraction the size of the PPNA settlement at Ein es Sultan. It contained houses and burials in the now expected styles, but lacked a town wall and tower. Their absence was as interesting as their presence eight miles to the south. For several thousand years of human history the wall and tower at Ein es Sultan were, as far as is known, unique in size and in the social complexity they implied about their builders. Why a defense system at one site and not at another? Strange that a threat would differ so greatly in the same pancake-flat valley. Who were the attackers?

Bar-Yosef studied topographic maps and reread the reports written by Kathleen Kenyon. He hiked in the valley. From every viewpoint the remarkableness of the town wall and tower at Ein es Sultan was undiminished. Studying the terrain, Bar-Yosef concluded the invaders' arrival was almost inevitable. People had chosen to settle alongside a spring within a mile of forested hills to the west and cut that forest for lumber and firewood. The invaders then poured down those hills. But the invaders were perhaps not an army.

To thwart them, people at Ein es Sultan took the revolutionary, necessary step of building a high wall. Whenever the defense system was in danger of being breached, it was strengthened: the town wall on the west, where the threat was greatest, became the thickest. As an extra measure of defense on the west, a ditch thirty feet wide and seven feet deep was quarried in bedrock just beyond the wall.

Given everything known about the attackers, these measures were practical, well-designed, the best available technology.

Bar-Yosef concluded that water and mud were the enemies.

They had poured down the hillsides with great force because the hills were largely denuded. The wadis were an efficient delivery system, against which a wall or a ditch was the only defense. Bar-Yosef offered his analysis in a paper published in 1986. In six pages he paid respectful tribute to Ernst Sellin, Carl Watzinger, John Garstang, and Kathleen Kenyon and some of her collaborators, and then went on to rewrite the probable history of PPNA. He noted the lack of archaeological evidence for organized warfare. A stone tower intended for military defense would stand, logically, outside the town wall, not inside where it was mostly hidden. And at Ein es Sultan, PPNA had been steady state, as one generation of mud-brick houses slowly collapsed onto the remains of its nearly identical predecessors. Military fortifications did not make an appearance in the material record for another thousand years; walls unmistakably designed to stop an army were not built until several centuries after 6000 B.C. Bar-Yosef took comfort from this. Human rivalries had apparently been insignificant during PPNA; warfare seemed to be invented only much later. If it were absent among the first permanent settlements in the valley, warfare might not be inevitably in the future, even in the Middle East.

The discovery of another town wall at another PPNA settlement will be the best test for Bar-Yosef's theory. Bar-Yosef is author of that suggestion, too. There is no reason to believe the inhabitants at Ein es Sultan would be the only people to formulate a response to a threat—whether it came from water or an army. Find another PPNA town wall, and you may learn more about the nature of the common threat. Hints have already been found. Ninety miles to the southeast, in Jordan, is the archaeological site called Beidha; it lies in a wadi where permanent settlers arrived during PPNB. A wall more than 150 feet long survives there, and it originally had an outside staircase. An outside staircase is no more sensible than an inside tower, unless the enemy were water. Bar-Yosef has suggested that a protective wall might also be buried at Netiv Hagdud or at some other site dated to PPNA—*ought* to be buried there and thus findable.

Because Peter Parr was late returning from lunch, one of his colleagues at the Institute of Archaeology in London waved me into her office. She was arranging pottery shards on a wooden table. In a hopeful tone she confided the shards were Roman and from Nebi Mend, in Syria, where Parr has excavated since the mid-1970s. Her task was to match shards with the notecards describing them. Amphora Rim 9 was described thusly: diameter 15 centimeters with inverted rim rounded to form semicircle above straight neck.

"If you are one of these people who knows about these things, you might be able to help me," she said.

On the table, Rim 9 was in pieces the size of pocket change. I saw no amphora, no rim.

Parr, my rescuer, was insignificantly rounder than his image in forty-year-old photographs, and his hair had become white but was still thick. In the photo from Jericho he was sitting atop a stone wall for a group portrait of Kenyon's latest crop of assistants—a solidly built adventurer, impressionable and eager.

In his office, Professor Parr smoked a pipe and wore a professor's tweed uniform. The Institute of Archaeology resides in an unredeemably plain building with the good fortune to face the stately trees of London's Gordon Square. In this building were the Great *Sitt*'s classrooms, the corridors she walked, and her offices.

Occupying the center of Parr's bookcase were the thick red-bound volumes by Kenyon et al. on Jericho. The work is remembered with pleasure, and a shudder at the thought of attempting to repeat it. Excavators now are as interested in patterns of settlements as in reaching bedrock at any single site. They seek bedrock of whole cultures in hopes of understanding reasons for cultural change. At Jericho, John Garstang was a bulldozer, Kathleen Kenyon a trowel. The current ideal calls for a finer, more delicate technique, archaeologist-as-pointillist, filling in a larger canvas.

Parr telephoned upstairs to invite Peter Dorrell to join the conversation. Dorrell is chief archivist of Jerichoia. He is a tall, very slender man, unhurried and watchful. He took most of the excavation's photographs, and he has created a subspeciality best called History of Archaeological Photographs. Indeed, his office upstairs is furnished, to the extent it is, with boxes of his photographs from Jericho. Our conversation turned to Ofer Bar-Yosef's idea that the people of PPNA constructed the town wall against water and erosion. At the Institute of Archaeology, the theory was heard as a challenge to the Great *Sitt* and, perhaps, to mental health. "I don't see why the walls aren't what they look to be," Parr said. "It seems like a lot of work to protect against water."

"What you're doing is substituting for a simple, unprovable theory a complex, unprovable theory," Peter Dorrell said. "Three or four meters thick, just to protect against rainwater?"

"It's a problem," Parr said. "Why do we have this one site with this tower and massive wall?"

"It must be a defense against something."

"Yes, defensive."

"Yes, there must have been marauding something around."

"I can't think but that the best thing we can do is leave it alone for the next hundred years, and then someone can try again."

During PPNB the inhabitants became more expert at the settled life. In the mix of animal bones, the percentage from sheep and goat is up from PPNA times, and the percentage from ibex, gazelle, wild boar is down. People were raising more of their protein in domesticated herds and depending less on venturing out to hunt for it.

The PPNB population then left the mound. Perhaps the soil gave out, as happens if it is unfertilized and hosts the same crop season after season. Or climate changed: it is believed the valley began to suffer a series of droughts and became warmer. The PPNB people may have gone to another, more favorable location, since the region was uncrowded and still without large-scale conflicts. Whatever the reason, for a long time—three hundred to five hundred years—no one was living by the spring. Then another, unmistakably different people arrived, bringing a culture that shakes one's assumptions about human development and one's understanding of "progress," or, if you will, "civilization."

The newcomers were troglodytes. They dug pits, six or so feet deep and about nine feet across, which were their homes. Kathleen Kenyon did not expect this or at first recognize it. The pits invaded the topmost strata from PPNB and contained a jumble of rubble. Seeing them, a rational person first thinks "quarry," not "dwelling." It is a living arrangement observed at many sites and that lasted, according to current estimates, about five hundred years. In some of the pits people hollowed out caves as side rooms, and some pits had benches. There probably was an aboveground level with walls made of animal skins or thatched branches, and a thatched roof. This is plausibly sensible architecture for people who have no central authority, have few immovable possessions, and are on the road as much as they are at home—a job description for herders. Herders can survive conditions that devastate farmers; when all crops have failed, goats and sheep may still find something to nibble. For the first time at the mound, the bones from domesticated animals outnumber their wild relatives. So the protein revolution had continued.

"Civilization" is, of course, the label we affix to a culture successful enough to leave a mark. A culture is a set of adaptations to conditions, a specialized organism in its niche. When climate turned cooler thirteen thousand years ago, the Natufians were the people whose experiments in food gathering were the most successful in the new conditions. When conditions changed again, other experimenters prevailed: the people of PPNA, then PPNB. Writing about the timing of change, Ofer Bar-Yosef notes that changes occur in society not for the sake of innovation itself but because they are necessary for human survival. If you survive you embody progress, whatever your way of living. And "progress" can differ from what we consider "improvement." The choices the PPNB people had made in housing and agriculture apparently were no longer sustainable when the climate turned dry and warm. In a sense, the PPNB people were too civilized—too well attuned to one set of circumstances. The niche had disappeared. By about 5500 B.C. the representatives of progress at Ein es Sultan were the pit dwellers.

They had arrived with pottery, the first ever at the mound. It is an enormously important addition. The ability to bake clay in prepared shapes creates a profession—the potter's—that affects every household in a community. The difference begins with efficiency, for making a vessel with baked clay consumes less time than shaping a vessel from stone. The potter can increase the number of containers and increase the variety of their shapes. With more shapes comes a wider choice of functions. Make large storage jars, and sufficiently large quantities of them, and the farmer can preserve the surplus from his harvest. A settlement has more merchandise for trade.

The first pottery was straight-sided and flat-bottomed. The potter mixed the clay with straw, and before the vessel went into the kiln he wiped the still-wet clay with grass. On the baked surface are the tracks and you still can all but see the hand that did the work. Those first pots were usually decorated in red, which was painted and baked onto a painted, baked cream. Later, the pottery was made without straw, and the surface designs changed, as did the rims. Every archaeologist beginning with Flinders Petrie has been deeply indebted to this and every subsequent change in aesthetic tastes. Changes in culture are embodied in the changing shapes of the vessels and the tinkerings with the manufacturing process.

A pottery rim is a legible signature of time and (with luck) place. The body shape and decorations are a home address. Writing would not appear for, approximately, another two thousand years. Four thousand years would pass before the first use of iron. The potters made the first goods that could be mass-produced (with the potter's wheel) and also be easily compared. The goods endured. A baked clay jar can break but does not rust. It will not rot. Unlike flints it allows expression of individual taste. A jigsaw puzzle of odd-shaped pieces of baked clay can be reassembled—even with an unknowable number of other pieces missing—to give a sense of the original whole.

The pit dwellers at the mound above Ein es Sultan mingled with builders of houses. Then were succeeded by them.

The newcomers placed plano-convex bricks atop stone foundations and, as should be expected, made pottery in new shapes. This was the last chapter of the stone age and an overlapping first chapter of the age of metals.

By 4000 B.C. the mound was again deserted. Or if not deserted, then nearly so. Another people arrived, within perhaps five hundred years, as the pioneers of the Early Bronze Age. It is hard to know precisely what they saw alongside the spring. The mound was in places already more than twenty feet high, and perhaps had the appearance of a building site already nicely prepared for them. Weathering could either uncover or bury the walls from PPNB. These pioneers built a town wall with at least one tower, and the purpose this time is without doubt military defense. By 3000 B.C. there was an era of relative wealth throughout the land.

Settlements had surplus crops. Agricultural surpluses allowed for more trade, and with greater commerce came trade routes worth protecting. So for the first time settlements needed bureaucrats. They had to design town defenses and have them built. Someone had to negotiate good relations with the next settlement along the dirt track. Principles of town planning gradually made themselves known. On the mound at Ein es Sultan, the houses first were built without regard to the buildings next door, each one on a different axis. People tossed garbage into the nearest open space, including the area between their houses. Later, people built their houses in neat rows and tossed garbage over the town walls.

Early Bronze ended with the valley deforested and, so it seems, agriculture in trouble. With crop failure, trade declined. City-states needed food and so did the herders. No one was lacking motivation for violence. The town at Ein es Sultan was destroyed. Whether it was attacked at this time or suffered a gruesome accident is unknown. But by happenstance or as part of an enemy's tactics, wood was placed against the outer face of the town wall. The wood ignited in about 2300 B.C. The fire heated the wall like the bricks of an oven. Everything leaning against the inside face sizzled and cooked until the settlement was in flames. Until Middle Bronze the mound was empty, again.

Some of the ever-present herders resettled themselves at the spring, or people arrived from the north (or both). Prosperity could be measured, then as now, by the sophistication of a community's defense system; and by that standard, the city-state at Ein es Sultan during Middle Bronze was wealthy. It was defended by a brick wall six to nine feet thick, atop a high artificial slope. Sellin and Watzinger estimated the wall had been more than twenty feet high, not including the fifteen-foot height of the slope. The original design is a matter of debate: Watzinger, Garstang, and Kenyon offered three possible reconstructions, and after studying their drawings, an Israeli archaeologist has formulated a fourth. Kenyon's assistants, before digging into still lower strata, photographed the Middle Bronze structures. In the photographs that last city from Middle Bronze appears more densely built than modern Riha. The construction is as good if not better. Kenyon uncovered a street six and a half feet wide that had a workable drainage system and climbed the slope of the mound with cobblestone steps.

Where the mound slopes toward the spring, Kenyon found ash three feet deep. The ash was what remained of buildings that had stood on higher ground. They had burned at the end of Middle Bronze. Rains had carried the ash downhill. Since no one rebuilt the city, or attempted to control the erosion, you can conclude that during at least part of the Late Bronze Age no one was there. For at least a century, no one. Another people did come in small numbers, eventually, to live on a small part of the mound—a community so poor that it reused some of the Middle Bronze tombs. It built very little.

It built no town wall.

The pattern is familiar—settlement, destruction, resettlement—and would not be worth special attention if Late Bronze were not the arrival time for the Israelites. It is when God assures Joshua that Jericho "with its king and mighty men of valor" are to fall into the Israelites' hands.

Garstang had discovered foundations of one Late Bronze building and a small amount of Late Bronze pottery. Kenyon found part of a floor from a single Late Bronze house, a small clay oven, and a small jug. "The remains were not spectacular," Kenyon wrote.

Nothing suggested the building of fortifications during the Late Bronze Age. Perhaps parts of the town walls from Middle Bronze had still been usable. Nothing suggested violent conquest or the arrival of a new people. Perhaps erosion had removed the evidence.

For fund-raising purposes, Kenyon had sometimes promoted the excavations as a modern pilgrimage. She would say the work was "to illustrate the bible's account with confirmation of the town's destruction by the Israelites." That goal sounded much like Charles Warren's dream as he slept at the base of the mound, and her words were little different from George Grove's to his earliest supporters. When the confirmation failed to materialize, Kenyon, writing for the public and not her colleagues, reported that a town *could* have existed during Late Bronze and then could have disappeared. She described the disappearance as almost fact, as if she were uncomfortable with her own findings. The Israelite invaders, Kenyon reasoned, would have been traveling light after living forty years in the desert. So light, their possessions decayed into nothingness. Thus the lack of evidence for anyone's arrival at Jericho. The lack of fortifications was left unexplained. In wanting to defer to the biblical account, Kenyon was following the lead of her most eminent colleagues, be they British, American, or Israeli.

In the end, though, she gave greater weight to the physical artifacts, and to the lack of them. She was not swayed by efforts, including her own, to make the findings "fit." She rejected using biblical testimony as a controlling authority for interpreting what she saw. Nothing at the mound suggested the existence of a great walled city during the Late Bronze Age: "nothing survives," she said, "to illustrate the biblical account."

Kenyon made an effort to keep theology separate from what she could examine with her hands and eyes. This was not a small accomplishment. She was, curiously, both a pioneer and distinctly old-fashioned. Unlike her successors, she was uninterested in biblical languages and made little effort to study the findings of other archaeologists. She was largely self-taught in her grasp of history and of her own field, and it showed. But in dirt, she was queen. As a field archaeologist, Kathleen Kenyon set the standard for her generation.

Her insistence on doing things her way played a large role in her subsequent failures. Not even she could live up to the standards she demanded. She spent most of each year in Britain. There were horses, hounds, and a country house, and by every material measure her life was always comfortable. What burdened her were the unwritten reports on her excavations. She had not yet finished writing about the work done in Libya in 1947, or published a final report about a project she had supervised in Britain in '52. One could always write another article for the usual journals about what one found during an excavation. No one could place full faith in the conclusions, however, or challenge them in an intellectually useful way, until the excavator published photographs of the artifacts and of the site, described in detail the method of work, and, in general, gave his or her colleagues enough information to make independent judgments. Otherwise it was better to leave a site untouched, everything intact for someone else to excavate.

She at least tried to write. Friends cite her habit of often working late into the night. But she seems to have arranged her affairs so that she never had time to finish any one assignment, or always had some alternative to that desk work. Another project was always waiting.

A first volume on Jericho appeared in 1960, with a promise of more to come. A year later, she began excavating in Jerusalem.

As always, she wanted to excavate narrow and deep and to record every detail. She was no less imperious, smoked more, drank more, and grew much heavier. She again chose to excavate a relatively small number of squares. From them, she would try to extrapolate the history of a large city.

Her techniques severely limited her finds. At Jericho she never managed to uncover any one building in its entirety. In Jerusalem she exposed an even smaller part of the whole. The smaller the area, the riskier the extrapolations.

And again she kept all responsibility for herself—raising money, negotiating with authorities, supervising an enormous staff. It was more than any one person could do. One team of young assistants could misread the all-important stratigraphy of a square that another young team had begun a season earlier—a problem that indeed occurred. One of her colleagues would later find that important drawings either had been lost or had not been made. There was also the turmoil of a war. When the Jerusalem project began, the area she excavated belonged to Jordan. A few weeks before her last season there, in 1967, the area was captured by Israel, and her regard for Israel was notably cool. She suggested Britain apply sanctions against Israel if it failed to give up the newly captured parts of the city.

Volume two of the final Jericho report appeared in 1964. Writing about the excavation would have been difficult for anyone, given the number of artifacts. Kenyon had kept some of the pottery, but a large quantity of it, after she was satisfied that she had properly classified it, went into the pond at her country house, to make an island for the ducks. Other volumes would be completed by one of her colleagues and published in the early 1980s, after her death. In 1978 at age seventy-two, Kenyon died of a stroke.

A person does not so much read the Jericho volumes as, sadly, struggle to excavate them. The largest part is devoted to lists. There are lists of bones and pottery and amulets and strata but few links among them, because Kenyon never synthesized her findings, despite more than twenty years of effort. The intellectual connections between the various trenches and squares were never made. She minutely analyzed many thousands of artifacts, but never found time to assemble them in some fashion and make sense of the recovered whole.

The results in Jerusalem were much more dismal. Kenyon lived long enough to learn that her early conclusions there were wrong. Fascinated with detail, reluctant to share authority, she accumulated more data than any one person could master.

Archaeology even at its best finds only fragments of something larger. Remains are only that: remnants of something else, and what has usually been lost is the meaning an object had for the people who made it, or who first saw it. Physical artifacts expand legends, undermine or revise them, and are never a complete historical truth. The mound at Ein es Sultan is one such artifact. In an important sense, Kenyon's findings supported the stirring tale offered by the Book of Joshua. For there was indeed a place in the Jordan Valley that had attracted people's attention beginning long ago. It was that high mound. No miracles were needed for it to become a rich source of legend. Without question, it inspired the compilers of what became the Old Testament. Seeing that large, high place covered with rubble—who could doubt it was once a great city? The Book of Joshua describes it. The mound testified to a powerful city's long-ago destruction and inspired people to believe in the greatness of their ancestors and in the power of the god who led them.

As told in Joshua, the Israelites destroy Jericho in the Jordan Valley, then raze the fortress cities of Ai and Bethel in the Judean hills, defeat a coalition of Canaanite kings in the southwest, and quickly turn to raid towns in the north. The Book of Judges contains a different version of the story: Joshua is dead (at the age of 110) and the Israelites struggle for generations to win control of the land. Until the Israelites finally succeed they live among the Canaanites.

Those are the texts. There are also the physical remains and the light they shed.

Some of the best analysis has been done by William Dever and Israel Finkelstein. They are, respectively, American and Israeli, attached to the University of Arizona and Tel Aviv University. Dever is sixtyish, with a white mustache and a white beard trimmed short, and is considered a fine excavator and an even better theoretician. He is combative and has a voice sonorous enough for radio. Finkelstein, who is two decades younger, helped pioneer field surveys that searched for signs of the Israelites' early settlements. He is less formal than Dever though no less confident. His dark beard is that of a grand rebbe, which is his status.

My summary of Late Bronze Age archaeological finds is William Dever's. The evidence for a new people arriving in Canaan in large numbers at that time is extremely limited; so is the evidence for anyone conducting a quick, violent conquest. Joshua and Judges give accounts of the destruction of sixteen cities. After many decades of excavations, ten of the sixteen have been identified with confidence. Evidence of destruction occurring at the time the Israelites seem to appear in the archaeological record has been found at three of those ten.

At the city of Ai the Israelites were initially repulsed—the Book of Joshua says—but then tricked the Canaanite army into marching out of the city into the desert. By the end of the fighting, Ai was smoldering and the victorious Israelites had killed twelve thousand men and women. Joshua hanged the city's king. "So Joshua burned Ai," the Book of Joshua says, "and made it for ever a heap of ruins, as it is to this day." And so indeed it was—a heap of ruins. Ai had been destroyed. But the destruction had occurred a thousand years before the Israelites. As at Jericho, anyone coming there during the Late Bronze Age would have seen ruins.

"Many [Late Bronze] sites were not destroyed at all," Dever has written. "Of those that were, more must be attributed to the Philistines or to unknown causes than to any groups to be identified as Israelites."

My description of an alternative method for the Israelites taking the land is Israel Finkelstein's. In his revised history of the Late Bronze Age, the people who would become known as Israelites had already lived for many generations in Canaan. The Israelites-to-be were among the herders of sheep and goats living on the fringes of the cities, ever since the economic and political turmoil at the end of the Middle Bronze. In Late Bronze this arrangement broke down. The largest settlements were under terrible stress, perhaps because of drought, perhaps because of conflict among the cities. The Amarna letters attest to the turmoil. When crops failed, and when food surpluses disappeared, the herders could no longer trade animals for surplus grain, as had been done for as long as people could remember. Out of necessity the herders moved with their flocks to thinly populated areas to become farmers themselves.

Finkelstein, surveying the hills north of Jerusalem acre by acre, identified the probable remains of those settlements. The herder-farmers lived in small communities without fortifications. They were apparently self-sufficient. Their pottery was similar to pottery found elsewhere in Canaan, though not identical. Their architecture was found elsewhere in Canaan, though some of the elements were changed as if to make allowances for the hilly terrain. A community of newly arrived foreigners would have had a material culture distinctly its own. Some of these people newly settled in the hills could have come from Egypt. Or they could have been joined by people who had traveled from there. But most had been in Canaan since their birth. So had their parents and the parents of their parents' parents.

The Canaanite cities, large and small, were conquered, eventually. It was not accomplished in one grand campaign. Over a period of several hundred years, the herder-farmers living mostly in the hills became the Israelites.

"I don't think there'll be a revival of the theory of these people coming from the deep desert," Israel Finkelstein said. "That's passé."

"There was no military conquest," William Dever said. "I think almost everyone agrees on that." Anyone wandering in the Jordan Valley at the end of the Late Bronze Age would have come across a freshwater spring, and rising from it a nearly deserted, high, lumpen mound.

V

Sheep Trails

Awad Njum is a shepherd in the valley. Whatever the steps that led to a more sedentary life, and led to the first cities and all that followed, some people ignored that path or came to it late. There are shepherds in the valley who wandered into a niche and have stayed there. They are not trapped, but they have not traveled far.

The Njum clan abandoned nomadism about fifty years ago to experiment with staying in one place. It is still only an experiment. The Njums mostly ignore the main flow of evolutionary traffic except to complain about it when they have a disagreeable encounter, as when city people inform them that the wholesale price for sheep and goats has dropped. A herder named Abu Od, a sometime friend of Awad Njum, described their chosen way of life. "Write down that the situation is garbage—garbage, garbage," said Abu Od. He and his flock were walking into a bone-dry field recently harvested of eggplants and squash. Every time a sheep took a step, there was a crunch of dry stubble, and the main crop looked to be a rubbery spaghetti of irrigation pipes. Abu Od was vainly hoping that Awad Njum would not mind the arrival of another flock.

Awad Njum had come to the field first. I crossed paths with him early in the morning on the highway winding along the valley floor, about a mile north of the mound. Crossing the road, Njum, his donkey, and his herd of about fifty sheep and goats were oblivious to the traffic. Njum wore sandals, dark pants, several layers of pullover shirts, and a white keffiya, and his staff was a length of irrigation pipe. I was driving with Hakam Fahoum and had to slow the car for the herd. We scrambled down a sandy embankment and Njum accepted our company as if we were a regular part of the flock. No questions asked, just a soliloquy about the lack of suitable grazing area and the baked dryness of the ground. He added that the dryness had been even worse the previous year, not to mention the year before that. One step, one complaint. "Dry ground, dry ground," he said. "It's like boiled shit." It was already hot, and every living thing looked to be suffering.

Herders were an offspring of the early farmers, themselves the offspring of the hunter-gatherers. People settled, and then learned to cultivate the land, and only with farming could food surpluses exist, to be used for feeding captive animals. Only then could a community keep animals as something other than an immediately pending meal. It was the farmer, not the hunter, who was in closer proximity to the different creatures and learned the greater amount about them and domesticated them, beginning with sheep and goats. The "how" of that first domestication remains a mystery, but it was accomplished by the people of PPNA and PPNB, beginning ten thousand years ago.

If the rains came, if the crops did not fail, if the human population survived, the crisis occurred when every few years the number of animals outstripped the feeding capacity of the lands lying within one or two days' walk. Some of the farmer-herders would then leave to establish a new settlement. Domestication of the donkey six thousand years ago provided the farmer-herders with a four-legged moving van. (Domestication of the camel—hardier, higher capacity than the donkey—occurred two thousand years later.) As the number of settlements increased, the farmer-herders necessarily spent more time on the move in search of pasture. Herders traded animals for grain and—when their own fields were dormant, or when the pasture gave out—moved again. For the first time herding became a full-time occupation.

Every morning Njum set out with his animals. They used to head west. Shepherds would climb from the valley into the hills and camp there from early summer until the first rains. When Israel gained control of the territory, the new authorities recognized the strategic value of near emptiness and designated the area a military training ground, closed to civilians. There was occasionally the sound of artillery or the rumble of transport planes flying low to drop the latest class of paratroopers.

Njum headed east, toward the river. The plain was crunchy sand with small dribbles of dull green weeds. On the opposite bank of the river rose the mountains of Moab, a smudge of blue almost lost in haze, like a vast becalmed sea. Since Njum usually had only the flock for company, he had found ample time to cultivate complaints. When he was not chasing the sheep and goats, hissing at them, shrieking at them, ordering the donkey into a chase, he complained about them. When he stopped cursing the animals, he cursed his life as a shepherd.

He had farmers on his mind. "If they see us eating the bananas, they kill us," he said, thumping the ground with the irrigation pipe. The flocks ate the crops that the farmer irrigated and worried over and prayed for in the hot sun. A flock given free reign would reduce his total return to a little randomly dropped manure. Njum's animals stopped at a line of banana plants and munched.

On cue, the farmer stepped out of the buggy green denseness.

Without the slightest pause Njum loudly announced he was in the company of officials from the United Nations. Big shots—a special team dispatched to study the desperate plight of the shepherds. Experts who were in *this banana grove.* With Awad Njum. It was a marvelous performance and included arm waving and more thumps of the irrigation pipe, and we were Njum's salvation. The farmer, as if confronted by a menacing army, offered a small wave before retreating into the green.

Njum made that speech his refrain for the day. "They were sent by the UN so they will tell us where we can herd and where we can't," he would say with a nod in our direction. Since we kept silent, the farmers were left to assume the animals trimming another row of vegetables were exercising their rights under international law. No one was much inclined to challenge outside authority because it was usually hostile and often came well armed. No one was going to mistake Hakam Fahoum, with a beeper on his belt, or me, wearing running shoes and a floppy gabardine hat, for shepherds. The animals feasted.

I thought of Claude Conder, who in 1873, as leader of the Palestine Exploration Fund's team of surveyors, encountered the same fearful respect. Fellahin who had never before seen a European fled their villages at the approach of the surveyors on horseback, until a story began to be whispered that the strangers were special representatives of the all-powerful sultan. The story took on a life of its own and cast the surveyors as good-hearted men sent by the Sublime Porte to document the poverty of the villagers. It was said the Europeans would then bring all poverty to an end. "And hence we became favourites," wrote Conder, "and every possible ruin in the village lands was shown to us, with the greatest eagerness, as it was supposed that taxes would be remitted in proportion to the amount of desolation." Never one to complain about an elaborate show of deference, Conder was surely pleased by the misunderstanding. On one occasion Conder's guide calmed two Bedouin—after one grabbed the bridle of Conder's horse, and for his impertinence was kicked by Conder—by introducing him as an English consul. This brought forth immediately a plea addressed to Her Majesty's eminent servant for large grants of water and vineyards. Conder responded with noncommittal phrases and a nod of his head.

We arrived in the desiccated field that was already emptied of eggplants and were joined by Abu Od. Slight to the point of gauntness, he wore a blousy blue-green jacket atop a well-worn shirt and purple trousers. He lightly gripped a crooked walking stick. He was tall and made to seem taller by his elongated face, a reincarnation of Pharoah Akhenaten—high forehead, narrow chin, with a long distance in between. Usually Abu Od spoke quietly and left the histrionics to Njum.

When Njum exaggerated, his voice rose at least one full octave. When he proclaimed his visitors were from the UN, he transformed himself from a baritone into a scratchy tenor. Njum was stocky, sturdier looking than Abu Od, and a handsome coppery brown. Neither man had attended school; their reading ability was limited to little more than the

Arabic script for their names. Njum's identity card said he was fifty years old. He shrugged and said he was born "in the year of the snow."

Njum and Abu Od shared certain qualities with the sheep. All of them spent much of their time in what appeared to be idleness, though the animals were busy eating and the shepherds maintained they were fully occupied with worries. Neither the animals nor the shepherds believed in boundaries, as if fences were created to be breached. When a sheep coughed, Njum and Abu Od coughed in sympathy.

The shepherds concentrated their worries on the thinness of the animals. Abu Od collared a sheep so we could feel its ribs poking through and join a round of tsk-tsking. Njum was anxious for the sheep to eat more to build up the energy to mate; there was much concern that none of the animals showed interest in sex. "There is no fucking here," Njum said. He interrupted the discussion by tossing a rock to frighten the animals away from a hedge of nubk. One sheep moved one step, which proved enough to convince the flock to return to the middle of the field.

The animals were looking for more shade than what was available from the field's solitary palm tree. Sheep are reasonably well adapted to the climate; their fleece insulates them from the heat. They pant rather than sweat and, to maintain a normal body temperature, can increase their rate of respiration tenfold, to three hundred breaths a minute. Given water, a thirsty sheep recovers many times faster than a dehydrated shepherd.

The only other available shade consisted of the small rectangles of shadow cast by the animals. The animals accommodated themselves to their means. Each sheep lowered its head under the hindquarters of another, into that small pocket of shade, and created a headless, panting mass in the middle of the field, a vibrating patch of dirty snow. As they panted, the field appeared to be quivering in an earthquake.

When hunger called, the animals would break away from the snowball. Awad Njum's flock mixed with Abu Od's. A third shepherd, a woman who smiled broadly, walked into the field, went immediately to the men, talked very quietly and apologetically about having come there—no other vegetation was to be found, it seemed—until Njum interrupted to demand very loudly that she take her herd elsewhere. Better for her to have said nothing; the men took the friendliness as an invitation to humiliate her. I looked for some identifying mark on her sheep but found none, and none on Njum's. On my behalf Hakam asked how shepherds could tell their animals apart.

"Mine are black," Njum said very slowly as if he were in the company of a creature even dumber than his sheep, "and Abu Od's are white." That was not the case, since each man had sheep of each color. Plus some of the animals were brown, plus there were the goats (brown and black). But no other explanation was offered, and I let the subject drop.

Shepherding required great patience and bottomless abnegation. After one day it was already possible to have an inkling of the full horror implied by the term *sheeplike.* In stories, sheep never played roles requiring a clear show of intelligence and were never the heroes. In the Old Testament sheep were a reliable metaphor for the hopelessly passive, the lost, the self-destructive; and in regard to sheep the Old Testament offered literal truth. Most shepherds were tainted by association. In the Old Testament no profession demanded greater responsibility or had as many misfits. Except for God Himself and a small number of His prophets, the shepherds were incompetent, irresponsible, or venal. Apparently everyone of that era could readily appreciate the image. God was chief shepherd, and though He was dependable, His flock was not. The problems were documented as far back as Abraham. Herdsmen in the clans of Abraham and Lot had quarreled, Genesis said, and the two clans agreed to go separate ways. Lot took the Jordan Valley, Abraham the western hills.

Rabbinic sages were intrigued by the story. The herdsmen had argued, but about what? In the fourth century Rabbi Hiyya bar Abba concluded that this primordial dispute had been caused by overgrazing and, based on somewhat involved reasoning, blamed it on the flocks belonging to Lot.

On occasion the biblical shepherds were brave. God led the Israelites out of Egypt as would a shepherd. Jeremiah, a shepherd, railed against Israel's leaders for incompetence and against the human flock for blindly following. More typical was the complaint of Ezekiel, who cataloged all the wrongdoings of shepherds to document human greed and laziness.

"The strayed you have not brought back," Ezekiel said.

"My people have been lost sheep; their shepherds have led them astray," Jeremiah said.

"Many shepherds have destroyed my vineyard," he said, "they have trampled down my portion, they have made my pleasant portion a desolate wilderness." Implicit in his observations was that peaceful coexistence between shepherds and farmers would begin about the time swords were beaten into plowshares and would be no less miraculous.

The most learned rabbis interpreted the biblical passages to mean the shepherd performed work that was extraordinarily trying yet important. Now it would be drug counseling: the clients are balky, the working conditions poor. The early sages charitably decided the job was designed as a test of patience and kindness. Then opinions changed, as they would if the counselor were discovered to be a small-time dealer. A later generation of rabbis advised people against buying anything from a shepherd because of the overwhelming likelihood that the shepherd had stolen anything he offered for sale. Presumably the sages had learned from experience. No one, the rabbis said, need listen to testimony from a shepherd accused of taking his herd into a prohibited area: the shepherd's word was considered not worth having. "The assumption," said a sage, "is that he is a robber."

Awad Njum and Abu Od all but swore that money was something they had heard of but never possessed. Every year was described as a losing one. They made bids on which year qualified as the pluperfect worst, who had lost more animals to cold, who lost more to heat.

The bulk of the herd was sold off twice a year, when the shepherd either walked the animals the twenty miles to East Jerusalem, or trucked the animals there, to the open-air livestock market, or dealt with one of the buyers who came to the valley. A major part of the financial dealings was the bartering of animals for feed. As more pastureland was closed off by farmers or was used for new housing, a shrinking proportion of the flocks' diet came from foraging, and more and more came from fifty-kilogram sacks of barley. If you kept the herd well fed, you had all the more reason to pray for a high price for the sheep to recoup the cost of the grain. In a cold year, or a dry one, the choice was to buy still more grain or watch the animals waste away. Awad Njum sometimes reached the point of trading animals for the barley needed to feed the remainder of the flock. Somewhere in the system, though, was enough cash to keep city people darting in and out as silent partners. During their college days Hakam and some of his friends purchased small flocks and by relying on country relatives to do the work made enough money to buy cheap cars.

Awad Njum had bought a donkey. It was the only vehicle that could reliably carry water to a flock grazing on a twenty-five-degree slope. It was chief water hauler, an assistant herder, and at times Njum's transport.

The shepherds saved their dinars and shekels one by one and practiced a sort of alchemy. When it was time for a son to marry, the shepherd produced a suitable stake of gold or of animals. But it was impolitic to talk of good times. Meeting one of Njum's cousins, Yousef Ibrahim, I made the mistake of praising the cousin's flock of more than fifty noticeably well fed sheep. "Yes," Yousef Ibrahim said in thanks for the compliment, "I lose a lot of money on all of them."

While their animals explored the vegetable field, Awad Njum and Abu Od began a contest for sympathy. "I don't remember even one single day of my life that was good," said Abu Od. "It was always bad. But we thank Allah anyway."

"I don't worry about my children as much as I worry about these sheep," said Awad Njum, father of fifteen.

"Not only is it hot, but at night the mosquitoes eat you up," said Abu Od.

He added that he was in need of a new belt.

Awad Njum, his voice rising an octave, countered that he suffered from intestinal problems. He announced he was unable to remember what he had eaten the previous night, so was also worried about the state of his mind.

Abu Od wailed that only Allah knew how they would stay alive.

Despairing of the conversation, I wandered to the western side of the field and headed toward a low wall. It did not seem to hold special promise. There was a dirt road to cross, brambles, and a pocket wilderness of knee-high brush. On the other side of the wall were large blocks of well-cut stone scattered in a sandy yard, the area like a construction site with the building materials in total disarray. There were short rows of pillars, no two pillars preserved to the same height, and more pillars broken into drums lay on the ground. This was, as a small sign outside the perimeter wall described, the site known—probably mistakenly—as Hisham's Palace; for it was here that the Arab rulers from the golden age of Islam built an extravagant hunting lodge and winter residence.

Hisham Abed al-Malikh was of the Umayyads, the first Islamic dynasty to emerge after the prophet Muhammad. Muhammad had died in 632 without leaving clear instructions for choosing a new leader. He thereby ensured that succession would rarely be peaceful. The first caliph ("successor") died after two years of rule. Caliphs number two and three were assassinated. Number four, Ali, was challenged on the battlefield by number five, Muawiya—governor of Damascus and member of the prominent clan called Umayyad.

Tradition says Muawiya was a figure of great resourcefulness. When his soldiers seemed in danger of losing their battle against Ali, they raised pages of the Koran on their lances. This produced one of the oddest cease-fires in the history of warfare. Seeing the holy book, Ali's men stopped fighting; some demanded that Ali allow religious judges to arbitrate his disputes with Muawiya. Ali agreed to let the judges intervene. They ruled in favor of Muawiya. Ali rejected the verdict as un-Koranic. The bloodletting resumed. A second set of judges found itself unable to decide whether Ali or Muawiya was the rightful caliph and so chose a third candidate. And in that way Ali and Muawiya found something on which they could agree. They ignored the arbitrators and established rival caliphates and ruled separately in relative peace. They might have continued to coexist if one of Ali's overly zealous supporters—convinced that Ali should have fought harder on the battlefield—had not stabbed him to death in a mosque. So began the Umayyad dynasty with Muawiya as sole caliph.

He was a born manager, immodest and manipulative. "Of him it was said," a later historian relates, "that, had he been shut up behind seven doors, he would have found a way to smash all seven locks." He created a royal court in Damascus, appointed talented governors, and kept a large pack of his scheming relatives in check. His armies reached Tunisia by 670, sailed to Cyprus and Crete, and headed toward India. He rarely bothered to make a show of piety, and for that the pious hated him. His death in 680 ignited another, fiercer round of fighting to determine the rightful heirs of Muhammad.

It must have been a terrible time. Fighting had already lasted for nearly a generation, Umayyads against Kharijites or Zaydites or allies of Ali. Hussein—son of Ali—refused to recognize the authority of the Umayyads. An Umayyad army energetically pillaged Medina for having sided with rebels, and besieged Mecca, catapulting stones into the holy area. In a battle at Karbala, in modern-day Iraq, Hussein and every member of his small army were killed.

To this day, the wounds have never healed. Arguments over who best embodied the qualities of Muhammad and best understood the Koran continue. Sunnis (followers of Muhammad's sunna, his "beaten path") are on one side with several doctrinal allies, on the other are Shia (followers of Ali and Hussein) and supporters of their own. Ayatollah Ruhollah Khomeini of Iran and Saddam Hussein of Iraq have been two of the many tremors along that fault line.

Hisham became in 724 the tenth Umayyad caliph. He inherited an empire he further enriched, his main talent being that of collecting taxes. He was dour and severe, and, perhaps undeservedly, earned a reputation for greed.

His family had for a long time chosen to build accommodations in the outback. The Umayyads preferred hunting and riding to spending time in Damascus, the capital. In Hisham's era, the family building program continued. For a sense of getting away from it all, Jericho was the ideal site.

The Umayyad architects chose as their building site an area northeast of Ein es Sultan. Over a period of many years workmen erected a structure that was part health club, part hunting lodge. It was an Umayyad palace of pleasure. There were sumptuous quarters for guests, a many-roomed bathhouse topped with cupcakelike domes, ornamental pools, a walled park that hunting parties had presumably found stocked with game. The style is High Boudoir. To wander now among the fallen masonry is to have the sense of intruding into a disheveled bedroom.

Almost every surface was decorated with frescoes or elaborately worked stucco, delicate looking, as finely detailed as lace. The dominant motif was pleasures of the flesh.

Most of the surviving sculpture is in Jerusalem at the Rockefeller Museum. There are freizes of human faces, a chorus line of bare-breasted slave girls, stucco monkeys climbing stucco vines, eerily naturalistic hands offering large bouquets of plaster flowers. A statue from the bathhouse facade was said to depict the caliph. He is rendered more as icon than person. He gazes straight ahead. Bare-chested, standing on a pedestal of square-jawed lions sitting haunch to haunch, he wears a belted coat over bright red trousers, Persian style. He grasps a dagger in his left hand, but his right arm has disappeared. Maybe because of the lions, he is distinctly bug-eyed.

In the late 1950s doubts arose as to whether the figure was Hisham. Indeed there was question whether Hisham had any connection to the palace: architectural flamboyance hardly fit his personality. His rambunctious nephew, Walid, seemed to be a more likely tenant.

Walid succeeded Hisham as caliph in 743. He was known chiefly for drinking, poetry, and as a devotee of excess. A writer of that day tells of the unsettling experiences of the singer named Utarrad, brought from Medina to sing for Caliph Walid at a palace that goes unnamed. Ushered into the presence of the caliph, Utarrad found him seated on the edge of a small pool. It was filled with wine. When the singer finished his performance, the caliph stripped himself naked, dove into the pool, and drank. So heartily did the caliph drink that Utarrad could observe a distinct drop in the wine level. Walid was hauled out, dead to the world. He recovered in time to listen to more songs the next day and take another dive.

At the Jericho palace are two small baths in a marble-lined room. It was noticed in the 1950s that the baths fit Utarrad's description of the setting for Walid's amusements. Hence the attribution of the palace to Walid, not Hisham. The baths and the riotous decoration through the palace would, at the least, befit a pleasure-loving caliph.

In 747 or 748—the several accounts date the events according to different calendars—an earthquake struck. Michael the Syrian tells of the ground in Damascus shaking "like the leaves on the trees." Elias of

Nisibus tells of the quake transporting a village the distance of four miles. No less wondrous than the distance traveled is Elias' statement that none of the buildings suffered even so much as a crack in its walls. The palace at Jericho was still under construction and collapsed in the tremors. The Umayyads barely outlasted it. Walid, after ruling for a year, was assassinated before the earthquake; and in 750 the fourteenth, and last, Umayyad caliph was defeated in battle and was soon thereafter murdered in Egypt.

The palace ruins became one of the oddly shaped mounds that so interested and puzzled Western travelers. Charles Warren recorded the local name for the place as Khurbet es Suman (the Dark Ruin). After bringing over his workmen to dig, he reported it to be an ancient church. Claude Conder heard the name was Khurbet el Mefjir—the Ruin Where the Water Breaks—in acknowledgment of its place alongside a deep wadi. Conder concluded it had been a monastery.

In 1894 Frederick Jones Bliss, a diligent, experienced American archaeologist who had worked alongside Flinders Petrie in Egypt and had then succeeded him in Palestine at Tell el-Hesi, made two trips from Jerusalem to Jericho to help pass the time while he waited for a firman for the Palestine Exploration Fund's latest projects. He saw workmen in Jericho building a government headquarters out of stone. He was told the stones had come from Khurbet el Mefjir.

On a first visit, Bliss speculated he had stumbled upon the remains of Herod's palace but after the second, was less sure about his discovery. People told him a tantalizing story about finding water pipes large enough for a man to crawl through. While pillaging, his informants had obviously come upon the bathhouse. Bliss methodically took measurements, made photographs, and collected a small number of decorated tiles and stucco sculptures. Studying the photographs one expert decided (correctly) the building was from sometime after the year 600 but could add nothing more; another declared (wrongly) that the structure was from the era of the Crusaders. Whatever had not already disappeared remained mostly buried until the 1920s. It was then that the Franciscans decided to build a monastery near Jericho. The builders wanted well-cut stone and apparently also wanted to cut costs, so carted away several of the columns and more than two thousand blocks. Other people did the same. The rest of the ruins stayed buried until a British team, beginning in the mid-1930s, conducted twelve winters of excavations. Given the persistence of local habits, the only way to preserve the sculptures was to move them into the Rockefeller Museum.

On a good day, a half-dozen cars turn from the main north-south highway to make the roller-coaster drive through the wadi to reach the ruins. The small printed sign said the admission fee was six shekels, a little less than three dollars. Abdullah Barah, the guard, did not have change in the cashbox for a ten-shekel bill. As usual, he said. He had worked off and on as the guard for twenty-five years. He produced the four shekels in change by digging into his own pocket. "I keep hoping tourism will improve," he said.

Barah was standing against a small building that housed an office almost bare of furniture, a cooler with soft drinks, and a pitifully arranged exhibit—flimsy display cases in need of dusting and containing goblets that had probably belonged to Caliph Walid. Barah generously shifted himself a few steps to share a small patch of shade and waved me onto a wooden bench. He left his head uncovered despite the sun trying to bore into us. He was tall and dressed neatly in dark blue work clothes, and nearly black in complexion. His adaptation to heat was to move slowly and only when movement was absolutely necessary. The Umayyad palace seemed permanently deserted, the grounds like a dried lake bottom marked by strange outcroppings.

I had once found him listening politely to a young Englishman seated on the bench. After establishing that Barah was indeed Muslim, the Englishman began a formal oration of several minutes ending with the question of whether Barah accepted Jesus Christ as his savior. Clearly this was a sermon the Englishman had made more than once. His companions, a man and a woman, listened intently for Barah's response. Three visitors, half the take on an average day. They had stopped within sight of the sign about the six shekels and proceeded no farther.

Barah handled the situation gracefully. He replied that Jesus was a great man—as was Muhammad.

Barah offered his good wishes when I left. It was almost midday, but his head was again uncovered. "The heat is the heat. That is one of the facts we all must accept."

During the slow walk home Awad Njum and his flock skirted by the Umayyad palace. He lived in a compound of mud-brick houses perched on a summit overlooking an extravagantly irrigated banana grove, a bright rectangle of green. Beyond it the desert was scorched a sickly yellow, ironed flat. In 1948 the Njum clan had walked into the valley from the Negev Desert as part of the general Palestinian exodus from the war. Members of the family had lived in one of the refugee camps but, despite the many hardships, held on to part of the flock. Some years later—no one concerned himself with dates—Awad Njum and his brothers and cousins built the family compound on the hilltop, land they took as their own. The dirt path was laid out by the goats.

When Hakam and I returned for another visit, Njum was in an agitated state and, greeting us on the porch, seemed greatly embarrassed. He had declared more than once—hand over heart—he would never stoop to ordering his daughters to care for the flock. Not even for a hour. But his oldest daughter was absent with the sheep while he was on the porch.

More troubling for him was the tall tale about our representing the UN. After getting so much satisfaction from it, Njum forgot the story was his own invention, so was worried about the consequences of it being true. He regularly showed up for the UN handouts of food but no longer lived in any of the refugee camps. He assumed our presence meant punishment was imminent. Since he had no deed or anything like one, there was also the issue of the hilltop. He was there, like the rest of the clan, with squatters' rights, which were none. Israeli soldiers had years before fenced off part of the summit, asked no questions, offered no explanation, but made no move to evict him. He had to hope the Palestinians newly in charge saw the land as properly his; otherwise, he had nothing.

A little unkindly, Hakam let Njum anxiously ramble on. He waved in the air the card identifying himself as a refugee and proceeded to indict, try, and convict himself, without a single word from us, for the commonplace offense of taking UN handouts to which, according to a close reading of the rules, he was not entitled. Once Hakam again explained who we were, Njum seemed more at ease.

We had a steadily growing audience as, one by one, Njum's two wives and seven of his fifteen children arrived to sit or stand at a respectful distance on the porch. One of his mothers-in-law, a tiny white-haired figure dressed entirely in black, sat on the hard-packed ground in front of the house. Wife number one was taller than Awad, showed a broad, welcoming face and stationed herself a considerable distance from us. Wife number two, slenderer and much younger, had brought us tea, shuffled to the far end of the porch without ever taking her eyes off the ground, and waited for wife number one to choose a spot. That done, the younger woman came a few steps closer. She momentarily ducked inside, returned with a large broom, and began a vigilant patrol against stray grains of sand.

Reassured that arrest was not imminent, Njum resumed bragging. More than once he pointed out his superior status as the only Njum of his generation to have two wives. During all this the women were a captive audience, imprisoned on the porch by etiquette. They were incapable of being ruffled; when their husband said loudly that he wanted a third wife, and added that unfortunately the financial burden from his children meant he could not afford another dowry, the wives held their fire. Then again, this was probably not the first time they had heard his wish. He sat cross-legged on the wooden floor of the porch, ruler of his kingdom, and was no less imperial than any pose I could imagine by Caliph Walid at his hunting lodge.

Njum expressed greater concern for the animals than for his children. He bemoaned his fate as a man ruthlessly oppressed by the appetites of others. What the sheep and goats did not eat, the children did. "A man gets a sack of flour and, God willing, can feed fifteen children for four days," he said to explain his belief that children required less care than the herd. His cost-benefit analysis held that eventually one child would turn out right—that is, be willing to take over the herd full-time and allow the honored father to relax into retirement. Sheep were income, children endless expense.

His profession was comfortingly familiar, and nearly as long established as farming, and picturesque when the sheep and goats slowly crossed the road or when you saw them on a hill. But I never heard a teacher or a merchant or a farmer express a wish to take his place. His station was low. A shepherd was wholly without security and dependent on the tolerance of others. Jericho's new self-importance was going to make his station lower. With the town growing, the pastoral backdrop was becoming smaller.

Njum made a new round of complaints about barley prices. Since barley was a necessity for the sheep, Njum had reduced his spending on the family. The children were weaned from bananas and other small luxuries. "The youngest didn't know what a banana was until he was five," he bragged. The family diet was mostly lentils and bread; it is possible that the people of PPNA consumed more meat than did the family of Awad Njum. "As long as we have bread everything is fine." Other than the matter of a third wife, his only pressing domestic concern was the house's roof, which was earth mixed with straw reinforced with tree branches. Every winter the rains threatened to collapse it. It could fall on one of the children and, as Awad saw it, ruin a marriage. A wife would be unhappy; capital would be lost.

In the autumn of 1871 the PEF completed plans for surveying all the territory lying between the Jordan and the Mediterranean. The plans consisted of choosing surveyors and wishing them godspeed. If the finds were spectacular enough, the necessary funds would duly arrive. The officer placed in charge was a Captain Stewart, to be accompanied by a Sergeant Black and a Corporal Armstrong. All were Royal Engineers on loan from the War Office. The PEF would bear the cost of their salaries but asked the government to provide some of the necessary survey instruments. In its formal petition to the House of Commons, the Fund gave equal weight to the public's great interest in the Holy Land and to the pledge that the expedition would save the government the cost of the men's pay and meals. In exchange the War Office would obtain accurate maps at no cost to itself.

The party reached Egypt safely in November 1871 but lost time by missing the fast steamer to Jaffa. "I suppose you will wish to hear of our safety so far," Stewart began his first letter to the PEF, "as we have got on our journey." He complained about the difficulty finding storage space in Jaffa for the luggage and the high cost of moving thirty cases of equipment to Jerusalem. And despite attempts to establish contact, Stewart had heard nothing from the fourth member of the party, Charles Francis Tyrwhitt Drake.

Captain Stewart led me on a long, ultimately frustrating chase; although I searched the PEF archives, reread letters and the minutes of almost every meeting, and combed biographies and memoirs, Stewart never stepped out of the shadows. I learned his initials—R. W.—but with them reached a dead end. It is one initial more than I found for Sergeant T. Black. When Black died, many years later, the PEF published an obituary in which his given name went unmentioned. Given the era it is possible that no one at the Fund had deigned to ask. The members showed paralyzing self-consciousness about social class and were no less sensitive to differences in age. The sensitivities were shared by members of the survey party. A lieutenant in the field writes of his concern about issuing orders to a civilian colleague who, by a margin of several months, happened to be his elder. At a public meeting, George Grove, the PEF's chief organizer, declares that Charles Tyrwhitt Drake deserved all the greater praise as an explorer since he was "an amateur"—not a commissioned officer. Corporal Armstrong avoids anonymity in the archives—becomes Corporal George Armstrong—thanks to his being appointed, many years later, the PEF's secretary.

Drake was always unlike the others. He was born in 1846, in a village a short distance west of London. He was a distant relative of the naval hero Sir Francis Drake and the son of an army colonel whose exploits at Waterloo were such that his sword became a museum exhibit. The son was privileged by that good name, and perhaps burdened by it. He was sickly, plagued by asthma. Growing up, he had reason to fear his contacts with exotic places would come only through books read in a sickbed. There seemed to be no way for son to emulate father. Drake developed a passion for ornithology, and to become the compleat ornithologist he became expert with a rifle and studied drawing. He was infected too with travel lust and with the public's enthusiasm for exploration of the Holy Land. By the time he entered Cambridge, he was interested most in the spaces that remained blank on the maps. To place one's finger on a distant, inviting place on a map could provoke a kind of ecstasy.

Always vulnerable to illness, Drake suffered through the winters. He decided not to endure another season of suffocating cold. His self-prescribed remedy was to leave Cambridge for travel in Morocco.

Drake got away from more than just the chilly English damp. He forever abandoned the conventional settled life. He never stopped signing on for extreme sorts of adventure, as if to escape from the personality of the infirm. A bird-hunting expedition in Morocco became the basis for his writing a semischolarly study on North African bird life. He learned Arabic. He wandered to Egypt, where he was appalled and charmed. "It is dirty and dilapidated as a rule," he reports of Cairo, "but that rather adds to the effect."

He chose in 1869 to join a survey party in the Sinai Desert. It was his brave attempt to make his travels more purposeful. The expedition there was already under way, led by Captain Charles Wilson. It was Wilson who had commanded the PEF's first work in Palestine. He now was busy mapping desert territories that, not by coincidence, began to interest the War Office about the time the French were completing the Suez Canal.

To catch up with the rest of the party, Drake traveled alone via camel for several weeks. The reward awaiting him was a first meeting with a gifted young linguist named Edward Henry Palmer—six years older, fellow Cambridge man, fellow asthma sufferer. Palmer had studied languages during his many periods of forced convalescence, and in that way he had discovered his talent and vocation. He had persuaded gypsies to teach him Romany, translated into English various writings from the Swedish, Finnish, and German, and helped revise a Persian translation of the New Testament. At Cambridge he lectured on Persian, Arabic, and Hindustani. There were also other, stranger talents: he was effortlessly skilled as a hypnotist and, to entertain friends, he performed tricks with cards and handkerchiefs.

Everything in the Sinai went well. Drake gained cachet within the small, self-assured club of British Arabists whose membership included Edward Palmer as well as Charles Wilson and Charles Warren. It was as self-conscious a group as any club at Oxbridge and taught the same lesson: the comfort of acceptance and of belonging. The best club was thought to be the one in which everyone thought alike. To a man they looked down upon Ottoman territories in the Middle East as hopelessly backward, and the inhabitants as primitive, even irrational, thus needing to be saved. The Arabists cast themselves as brave scouts collecting place-names and drafting maps. And thought themselves to be cutting trails in a wilderness, civilizing it.

As a reward for the work in the Sinai, the PEF asked Palmer and Drake to journey through the Negev Desert for purposes of making another survey. Charles Warren was already tunneling through Jerusalem, while the survey of all of Palestine was still two years in the future. Charles Wilson gave both Drake and Palmer a brief course in mapmaking and desert survival, and Drake obtained a grant from Cambridge to help pay his way. And for once-sickly young men, they gave themselves remarkable tasks: in late 1869, Palmer and Drake left Port Suez without guides, and on foot. They traveled with four camels that carried the tent, the equipment for surveying, and the great bulk of a camera. There was tobacco, tea, flour, and bacon, and a three-month ration of brandy. Their only escort was the owner of the camels, though the escort and the camels changed each time the Englishmen entered the territory of a different tribe of Bedouin. In dress, the Englishmen were indistinguishable from the occasional Syrian making a desert crossing. "The prevailing opinion," Palmer said of their reception at various outposts, "is that we are harmless lunatics."

They hiked across the northern Sinai, then into the Negev, carried on to Jerusalem; after a break, they explored the mountainous regions east of the Jordan and returned to Jerusalem: in all, six hundred miles on foot. Palmer described the adventure in *The Desert of the Exodus,* which was illustrated with paintings and sketches by Drake but made memorable by Palmer's unromantic comments about the Bedouin. For this most scholarly of travelers, the desert native was of the lowest possible class. "Wherever he goes, he brings with him ruin, violence, and neglect," Palmer said. "The sympathy already wasted on the Red man of North America warns me that I am treading on delicate ground, but I must nevertheless state my belief that the 'noble savage' is a simple and unmitigated nuisance. To the Bedawi this applies even more forcibly."

His opinions were colored by constant frustration. To secure safe passage through the territory of the Taiyahah tribe, Palmer had needed two days of shouted negotiations. Some problems were compounded by his showing inordinate pride at speaking the language of the natives; the modesty of ignorance sometimes served the traveler better. The Taiyahah subsisted on the protection money paid by anxious pilgrims making the desert trek to the Gulf of Aqaba, on the way to Mecca. The other occasional source of income was plunder. In a good raiding season, the tribe could steal six hundred camels. Palmer's recommendation to future travelers was that they negotiate terms with the various tribes with great firmness. As a more lasting measure, he proposed, in complete seriousness, a large-scale military expedition to seize the Bedouins' animals. In this way the Bedouin would be forced to choose between starvation and adopting what Englishmen thought a more acceptable profession, which was farming. Where suitable land was to be found was an aspect left undiscussed. Palmer writes, "Such a plan would probably entail some hardship and injustice at first, but a virulent disease requires a strong remedy."

In the photographs they took of themselves, Palmer and Drake are easily mistaken for Arab traders. They are dark-skinned and wear long robes and simple sandals, with keffiyas wrapped around their heads for protection from the sun. Their beards are of William Morris length and density. Drake—thin-lipped, long-faced—poses cradling a rifle. A photograph taken in a small paved courtyard, most likely in Jerusalem, shows Palmer and Drake each wearing a fez, and Drake grasps the pipe of a hookah. The hookah locates them a world away from lecture halls at Cambridge. This is less snapshot than idealized portrait, for in every sense the two travelers are posed. The props were surely chosen with care, for effect. There is a stereotype to fulfill, as one does by mailing home a postcard of the Sphinx. The traveler wants to leave an intelligible footprint to be admired by everyone at home. The young men pose as Brave Travelers, which was a real part of their identity. They surpassed the stereotype. They appear experienced, wise, weathered, and not at all young; and in that year Drake turned twenty-three.

Shaking hands with David Tyrwhitt-Drake Clark, I thought I saw in his longish face a hint of Charles Tyrwhitt Drake's mouth. Clark is Charles Drake's grandnephew and chief archaeologist of the family. The nineteenth-century photographs had belonged to a relative who showed no great interest in family lore but "who needed money in the worst way—to meet his creditors, as you call it." Clark's mother offered the penurious relation cash for the photos, to keep them in the family; from the photos had come Clark's interest in Great-uncle Charles.

Clark had recently retired as director of the municipal museum in Colchester, and agreed on the telephone to detour from visiting a new grandson to meet in London. His handshake was very firm. It was indeed the same mouth.

Charles Drake had been a very reserved young man. He was a fine linguist, observant, and without doubt highly intelligent. He was also a snob. In his writings he displays contempt for people different from himself, an attitude that could have only been reinforced by being in the company of his great friend Edward Palmer. Drake wanted to see the world by camel and on foot for excitement's sake. "He was sort of a nutto," Clark said as we talked about Drake's adventures. "He liked going to those odd places, and somebody was willing to pay for it."

Clark has made his granduncle's life something of an avocation, and his explorations into family lore continue. Young Charles Drake had lived in a cottage outside London that Clark suspects still exists, and for which he is searching. There is a newly discovered list of antiquities that Drake had purchased in Jerusalem, complete with the prices he paid, but no trace of the goods as yet; and in addition to the photographs, Clark has about a hundred of Drake's watercolors. His painted deserts are sunlit yet foreboding, Middle East landscapes by Edvard Munch. They are dense with emptiness and more oppressive than liberating and in that way, truer to life than any photograph.

"Charles does seem to have been very much the loner," Clark said. "Whether one would have hit it off, I don't know."

From Jerusalem, Palmer and Drake rode to Damascus, arriving finally in the village called Salihiyeh. It served as a summer home for the British consul. They appeared in his garden carrying their tent and in that way met Captain Richard Burton, consul and glorious adventurer.

No portrait of Burton could be too bright or fantastical, for within the imaginary club of Arabists he was unchallenged for intrepidness. As a young lieutenant stationed in India, Burton had disguised himself as a dervish to carry out military and spiritual explorations, and enthusiastically lived the life required by the disguise; in Arabia, he risked his life by traveling as a Muslim pilgrim to the holy city of Mecca, forbidden to nonbelievers; in Africa, he joined the daredevil competition to discover the source of the Nile. It was said he spoke twenty-nine languages. He would help introduce the *Kama Sutra* to the West and translated the writings published as the *Arabian Nights.*

The appointment to Syria was, to say the least, unexpected. He learned of his new post when he was underemployed, unhappy, and drunk in Peru. Burton and his wife, Isabel, arrived in Damascus to take up his new post but found the walled city claustrophobic. They spent their time in Salihiyeh. Isabel's salon was held every Wednesday. A pet leopard was part of the household. The summer residence, which was in the mountains at Bludan, was four hours from Damascus by fast horse, ten hours by mule.

Having found someone to admire, Edward Palmer and Charles Drake settled in for a long stay.

Life with the Burtons could surpass the most romantic stereotype of Middle Eastern adventure. There were cool nights spent in the desert with the Bedouin outside their great black tents, circled around a campfire, the men dancing, the camels grunting in the shadows. Burton would entertain the audience with readings from the *Arabian Nights.* Palmer, true to his linguistic talents, recited poetry, and Isabel Burton later recalled "Charley Drake" performing magic tricks much to the pleasure of everyone else. Isabel writes, "I have seen the gravest and most reverend Shaykhs, rolling on the ground and screaming with delight in spite of their Oriental gravity, and they seemed as if they could not let my husband go again."

In London the PEF was meanwhile growing interested in exploring the Syrian countryside. Edward Palmer persuaded the Fund to assign the work to his new young friend. It was a worthy assignment that assured Charles Drake and the Burtons of another season of pleasureful rides. Such was Drake's understanding. For more than a month in 1871 he rode an average of seven hours a day to sketch ruins, make rubbings of inscriptions, paint more watercolors. He collected more birds. It was decided, Isabel said, "that we should do a little geography." So Drake learned the use of survey instruments. Wearing desert gear, Burton and Drake could be mistaken for father and adult son—the older man six feet tall with a craggy face scarred by a spear wound, Drake leaner, as if not yet eating full portions, the face unlined. They were adventurers practical in their thinking. Syria was a fine entertainment. For Drake, there were valuable lessons about the authenticity of much-heralded finds: he was reverently shown the sacred, true, final resting place of John the Baptist—first in Damascus, then in Homs.

And then, in a curious turnabout, the PEF severed its connection with the work. It never made the payments that Drake expected. Money problems had already plagued Charles Warren's diggings in Jerusalem, and members of the PEF were for good reason worried about paying for the survey of all of Palestine, which was about to begin. No one really knew how to estimate the expenses or how the money would be raised, whatever the amount. George Grove, whose record in these matters did not inspire confidence, predicted that Captain Stewart would need three years in the field plus one year at the writing desk, at no more than three thousand pounds a year. And after the four years he would be able to deliver photographs, lists of place-names, and the finished maps. But Richard Burton scoffed at this.

Nine years, Burton said; not four.

In his gruff way he was scrupulously honest. He never bothered to hide his scorn for people in London thinking themselves expert about conditions in the Middle East. Societies of armchair explorers were run, in Burton's caustic judgment, "by Messrs. Feeble-mind and Ready-to-halt." Meanwhile, "the real explorer, the true inventor, the most learned writer, and the best artist"—he presumably had himself in mind as well as Drake—went unheralded. He was more right than wrong in regard to the PEF. Charles Warren himself, frustrated by Grove's management and not a little horrified by the PEF claiming credit for discoveries that should have been credited elsewhere, had severed his ties with the organization. So one can only believe that the real target of the PEF in deciding not to pay for the work in Syria was Burton—who dared to speak his mind—and not poor Drake.

Keep the money, said Richard Burton.

He and Drake sponsored themselves. Burton gloated that the cream of the discoveries would be theirs instead of the stuffed shirts' in London. The results—a hybrid of travelogue, Drake's cultural observations, and a diatribe against the Ottomans—were published two years after the desert rides began, in two thick volumes by Richard F. Burton and Charles F. Tyrwhitt Drake, and entitled *Unexplored Syria.* With the pride befitting a father introducing a gifted son, Burton declared that Drake had methodically explored an area that even on the best maps was "a pure white blank." He had put his finger right there, on that spot on the map. Drake then redrew it in the image of his own labor.

Burton was fired from his job as consul in August 1871. The firing was less surprising than his having been appointed to the post. Isabel had used her whip to strike the son of a local sheikh in retaliation for an insult. The consul himself caused offense to the small Protestant community, the Greek Orthodox bishop, the Jewish moneylenders, the Muslims. He and Drake were preparing to ride out from Bludan when a messenger handed Burton the letter announcing the dismissal. Disgraced and upset, Burton left the country by himself. It was Drake who escorted Isabel on board the steamer in Beirut and oversaw shipment of the furnishings. He wanted to stay, since by then the Middle East seemed more welcoming than Britain. But he needed a purpose in his life and he needed more income. Thus at the end of September 1871 his letter to the PEF—the organization that had caused him such embarrassment—soliciting a position with the surveyors about to embark for Palestine.

> I am sorry I am not in a position to offer my services gratis but if the Committee should think fit to give me a small grant & to pay my expenses I will do all I can to assist

> them: this I feel myself somewhat competent to offer owing to a residence of more than 12 months in this country, most of wh. has been spent in traveling, & the knowledge of the language.

He accepted the organization's terms of one hundred pounds a year plus expenses. Captain Stewart and the rest of the party had already landed in Jaffa, knowing not a word of Arabic. Drake was to be responsible for recording Arabic place-names, sketching any finds of interest, and recording his observations of local customs. Captain Stewart would oversee the technical survey work needed for drafting the maps. In Jaffa, Stewart was already trying to learn when Drake might be arriving from Damascus to rescue the survey party from its ignorance.

Edward Palmer in the years ahead became a flickering light in the firmament of Arabists, a figure his admirers believed to shine with wisdom. Cambridge University thought otherwise, unfortunately; in 1871 it chose another candidate to become its professor of Arabic, forever embittering Palmer. He tutored students, wrote reviews for the better magazines, and worked four hours a night for one or another of the London newspapers. He both needed money and wanted adventure. So he was flattered, in 1882, when the War Office sought his advice about the Bedouin of the Sinai Desert. A nationalist uprising in Egypt was endangering the trade routes to India by threatening—so the Intelligence Department believed—the Suez Canal. The revolt's leader, an army officer named Ahmed Arabi, encouraged his followers to believe they would be impervious to a Christian army. More than ten thousand Europeans fled to Alexandria for the shelter of a gathering fleet of French and British warships. A British invasion force was being readied. Because Palmer knew the region, his services were courted. Envisioning glory, he volunteered to travel again into the Sinai, as in the long-ago days with Drake. Palmer was assigned the job of persuading the Bedouin to take the side of Britain, at least not to interfere. He was to persuade them with bribes paid in gold. Stories were put out that he had returned to the Middle East as a special correspondent for the London papers, then as a buyer of camels for the army. Friends heard he had gone abroad for his health.

A first venture into the desert convinced Palmer the assignment was an easy one. He wrote in his diary, "I am very glad that the war has actually come to a crisis, because now I shall really have to do my big task, and I am certain of success." On his shoulders, he believed, was the security of India. The Royal Navy appointed him Interpreter in Chief to Her Majesty's Forces in Egypt. "My position seems like a dream. . . . I have servants, clerks, and interpreters at my beck and call, and in short I could not be in a better position." It seemed to him that Bedouin were as easily cajoled as sheep. He confided to his diary that he believed himself capable of hypnotizing all of them. "I can have every Bedoui at my call from Suez to Gaza." As an extra measure of safety he hired a sheikh named Abu Sofieh as a guide. Abu Sofieh was presented as the leader of a powerful tribe.

On a second trek Palmer left Port Suez with Captain William Gill of the Intelligence Department, a cook, another officer, and Abu Sofieh. Palmer carried with him three thousand pounds in gold.

No further word was heard from Palmer.

Charles Warren was the officer sent from London to lead the search party. After two months of dangerous adventures he found Palmer and his companions. They were a short distance from Port Suez at the bottom of a deep wadi. Lowered by a rope, Warren picked through a scattering of well-gnawed ribs, one skull, a truss belonging to Palmer, and Gill's socks with the feet still in them. As established by the search party, Palmer had been ambushed at night by Bedouin, who fired several shots. As soon as the firing began, Abu Sofieh fled with most of the gold. He returned after daybreak to find the men surrounded by their captors and stripped of any protection from the sun. Palmer pleaded for his and his colleagues' lives, saying there was money to be had. Abu Sofieh is said to have promised camels to the other Bedouin if they released the Englishmen. He did not offer the gold. He kissed the Englishmen. Then he left.

Palmer was shot and finished off with a sword, then was dropped into the wadi. The others were pushed, then shot from above.

In searching for the murderers, Warren encountered terrible difficulties from the first day. No tribe was eager to provide information or to provide the camels he needed as transport. He obtained goodwill by resorting to the purchase of sheep; but in instances when help was still not forthcoming, he took hostages. The British officers became delirious during the desert crossing from lack of water. Even the camels collapsed. The party fought off vultures attacking people who were not yet dead.

Abu Sofieh surrendered. Men suspected of having carried out the attack were eventually tracked down, and in organizing the trial the British left nothing to chance. Warren was convinced of the suspects' guilt and clearly wanted the trial to go accordingly. The president of the court proved reluctant to follow the script and adjourned the proceedings almost as soon as they had begun. The next day, Warren himself escorted a new president into the courtroom, and while the trial was under way Warren suggested the proper lines of inquiry.

Five men were sentenced to death, and seven others received varying terms of imprisonment. Abu Sofieh had meanwhile died in prison (of natural causes, according to the physician who conducted the autopsy). To impress upon everyone the sure workings of British justice, Warren invited the sheikhs of every tribe to observe the hangings. This offer the sheikhs were not permitted to refuse. The compliant Ottomans awarded Warren the Khedive's Star and membership in the Order of the Medjidie (third class). Opposition members in Britain's parliament described the proceedings as "judicial murder." The government of Mr. Gladstone warmly praised him.

Warren informed the War Office in his final report that Edward Palmer, who so disdained the Bedouin, had fatally underestimated them. He had been the wrong man for the job. He talked too freely about the gold in his luggage and placed too much faith in his own judgment. Abu Sofieh had proved not to be the leader of a vast tribe but the head of small breakaway clan wholly without influence. Supremely self-confident, Palmer had seriously misjudged him. Palmer the gifted linguist had misunderstood his perilous situation.

Four weeks after Palmer's disappearance the British—without interference or assistance from Bedouin in the Sinai Desert—defeated the forces of Ahmed Arabi in a battle lasting less than three hours.

In November 1871 Captain Stewart rode from Jerusalem to the Dead Sea to pass the time. Still no sign of Charles Drake. Still no firman from the Ottomans. Rather than spend the PEF's money solely on waiting, Stewart purchased tents and hired a cook and a dragoman-interpreter, who led the party onto the coastal plain to the town called Ramleh. It was known to every traveler for its gnat-infested inn. And on the twenty-third of November the surveyors unpacked their equipment—chains, theodolite, the theodolite's bulky legs—to begin measuring with the greatest possible accuracy a straight line four miles long. It was the true starting line for the work to follow, the touchstone for every measurement: from that baseline four miles long the surveyors would triangulate the rest of the countryside, and from the triangulation draw their maps.

"Our future plan of operation was decided upon," said Stewart, "and all seemed prosperous." That was a Thursday.

On the Saturday, Stewart fell so ill he could no longer work. Then could hardly even stand.

After packing and booking passage on a ship, once he received the telegram reporting Stewart's illness, Charles Drake arrived in Jaffa. He found Stewart somewhat recovered. They rode through a cold wind to Jerusalem to consult the English physician in charge of the only institution in Palestine that resembled a hospital.

Dr. Thomas Chaplin, as judged by accounts from his own day, was one of the animating figures of nineteenth-century Jerusalem. He was author of a grim study called *Fevers of Jerusalem* and, within the constraints of existing knowledge, was expert on leprosy and malaria. He labored in Jerusalem for twenty-five years as a Protestant missionary among the Jews, though without significant result, and directed the English Missionary Hospital. In his widely shared opinion, the city was "shamefully and abominably dirty." Chaplin and others already understood that the rotting corpses of animals lying in the streets and the never-cleaned cisterns and the accumulations of sewage and rotting food all played roles in making Jerusalem one of the least healthful of cities.

He forbade Captain Stewart even to sit up in bed.

"Dr. Chaplin has ordered me to England, as he finds there is no prospect of recovery here," writes the captain, apologizing for using pencil, since ink would have required him to sit. "I go via Southampton, handing over everything to Drake."

On New Year's Day 1872 the survey resumed with Charles Drake in charge. For the first time the party had a member who knew the language of the country. Drake discovered that the dragoman had been inventing names for places he didn't know. For the dragoman this was merely normal practice and good business sense. With tourists, you told them what they wished to be true, then moved on to the next holy site. Dismissed. Without Drake, the other men would have in every sense been lost.

He established the routines. The surveyors would choose an observation point on which to stand the theodolite—like an abbreviated telescope, and the most advanced survey equipment of the day—and when necessary build a stone tower eight or nine feet high to make the spot visible from a great distance; and from there they recorded in their notebooks details of the topography that they could see. Drake would ride off to talk with the locals, to learn the place-names. More information was collected later by everyone riding, more or less methodically, over every mile of the countryside—through swampland, across fields of boulders, into nubk hedges. On Sundays the party rested. A full day would be spent drawing everything onto the map. And then to a new camp. In six months the party surveyed a strip of territory between Jaffa and Jerusalem and moved into the stony hills between Jerusalem and Nablus, where the natives were less welcoming. But Drake was unimpressed by the sights and even less by the people.

In the reports sent to London he sounds bored. Having traveled with Edward Palmer through the most dangerous hinterlands, then with the fearless Richard Burton, he was more irritated than intrigued by the settled areas of Palestine. He was the only Arabic speaker in a small company of greenhorns. Everything about the territory disgusted him, even the architecture. The houses ("generally miserable huts, dark, dirty, and comfortless") were identical in architecture and construction to the house Awad Njum would build 120 years later. Then as now the greatest danger was that the earthen roofs would collapse during the winter rains.

In the reports, Drake is a serious-minded young man who travels in the Middle East observing it closely but without ever desiring to be a part of it. His Oriental ways were no more profound or lasting than the keffiya draped over his shoulders. He views the region as a theater of the bizarre, a dusty storehouse of the needing-to-be-fixed; and there is no empathy for the inhabitants. They are curiosities, like the landscape. There is never a generous word except for the presumed superiority of the Westerner. Drake the Arabist found Arabs repellent, which comes across most clearly in his first letters, in which he offers an introductory course on ethnology and geography to members of the PEF. The least contemptible natives for him are the city dwellers. One rung down are the Bedouin, and the lowest of the low are the fellahin, the group that includes every villager.

On this subject Drake considered himself expert. "The fellahin are all in all the worst type of humanity that I have come across in the East," he informs his employers. "To one who has power he is fawning and cringing to a disgusting extent, but to one whom he does not fear, or who does not understand Arabic, his insolence and ribald abuse are unbounded." That the fellahin's behavior might be a reflex of self-protection is a possibility that Drake ignores. There was almost every year a new Ottoman governor, who, to obtain his position, would make a promise to the sultan to collect more taxes or draft a larger number of soldiers; every year, someone new with agents whose favor had to be won. Flattery and servility were the only bribes the fellahin had to offer. No villager was going to risk offending a stranger until the stranger turned his back.

Drake had already endured several harrowing episodes, and my suspicion is that these were some of the sources for his venom. In the Sinai he suffered an almost fatal attack of dysentery. He and Burton, riding in Syria, had narrowly escaped an ambush by Bedouin. In Palestine, the fellahin repeatedly attempted to steal the survey party's horses. During one three-week period, the surveyors were attacked four times. As an early warning system against intruders, Drake kept two bullterriers: fearless Jack and Jill. Drake was also necessarily engaged with local authorities in endless dickering. There were constant rumors that Muslims were plotting to massacre Christians, and Christians were rumored to be plotting their revenge. Travelers were exhausted both by fearfulness and by the physical hardships. In all of Palestine only one road was wide enough for a carriage, but it was so rough as to smash the carriages to bits. No governor could be bothered to make repairs unless the arrival of a foreign dignitary was imminent. Every visiting prince presumably expected a grand tour of a land that was rich and polished. So it might be hurriedly polished. To smooth the roadway, the fellahin unfortunate enough to be drafted as forced laborers used stone columns like rolling pins—the columns pilfered from the various ruins along the route.

And Drake's prejudices accurately reflected the jingoistic sentiments of his employers. Every dismissive comment made by the PEF's socially prominent members about the hapless Turks reinforced the belief that the survey was a mission for Britain and for Christians everywhere. Drake sounds always annoyed with Palestine. If he was tired, or tired of danger, he had a right to be. His dilemma was his preferring danger to its absence and to life in Britain.

Efforts to obtain even the simplest information from the fellahin became for Drake maddening exercises in frustration. Assurance had to be offered, first, that the survey party was not attempting to confiscate the territory. There were problems, next, of "denseness," which Drake illustrated by the exchange he endured to learn the name of a wadi:

> I ride up to a man ploughing in a wady and say, "What do you call this wady?"
>
> "Which wady, where?"
>
> "Why, the one we are in; here."
>
> "What do you want to know for?"
>
> "To write it on the map, &c."
>
> "Oh, this is called El Wad" (the Valley).
>
> "Nothing else?"
>
> "No."
>
> "Well, the men here must be illiterate donkeys! . . . Why, when you go home and say that you have been ploughing in the "Wad," perhaps they'll think that you've been on the side of that hill yonder."

(In a tone of pique) "Oh, no! I should say I've been in Wady Serar."

"Then you call this Wady Serar?"

"Yes, that's what we call it."

Other conflicts were more serious. When fellahin threatened to attack Drake's servant, a Christian Arab named Habib, Drake called in Turkish soldiers.

The argument seems to have been over the presence of the Christian heathens. Drake demanded an apology from the local sheikh, who predictably refused. No less predictably, the soldiers took into custody the village elders. With their prisoners in tow, the soldiers rode away in the direction of Jerusalem. The calculated hostage taking had the desired effect. Fellahin fared poorly in Turkish jails, and being hauled away on the complaint of an Englishman could only make a prisoner's dire situation worse. So the apology was forthcoming. The villagers presented a written pledge of future cooperation—whatever the distinguished visitor wished and his distinguished servant Habib wished. Drake writes of the village, "We now are on very good terms."

Drake's letters show him to be knowledgeable and invariably businesslike, but his anxieties about his future status with the PEF sometime show through. There are hints too of physical exhaustion. A sense of romance is almost entirely absent. His feelings are hurt by the lack of praise or encouragement from London, and from time to time he seems compelled to write a politely worded reminder that he is indeed working hard.

He asks Walter Besant, the PEF's secretary, to acquire for him a more comfortable saddle. He wants a carbine plus a copy of Charles Warren's *Jerusalem Recovered.* For a year he pleads for a better thermometer. Compliments are offered to whoever chose the sherry included in the previous shipment. Newspapers from London were still addressed to Jaffa, not Jerusalem, delaying delivery by weeks—could Besant attend to that?

"The work is thoroughly to my taste, and I feel I am doing good work," Drake writes, to prepare Besant for a request for more money. He has reduced expenses—always important to the PEF—by dispensing with the dragoman and hiring a cheaper cook. His own salary of £100, however, is only one fifth of Captain Stewart's, whose work Drake has inherited, and less even than a corporal's. Unlike the other members of the party, Drake has provided a horse for himself, plus bedding, plus a tent. He asks for an increase to £250. Penciled across the upper-left corner of his letter, which is in the PEF archives, is this word: "Granted."

In six months, the party surveys five hundred square miles. Drake reports that the maps will be ready in another three or four years but only if the PEF sends more surveyors. Otherwise, ten or twelve years. Since the PEF was as always struggling to raise money, this prediction could have only horrified the men in London. And one imagines that the membership felt great relief, and congratulated itself, on obtaining from the Royal Engineers another officer. He would be the real replacement for the unfortunate Captain Stewart and take over command from Drake, and this new man, it was assumed, would reach a less alarming conclusion about the party's needs.

Claude Reignier Conder is "jolly as a sandboy" when he reaches Paris. At the beginning of his travels he writes home almost every day. Traveling with him is Jonah, a white terrier who, to his owner's alarm, is almost strangled when a Parisian trods upon his leash. Conder is bored by fifty-six hours of train travel to Turin and Brindisi; at the end of the sea voyage to Egypt he is "awfully jolly" once more.

Conder had been unlike most other cadets at the Royal Military Academy at Woolwich. He had used his spare time to learn Hebrew and to study the history of Jerusalem. Church ritual was his avocation, further distinguishing him from his peers. He was unabashedly hungry for fame now that he was a freshly commissioned lieutenant. He was enormously eager, well traveled since he had spent part of his childhood in Italy, yet unworldly. In Cairo he was most impressed by the bustle ("just like *Arabian Nights*") and the beggars jabbering Arabic ("just like Italian only you can't understand it").

"Dear Mamma," he writes the day he arrives in Jerusalem. "Here I am well & happy making friends all round. . . . I am very well & feel so jolly to find I really shall be able to make a name here." Back in England the local postmistress, not knowing Jerusalem to exist outside the pages of the Bible, placed the first outbound letters from Conder's family on a shelf, for eternal safekeeping.

Since Drake was away in Damascus tending business, Sergeant Black was the one to lead the new man from Jerusalem to the camp near Nablus. Jack and Jill immediately set upon Jonah. Conder examined the three tents for sleeping plus the tent that was used by the servants as a kitchen, and apparently was pleased with what he found. Drake rode forty miles the next day to greet his new colleague. The man Conder watched dismounting was intimidatingly tall and very tan, with an enormous beard, and wearing tweeds and knee boots. A keffiya covered his head. Everything about Charles Drake was exotic to a man newly arrived in Palestine. Habib, in big boots and a gray jacket in the ornate style of the Ottomans, was even more impressive. Claude Conder was twenty-three—two and a half years younger than Drake—and now the man in charge. At the first opportunity he assured the PEF he was not suffering from "'Holy Land on the brain,'" his guarantee he would be professional and calm. He was an officer, fresh and confident that with him the party could work faster and that members of the PEF would express their gratitude.

VI

"Working Like Smoke"

The better read you the traveler were about earlier explorers the more frightened you were entitled to be. In 1805, Ulrich Seetzen, a German physician, had journeyed to Damascus and into Palestine disguised as an Arab sheikh and as a beggar. He found the ruins of Roman cities last known from the writings of Josephus, reached Jerusalem and Jericho, and became the first Westerner to venture around the entire circumference of the Dead Sea. It was overheated territory of salt plains and mountains. In a brief account published in 1810, Seetzen could not entirely suppress his shock at having been abandoned by his guides. There were other difficulties. Reaching the western shore of the Dead Sea, he had consulted a map showing a river to be nearby but discovered the river to be the mapmaker's invention. "I was very sorry it was not to be found," Seetzen wrote, "for we were suffering extremely from thirst." The party subsisted for a time on grass.

One of Seetzen's admirers was Jean-Louis Burckhardt, a Swiss scholar who presented himself in his travels as an Indian gunpowder merchant, a Greek Orthodox priest, an Arab physician-herbalist. In 1812 he became the rediscoverer of Petra, the abandoned, dreamlike city carved in a desert gorge southeast of the Dead Sea and unseen by any Westerner since the Crusades. Seetzen and Burckhardt each joined the forbidden pilgrimage to Mecca. Each man traveled in the Nile Valley and studied for journeys deeper into Africa—the Middle Eastern travels were intended as only warm-ups. But Seetzen died in Yemen, probably poisoned; Burckhardt succumbed to dysentery in Egypt.

Claude Conder's first impression of Palestine was that everything in it was broken. He mistook villages for abandoned ruins, and wondered where the people lived and why they had taken the trouble to hide the houses. He was even younger than his age.

With instructions from Drake, he learned the workings of a hookah and the local rules of hospitality, so he was duly charmed by the solicitude of village elders. They inquired as to the good health of Your Excellency, if Your Worship was comfortable, if Your Lordship had any unmet desires. He welcomed the attention but refused to drop his guard; the warm welcome, he said, "made one forget for a time that we were dealing with ignorant and degraded peasants." Since Conder initially knew little or no Arabic, the conversations were mediated by Drake. While everyone indulged in cigarettes and the hookah, Drake regaled the audience with stories about the fantasy world called London. He usually let slip that the Queen of England—sovereign over India—ruled more Muslims than did the sultan. This was found no less wondrous than the Englishman's descriptions of enormous steam-puffing beasts called trains.

The new man's first problem was a constant roaring in his ears. He blamed his pith helmet; it was replaced with a keffiya. In the first ten days he wrote three long, highly detailed reports to the PEF and, by then, had endorsed Drake's view that their employers had grievously underestimated the work to be done. He asked Walter Besant to send books about the Middle East, blankets, plus the thermometers for which Drake had been pleading, galoshes, foolscap and a dozen bottles of black ink, garters, a tent, and a mackintosh. And Conder, ten days after arriving in the country, pleaded for more men. "In England," he writes Besant, "you have no ideas of the difficulties." Additional members of the party should be strong, young and active, not given to drink, and junior to Conder. He advised that they leave their pith helmets at home.

Everything except the manpower was on its way.

Conder reveals himself in the reports and in the determinedly cheerful letters home as sensitive to slights, prideful, and incapable of hiding his ambition to become somehow more than just another junior officer of the Royal Engineers. He dreaded the normal career in which one dutifully supervised the construction of fortifications and roads in a succession of colonial outposts until retirement. Or in which one was banished to an actionless post in Britain. His hunger for approval was enormous. With the PEF, he would test his opinions by writing privately to Walter Besant and only later sending a more judiciously composed letter marked "official."

Officially, he had high praise for Drake. Privately, Conder was taken aback by his "very injudicious" writings about Arabs and other topics, but he was sensitive enough to recognize Drake's unhappiness at having to surrender command of the party. "He was very sore when I came first and has had a very hard time of it and done his work like a man."

Yet Conder is also resentful, niggling, constantly fearful that his own status is in doubt. "I should feel obliged if you would direct letters on official subjects, with regard to the survey &c, here to *me*," he tells Besant. He requests that future correspondence include, along with his name, his title: Claude R. Conder R. E., in Charge of Survey of Palestine. "I assert no authority over Drake as a civilian, but over the rest of course I am supreme." His is the outlook of a person convinced that the greatest dangers come not from disease or the Bedouin but from the ambitions of others.

He always insisted on riding at the head of the little caravan, on a chestnut colt he purchased from a sheikh. In the one photograph that shows all the British members of the party from this chapter of the survey, Sergeant Black, Corporal Armstrong, and Charles Drake are seated together on a stone wall in front of a shuttered house. Lieutenant Conder stands in front, apart from the others. It is the pose of a man wanting to assert his importance. He has a mustache, is without a beard, and is also clearly the shortest member of the survey party. And however mundane the thought, I could not but wonder if he had been sensitive about his height—if that is another reason he demanded trappings due an officer commanding an army.

Before taking the party into the valley he wanted more experience and cooler weather. In the meantime the surveyors were mapping a hundred square miles a month, up from eighty. "I believe the climate and the work suits me wonderfully well," Conder writes home. "The hard riding is very good for one's liver, and I have a big appetite for goats meat." Everyone was awake by 6:00 A.M. for strong tea and rode out by 7:00. At each new camp Habib, the head servant, would dress in his gaudiest costume and ride to the nearest village to introduce himself to the elders and show them the party's impressive-looking firman from the sultan. Habib would solemnly declare the party's peaceful intentions. For this peacemaking he always carried a shotgun and two pistols. The notables would soon thereafter visit the Englishmen to demand an exorbitant sum for the right to survey lands that, in the elders' descriptions, had become no less sacred than Mecca. Negotiations were conducted during the drinking of coffee. The notables always settled for a pittance.

In some of the remoter villages, the fellahin suspected that the Englishmen so busy building cairns as observation points during the day were marking the place of buried treasure. Clearly the foreigners planned to steal the hidden riches. During the night the fellahin would tear down the cairns and dig.

Still stranger was the theodolite.

It is now in residence in the basement of the PEF's office in London. The theodolite—it is the second or third of the several used by the survey party—rests in its original wooden carrying case, a bulky cube that is itself worthy of an exhibit on nineteenth-century craftsmanship. Its mitred joints are buttery smooth, the interior plush with felt shaped to accommodate the theodolite, like fitted luggage for a handsome carriage.

Lifted clear, the theodolite is a factory's worth of small gears attached to a polished brass tube. It is a small telescope one could mistake for the barrel of a stumpy gun. It has the polished innards of a fine clock. Conder, Drake, and all the officers to follow measured distances and elevations through the eyepiece; in that way, Palestine was committed to a map. As an emblem for the survey party, the PEF used a pen-and-ink sketch showing a Royal Engineer—a revolver strapped to his waist, a keffiya on his head—peering through a theodolite on a tripod resting on rocky ground. In the sketch, a large umbrella shades the mechanism, the Royal Engineer at the controls, and a fellow Royal Engineer seated on the ground with an open notebook and pen.

Whenever the weather turned hot, the theodolite became nearly useless because of the mirages. Waves of heat, Drake said, made a hill observed through the eyepiece "undulate like sea during a heavy ground-swell." When the day's work was finished, the wooden carrying case with the theodolite inside would be strapped to the back of a mule. Sometimes the mule lost his footing or the straps came undone, letting the instrument tumble onto the ground.

By seven in the evening everyone was back in camp for dinner. There would be soup, then goat, mutton, or partridge, then figs. Conder wrote home that he felt even stronger than in England. By ten everyone was in bed. Conder had never been more confident: "I will make a name on my return which will throw my predecessors in the shade."

For glory, Conder in the autumn of 1872 was counting on a large, startling collection of terra-cotta figurines in the hands of a Jerusalem antiquities dealer. The sculptures' provenance was unknown. In the hothouse that was the European community in Jerusalem, people brushed aside all the questions about the figurines' age and how they had come to be in the dealer's possession. For every traveler dreamed of not merely seeing the land of the Bible but discovering a long-lost remnant of it. Ideally, the remnant would be of portable size and suitable for shipping home. No one at the PEF was wholly immune to that desire; a collection of authentic biblical antiquities would undoubtedly impress potential contributors more than would another dry report in the organization's quarterly journal. In the chance to acquire the figurines for the PEF, and for Britain, Conder believed he saw a safe straight road to fame.

No one could fail to notice that one of the sculptures was a phallus with a face. Another was a female figure with an obscenely prominent vagina and anus. Figures were horned, wore odd-shaped crowns, were studies in the erotic and grotesquely anthropomorphic. No less striking was that many of these "bodies" were inscribed with letters belonging to an exotic-looking alphabet. At the first opportunity agents for Prussia bought some of the figurines for the Imperial Museum in Berlin. Learned men sought to translate the inscriptions, and alternate readings were debated in print. A competition for national glory was under way.

The Great Powers regarded archaeological finds in much the same light as conquered territory. One was no more willing to give away an artifact than land. No one willingly shared credit for an object's discovery. An ugly incident had already occurred at the end of the 1860s during the sojourn of Charles Warren. Through no real fault of his own, he became embroiled in a race with representatives of Prussia and France for possession of a block of polished black basalt.

Two feet wide, about three feet high, not unlike a large grave marker in shape, the stone was covered on one side by a lengthy inscription in what appeared to be an ancient alphabet. Bedouin had found the Moabite Stone, as it came to be known, on a dry, rocky plateau east of the Jordan. The stone would eventually come into the possession of France in the climax of a drama involving bribes and stealth, and in which the leading role was performed by a junior member of the French consulate in Jerusalem, Charles Clermont-Ganneau.

Clermont-Ganneau held the lowly position of dragoman-translator. Expert in paleography, he had been a distinguished student of the most distinguished Orientalists in France. When the drama began, he was twenty-two. The Bedouin east of the Jordan had first shown the stone to a missionary, who then brought word back to Jerusalem of having seen a most unusual artifact. The news exerted a pull akin to that exerted, in a later era, by rumors of a vast new oil field. In the race for the stone, the chief competitors were Clermont-Ganneau and agents for Prussia. Over a period of months, the Prussians sought to persuade the Bedouin to sell the artifact, made elaborate arrangements for it to be transported to Jerusalem, but always had something go wrong. Clermont-Ganneau meanwhile dispatched messengers to copy the incised writing. They became embroiled in a fight among the Bedouin and, in their understandable haste to escape, tore the copy of the inscription. They delivered to the Frenchman a paper ripped into seven pieces. The Bedouin, having received such lavish attention, became suspicious, then greatly annoyed, and broke the stone into fragments.

With disinterested help from Warren, Clermont-Ganneau managed to acquire fragments that accounted for perhaps 60 percent of the original stone. He also possessed his paper copy of the writing, albeit on paper that was not especially legible. He applied his own considerable skills to determine what the inscription said.

George Grove of the Palestine Exploration Fund would have had everyone believe the starring role had been played by Warren. For reasons of national pride, and to promote the PEF, Grove announced to the British press that Charles Warren was the true discoverer of the Moabite Stone. Not a word about Frenchmen or Prussians. It was that false claim, and the subsequent round of misaddressed congratulations and queries, that so embarrassed and angered Warren as to bring about his resignation from the PEF.

For translating the inscription and recognizing its authenticity, Clermont-Ganneau became a celebrity. The Moabite Stone was no less of one. "Like a lucky actress or singer," said an admiring British journal, "it took us by storm." Its inscription told of a victory by Mesha, king of Moab, over the armies of Israel. Mesha and his battles with Israel were also known from the Bible: chapter 3, Second Book of Kings. There was Mesha, king of Moab—in the Bible and inscribed in stone. That the stories were different hardly mattered. In the Second Book of Kings, Israel defeats the Moabites; the Moabite Stone tells of Mesha triumphing over Israel.

To discover within biblical territories an independent, written account of a biblical event is notably rare. The area is as infamously poor in preserved inscriptions as Egypt is famously rich. Ancient Israel and Judea and the domains to the east were small kingdoms of modest wealth and, excepting the Bible, modest monuments. The Moabite Stone was the first artifact found in those territories to "speak" at any length of characters described in the Bible. For a long time the Moabite Stone was also the only such artifact: the discovery of what may prove to be the second occurred 125 years later, in 1993.

Clermont-Ganneau had captured the Moabite Stone for France; Conder now was worried that events were about to repeat themselves with the terra-cotta figurines. Prussia had bought several of them while Britain did nothing. Drake and Conder sent sketches to the PEF, and Conder called the objects "extraordinary." He dismissed skepticism expressed by curators at the British Museum ("I have heard other instances of men there who could not translate a Greek inscription") and wanted the PEF to buy what it could. At least to publish the sketches.

Before committing the PEF to the cause, Walter Besant wanted the opinion of someone more expert. Charles Clermont-Ganneau was the expert. Examining the sketches while he was in London, the Frenchman concluded the sculptures were fakes, the inscriptions on them gibberish. When he returned to Jerusalem he tracked down a potter's frightened apprentice, who confessed to having helped make hundreds of figurines and bathing them in saltpeter to give them a suitably old appearance. The apprentice said several of the local potters had participated in the fraud. Clermont-Ganneau collected statements from various potters confirming that members of the close-knit community of artisans had worked together much as the apprentice reported.

But this strange affair never really ends. Their money and pride at stake, the Prussians rejected Clermont-Ganneau's findings and launched their own investigation. Questioned again, the potter's apprentice retracted his confession. The local potters repudiated their sworn statements and volunteered that Clermont-Ganneau had offered them bribes to lie. They swore on their sacred honor—may our right hands become crippled—that they were strangers to each other. And would never conspire to make money.

Claude Conder did his reputation little good because he kept switching sides. He asserted that the figurines were genuine antiquities, then perhaps not, then that the matter was too muddled to be worth the attention of a Royal Engineers lieutenant. The odd behavior was fueled by jealousy of Clermont-Ganneau, feelings Conder could not hide. Here was the *British* survey team in the dangerous countryside of Palestine, and "working like negroes," he complained, but the PEF consults a Frenchman who interferes.

Of Conder, the best that can be said is that his wanting to bring the figurines to public attention, and his wanting credit, were only human.

He so much wanted to be noticed. Nor is the hero in this affair Clermont-Ganneau: in hindsight, he was too sweeping in his judgment that all the sculptures were worthless forgeries. The hero is Charles Drake.

He observed that some of the first figurines to reach Jerusalem were made of a distinctly different clay than those offered for sale later. Those first sculptures had no inscriptions. Drake believed that the first artifacts were genuine and that their sale to the Prussians had inspired forgers to enter the manufacturing business to exploit an eager market. To increase the desirability of the products, the forgers had added nonsense inscriptions in the alphabet known from the Moabite Stone.

Evidence has been found to support him. An archaeological team working at a site named Horvat Qitmi, in Israel's Negev Desert, found a cache of figurines that were horned, wore odd-shaped crowns, or were grotesquely anthropomorphic. The discovery was made in 1979. None of the sculptures had inscriptions. The artifacts were dated to (approximately) the sixth century B.C. and identified as part of a shrine probably associated with the Edomites, one of the peoples from east of the Jordan. As it happens, the sculptures show a striking resemblance to some of the figurines sketched by Drake and Conder and declared by Clermont-Ganneau to be forgeries.

If Conder was fooled into believing all the figurines were genuine antiquities, so Clermont-Ganneau was fooled into rejecting the real along with the fake.

As the weather turned cooler, every week seemed to deliver some new tribulation. An olive tree fell onto the camp, just missing the servants. Jack barked at a herd of cows, eliciting a shower of stones from the fellahin. Poor Jill went mad and had to be shot. Corporal Armstrong was sore from too much riding, and Conder had a lingering cold. Conder meanwhile faithfully read the letters from home to Jonah, who gave birth to puppies. Still ahead was the descent into the valley; and the valley, Conder wrote home, was surely going to make everything the expedition was doing now seem like child's play.

The surveyors sketched tombs, aqueducts, roads. They recorded observations on geology, sent home detailed reports on the customs of the fellahin, described the status of women and the territorial boundaries of various Bedouin. But wrote almost nothing on Palestine's Jews. Jews failed to conform to Western expectations so were largely ignored.

The Jews in Palestine ruined the Middle Eastern landscapes imagined in London—brightly colored scenes in which Palestine's inhabitants, in dress and other customs, were living artifacts from the Bible. You traveled to the Middle East or read accounts by explorers to glimpse that biblical scenery. You contributed money to the PEF to have the picture drawn for you. Even before the setting was described you believed you knew it intimately. There was a mirage of fanciful nostalgia. The Bedouin reminded Westerners of the Israelites who wandered forty years in the desert, or of Abraham with his flocks. Fellahin half starving in the countryside were regarded as an affecting *tableau vivant* for the story of Ruth, gleaning the fields of Boaz. After touring North Africa, the painter Eugène Fromentin wrote of Arabs emanating "that something we call 'Biblical,' like a perfume of ancient times." And like imaginative artists, the explorers and their patrons helped invent a Middle Eastern "realism." The region was said to embody indolence, decay, an Oriental voluptuousness. But Palestine's Jews ruined the portrait. They lived in the crowded cities, not a romantic desert. The men wore fur hats instead of keffiyas, and mostly black instead of gaily colored gowns; and many of the Jews seemed in every way more of Europe than the Middle East. Except for them, the landscape was regarded from far away as delightful, something to marvel at like a circus with half-tamed beasts.

Thanks to the diplomacy of Charles Warren, the surveyors and the Jews maintained cordial relations. Warren, despite his having tunneled under parts of Jerusalem, convinced the Jewish community of his respect for Jewish graves, and he had fortunately left its cemeteries undisturbed. He spoke of the community offering "much kindness." When he accepted an invitation to attend a synagogue, the rabbi added a prayer for the Palestine Exploration Fund.

Of the survey party members, initially only Drake regarded the Jews as worthy of serious attention. His curiosity had been aroused by his seeing their first organized experiments with farming. They were taking place at Mikveh Israel, an agriculture training school a Jewish philanthropy had opened near Jaffa in 1870 on land leased from the Ottomans. The first pupils included four gardeners, three shoemakers, two carpenters, a blacksmith, an accountant. To end a babble of Russian, Polish, German, and Spanish, the imposed common language was French. In time, Mikveh Israel would become an important proving ground for new theories about farming and Jewish settlement. But it also offered a sort of preview of tension between Jews and Arabs. Though the property was the government's, the fellahin in the closest village complained about losing farmland to the new institution. Eventually, authorities compensated them with other lands nearby.

Drake approvingly examined the school's orchards and vegetable fields and noted the plans that existed for adding olive trees and increasing the number of pupils to a hundred. The fellahin, he concluded, could profit by learning from Mikveh Israel's good agricultural example. If the Ottoman government allowed more such schools, it would be "a most excellent thing."

Conder, fresh to the Middle East, placed his full faith in stereotypes. He found Jews notable for "high religious zeal, endurance, energy, and courage of peculiar kind"—and "love of money, craft, exclusiveness, and lying." He disdained the Jews he met aboard ship as "essentially and incurably dirty." But as Drake had before him, Conder gradually became an advocate of Jews as agents of positive change. He believed that a large Jewish population in Palestine would help create a modern economy. In widely circulated articles and books, Conder would promote the idea of Jews leasing a large tract of land from the Ottoman Turks for Jewish settlement. The new inhabitants were to support themselves through agriculture or crafts that would produce goods for export. Such a scheme, he said, would provide the income needed by the Sublime Porte to pay its international debts and to finance desperately needed reform. And the colony-by-lease would become a destination (more important, a destination other than Britain) for the many thousands of Jews wanting to leave czarist Russia.

Conder's ultimate prescription for reducing the abject poverty of Palestine was a mix of Jewish capital, British management, and a network of responsible Arab chiefs, whom he regarded as the only people capable of motivating the fellahin. "The energy, industry, and tact, which are so remarkable in the Jewish character, are qualities invaluable in a country whose inhabitants have sunk into fatalistic indolence," he wrote in an article contributed to Britain's leading Jewish newspaper. Since Jews were Palestine's "rightful owners," and since land was cheap, he speculated that Palestine would attract middle-class Jews, either their person or their capital.

Proposals similar to Conder's—reformulated, and offered with greater intellectual and emotional force—later became known as Zionism.

He was endearingly naive. The most vexing issues were beyond his field of vision: no regard was given to whether the Arab population would welcome Jewish immigrants or welcome the British as replacements for the Ottomans. Almost every issue was treated as a straightforward engineering problem that would be no more difficult that those the Royal Engineers faced when designing a road. Economic issues were never linked to politics. Conder optimistically suggested new routes for railroads in Palestine along with the preferred type of locomotive. Then he was mystified by the slow rate of change. Why, he asked in his articles, was Britain so ponderously slow to act? In the making of his idealized Palestine, the only weapon one might need would be a theodolite. In his eyes, colonialism was an enterprise wholly beneficial to the governed and to the governor, as long as the governor were British.

When the party reached Nazareth, Drake fell ill. Sergeant Black developed the same mysterious malady, and there were drenching rains. "I have just been suffering from congestion of the liver but I think I am getting over it," Drake writes after a week of high fever. "A few days ago it was bad." At first the men were reluctant to complain in their letters. Conder was anxious to demonstrate to the PEF that he was indeed the right man for the job. And Drake, given his childhood illnesses, was never one willingly to bring attention to his health.

The party wintered together in a rented house in Haifa. After laboring over the maps during the mornings, the Englishmen spent the afternoons shooting and riding for pleasure. Conder and Drake raced each other on horseback from Haifa nearly to Acre—fourteen miles in an hour.

But Drake had not fully recovered from his fever. He believed that for his health he needed time away from Palestine and away from the survey. With Conder's consent, he decided upon a sea voyage to Alexandria as the best therapy. Drake rejoined the fieldwork after a month but was still not well. So in May 1873 he left for a second, longer leave.

One needs no special sensitivity to understand the unfortunate events that occurred when Drake finally returned in October. For the expedition's other members, the sense of isolation had not abated during his five-month absence, nor had the feeling of being trapped between corrupt authorities in Palestine and tightfisted aristocrats in London. The PEF seemed stone-deaf to any request that involved spending even one pound. Just knowing that Drake was about to reappear ignited a tantrum by Conder. For him, Drake was not so much returning as invading. Conder was having to face the prospect of being once again in the company of someone who was senior in experience and age, who was more knowledgeable about Palestine, who was a Cambridge man. Worse, who wasn't even an officer. In Conder's view, anyone needing long leaves lacked the stuff for it.

Drake knew of the chilly reception awaiting him. From Conder, he had received a rudely officious letter announcing that he was no longer to issue orders to other members of the party. Even Habib would henceforth receive his instructions from Lieutenant Claude R. Conder. Conder meanwhile complained to Walter Besant about Drake's bookkeeping, composed a formal list of each man's duties—as if the survey party were a thousand-member army—and remained in a huff about not being addressed by his full title.

In this clash of ambitions, each man shows the worst of himself. "I am in no wise wishing to complain of Lieut Conder," Drake tells Walter Besant in response to this new division of authority, "but of course it is very difficult for an exceedingly young man like him who never had any public school trial or experience of life or traveling to find himself in charge of a party like the Survey."

Drake is snobbish. Conder has a streak of authoritarianism. In this instance, though, Drake is the person wronged and yet the one more anxious to repair the damage. In the letter to Walter Besant, Drake suggests that all sides show "a little courtesy."

His letter continues, "I shall studiously avoid any possibility of disputes with [Conder] as far as I can without neglecting the interests of the Fund but I *must know* as soon as possible on what footing the Committee wishes me to stand." In a postscript Drake adds: "It seems that having used me for a time he now wishes to shelve me. For the sake of the Survey I have said nothing yet & shall remain silent as long as I can: but I cannot silently see this management going on, nor can I stand *too* much dictation."

Nothing in the archives suggests that the PEF offered any response other than a silence that forced the men to resolve the issue by themselves. "We are all well & jolly & working away like smoke," Conder informs his mother. "It is very encouraging. Drake has rejoined us but I have put him in his proper position & we get on very well." The younger man had prevailed.

When Drake returned, the Englishmen were about to make a final stop before descending into the valley. They were riding east from Bethlehem to the edge of a vertiginous gorge, on which clung the monastery called Mar Saba.

Even now it blurs the line between the natural and the built. Mar Saba overlooks a wadi, five hundred feet below, but appears to be attached to the face of the cliff by just a fingertip, like a trapeze artist with a tenuous grip on the bar. Blue cupolas grow out of rock. Rock seems to sprout from the chapels. The stone buildings look to be anchored by nothing more than the prayers of the monks or a whimsy of gravity.

In the year 478, the man who would become known as St. Sabas came to the gorge to live alone. But such was his reputation for wisdom and devotion to God, after Sabas had lived in a cave for five years, other monks insisted on joining him. They would establish a city of cave-dwelling monks. It was said that Sabas could bring rain and could heal the sick. His followers would build chapels allowing them to pray together in the desolate place the Arabs began to call Valley of the Monk. Tradition says that in those days the number of monks reached at least a thousand—a plausible number if one includes monks from all fourteen of the monasteries established by Sabas or his disciples.

The community of monks survived the monastery being pillaged during the Persian conquest, the arrival of Islam, survived ransackings that accompanied the several defeats of the Crusaders, earthquakes severe enough to collapse some of the buildings, and early in the nineteenth century, a wave of anti-Christian riots. For the monastery's first thousand years, the monks occupied themselves by expanding the chapels, or repairing them, and housing the pilgrims who provided most of Mar Saba's income. Fellahin supplied wheat and eggs; from the monks the fellahin received gifts of bread.

Not everyone, though, was equipped to lead a saint's life. Some monks were at Mar Saba as punishment for various offenses. Once there, the monks energetically acted out the rivalries that beset the Orthodox Church, a ceaseless competition between Russia and breakaway parts of the Ottoman Empire for influence in the Holy Land. Russian monks painted Russian inscriptions; Greek monks painted over Russian inscriptions with inscriptions in Greek. The ecclesiastical contest seemed without end. By the mid–nineteenth century, Mar Saba was less a monastery than a penal colony. Boredom had taken the place of contemplation.

Claude Conder found the monks emaciated, most of them illiterate, some clearly mad—"more like dead bodies than living men." He had arrived with all the common prejudices against the Orthodox Church and firmly believed it to be theologically corrupt. He claimed to glimpse in the faces of the monks the true nature of the Eastern church—"its blasphemy, immorality and dishonesty." Yet what impressed him most was the oldest of the chapels. High ceilinged, hewn from the rock, it had been made from the cave said to have been inhabited by St. Sabas. There, on the far side of a metal grill, Conder saw a jumble of skeletons. For there lay the many previous generations of monks.

Driving there, I always stopped at least once to ask if the road truly went to Mar Saba, so many were the curves. Everyone in the villages would wave the car forward into hills that were the coarse brown tweed of the dry season. Two stone towers would be the first objects to appear, then a sinuous stone wall worthy of a king's fortress and in which there was a small blue door.

"Orthodox?" asked the monk standing one step beyond it, when I parked the car and walked toward him.

He held up his hand as a sign to stop.

"Not Orthodox?"

It did not seem to matter, because he struck a bell with a mallet to signal that a visitor had arrived and sounded the bell again as he pointed down a staircase, toward Father Nicholas.

Since the 1970s, the Greek Orthodox Patriarchate had managed to maintain the population at twelve. Father Nicholas, who looked to be in his early thirties, had lived at Mar Saba one year. First, he showed the way to the glass-sided coffin containing the body of St. Sabas, and lifted the cloth draped over it. The small wrinkled figure inside appeared to be clothed in silk. In another of the chapels, Father Nicholas pointed to the metal grill that Conder had seen, and the grisly chamber of skeletons beyond it. He did not encourage a long look. In the rear of the chapel were well-lit cabinets displaying the skulls of forty-nine other monks, some of the many killed during the era of the Persians. Outside, Father Nicholas stood in a courtyard that was part of the mountain but projected from the face like a window washer's ledge. A cupola floated at eye level. Another levitated above his head. Across the gorge was a cliff face pockmarked with caves, which the monks had reached via a network of ladders and narrow trails. Below, green water foamed with whitecaps through the gorge.

Gazing at the water, Father Nicholas remarked that he had always liked fishing. It was one of the few activities left for the monks; all the repairs were now the responsibility of contractors from Bethlehem or the villages. But he said the fishing was extremely poor.

The whitecaps were soapsuds and sewage from Jerusalem. Farmers upstream bragged to Father Nicholas about harvesting peppers and onions that were twice the normal size. The farmers attributed this success to skill.

"I ask them, 'Are you crazy?' It's the sewage," Father Nicholas said. "I would prefer fishing somewhere else."

On the fifteenth of November 1873, in the rain, the survey party loaded the pack animals at Mar Saba, and the ride to Jericho consumed the entire day. The guide in charge of the mules carrying the tents and most of the food was presumed to know the route better than anyone else, but wandered off the trail into the hills. So the first to reach Ein es Sultan were the surveyors, without food.

Tired, grumpy about the lack of a proper dinner, Conder took a long drink from what he assumed to be a bottle of wine. Instead of claret he ingested pickled olives, his first meal in Jericho. From a distance, he had seen Ein es Sultan as a calm green lake surrounded by a vast sandy beach. At dawn he realized the groves he had admired from the hills were only hedges of nubk. A few steps from his tent was the mound.

He found it shapeless. To walk at a normal pace all the way around the base of it, through the thorns and scrub, required a full quarter hour. No one climbed straight to the highest part without getting out of breath—seventy feet, almost straight up. It was a beast asleep, lying north-south, broadest at the middle of its great length, in fact so long and broad that no one standing at one end could clearly see to the other. Everything appeared to be rock, baked clay, coarse sandy earth.

After some reflection, Conder believed he saw similarities between it and mounds that travelers had noticed in India. He remained faithful to the idea for years though others quickly abandoned it. In India, the mounds were where brick makers had labored generation after generation at their trade; and fragments of the bricks, and the leftovers of the brick makers' failed experiments, gradually accumulated into a sort of platform. Conder suggested that the same explanation could apply to the odd formations he saw in the valley.

No one had yet dared to speculate that a mound could contain an architectural whole—a well-ordered city of streets, houses, cemeteries. It would be a still more daring leap to suggest a hill was not one city but an accumulation of many. Flinders Petrie's imperfect science of stratigraphy remained in the future. The archaeologists Ernst Sellin and Carl Watzinger would arrive still later. Consider it a measure of archaeology's slow progress that the discovery of pottery's ability to narrate ancient history is made after, not before, the invention of the phonograph, of the incandescent lamp, of the first horseless carriage.

Charles Warren believed, as we know, that at Ein es Sultan he had come to a knobby natural rise upon which someone in the distant past had erected one or more large buildings. Their purpose and design were assumed to be recoverable, if one were to dig. Like Warren, Claude Conder observed the mud-bricks and the bits of pottery. But he stuck to his theory that the key to Ein es Sultan was India; he was offering a rational speculation that could be neither easily discarded nor proven right.

What he saw was a high rocky embankment with the spring at its foot, the water collecting in a small artificial pool. In the few photographs from that time, it is a square, utterly calm pond bordered by large rocks, and behind that pond is the mound, and in its face several courses of stones. They looked to be a remnant of a curved wall, perhaps originally a stone backdrop for a fountain, and the curved wall may have been from Roman times; by 1900, all traces of it would disappear. A woody fig tree grew from the embankment and spread its shade near the pool.

Conder sketched the scene at Ein es Sultan for his mother. In the drawing, two women stand in the water washing clothes, a third appears to be soaking her feet, and a fourth has come there with two donkeys. In the background is the mound. Proud of his powers of observation and his improving skills as a draftsman, Conder drew the several short rows of stones poking through the face of the mound, and drew what appear to be mud-bricks—parts of walls.

I came to admire Conder's great energy and I forgave him his pride and the nakedness of his ambition. At great cost to himself he would encounter men far more selfish and driven. In his essays and his earliest books, Conder cannot resist self-congratulation, and he is guilty of shameless self-pity, a hundred times over. Yet he manages to convey the aura of risk in his adventures, his virgin wonderment at the stark settings, the boyish pleasure in uncommon experiences. No other territory moved him this way. His audience can sit on the cliffs overlooking Ein es Sultan to watch the grackles swoop and feel the solitude that so frightened and inspired him. But I found his missteps in Palestine more affecting and memorable than his successes. So many rewarding paths not taken! So many humbling might-have-beens! He was physically courageous, worried about his position in the world, terribly anxious to please. But if only he had looked again at what was in front of him. From that first morning at the spring, bricks and walls were in front of him.

Once again, Drake was more observant. It was Drake who saw that the mud-bricks and stones above Ein es Sultan were in well-laid courses, and whole. They could hardly be the leavings of a brick maker's failed experiments.

Conder, thanks to Drake, gave the matter more thought.

He allowed that the mounds were "accumulations." He went so tantalizingly far as to wonder if the accumulations represented the works of more than one people. He had within his grasp a sense of there being buried strata, and a relationship between strata and contents. But Conder did not find those ideas worth pursuing. That anything could be gained from digging struck him as contrary to the work of the true explorer. "*Entre nous,*" he informs Walter Besant after three months in the country, "there is hardly anything to be found in Palestine; all is smashed to powder." Conder regarded himself a careful scientist, and his first axiom was that topography counted more than excavation. What one could see on the surface was the only thing worth seeing at all. So Conder's vague divining of strata within the mound slipped away.

Riha looked best to the Englishmen before they actually arrived. Until then they were able to imagine it being more than the scattering of mud-brick hovels and the goat-hair tents of one of many clans of the Ghawarneh, the ever-present Bedouin. Corn grew on the plain, and vines compliantly draped themselves over trellises. But no one took much care to maintain the irrigation canals. The water from Ein es Sultan fed a swamp that supported a noisy multitude of frogs. A chorus of nightingales hid in the nubk. So profound was the torpor of the people that they appeared to be drugged, or part of an exhibition on indolence. In a *tour d'horizon* for Drake, the local governor explained that to rouse the inhabitants "you must take a stick, to make them work, a whip." Such was the Ottoman theory of local government.

Conder and Drake sought to account for the contrast between that dismal present and the earthly paradise that had been described by Josephus. It is a noteworthy effort, because it implied that to understand conditions at Jericho one needed to look beyond prophecies in the Bible and beyond catastrophism. Neither of those sources left much room for human influence, human willfulness, or for mistakes that might be corrected. God commanded. Or, "things happened." As late as the end of the eighteenth century, travelers who visited the valley returned with descriptions of a land of volcanoes, the mists rising from the Dead Sea proof that underground fires were still burning. Common wisdom—as expressed in 1849 by the *Theological and Literary Journal* of New York—held that the desolate countryside was proof that Palestine was smitten by God's curse: the harshness of the Judean desert was a "conspicuous and terrible demonstration to the eye of the whole world that God reigns and verifies his word."

To their great credit, Conder and Drake rejected the apocalyptic. They were among the first to make a well-reasoned argument that all of Palestine was unchanged in its climate and natural resources since the era chronicled by Josephus. Forests had indeed disappeared, but they could be restored. With proper irrigation, the surveyors said, the fields near Ein es Sultan could be as fertile as in the days of Herod. The British survey team helped change the valley from a place of miracle and calamity to an earthly geography, a place where mortals lived.

"To sum up," Conder writes, "the change in Palestine is one of degree only and not of kind. The curse of the country is bad government and oppression." Problems were due to greed or to ineptitude—just as in Europe. One did not need to attribute the conditions to retribution by anyone's god. In that way, Conder and Drake extinguished, then made wholly imaginary, the last volcanoes.

The governor at Riha had to share his authority with Sheikh Jemil, the leader of the local Ghawarneh. Of the two men, the sheikh had the greater power. His tribe, depending on one's point of view, either employed or had enslaved another, smaller clan that did much of the farming and all the other labor. He was both the largest potential threat to public order and the only effective policeman. Conder and Drake knew him by reputation. He had provided services in the 1860s to the Reverend Henry Baker Tristram and much impressed the Englishman with his abilities as both a hunter and a self-taught naturalist with a particular talent for distinguishing species of mollusks. With training, Tristram reported, Jemil would make a fine zoologist.

As demanded by etiquette and good sense, the survey party hired Jemil to provide protection. He asked after the Reverend Tristram's health. He rode a camel that, at the cost of shaking its rider into a blur, kept pace with Conder's horse. His men served as guides, grilled ibex for dinner, and shot birds. Of all the tribes, the Ghawarneh—the name embracing all the Bedouin near Ein es Sultan—were the most endearing to the traveler and the most businesslike. ("They were kindly, good-natured, and obliging fellows, those Ghawarneh," said Tristram.) This helped offset everyone's revulsion for the Jehallin, whose territory began where the Ghawarneh's ended, at Mar Saba, and extended to the southernmost reaches of the Dead Sea, and beyond, into more desert.

Even the name was inauspicious. *Jehallin* meant "the ignorant ones," after the Arabs of the Jehalliya, "the period of ignorance" before the prophet Muhammad. Tristram complained of an unendurable odor due to the Jehallin's reluctance to bathe. They were "degraded," "wild," barely half-clothed, superstitious enough to believe that a Westerner could change the weather. They wore sheepskins during the day, then at night kneaded flour on them to make a coarse bread. Reattired the next morning in a sheepskin-breadboard, each man lived in a cloud of insects.

Abu Dahok was the Jehallin sheikh—elderly, mild mannered in camp, a fine conversationalist. When he had been with Tristram, he had liked to camp at the place where he had killed eleven men. Between him and the Englishman there was eventually something like a friendship, for Abu Dahok invited him to join the tribe. Tristram, who had a wife and seven children in England, was promised a goat-hair tent of his own and Abu Dahok's fifteen-year-old granddaughter as a wife. If the Englishman later chose to leave, the sheikh pledged, he could divorce the new wife and return to the one in Britain. "Tempting offer," said Tristram. But he declined.

The prayer leader at the old Jericho mosque was unsure whether any of the elders who had known Sheikh Jemil were still alive but told us where to look. He spoke favorably of Sheikh Jemil's branch of the Gha-warneh as a people who always took time to pray. Look in Al Auja, he said.

Even close up it was no more than a green smudge on the plain, the first village north of Jericho. Al Auja fancied itself the capital of ba-nanas, and had its own freshwater spring that emerged from a palm grove in hills to the west. One of King Herod's canals had carried the water from Al Auja to the plantations at Wadi Kelt. From the highway you saw about a dozen low houses that were stained by exhaust fumes and by the dirt, and the land seemed to be rolled flat. Everything else was dirt road and banana grove. Jericho was the great metropolis. The air was as heavy as steam. But however poor Al Auja looked, the ba-nanas were the most profitable crop in the valley and had made the landowners rich.

Hakam Fahoum conferred with a man along the highway who di-rected us to the mosque, an utterly charmless building made of stone—flat roofed, with two metal doors and a deep porch, set back on the road that led to the river. We waited until the end of midafternoon prayers. When the worshipers filtered outside they helped a man bent with age take slow steps past the doors onto the porch. He needed a long time to reach us.

Ahmed Nassallah had a pure white beard, trimmed as neatly as a pharoah's. His robe was black and his headdress white. He believed he was about eighty-five. He was unsteady on his feet and fragile, and was hunched like a great black bird at rest but with a raptor's bright flinty eyes. I wanted to make sure he was the right man, that he had met the right Sheikh Jemil. Since Ahmed Nassallah's hearing was not what it once was, Hakam shouted the questions.

The Sheikh Jemil of whom Ahmed Nassallah had heard many stories was a favorite of the English, he said in a voice pinched and reedy as a boy's. Sheikh Jemil guided many tourists to the river; he excelled as a hunter of birds; he had known a smattering of English, which he learned from a minister, or so said everyone in the clan. Though he stood very close, Hakam had to repeat the questions many times, until Ahmed Nassallah produced an ear trumpet from within his robes. Hakam still had to shout. Laughing, some of the men on the porch formed a circle around us, as if to catch the old man in case he collapsed from expending so much energy.

Ahmed Nassallah's clan had lived alongside the sheikh's and wintered together in Al Auja and the *zhor,* the grassy strip of land closest to the river. In summers they moved to hills near Jerusalem. He remembered Sheikh Jemil as old, infirm, at the end of his life senile. "He could barely move. I was sucking my mother's milk when this man died."

My wishful theory was that Reverend Tristram was the minister who had taught Sheikh Jemil English, but I never found proof. Adorned with an impressive length of untrimmed whiskers, Tristram had been known to Sheikh Jemil as Father of the Beard. I was disappointed but hardly surprised that no one at the mosque had heard his name or the names Conder or Drake.

Hakam murmured when we left that he was "my" Jemil. I was "his" foreigner, resurveying territory of the Ghawarneh. Hakam's family owned one of the banana groves, and he was accorded the deference due a young sheikh. My presence barely mattered except as a curiosity, the same as had been true of the survey party. The foreigner was warmly welcomed as a guest, and in the nineteenth century was also an important source of income. But to linger raised suspicions. In the desolation of the valley, what did the foreigner see that the Bedouin did not? What secret treasure did he divine? Little wonder that some tribes had believed Westerners could control the rains. A guide kept suspicions at bay and kept the peace. Hakam made sense of my maps as Sheikh Jemil had helped Conder and Drake, the mapmakers, make sense of the plain, when it had looked to be empty even of history.

For hundreds of years travelers had searched north of Jericho for a village that had been founded by one of Herod's sons. The son, Archelaus, named it Archelais, in honor of himself. Water was diverted there from the spring, the palm trees produced excellent dates: what little is known was told by Josephus and Pliny. Riding north, the survey party saw no trace of the village.

A telephone crew, laying an underground cable, found the probable site in the mid-1980s, in Al Auja. Digging a trench perpendicular to the highway, the laborers struck a mosaic floor, kept working until the trench cut across the floor's entire width, then notified the authorities responsible for antiquities. Improvements to telephone service were temporarily halted. A proper excavation uncovered the ruins of a sixth-century church belonging to a hitherto unknown community. Some of the building's materials showed signs of earlier use; that is, use before construction of the church. One thousand four hundred years old, the church was the "after." Current theory is that the "before" was Archelais. I passed by a dozen times before noticing the new high fence, the custodian's shack, and the dirt road going directly to the site. It is not for me to criticize the surveyors for having seen nothing. In the nave of the church, the floor cut by the telephone crew portrays flower buds and curling vines; it was, despite the many rips and tears, a fine thick carpet covering the earth.

A few of the tribes prospered into modern times but not the Ghawarneh. When British soldiers took the place of Ottoman governors at the end of World War I, everyone was placed more nearly under the rule of law. The new authorities persuaded some tribes to surrender their weapons (tricked the tribes, the Bedouin say). In Transjordan, British advisers to Emir Abdullah enlisted members of the Bani Sakhr tribe—never shy about raiding farms in the valley, or "borrowing" camels—into a desert army that brought pillaging to an end. Riding camels, Bedouin could not outdistance authorities arriving by armored car. No one could cross the redrawn borders at will. Sheikh Jemil's clan stayed near Jericho through British times, survived the wars in 1948 and 1967, then were bystanders to the first skirmishes between Israeli soldiers and the *fedayeen.* But after one especially bloody clash, the riverbank became a no-man's land planted with mines. The Ghawarneh were ordered into houses in Al Auja, mud-brick quarters hastily built near the mosque. Most of the Ghawarneh chose to cross the river into Jordan. Their children would grow up there, in the cities. In Al Auja the houses of the Ghawarneh are mostly empty. Walls have collapsed and sprouted weeds; the buildings are fissioning into sand and straw.

The Jehallin fared no better. Their encampments are along the

Jerusalem-Jericho highway. They could be mistaken for part of a tourist display or a remnant of prehistory. One saw a littering of tents and goats alongside shallow wadis, everything rendered small by voluptuous hills rounded into breasts, buttocks, sinewy thighs. The landscape was Rubenesque. It was a sensualist's dream of naked hills in repose. I was expected at dusk at the tents of Abu Hassen.

His compound accommodated two wives, sixteen children and daughters-in-law, and their goats. The second-oldest son, thirty-five-year-old Nasser, led the way into the largest tent and to the place to the right of his father. "A house that has no door is more generous than a place with many doors," Abu Hassen said as a welcome. The tent—goatskin and canvas—could cover a boxcar. Most of the light came from a kerosene lantern, though a nearly smokeless fire was at Abu Hassen's feet. The women and a wailing infant made themselves heard on the other side of a goatskin divider that protected them from being seen. Some of the women were outside coaxing the goats into a pen.

Abu Hassen observed the traditions of hospitality with the devotion other men reserved for the mosque. He was small, even delicate, handsomely dark, and in his sixties. If not for his white beard he could have passed for thirty. He said his father had recently died at the age of 120. Abu Hassen rolled cigarettes filled with tobacco pinched from a bulging green pouch, offered them around many times, and joked about hashish being better for one's health. Between puffs came much hacking and spitting. Some of the younger sons sat by the fire through three rounds of coffee, after which one of the boys picked up some of the embers with tongs and disappeared into the women's side. An hour later he returned bearing glasses of sugary tea. Everyone sat in the fire's soft light. Jericho would just then have seemed loud, overbright.

In Abu Hassen's retelling, Ottoman times were retouched to place the Jehallin in retrospective control of a vast territory. Everything between Al Auja and Hebron became theirs. Every rival—gone. It was accurate to the same degree as stories about volcanoes in the valley, the craters still smoking. Great affection was expressed for the Turks, since their era was no longer part of living memory; less for the British; none for the Israelis. It was too soon to have an opinion on a government run by Palestinians. The Bedouin romanticized Ottoman times just as travelers had romanticized the Bedouin. Seen in the firelight, the past was an era of noble deeds and fearless people.

"In Turkish times the Turks were in control of nothing," Nasser said. "The people were in control of themselves."

"The old times and the good times are gone," Abu Hassen said.

At the end of the Ottoman era conditions were in fact extremely dire. Bedouin in the valley attacked strangers merely for food they might be carrying, the Bedouin having almost none. There were raids by the dreaded Bani Sakhr, who would escape across the river with stolen livestock. "If we had enough force to go after them we would," Abu Hassen said. "If not, it was gone." Almost every family, though, had a goatskin tent, a dozen camels if not more, and land for the camels to graze. In every family the patriarch had a horse and gun. In winter, home was alongside the wadis in the desert between Beersheba and the Dead Sea. In spring Abu Hassen's father would move to the hills above Jericho, then would spend the summer near Hebron, to escape the heat of the valley.

All the lands near the Dead Sea were lost after 1948. Tribes had long agreed among themselves about the ownership of land, the agreements extending to the plots for individual families, and needed no written deeds and only rarely encountered anyone to offer a challenge. But the first governments of Israel expropriated large tracts. Without formal deeds the tribes were shunted elsewhere and their claims ignored. In the tent of Abu Hassen, the story was told about a rival tribe having tricked the Jehallin by falsely denouncing them to the new authorities. In that way, it is said, the Jehallin's lands were stolen.

The story has already been passed from father to grandson. Since 1967, the tribe has been restricted to the hills between Jericho and Jerusalem. The young men, coming back each night to the tents, took jobs building high-rise apartments in the cities. The women continued to tend the goats. "This is my quarters since that time," said Abu Hassen, a wave of his arm taking in hills where no one used to live. "I do not move one single step."

First, Claude Conder was charmed by Arabs in Palestine and especially by the Bedouin. He believed the Bedouin to be more polite and refined than the fellahin, their life "really nearer civilisation." But except for Sheikh Jemil, he almost never rendered Palestine's inhabitants as individuals or people of complexity. There were only "types." Because the Ghawarneh happened to conform to Western expectations, Conder complimented the members of the tribe as "real Arabs and good sportsmen"; they were "capital fellows." But they and other Arabs, in the survey reports, were virtually indistinguishable from likable pets. They were strong willed, likable, but, alas, prone to misbehave and in need of discipline. "They are good-natured and very docile under recognized authority," Conder said, a description just as suitable for Jonah and her puppies. Arabs were said to be clever, energetic, blessed with physical endurance, and able to bear great amounts of pain—qualities suitable for servants, shepherds, hewers of wood.

Then, the Bedouin disgusted him. Later still, the disgust was tempered to disappointment. Conder knew them as "hating, backbiting, slandering, envying, quarrelling, cursing, lying, running away; cringing, bullying, flattering, turning the cold shoulder; flirting with maidens, beating (or stoning) wives; weeping over the dead; swearing brotherhood (and forgetting the oath) . . . grasping, avaricious, untrustworthy, even stupid, but also lavish and courteous, intelligent and full of information; superstitious and sceptical, fearing God and conscience, or without regard to either; rich and poor, good, bad, and indifferent." They were as noble as a London chimney sweep. They were trusting like the nations of Europe. They were as moral as a married duke with his mistress. Conder had the wit to observe that a European should immediately feel at home among the Jehallin or any other tribe.

Conder would ride out each day from Ein es Sultan in one direction and Drake usually in another, to cover ground faster. They were trapped in the stressful race against the PEF's impatience for results and its anxieties about expenses. In London, Walter Besant still served as the men's secret confessor, but it was Besant who also conveyed the PEF's dissatisfactions. Conder had to justify having bought clothes for the men—the first new clothing in nearly two years—and buying a new muzzle-loading gun, his leasing four mules, his spending more on barley in autumn 1873 than the party had spent in 1872. No one seemed to appreciate—so it seemed to Conder—that he had haggled for the best price on the clothing, that the gun was used to get birds for the PEF's own collection, or that the mules carried supplies from Jerusalem into the valley, that barley prices had nearly doubled. The harder he tried to explain himself, the more petulant he sounded. Besant was meanwhile pleading for still more economy measures. Conder did his own cause little good by demanding tartly that the economies begin with a cut in office expenses in London. "You in England," he told Besant, "don't know at all when you grumble so much how wonderfully cheap you are doing the Survey.

"And now good bye & do try & keep people from worrying me or I shall knock up and then everything will go to smash."

On the twenty-fourth of November 1873, during one of the ventures made from Ein es Sultan, the party rode south and then a short distance west into the hills, until reaching a building that was singularly imposing. It might have been mistaken for an abandoned fortress from a forgotten war. The fellahin venerated it as the tomb of Nebi Musa—the prophet Moses. Everyone knew the building by that name, Nebi Musa.

The building has a roof of squat domes, like an array of radars. Nebi Musa stands alone on the edge of a deep wadi frequented by hyenas, is two stories high, and is roughly rectangular in plan. It has a plump minaret, everything built of stone. All around are reddish brown hills with rock so rich in petroleum it will burn. The fellahin called the rock "Moses stone," and from it they carved ornaments they sold to travelers, and in desperate times used it as a firewood, choking everyone with oily smoke. The rock smells of oil—rock that is black inside from the plants and animals in seas that had covered the valley. In the uppermost hundred feet of the hills, one hundred million tons of proto-oil.

In front of Nebi Musa is a driveway, narrow and pitted, and a car stripped of its wheels. When I arrived the only sound came from a radio blaring music from the upper story. Then Muhammad al-Jamal stepped into view: he shouted upstairs to his wife, and the radio went dead.

Al-Jamal had been Nebi Musa's caretaker for, so far, eleven years. For all that time he and his wife were the only tenants; and al-Jamal, who was in his mid-forties and seemingly in good health, said he expected to remain until he died.

In the nineteenth century, his would have been a privileged position. Nebi Musa had been revered ever since the early years of Islam. Pilgrims journeying from Jerusalem to Mecca would reach the reddish hills at the end of the first day of travel. From there the travelers could see across the Jordan River to Mount Nebo, the peak from which the God of the Hebrews had given Moses his only glimpse of Canaan.

In the Old Testament story, Moses dies soon after his ascent of the mountain and is buried in a place never found by man. Alternative endings came from mystics and the fellahin. In one, Moses, knowing death is near, rushes westward across the Jordan into Canaan, where he finds angels digging a grave. Stepping into the grave to check its size, he finds himself trapped. It becomes his burial place. In another, Moses is buried east of the Jordan, as in the Old Testament, but becomes dissatisfied with his assigned place of rest. He rolls himself underground and under the river, to the outskirts of Jericho. Hence the shrine in the reddish hills.

What is almost certain is that Bedouin, sometime in the distant past, began to venerate a grave in those hills. It came not to matter whether it was the grave of a clan leader or whose clan it was. Rather than denounce that worship as pagan, the rulers of Palestine appropriated the site for Islam by building, in the thirteenth century, a mosque around the grave. Then came spacious quarters for travelers. Then stables, then an immense courtyard in which merchants could sell food to the pilgrims.

By the mid–nineteenth century, the Ottoman governors began promoting weeklong pilgrimages to Nebi Musa. It was an example of enlightened government, because the pilgrimages were timed to coincide with Easter, to keep Muslims and Christians apart. As Christians poured into Jerusalem for their holy week, Muslims would be leaving for the valley.

For part of the way, the governor himself would lead the procession. Just behind his uniformed retinue came various sects of dervishes, who worked themselves into a rapture banging tambourines, singing, whirling—like churchgoers about to speak in tongues. They fought for the honor of being the first to enter the shrine. Every hillside became a crowded campground. At the shrine the mufti, the most senior religious official of Jerusalem, always took over the grandest apartment; and with his many attending sheikhs, the mufti granted audiences to pilgrims wanting his ruling on questions of religion, business propositions, affairs of the heart. Because not everyone regarded the religious aspect with total seriousness, there were horse races and other contests. There was a chance to visit friends for a full week. So numerous were the pilgrims, their procession would fill the road from Jerusalem for twelve miles.

After World War I, the annual pilgrimage abruptly changed character to become a celebration of Arab nationalism. Nebi Musa, so popular among the uneducated and the poor, helped make Arab political demands known to fellahin in even the smallest villages. Instead of defusing tensions, the procession now was increasing them; for this new nationalism of the Arabs was in competition with the nationalism of the Jews, and inevitably came into conflict with the British, the new rulers of Palestine. In 1920, the march degenerated into a three-day riot directed against the Jews in Jerusalem. At least six persons were killed. And from that time forward, the annual pilgrimage became an incendiary forum celebrating the political strength of a young new mufti, Haj Amin al-Husseini.

No one was more vociferous than Haj Amin in opposing Jewish immigration to Palestine. He was implacably hostile to Zionism and eventually to British rule of Palestine as well. His hostility also extended to Emir Abdullah of Transjordan, a rival for political leadership. For anyone sharing the mufti's views, Nebi Musa during the 1920s and '30s represented an ideological home. In 1937, Haj Amin fled Palestine to escape arrest by the British. (He never moderated his uncompromising views during an exile—spent mostly in Cairo and Beirut—that lasted until his death.) But to attend the celebrations at Nebi Musa remained, for a long time, an endorsement of his uncompromising politics.

Muhammad al-Jamal, the caretaker, has had the shrine mostly to himself. During the 1948 Arab-Israeli war, Abdullah gained control of the West Bank, and not surprisingly discouraged a resumption of the pilgrimages so closely associated with his opponent. In 1960 the Jordanians commandeered the building as a military post. Officers' quarters and an armory went upstairs, stables on ground level. Some rooms still smell faintly of horse manure. Since then, al-Jamal has converted another wing into a pen for his goats. The miles-long processions from Jerusalem have never resumed.

"It was a very nice place, what can I say?" al-Jamal shrugged as he showed off the main courtyard. One week every year it had been an overcrowded city with even its own clinic. Merchants fought to get favored positions in the courtyard. Each stall was just wide enough to accommodate a horse-drawn cart. Like scribbled petroglyphs, the names of the merchants were still faintly visible on the walls.

Haj Amin al-Husseini had received his guests upstairs. Even empty his salon is hauntingly lovely: a vast, white, high-ceilinged room lit by ten large windows opening onto red hills and white domes. No great feat of imagination is required to picture it furnished with couches and plush armchairs, and seated on his divan the mufti waving forward the next supplicant. Because of the airiness, anyone entering the room seems to float high above the landscape.

The hills are a densely populated necropolis but one so badly eroded as to be barely recognizable for what it is. Al-Jamal said the graves numbered at least fifty thousand. Most are pilgrims who had wanted to lie near a great prophet. Bedouin from throughout the valley had brought their dead there too: the shrine had served as a sort of home address where clans left messages for each other and could always depend on finding water. A large monument honors a Jericho man said to have worked at Nebi Musa for a hundred years. Another honors a woman who spent lavishly to repair the buildings. The wind has reduced most of the graves to small lumps, the hills to boulder fields. To this day, people from the villages still ask to be buried there. "There are seven mountains that are full. We begin the eighth."

Al-Jamal led the way through the courtyard to the tomb ascribed to Moses. It was under the highest dome. A foot-long metal spike unlocked the door, and the sarcophagus inside was chest high and wider across than you could reach. It so nearly filled the room, you could not see over or even around it. You saw only a big stone chest draped with hundreds of layers of green silk reaching to the ankles of the stone. The silk coverings had always been the responsibility of the caretakers. Al-Jamal did not know the age of the bottommost layers; the lightest touch turned a small part into dry green crumbs. He had sewn the topmost silk seven years before. He was about to begin work on another.

Moses was unlikely to be the person inside the sarcophagus, al-Jamal said. Al-Jamal's father, who was the prayer leader at the mosque in Jericho, had said the same thing without any obvious concern. "The old persons believe, not the educated," al-Jamal said. But if it were not Moses, it was some other good and righteous man, he said. He had watched dust storms skip right over the shrine. Earth tremors never damaged it. Rain never leaked through the domes. For al-Jamal, those were sufficient proofs of sanctity. "It is free for you to believe or not to believe."

On the day the party visited Nebi Musa, a thunderstorm ushered in the first autumn rains. Claude Conder gallantly escorted to Riha four ladies who had lost their guide, and then dined with them under a leaky roof. The other surveyors were searching for Conder while he dined, and became trapped in nubk.

A few nights later, Charles Clermont-Ganneau arrived. He too had promptly gotten lost. Already celebrated for his decoding of the Moabite Stone, Clermont-Ganneau was now in the temporary employ of the PEF. His was the reputation that Conder hoped eventually to match or even surpass. In the darkness, the Frenchman had wandered from thorn bush to thorn bush because the Englishmen's campfire was obscured by the great mound. Later he would say that his hosts gave him "the warmest welcome," but he found Conder cold and gloomily serious—not at all confident, and not very entertaining company.

Clermont-Ganneau brought with him two fellahin who had worked with Charles Warren, and he soon busied himself like an emperor examining a new conquest. At Ein es Sultan, the Frenchman ordered the workmen to uncover more of the stone wall behind the small pool, until people from Riha—worried he would cause the spring to dry up—insisted he stop digging. In Riha itself, he saw broken friezes and old sarcophagi being used as construction materials. All very promising, except for the lack of ancient inscriptions. So Clermont-Ganneau, preeminent paleographer, suggested demolishing all the aqueducts and sifting their rubble to improve the chances of discovering inscribed stones.

His suggestion fortunately was ignored; he otherwise would have destroyed one of the marvels of engineering created by the Hasmoneans. Breaking up the irrigation system would also have deprived the inhabitants of Riha of the livelihood they eked out from farming.

To his credit, Charles Clermont-Ganneau understood, as had Charles Warren, that the plains and the seemingly misshapen mounds near the spring were no less worthy of investigation than were the famous edifices of Jerusalem. In the valley, the real problem was deciding where and how to look. "A perfect mine of antiquities is there waiting to be worked," the Frenchman advised the Palestine Exploration Fund, "and I commend it to the attention of future explorers."

He was at his best when he knew in some detail what *ought* to be present. It was one thing to examine a place already suspected to be of great antiquity, as was the case at Ein es Sultan. It was much harder work to judge the merits of something previously unknown. Why, you might as well arrive wearing a blindfold. So the explorer-archaeologists went where they believed the Bible led them. It was always easier to interpret finds in light of what the Bible led one to expect. If the Bible seemed silent about a particular site, a person could more easily convince himself that nothing of interest was there.

Clermont-Ganneau spent a day with Charles Drake riding south, and their trip is noteworthy not for what they saw but because of all they failed to imagine. Nine miles from Ein es Sultan, they reached a limestone plateau. It formed a sort of broad shelf overlooking the shore of the Dead Sea and lay like a stepping stone against the mountains. As anyone could see from the plateau, the mountains were honeycombed with caves. On that limestone shelf were orderly courses of stone; no great expertise was needed to realize they had once been part of a building of some sort. Near the rubble was a cemetery where the graves were arranged in neat rows and marked by more stones. Bedouin called those ruins Qumran.

In 1947, a teenage member of the Ta'amireh tribe would find in one of the caves above Qumran several soiled, somewhat leathery bundles and two tall jars. Scholars made the bundles known to the world as the first of the Dead Sea Scrolls, the jars the containers in which they had originally been placed for storage or hiding. In 1951, Qumran would be identified as the community where, more likely than not, the writers of the scrolls had lived and worked.

Clermont-Ganneau and Drake stayed at Qumran almost certainly for several hours. Until their visit, only one other Westerner, Louis-Félicien de Saulcy, had described the ruins. De Saulcy—French artillery officer, expert numismatist, confidant to men of letters, future senator of the Second Empire—had visited Qumran in 1851 during the course of several weeks' travel in the Dead Sea region; and, in a two-volume work published in 1853, he reported having found traces of an ancient settlement there.

But de Saulcy also declared that Qumran was really Gomorrah, the famous city of iniquity. He had interpreted the finds in light of what he believed the Bible promised. For Genesis said, albeit none too clearly, that Gomorrah had lain somewhere in the valley. De Saulcy announced that Qumran met all the biblical specifications for being the destroyed city. Critics in Paris dismissed his conclusions, and doubts were expressed as to whether de Saulcy had even made such a trip. It was unkindly suggested that in writing his book he had relied solely on his imagination.

Clermont-Ganneau and Drake found the site unremarkable. "The ruins are quite insignificant in themselves: a few fallen walls of mean construction; a little [pool], into which you descend by steps; and numerous fragments of irregular pottery scattered over the soil," Clermont-Ganneau reported. At his orders, the two fellahin who had ridden with the party exhumed a corpse from the cemetery. Contrary to Muslim practice, the body had been oriented not east-west but north-south. Perhaps, said Clermont-Ganneau, the cemetery dated to an era before the arrival of Islam in the seventh century. With that his curiosity apparently was exhausted.

How odd that neither he nor Drake made any mention of the caves. Some of them were clearly visible from the cemetery, and the explorers had already noted caves and crevices elsewhere, and recognized that many had served as places of habitation. In the cliff face at Qumran were more than two hundred openings of various shapes and sizes. At the foot of the mountains less than a half mile away were traces of an aqueduct. But to notice those features, you had to believe that in a distant past people would willfully choose to live somewhere remote and unwelcoming. You had to recognize that those qualities could be the landscape's strongest attractions.

In 1902, Gurney Masterman, the English physician who on behalf of the PEF periodically measured the Dead Sea water level, stopped at Qumran long enough to observe that the ruins occupied a site offering a clear view of a freshwater spring and of all the approach roads. Masterman found that even on a hot day the limestone plateau captured steady breezes: Qumran enjoyed "a fresher, healthier situation than any spot in the plain below." He discovered the remains of the aqueduct system and surmised that the area, sometime in the past, was "in no considerable degree inhabited." Masterman refrained from speculating who the inhabitants were.

Discovery of the first Dead Sea Scrolls did not by itself bring recognition of Qumran's importance. In 1949 the future excavators, after a first brief examination of the site, concluded the ruins had been a Roman fort without any link to the scroll writers. In 1952, these accomplished excavators spent three weeks working within one hundred yards of the largest cave in the limestone plateau without detecting it, and learned of its existence only when the Ta'amireh arrived in Jerusalem to sell more scrolls. Charles Clermont-Ganneau and Charles Drake—for having failed in 1873 both to discern Qumran's importance and to explore the caves—were in distinguished company.

Conder suffered not from excessive caution but from overeagerness, as when he beseeched the PEF to buy the exotic-looking figurines from the antiquities dealer in Jerusalem. Now, he declared he had found Gilgal.

In the Book of Joshua, Gilgal was the first campground of the Israelites after their crossing of the Jordan. It was the place from which they launched their attack on Jericho, the Bible said, and where they had brought twelve stones from the Jordan to mark the safe passage into

Canaan. To be the discoverer of Gilgal, Conder knew, would be at least as great an accomplishment as any of Warren in Jerusalem or Clermont-Ganneau with the Moabite Stone. Yet every reader of the Old Testament had been stumped by that book's one, maddeningly imprecise phrase about the location. Gilgal, said the Bible, was "on the east border of Jericho."

Flavius Josephus placed it ten stadia—somewhat more than one modern mile—from Jericho but did not clearly specify whether he meant the Jericho built at Wadi Kelt by the Hasmoneans and Herod or the "old" Jericho that was the mound at Ein es Sultan. Christian pilgrims said it was "near" old Jericho, no direction given. Or one mile from Jericho (but which Jericho? one mile in which direction?). Or two miles east. Five miles east. Seven miles from Ein es Sultan (again, no direction given). Some of the distances were presumably calculated from the "new" Jericho built sometime after the year 70.

We know that pilgrims told of seeing the house of Rahab the prostitute and the sycamore that Zacchaeus had climbed to catch sight of Jesus. Not surprising, then, that they spoke of Gilgal. In the Bible it is an outdoor place marked by stones of unspecified size but a site otherwise undescribed. None of the early pilgrims said unambiguously that he had actually been there. None described it. The accounts offered itineraries—a particular distance from Jerusalem to Jericho, another distance to Gilgal, so many miles to the Jordan. There were already guidebooks containing guidebook rote. Travelers who had survived the trek to Jericho settled for pointing a finger east; they said Gilgal was to be found . . . somewhere close.

The anonymous pilgrim from Piacenza—he is already known to us—reported visiting "not far from Jericho" a church displaying twelve large stones behind its altar. He had traveled into the valley in about the year 570, and his is one of the first mentions of the stones and of a church. A century later the pilgrim Arculf described a church in which six stones were on one side and six on another. So heavy was each stone, Arculf said, two strong men were required to lift just one of them.

What had excited Conder was hearing a name that was *like* the name Gilgal. First with Clermont-Ganneau and then on his own, he had searched for a place rumored to be called Jiljulieh. "Jiljul"—so nearly

"Gilgal"—fit his stubborn confidence in the primacy of names. Conder preferred hearing an ancient-sounding place-name to discovering pottery, certainly to the onerous work of excavation. A well-done field survey, he always advised, guaranteed a person more knowledge than would any amount of digging or literary exegesis. Work by textual critics earned nothing but his derision because such work "smells of the lamp" and not of a desert valley traversed by an experienced explorer. "Library scholars and the conductors of exploration parties," he proclaimed when his reputation was at its peak, "are not always made of the same stuff." For Conder, the stuff of anyone but a Royal Engineer equipped with a theodolite was manufactured, pale, inferior. Riding out each day from Ein es Sultan was for him the survey at its most sublime. Imagine then his excitement at hearing "Jiljulieh." He found the place marked by a large tamarisk tree about a mile east of Riha; there were several low mounds and a stone pool. Conder, acknowledging "a certain amount of doubt or difficulty," reported to London he had found at Jijulieh the Gilgal of the Israelites.

The response could have only disappointed him. In London, Charles Warren sniffed that he had "not myself the slightest faith" in the purported discovery; Clermont-Ganneau, conducting "a few little excavations," had found at Jiljulieh glass and bits of mosaic, which was evidence of a building of some kind, but "nothing for or against the identification of Gilgal, which appears to me still a doubtful point."

For the rest of his career, Conder would insist that the work at Jiljulieh was one of the grandest moments of the PEF. He paraded his claim like a battle ribbon from a hard-fought war. He believed he had won.

What had he found? Most likely ruins of the church where the early Christian pilgrims had indeed seen twelve stones. The church had undoubtedly commemorated Gilgal. But whether the Israelites had ever camped there, and when, and under what circumstances, would have been as unknown to sixth-century pilgrims as to the PEF survey team. A monastery may have stood near the church, and excavations in the 1950s would uncover part of a mosaic floor. A photo from that time showed the tamarisk tree that Conder used as a marker, and the little that remained of the floor. Within another two decades the remains had been looted, or farmers had plowed over everything. The tree is gone.

"Jiljulieh" as a word was plausibly linked to "Gilgal"—in that, Conder had been right—but Jiljulieh was not the only such name: a later survey found *fourteen* sites with names that were philological cousins of "Gilgal." Pilgrims had wanted to believe they had found some special place, and so had Conder. The sight of it could justify the pilgrims' hardships, or cure the self-doubt of a young explorer. No one would easily convince the pilgrims that the twelve stones might have been placed in a church to meet the pilgrims' expectations. No one convinced Conder he had seen anything other than the true Gilgal.

On the third of December 1873, having spent five days in the valley and satisfied his curiosity, Clermont-Ganneau left for Jerusalem. Conder rode to Jerusalem the same day to make arrangements for a winter camp and headed back to Jericho the following night, a Thursday. With the light of a full moon, he let his horse gallop the last distance to the campfires. What surprised him at the tents was the silence: no one shouted a greeting or even peered outside at the sound of the horse. As soon as Conder glimpsed the men he understood the reason: during his brief absence, almost everyone in camp had been attacked by fever. He had returned just in time to care for the sick.

Drake seemed the worst off but the sick list also included a corporal, five of the servants, two of the Bedouin. Two days later, on Saturday, Conder sent a messenger to ask Dr. Thomas Chaplin, the physician who had cared for the unfortunate Captain Stewart, to ride to Ein es Sultan.

Unfortunately, Dr. Chaplin was himself much too ill to leave Jerusalem. Another physician, though unsure of the way, volunteered, and after the soldier who was supposed to act as guide deserted him, set out on his own, on Sunday. Drake was delirious throughout that day but in lucid moments was pleading for a doctor. Conder kept assuring him the doctor would arrive any moment. But traveling alone, the poor doctor wandered for all of the day and most of the night; in the darkness he fell off his horse. He arrived sometime after midnight, his head badly cut, as ill as anyone in the tents. Conder treated the doctor's bruises with vinegar and put him to bed.

After two more days, finally, a mule litter carried Drake to Jerusalem;

he was again delirious. Dr. Chaplin roused himself to join Conder in watching over him in Jerusalem through the night.

It was now that Conder grew into his job; the change was as striking as if he had donned a new uniform made of a better cloth. He was all business. All the self-pity disappeared. "I shall never remember the Sunday at Jericho without feeling how important a day it was in my life," he would write later. For the first time the men's well-being was unmistakably in his hands alone; he saw that unless he acted responsibly, there might be no survey team. He had often secretly worried that someone would suffer terribly, would *have* to suffer and maybe even die, as a sort of price for the survey team undertaking its work. It was a superstition he never entirely abandoned. As he saw it, every expedition in Palestine was fated to endure at least one disaster. One of Reverend Tristram's companions had died; one of Charles Warren's corporals died in Jerusalem; none of the expeditions to the Dead Sea had been without some human tragedy. Conder had consoled himself that Captain Stewart's illness during the very first week of work had meant that the party's unavoidable debt was already paid. Drake's delirium seemed to show otherwise.

Conder saw that he himself had been spared—miraculously, it seemed to him—and he took charge with the confidence of a person newly infused with the belief he was immune to any serious harm. Someone *else* had paid. Conder began to justify the title he wanted: in Charge of Survey of Palestine.

That terrible Sunday in Jericho, the cook had wanted to quit to save himself from the fever. Conder, the newly strengthened Conder, threatened to shoot him. The cook stayed. For Drake, Conder found a full-time male nurse. Everyone else received orders to leave Ein es Sultan soon after Drake was carried away by litter. "I am glad to report that I have been able to arrange so that the work has not been actually stopped for a single day," Conder informed the PEF. "I have now ordered the party to follow me to Jerusalem where work will be continued until Mr. Drake's state of health allows me to leave him." Then the expedition would return to the valley. Drake's future would need to be decided with counsel from Dr. Chaplin. But Conder offered advice that seemed motivated less by his old rivalry with Drake than by genuine concern and a new sense of responsibility:

> If Drake's health does not get better he ought to give up, as it will seriously hinder his work. If he is in tents in winter he *must* get asthma and probably fever again, which will certainly kill him. He has had a great squeak this time. Nothing but great care & a good doctor got him through. At all events he should rest for a time.

But he couldn't resist crediting himself with foresight:

> I told you before, he ought not to come out unless quite well, and was fully expecting him to knock up as he has done, poor fellow.

The men called the illness Jericho fever or malaria. They in fact were two different diseases; the men probably had both.

Jericho fever accounted for the large sores that took months to heal. Sergeant Black had been troubled by "a very bad place" on his hands; Conder complained of an ulcerous sore that kept growing on one hand until the whole arm was painful; Drake was so plagued by sores on his feet, at times he could barely walk. Any newcomer would mistakenly think the sore was a boil, or the result of irritation of some kind, but not a disease. When it healed it left a large scar. Then you would notice, among people in Riha or in dealings with the Bedouin, that almost everyone in the valley had on his hands or face at least one large ugly scar.

Cutaneous leishmaniasis was, much later, the name assigned to the disease, to honor Lieutenant-General Sir William Boog Leishman. He was surgeon, pathologist, tropical disease specialist. At age twenty-one, in 1887, newly ordered by the Royal Army Medical Corps to India, Dr. Leishman took the then extraordinary step of adding to his luggage a microscope. In 1900 he would discover the parasite responsible for a large family of tropical diseases, including the illness manifested by the open sores. The pathogen and its many cousins are notably well traveled; depending on your itinerary you can encounter *Leishmania mexicana, L. amazonensis, L. tropica* (in India), or *L. aethiopica* (throughout

Africa). Within the genus *Leishmania* are also the species *braziliensis, guyanesis, panamensis,* and *peruviana.* In the Middle East, travelers knew cutaneous leishmaniasis as Jericho Fever, Baghdad Boil, Aleppo Evil, Oriental Sore.

In the 1870s the route of infection was not merely unknown but almost beyond imagination. That something microscopic could cause disease had only recently been established, by Pasteur and others. No one would discover until 1875 that the agents of illness could be protozoa. Disease was thought to be the product of humors gone out of balance, or fatigue, or water that in some unknown way was "bad," or a "bad" air that emanated invisibly from swamps. In 1928, researchers would establish that the parasite responsible for cutaneous leishmaniasis was transmitted by sandflies. At Ein es Sultan, as it happened, the survey party camped in sandfly paradise.

As their habitat, sandflies prefer crevices in walls and the crannies formed by rubble close to the ground. Imagine the possibilities offered by a crumbling mound of mud-brick and bits of pottery. Imagine the opportunity afforded by a constant water supply.

The flies ingested the parasite by feeding on an infected mammal; the parasite then multiplied within its new host. With the next insect bite, the parasite was transmitted to its next victim. And interestingly, given the attention Conder lavished on Jonah and her puppies, the parasite's preferred carriers were dogs. And jackals: in the 1980s, jackals would be blamed for the disease becoming a near epidemic outside Baghdad.

Jericho fever's legacy was usually only the scarring. A severe case could disfigure your throat or nose, even destroy the outer part of an ear, or be mistaken for leprosy. People judged it an unavoidable side effect of life in the valley. They realized that a first sore usually gave immunity to having another. With luck your first scar was your last. Once the role of the sandfly became known, mothers would expose the buttocks of young children to the flies—to ensure that the first sore, and the first and maybe last scar, would be in the least conspicuous place. Doctors offered the same therapy by injecting children with the live parasite to produce a sore and the hoped-for immunity; but because not all the induced sores healed, the practice was abandoned.

Other threats to health were more serious. In 1918, Gurney Masterman, the physician in the sometime employ of the PEF, cataloged the most prevalent diseases in Palestine and, by doing so, sketched the portrait of a country of striking unhealthfulness.

Cholera was decimating entire villages. Smallpox brought "very high mortality." People from Europe seemed especially susceptible to the country's endemic typhoid. Tuberculosis had increased to an extent Masterman considered frightening. But *the* disease of Palestine—in the expedition's day, as in 1918—was malaria.

People knew it as swamp fever. Remittent fever. The ague. "Practically speaking," Masterman reported, "it occurs all over the land and affects every class of its inhabitants." Malaria's victims suffered enervating cycles of intense chills and fevers that drenched them in sweat. A high fever that returned every twenty-four hours, or every forty-eight, or every seventy-two was the telltale symptom and was as regular as clockwork. And malaria was not a "modern" disease that could be attributed to changes in society or blamed on one territory. A practitioner of the medical arts in China had recorded malaria's symptoms in 2700 B.C. So did the writers of sacred Hindu texts in 1600 B.C. In the Bible, Moses warned that God would punish the disobedient with fever, inflammation, and fiery heat; that too is plausibly malaria.

Dr. Thomas Chaplin, the local expert, knew not significantly more about the affliction than did Hippocrates, in the fifth century B.C. True, quinine, found in the bark of the South American Cinchona tree, had reached Europe in the seventeenth century as the first effective antimalarial drug. (Until the 1940s, quinine remained the only such drug.) But Chaplin, like the ancient Greeks, held that the disease was caused by a miasma, a dankness originating from the marshes and terrifying to anyone believing in its power. For over two thousand years, the medical profession hypothesized the miasma's existence: invisible, penetrating, selectively poisonous. Convention held that it poisoned both soil and air. That the innocent traveler risked being contaminated by a cloud of it. That the malarious districts of Palestine could be rendered safe, if ever, only by the heavy winter rains thoroughly washing the land. It was no less a known part of Dr. Chaplin's world than, say, ionizing radiation is a known part of ours; one worried about exposure to it. Conder told of lands in the valley that "reek of miasma," and his descriptions placed him in the scientific mainstream. Anyone in search of proof of the dangers needed only to cite Drake's dreadful illness. For the survey party had camped at the small marsh formed by Ein es Sultan and, compounding the danger, well before the end of the winter rains.

Fatigue was presumed to be a contributory factor. So were rapid changes in climate, like those experienced riding from Jerusalem to the ovenlike temperatures of Riha. So were chills. Charles Warren had attributed his own case of malaria, albeit mild, to having removed his jacket for an impromptu horse race across the plain to Al Auja. He had gotten rather chilled. His health advice was that a traveler should drink when thirsty, eat when hungry, and avoid strenuous activities on an empty stomach. Plus one extra item of advice that later knowledge makes more interesting.

The traveler, Warren said, should sleep with his head wrapped in a muslin bag.

As protection against the invisible miasma? Against mosquitoes? Warren didn't say. Mosquitoes were infamously populous in the valley. It's logical Warren would suggest a way to avoid their nighttime torture. Logical too for us to assume that he did not suspect that the mosquito played the key role in transmitting the disease. The miasma theory was still in good health. Only in 1880 would a French army physician, Alphonse Laveran, discover that the disease could be traced to a microscopic parasite. Only in 1898 would another physician, Ronald Ross, find proof that the parasite was delivered to humans by the water-loving *Anopheles.* Until then you wrapped yourself in muslin as protection against the nuisance of the insect, not against disease.

Conder blamed the fever on Drake having overtired himself riding from Ein es Sultan into Wadi Kelt on an especially hot day. Recognizing the illness for what it was, he gave Drake quinine that the party carried in its medical kit.

Dr. Chaplin doubted that Drake would survive. By the middle of December, though, two weeks after he fell ill, everyone was marveling at his recovery. After two weeks in a sickbed, Drake, saying he had "been at death's door" and was "only just now able to creep about," wrote the PEF to tell of the wonderful care that had been shown by Conder, but also to let it be known that now Conder himself was sick. He had not been miraculously spared after all. "Don't tell his people or they will be alarmed," Drake cautioned. "He is obliged to keep in his bed still."

Conder's fever was less severe. He thought the illness was due in some small part to change in climate, but mostly to his employers sending more letters of complaint about expenses. There were questions about the bookkeeping. As a way to save money, there was even talk of reducing the size of the expedition. Conder found the stress from illness and bad weather—and now money—almost impossible to bear. He said he was at his wits' end. "I am so driven that I fear if I don't get rest soon I shall break down," he told Walter Besant. And all his old petulance returned. He divided his anger between the blithely comfortable men in London and the largely innocent Drake. Even as Conder expressed his own desperate need for rest, he was insinuating that everyone in the party except Drake wanted to return to work and was ready, that Drake alone was responsible for any delays.

Much later, Conder wrote that he and Dr. Chaplin at precisely this time had counseled Drake to leave Palestine. They told him it was his only chance to recover his strength. Though we have only Conder's version of these events, there is no compelling reason to doubt it. He had good reason to feel anxious about the work to come, and common sense would have told him, and should have told Drake, that no one in a seriously weakened state should make another long stay in the valley. You didn't need to know the true etiology of malaria to realize that, given enough time near Jericho and the Jordan, and given normal luck, malaria would find you. Dysentery and the sores that never seemed to heal awaited you too. But Drake planned on returning to work.

He felt better than he had in months. It's possible that for him the most recent fever had seemed no worse than past illnesses; he had visited death's door more than once. He had told friends that he certainly didn't expect to live to an especially venerable age. He saw no reason to leave the survey. It was his chance—his last, as it turns out—to do work that might be remembered.

It was a horrible winter, so cold and with so much snow falling in Jerusalem that the survey party felt imprisoned. When there wasn't snow, Conder and Drake rode out but found the hills nearly impassable and too exposed to the winds to allow camping or sustained work, and the coastal plain half-submerged in water. The Jordan Valley was a quagmire. "The most severe winter in Palestine ever remembered," Conder writes in January 1874. "We have no stove so it is cold." They lost more than two months in Jerusalem. Only at the end of February could the expedition return, finally, to Ein es Sultan.

As the first order of business Conder and Drake rode from the spring to the northern end of the Dead Sea, carrying with them two long iron poles prepared during those frustrating weeks in Jerusalem. Each pole had marks every six inches along its length. Drive the poles into the lake bed, and you could measure with some precision the changes, if any, in water level. It seemed a practical, indeed infallible method of answering long-pending questions about the lake.

The first pole went in easily enough at the water's edge. Driving in the second, in five and a half feet of water, was more trying, as Conder, floating on his back, held the pole upright with his feet, while Drake hammered it with an enormous mallet and swam at the same time. When the pole was partway in, Conder climbed onto it and hammered it some more. After nearly an hour in the water, Drake emerged exhausted.

Unfortunately, the fellahin or the Bedouin could always earn a good price for iron. Within a week the infallible measuring devices—definitely not washed away, but pulled out—disappeared.

The survey party did not bother trying to replace them. If the maps were ever to be finished, the whole northern half of the valley had to be surveyed, and all the ruins looked at and sketched, before the return of hot weather. Or the niggardly powers in London would realize the project was falling expensively behind, maybe even decide against finishing it. From Ein es Sultan the men moved north, out of Sheikh Jemil's territory and into the domain of a tribe decried as "good for nothing"—worse even than the Jehallin—and to a new camp judged as simply horrible. The drinking water was salty, the land a giant bog.

They kept traveling north. Drake, because of his open sores, and in an effort to conserve his energy, no longer rode except when absolutely necessary. Yet he sounded cheerful enough in the correspondence, interested and perceptive about the work, his ample curiosity well fed.

He portrayed the countryside as exceptionally beautiful. Thanks to the heavy rains, the crop of wildflowers was unusually rich, and the grasses thick enough to feed the horses and mules and save the party the price of barley. You could wonder if he and Conder were traveling in different seasons. One man recounted small adventures and lessons learned, while the other would have Walter Besant believe every day was an utter misery. Drake sought to play down his discomfort. Conder, without doubt enjoying his responsibility, sought to make his job seem even larger. Expectations, personal relationships, temperament, the message you wanted to convey—the message that you were fully fit, or that you were leading an infinitely dangerous enterprise—what you "saw" was not the only factor coloring your vision of the landscape. Conder told of insects so numerous he was breathing them. Another ten days were lost to rain.

But Conder was soon in good spirits as well. The PEF had chosen to grant him his first leave since his arrival in Palestine nearly two years earlier. "Time flies & flies, and already I can count not much over a month before I start for *HOME*," Conder writes his mother. Beloved Jonah would be traveling with him. Drake was to be in charge of putting the equipment in storage. During the hot months he also planned on revisiting parts of Syria while the other men labored over various reports and the maps. And on the twentieth of April 1874, the expedition completed, for that season at least, its work in the valley. So far, three thousand square miles surveyed—roughly half the country. Riding toward Jenin, a none too welcoming town in the northern hills and never known for beauty or comfort, Conder felt he was returning to civilization. "The worst is now down and I hope we have broken the back of the Survey of Palestine."

Later, Conder would say that even before sailing for Britain he felt a sense of foreboding. He wrote Drake's friends in Damascus to advise that they not let him travel alone, because hot weather always proved bad for him and he was perhaps weaker than he would say.

Conder reached home by the end of May.

In mid-June, Dr. Chaplin wrote to inform him that Drake had suffered a relapse. The fever this time was far worse. Dr. Chaplin had put

Drake into the Mediterranean Hotel, a well-kept establishment and the most comfortable indoor quarters available, and five doctors examined him. He exhausted the nurses charged with watching over him because, whenever the delirium abated, he insisted on leaving his bed but then became frightened. In lucid moments, Drake asked for Conder. He also asked for Habib, his servant from the grand days with Richard Burton, and shouted orders for him to pitch the tents on Mount Zion. "I cannot now report otherwise than very unfavourably of his case," Chaplin wrote. "I shall not be surprised if in my next letter I have to communicate very sad intelligence. . . . We just now know not what to do. . . . I have told him of my intention to write and he sends his kind regards."

Drake was delirious forty-two days. Even Dr. Chaplin was exhausted at the end.

One of the guests at the PEF's annual meeting, held in London in June 1874, was Claude Conder. Most of the speeches cast him as a hero. George Grove, the PEF's founder and chief drum beater, went so far as to compare him favorably to Sennacherib, the Assyrian king whose army had besieged Jerusalem. Lieutenant Conder, Grove said, had not turned back at obstacles that had stymied the Assyrians. Another speaker congratulated the survey team for performing as magnificently as an army winning a major campaign. The audience cheered.

Only then did Grove begin to talk about the organization's problems. "I do not think that any of you now present, or any one that thinks of these things in England, can realize the fact that we are *in want of money.*" In truly desperate want. For income, the organization depended on dues-paying members, and on support drummed up by the local chapters in more than a hundred towns—from Aberdeen to York—plus the efforts of its Ladies' Association. But the PEF had almost nothing tangible to show for its work of the last two years except the young mustachioed lieutenant who was just then in the members' presence.

His audience was sheltered from knowing the worst ignominies. Since the PEF could no longer pay the bills, the printer who published its quarterly journal was extending credit. A board member had extended a large loan. If not for the loan, the PEF would probably have

The mound at Ein es Sultan, photographed in 1867 by a member of Charles Warren's excavation team. *(Reproduced by permission of the Palestine Exploration Fund)*

Lieutenant Charles Warren *(left)* with his assistants from the work in Jerusalem and Jericho, 1867. *(Reproduced by permission of the Palestine Exploration Fund)*

Members of the PEF survey team in Palestine: Charles Tyrwhitt Drake, Lieutenant Claude Conder, Corporal George Armstrong, and Sergeant T. Black, in a photograph taken by Drake. *(Reproduced by permission of the Palestine Exploration Fund)*

Edward Henry Palmer and Charles Tyrwhitt Drake in 1870 after their walk through the Sinai and Negev Deserts. *(Reproduced by permission of the Palestine Exploration Fund)*

Claude Conder at Ein es Sultan, photographed by H. H. Kitchener in December 1874 or January 1875. *(Reproduced by permission of the Palestine Exploration Fund)*

Lieutenant Horatio Herbert Kitchener, Royal Engineers. *(Reproduced by permission of the Palestine Exploration Fund)*

The Jordan River near Jericho, photographed by H. H. Kitchener during the PEF survey. *(Reproduced by permission of the Palestine Exploration Fund)*

Claude Reignier Conder, "*par excellence* the Surveyor of the Holy Land." *(Private collection)*

Riha (Jericho) sometime during the last quarter of the nineteenth century. *(Reproduced by permission of the Palestine Exploration Fund)*

Kathleen Kenyon alongside an Early Bronze Age wall uncovered at the mound in the 1950s. *(British School of Archaeology in Jerusalem)*

The Ein es Sultan refugee camp, adjoining the northern edge of the mound. The square-topped mountain in the background is the Mount of Temptation. *(UNRWA)*

Pump house, and its inelegant pipings, at Ein es Sultan. *(Nitsan Shorer)*

Modern Jericho and *(above center)* the mound. *(Nitsan Shorer)*

already collapsed. Meanwhile, monthly expenses for the survey party were two hundred pounds—several thousands of today's dollars—with an additional amount sent each month to Charles Clermont-Ganneau. Meanwhile, here was Claude Conder. Walter Besant, in private, asked other members of the board to advance enough money to keep the Fund, and the survey, afloat.

The necessary money arrived in drips, not a flood. Six years would pass before the last loan was repaid.

Conder's remarks at the meeting, at least on the page, are strangely bland. They are so drily ordinary as to make one wonder whether he had been warned not to mention the hardships, and in retaliation edited out all sense of adventure, and the color of the country. They contradict everything he was writing from the field. Strangest of all are his brief remarks about the party's health.

They contradict what he knew to be true. "Hitherto the men have hardly had a day's illness," Conder told his audience, "and I think we may hope that with due care and the invaluable advice of Dr. Chaplin, the open-air life may continue to enable them to stand the effects of the work." Conder was speaking in London on the twenty-third of June 1874, and it was the day Charles Francis Tyrwhitt Drake died in Jerusalem.

VII

Pious Ambition

In the desert the only distraction was sky. Every overheated day reminded you of your human frailty. The quiet was like a tomb's. The early Christian philosophers judged all that to the good since they believed the valley was close to heaven, somehow open to it, in the sense that your every act was exposed in all that bright light. You were the actor, the valley was the stage. Someone in heaven could watch how you coped. Father Chrisostomos Tavoulareas said he had wanted the quiet. By earthly standards he was coping well.

He never told me much about his past except to say his decision to become a priest was made at an early age. Some unspecified family problem when he was a boy had led him to the safekeeping of the church. As a young priest he lived in Jerusalem, then at a monastery in Bethlehem, but wanted more solitude. Too many people in Bethlehem. Too much commotion. Mar Saba, the cliff-hanging monastery where the population was limited to twelve monks, was what he had in mind. What the Greek Orthodox Patriarchate offered was a monastery in the plain between Jericho and the Dead Sea, where the population was zero.

Hajla, people in Jericho called it. Few had actually seen it. The driver bringing Father Tavoulareas for a first look had to stop a mile away for lack of a road. Hajla had no water, either. No one lived within sight of the building. On even the brightest day it was intimidatingly somber, because the stone was dark and poorly cut, the building from the outside a single large cube, the windows gun slits. Trespassers were scared away by the bats. It was on a dry white plain cut by deep wadis like troughs in a stormy ocean, and hemmed in by the Jordan and the hills. There were only a few islets of true flatness. Father Tavoulareas, by the time I saw the monastery, had made it a private duchy, in which he was the ruler. There were acolytes and large busloads of pilgrims to see the many works of the desert priest.

A monk named Gerasimus had founded the monastery in about 455. He too had come for the quiet. Gerasimus was the famously kindhearted saint, tradition says, who removed a thorn from the foot of a lion and was rewarded with the lion's lasting devotion. At Hajla, Gerasimus created the first desert monastery where monks lived alone during the week—in natural caves, or in small chambers the monks carved into the banks of the wadis, or in freestanding huts built on the plain—and returned to a central building for weekend mass, and to obtain supplies for the week to follow. In that way the monks had both solitude and community. A one-person cell in the wadis would serve for most of the week as a monk's church, refectory, library, bedroom. No cooked food was allowed in the cells. No more than one set of clothing, plus a cloak and a hood. Except on the sabbath, the diet was restricted to bread, water from a nearby spring, and dates. The monks prayed and sought to perfect their self-discipline.

Pilgrims came to see the holy sites and to demonstrate religious faith. They tested their faith on that well-lit stage by depending on God to help them survive the hardships, and they followed predictable routes.

One of the pilgrim highways led, of course, to Jericho and the Jordan. The monasteries evolved into rest stops, the only safe or comfortable shelter. Pilgrims contributed what they could, or bought baskets the monks wove from palm fronds in their cells; or they acquired holy water, clumps of sanctified earth, or the small flasks of holy oil that were another mainstay of the relics business. The monastic standard of living rose. For their time, the central buildings were large, uncrowded, and built with the finest materials. Only a monastery or the household of the notably rich could afford a tile roof. A private home was unlikely to have imported marble, stucco decorations, frescoes. Becoming a monk gave you security and, perhaps, a more comfortable material life than in the secular world, and it gave you prestige; and this is to leave aside all matters of the spirit. In this era—the fifth, sixth, and early seventh centuries—monasticism crested in the Judean desert.

In the 1980s, Yizhar Hirschfeld, an Israeli, spent much of his time "collecting" monasteries. With his archaeo-colleagues, he would awake at 3:00 A.M. in order to reach the southern half of the valley or the Judean hills by dawn; and for the next five or six hours the researchers hiked, measured, sketched, drank coffee, photographed. "Then home," Hirschfeld said. "Siesta time." The work sufficed for Hirschfeld's doctorate, then an exhaustive book, and a doctorate for one of his colleagues.

Hirschfeld identified sixty-four Byzantine monastic sites within the desert. No one is more knowledgeable than Hirschfeld about the settings or the living arrangements of the monks. At Hajla, during the sixth century, you were within two miles of twinned monasteries called Elias, one mile from the scattered cells of the monastery Calamon, less than a mile from the monastery Pyrgoi. Within an hour's walk were the monasteries Chorembe, Soubiba, Petrus, Penthucla, St. John: all of them in the small scrubby wilderness between Jericho and the Dead Sea. They were largely apart from the world but together in their isolation.

In the wadis near Hajla, Hirschfeld rediscovered about a dozen of the small cells inhabited during the age of Gerasimus. I wanted to find the most striking of them, a group of five cells that was carved high in a cliff. In Hirschfeld's photographs, the cliff was opposite a copse of palm trees. Find the palms by pacing off a grid, I decided, then narrow the search for the monks' cells, though I needn't have been so serious about it. The palms were the only trees to be found near Hajla. They grew from a seep hidden in a wadi; and just there the landscape seemed to dive in a free fall, tearing away one bank of the wadi but leaving the other to tower over the trees. The surviving bank was the cliff. The cliff top was as spongy as fresh cake. I lowered myself from the crumbly edge by my fingertips, then just dropped, my small leap of faith, to land somewhat shakily on the ledge the monks had made, twenty or so feet above the ground, in the cliff face. The ledge was their sidewalk. The cliff face was soft marl, striated and milky, like whipped batter in a giant bowl. It powdered hands white, shoes white: everything was white as if floured. In the fifth or sixth century, the monks had carved, scooped, whittled the marl to make cells roughly three feet deep, seven feet across, six feet high. In each one is a low shelflike niche that served as a place to sit, and at least one small window. From their cells the monks looked out on a world of white marl with a pocket of dull green around the seep and a background of washed blue sky striped with a darker blue from the mountains of Moab. The world was a few small patches of color nearly lost in a field of white.

And some found even that insufficiently ascetic. The monk George, living in Wadi Kelt, restricted his diet to the crumbs from the communal Sunday meal, table sweepings he molded into balls that he baked in the sun. The monk Chariton insisted on staying awake most of each night to read aloud from the Psalms. Gerasimus himself had lived alone near the Dead Sea on a diet of wild plants. Tradition says Sabas lived alone for five years in one of the caves that became Mar Saba. In the end, though, these self-effacing men became members of large communities and in some case their founders. Gerasimus, and those like him, concluded that the truly solitary life was less exemplary, or impossible. A life truly alone in the Judean desert would have made for inspiring biography, but living it was too hard. Even in striving for abnegation, a monk was better off setting modest goals. Whatever our images of a desert hermit, only the most determined Byzantine monks lived entirely alone in the valley.

The Jews in the valley coexisted with the monks or usually tried to. A synagogue was built near Ein es Sultan during the sixth century, and another was built a few miles north at the long-established community called Na'aran. In monasticism's earlier days some of the Jews and monks near Na'aran fought each other in a dispute that was perhaps overtly about religion, or about land, or over the water the communities had to share; the chronicler does not say. (If the dispute sounds uncannily familiar, it should, because of reenactments during the mid-1990s. Jewish settlers have marched en masse to the remains of the Na'aran synagogue and—more often—come to the remains of the synagogue near Ein es Sultan, to protest Israel's ceding of land to Palestinians. The disputes over religion, land, and water have never adjourned.)

Sometime after the sixth century Na'aran and its synagogue were abandoned, then entirely forgotten. They were rediscovered in 1918 by an artillery shell. The Turkish army was firing against an encampment of British invaders. An errant shell struck an undistinguished patch of vegetation, exploded open a crater, and in that way uncovered parts of the sixth-century synagogue. To the unknown gunner goes the credit for being the first to excavate Na'aran.

In the seventh century, Palestine was invaded by Persians and then by the new armies of Islam. Most of the monasteries were abandoned and sacked; the monks were killed or went into hiding. At the end of the eleventh century the Crusaders made their violent arrival in Jerusalem, and monasticism began a temporary revival. The stones from whatever was left of Hajla went into the construction of a new, second Hajla. It stood a few hundred feet from the site of the first, the building that had been known to Gerasimus. At nearby Calamon, the wave of pilgrims that followed the Crusaders began to attribute miracles to a painting of Jesus. Two churches were built on the highest cliff overlooking Ein es Sultan. The medieval pilgrims believed that mountain to be the place where Jesus had fasted forty days; and it was at that high place, monks began to say, that the devil had tried to tempt Jesus by giving him a glimpse of all the physical wonders of the world. So here was the Mount of Temptation. To reach the two churches, pilgrims crawled up a steep path on their hands and knees. And almost every pilgrim, whatever the hardships, sought to reach the Jordan. Nowhere else was the record of miracles as fresh, as rich, so well attested. In Byzantine times, it was said, the river had reversed its course and stood wondrously still whenever the priests blessed the water at the beginning of the baptismal service. The river would not resume its flow, it was said, until the priests finished their prayers. Anyone entering the water sick had emerged healed. Anyone healthy and devout was rendered stronger. The devout had written that it was so. For medieval pilgrims, Byzantine times seemed nearly as miraculous as the days of Jesus.

The final defeat of the Crusaders brought the monasteries into a longer season of ruin. By the fifteenth century, Felix Fabri, the pilgrim from the German city of Ulm, would remark that the woodwork at Hajla—the "new," second Hajla—was about to collapse. The whole building seemed to shake with every step of the pilgrims. Animals wandered through the rooms. Everyone was frightened by the hiss of snakes and by stories of bats capable of biting off a human nose. "Men who have long noses are in greater danger than others," said Fabri. "When we heard this, we kept careful watch over ourselves, covering our noses with our hands." Rather than spend the night in that place, Fabri chose to ride a long distance in the dark to another camp.

Claude Conder, in the 1870s, knew the name Hajla when he was slowly riding about the plain as head of the Palestine Exploration Fund survey party. No one, though, knew much about the building he found. The stout wall surrounding it had crumbled away on one side, and the leftovers of the structure amounted to two large chapels, a deep cistern, an underground third chapel, and frescoes depicting Jesus, who looked down from a dome, and numerous saints. Most of the figures and medieval inscriptions had been defaced but it was a "fine old religious fortress," Conder reported, and he spent two days measuring and sketching. He was well-read in the classic pilgrim literature (so much so that he contributed later to a well-received series of translations rendering the pilgrims' stories into English) and knew that a monastery associated with Gerasimus had once stood somewhere near Jericho. But he assumed the building was to be found at some unknown elsewhere, not at Hajla. He wrongly believed the monastery of Gerasimus was still awaiting its discoverer.

Conder returned to Hajla more than once, over a period of several years, but the visits gave him no pleasure. A century in advance of Father Tavoulareas, a solitary monk had come from Mar Saba to try to return the monastery to usefulness, but he did not impress the Englishman. In 1882 Conder found a larger delegation of monks busy rebuilding and redecorating. They began by obliterating the medieval frescoes and inscriptions.

Father Tavoulareas engineered a water supply for the building in the 1980s, and the Patriarchate convinced secular authorities of the need for a road. A donkey path was widened to accommodate the buses bringing pilgrims and it was paved when someone tired of the buses whipping up dust storms. It was the same pilgrim highway known in the fifteenth century to Felix Fabri. It leads to the sites known in the fifth century to Gerasimus. The only radical change was the effort required of the pilgrim.

One no longer needed to crawl up the Mount of Temptation but walked on a wide zigzag path. "Going upstairs," Abu Issa called the hike. He had worked thirty years in the monastery—upstairs—until retirement and now lived at the base of the cliff in one of the sturdier-looking huts. It was half mud-brick, half stone. Attached to one end was a ramshackle shed that the dust colored the same powdery brown as the mountain, like weak sandy tea. Abu Issa seemed hale but a little bored with retirement. His paunch severely tested the stitches of a *galabiyah* colored that same dusty brown. To amuse himself, he clocked the tourists gasping up the path. Ten minutes if the hiker were fit and oblivious to scenery. During his harrowing climb, Felix Fabri had encountered a fearsome man armed with a club who demanded the pilgrims pay him a toll. Abu Issa, when he felt energetic, hawked colas and bottled lemonade from a battered refrigerator in the shed.

From the bottom of the cliff, the monastery was a small papery nest, something hornets had suspended from a fissure in the rock. Or just a wide stripe someone had painted in a long dry stroke of brown onto a dark brown background. The monastery looked no more substantial than a smear of color; it was a shimmering weightless band of brown light. A priest wearing a black cassock opened the black metaled door, but long before he reached it, you heard him shuffling down a long flight of steps in the syncope of the elderly. He always leaned outside to see if anyone was climbing the path behind you.

Some of the rooms were caves inhabited off and on by monks since the middle of the fourth century; the other rooms were built during the 1890s and were cantilevered into open air. Whenever the monks fled, or died out, shepherds stabled sheep in the caves and used them as silos for corn, as hideouts from tax collectors or from soldiers forcibly recruiting young men for the Turks' wars in the Balkans. During the nineteenth century a small number of Coptic monks would come from Jerusalem at Lent to fast near the cave where they said Jesus had fasted. Now, the switchback path passed the metaled door and formed the corridor between the caves and the rooms cantilevered from the face.

Past the monastery, the path resumed its zigzag to the summit.

It was a temporary home of the devil, in some ways magic, also sanctified ground. On that summit the Hasmoneans built a fortress. A Dead Sea Scroll names the summit as a hiding place for tons of gold and silver. In the twelfth century, a pilgrim-monk writes of seeing on the summit the rock where the devil sat while tempting Jesus. On the summit was one of the churches to which the pilgrims crawled.

Heaped together there is a junkyard's worth of stone capitals and broken columns—everything that is left of the church. In 1914, the Patriarchate began building another sanctuary but got not much farther than a wall that the cliff top wears like a jaunty hat. Beyond the wall is a foreboding ditch quarried in bedrock and the stump of a stone tower; they are remains of the Hasmonean fort.

And from that summit, you look down on a small bright paradise. It is one of the most beautiful views of the valley and one of the most deceptive. Paradise has iridescent banana groves and jeweled irrigation ponds that reflect the sunlight. Grackles dive-bomb crevices in the rock, swallows attack miniature trees in a miniaturized world, so high is the cliff. You grow invisible wings; staring down you are in steady flight. The great mound by Ein es Sultan is flattened to a small ruffle in the ground. A crescent of silvery water is the Dead Sea. A valley without saltiness or heat, a beckoning false world of rich green and precious silver.

The priest, after a minute or two, always sighed or began to pace. He would knead his beard and fidget in every other way available to him in the monastery while visitors chattered about the view from the windows. Everyone was waved back along the stone corridor to the door. He would wordlessly lean outside, again, to see how long he would have before someone else pounded on that door.

Father Tavoulareas built a world made comfortable by servants and admirers and privacy and space. One of the young men living at Hajla served tea and apologized for Tavoulareas being absent; there was a problem with the water supply or with the planting of one of the fields, the young man was unsure. Another half-dozen men commuted from Jericho to do most of the manual labor, and three or four young women from Greece lived at the monastery and seemed to tend the chapels. For the women the hardest work was to ignore glances from those men. Showing me some of the rooms upstairs, the young man pointed out icons and then a large portrait of Tavoulareas, his portrait larger than any saint's.

He wasn't absent after all, just sitting outside and reading a diocesan newspaper. He sat next to an aviary filled with doves and canaries that never stopped singing. An aviary was as typical of the valley as a giraffe. Given the incongruity of the birds, and then the presence of another young man who held a bowl overflowing with fruit, and the arrival of a third with coffee, Tavoulareas seemed less the solitary priest than a potentate enjoying his domain, an impression the languidness of his greeting did nothing to dispel. He stayed seated. He nodded his hello. His beard was full and dark, his hair halfway down his back, his fingers stained by cigarettes. He told an odd story about an argument of some sort having given him a headache that had now lasted several days, as if he were under the power of a curse; he had fainted and, to relieve that sensation of terrible pressure in his head, he had allowed one of the young men to bleed him with a deep cut on one ear. His blood came out black, he said. He spoke with the extreme softness of someone accustomed to having the full attention of his audience. He found Jericho attractive for its smallness and poverty: there was much a willing priest could do. There were immodest remarks about his donations of clothes to young men and to the sick, and the jobs created at Hajla. If water could be obtained to irrigate all the property, the staff might grow to forty. Authority seemed more attractive than solitude. One could do more than open the door for visitors to a mountain chapel. "We are supposed to work and improve."

Gerasimus' Hajla—the first Hajla—is thought to be a short distance to the east. After the Crusades the building was "lost"; it was rediscovered in 1903 by an insightful scholar named Jean Louis Féderlin when he came to the valley, but was lost again until Yizhar Hirschfeld's work in the late 1980s. East of the "new" Hajla were two long arms of earth rounded and low like a freshly filled grave and curved like arms of a horseshoe. Unless you were cued to search for it, you could walk across the horseshoe without detecting it. Claude Conder either did not know to look or, more likely, saw nothing there to interest him, saw nothing he knew how to recognize. You need to be on hands and knees. Brownish pebbles embedded in the dirt turn into pottery shards. A speck of red, pulled clear and dusted off, becomes a broken handle. I should have left the fragment there but did not. I do not know whether the fragment is truly from the time of Gerasimus but I choose to believe it is very old; and one face of it is fluted and makes the shard comfortable to grip and, in some inexplicable way, comforting. Tavoulareas knew only vaguely of there having been an older Hajla before "his" Hajla but was unsure where.

A young shepherd was on the path between Hajla and Calamon and he insisted on sharing tea. His hospitality was unfeigned. He looked to be no more than thirteen and was thin and caked with dirt, and he said his name was Dhib. Through vigorous nods, we concurred this was a fine, wet, grassy, empty day to be a sheep. He built a fire with twigs, and his black kettle held just enough water to fill his one cup, which he vigorously polished with his fingers. He refused everything but the last few sips of the tea.

Calamon, like Hajla, had depended on a small freshwater spring the monks knew from the Book of Joshua. In Old Testament times the spring, and the settlement that was presumably nearby, were called Beth-Hoglah. The spring marked part of the boundary between the tribes of Benjamin and Judah. The name Hoglah would be preserved as . . . Hajla. Hence the current name of the spring: Ein Hajla. It had made life viable on the plain. "The water wells up in a masonry well about six feet in diameter," Claude Conder reported. "It is a dark blue colour, but fresh and cool."

A forest of high reeds marks the place. The masonry enclosure was almost flush with the ground but intact, the water barely percolating. What remained of Calamon was one cave. Another path had led to the two monasteries that shared the name Elias. No one knew of any trace of them until the PEF survey team, in 1873, found on the plain "walls and heaps of masonry." In 1903, after detecting traces of a courtyard and garden, Jean Louis Féderlin suggested that place was in fact Elias. The church pillars were said to have been carted away to Riha as construction material for a hostel intended for Russian pilgrims on their way to the Jordan. By chance, Charles Clermont-Ganneau—archaeologist, expert paleographer—saw the hostel being built. He had observed laborers in the shambles that was Riha using stones engraved with the cross. Stones probably from Elias.

The hostel is still standing. People on the street shrug when asked about Russians, and know the building only by one or another of its many subsequent lives. You are directed to the local UN offices, which used to be offices for the British, which used to be offices for the Turks, which used to be the Russian hostel. It is stone, of course, and the interior has overwide corridors and a hospital's starkness. Cyrillic lettering almost hidden by grime welcomes you to the Russian Spiritual Mission.

As for Elias, everything has disappeared from the plain except for an earthen berm and small scattered stones.

The river of pilgrims always flowed toward the Jordan. They would spend the night at Jericho and be awakened at 3:00 A.M. and reach the traditional baptism site shortly after dawn. They donned robes they hoped to use as burial shrouds, or stripped naked; some brought soap and worked up a lather. A typical nineteenth-century Easter at the riverbank produced this log of crime and accident: one pilgrim robbed by Bedouin when he fell behind, one pilgrim accidentally shot to death by a soldier, an unspecified number of pilgrims injured by falling off horses or donkeys, plus three drownings. From the 1850s until the outbreak of World War I, the largest number of pilgrims were Russians. They were poor even by the standards of Palestine and were making the one great voyage of their lives. Unknowingly they were also carrying out the czars' imperial desire to compete with Britain and France in influencing the Ottomans. From Russia came royal grants and public subscriptions that paid for the rebuilding of monasteries and the construction of the hostels; and on behalf of the pilgrims, Russia, like an imperial travel agent, negotiated group rates with steamship lines.

The hardships were endless but still the Russians came: in 1900, more than ten thousand Russian pilgrims. A few years later a British journalist named Stephen Graham sailed with pilgrims leaving from ports on the Black Sea, and wrote a respectful, harrowing account of faith and anxiety. What impressed him was the pilgrims' fervor. For food, most of them had only the bread crusts they had saved in the weeks before the trip. During the fifteen days the ship needed to reach Jaffa, a storm shattered the masts and washed away one of the lifeboats. An enterprising priest declared that his prayers to St. Nicholas had saved the ship, and the priest harvested bountiful cash from thankful passengers. A train took everyone from Jaffa to Jerusalem. From Jerusalem, everyone walked to Jericho.

Stephen Graham was directed to the stone hostel there, as were a thousand other pilgrims. The hostel could comfortably accommodate fifty people. On this occasion it uncomfortably accommodated several hundred. In the morning everyone walked to the river, and since heaven just then seemed closer, all inhibition disappeared. "For a whole hour," Stephen Graham wrote with evident awe, "there was a scene that baffles description, the most extraordinary mingling of men and women all in white, dry and gleaming, or wet and dripping." Everyone rested at Hajla during the afternoon or toured the Mount of Temptation. Those unable to contemplate another night at the hostel began the long walk back to Jerusalem.

Dr. Amba Abraham, the Coptic Patriarch of Jerusalem, graciously ferried me to the river by air-conditioned Mercedes-Benz. Dr. Abraham, recently of Zurich and new to his job, wished to see the Coptic monastery that stood on the shore of the river. There were six monasteries or convents within sight of the water, all of them closed since the 1967

Arab-Israeli war and, at the time of our visit, part of a vast minefield. Shmuel Hamburger, representing the government of Israel, shared the car to guide the driver between the mines.

Religious rivalries, as if nourished by water, thrived at the riverbank. The Greek Orthodox Church owned property on one side of the road leading to the baptismal site; the Franciscans held title to the land on the other side. The Coptic, Romanian Orthodox, Syriac Orthodox, Russian Orthodox, and Ethiopian churches clung to other territories downriver. The Greek Orthodox Church owned the only path descending to the water and allowed no other sect to use it.

Amba Abraham, fingering a large, jeweled golden cross hanging from his neck, listened as Shmuel Hamburger pointed out each building. The Romanian convent was no larger than a guard shack. The Russian Orthodox monastery had been reduced to a doorframe whose lintel supported a cross tilted thirty degrees. The Coptic monastery was a small concrete barracks surrounded by weeds. It had been empty since the three resident monks fled to Egypt, in '67.

Dr. Abraham unfolded himself from his car and paced on the roadway. Every few steps he was reminded not to stray. He asked Hamburger to see to it that signs were erected in the field of weeds to proclaim clearly this to be property of the Coptic Church. He asked too that Hamburger arrange for a path to be cleared from the monastery to the river.

Erecting signs, said Hamburger, would be impossible until the minefields were cleared. Clearing a path to the river was out of the question for the same reason.

The patriarch repeated his requests in the gentlest of voices. "I will appreciate it," he said.

Hamburger explained a second time.

"Not so close to the building will be fine, but I want the signs," the patriarch said. A mine explosion seemed to have already rendered both men deaf.

Hamburger promised to inform higher authority. Nothing was said of the absolute certainty that the requests would be denied.

"Just for a few hours, the path to the river," the patriarch said. "Is it not a simple matter, going to the water?"

In September 1874, after his three-month leave in Britain, Claude Conder returned to Palestine. The trip was fast—only nine days. "I am in harness again, well and jolly," he writes his mother from Jerusalem. Habib, the head servant since the expedition's earliest days, duly flattered Conder by saying that during his absence the survey party had been like a family without a father. Before returning, Conder had rather gracelessly reminded the PEF of his own hard work, the burdens of responsibility, his imperfect health. He lobbied the PEF to send a replacement for poor Charles Drake and recommended that the new man be clearly designated as the junior officer. The new man, he said, should take the dross and in that way free the commander for whatever demanded experience, intelligence, expert judgment. And Conder tried to influence the PEF's selection by suggesting a young officer he liked and knew to be available.

Great friends, those two. They had met in 1867 in the London house of the Reverend George Frost, renowned specialist in preparing young men for army entrance exams. The two young men were enrolled in the same crash course before taking the exam for the Royal Military Academy at Woolwich. Thus Conder made the acquaintance of Horatio Herbert Kitchener. On the entrance exam, Conder placed ninth; a year later Kitchener placed twenty-eighth. At Woolwich, Conder introduced his friend to the spare-time study of Hebrew and to the idea that interesting work might await anyone clever enough to wrangle an assignment to Palestine. It was still a place mostly blank on the maps.

Now, in 1874, Conder was campaigning on Kitchener's behalf to have him appointed the survey party's number two. It was the largest mistake Conder ever made in regard to his own career. Take it as evidence of how badly Conder misjudged the nature of their friendship and the personality of his friend.

The kindest thing one can say about Herbert Kitchener—as a person, not as a military leader—is that he rarely let himself down. *He* was going to succeed; he was determined to see to that. He almost always reached his goals. Joining the PEF survey party happened to be one of the small, early ones. He was future Governor-General of the Sudan, a favorite of Queen Victoria, future commander-in-chief in India, de facto ruler of Egypt, Secretary of State for War. "Thorough" was the family motto and it was a good fit: he was thoroughly, wholly ambitious.

His mother was already sickly when he was born in 1850, and Kitchener was fourteen when tuberculosis killed her. His father was imperious, foulmouthed, a horrifically strict disciplinarian at home, an army officer who believed himself shortchanged in his career. He commanded his household like a drill sergeant. The son inherited from the father a willingness to flatter and to pull every string and to go behind the back of a superior, if that might advance one's career. After Woolwich, Kitchener served briefly with the French in the Franco-Prussian War, so anxious was he to begin active service and to break away from the pack of his classmates. Back in Britain, he was reprimanded by his superiors for having tried to fight someone else's war, but they admired his spirit. And it was hard not to be impressed when he came into a room: Kitchener was six feet, two inches tall and handsome by anyone's standard. He was exceptionally neat and so calm he might have been bloodless. His aloofness was always taken for boundless self-confidence. In 1871 he was commissioned as a lieutenant in the Royal Engineers and began specialized studies at the army's school for engineering. As a new graduate, his first assignment was to train enlisted men in Britain. He was terribly bored.

By summer 1874, he considered volunteering for the grim business of subduing a revolt in West Africa—anything to escape the tedium. It was the summer Conder was on leave in Britain and wanting a new number two. Palestine, Conder assured his friend, was a reasonable place. It was not so near the edge of the map as West Africa, so a better career step. After Conder's lobbying, the Royal Engineers agreed to loan Kitchener to the PEF.

Conder was lonely, anxious, "very melancholy." The survey no longer had the character of a boy's adventure. He seems to have felt the full force of Charles Drake's death only after he had to go through Drake's personal effects in Jerusalem: tents, the tarpaulins that had been so long in arriving, a compass, and Drake's little shelf of books.

He felt the loss again when he had to resume the fieldwork, because he missed Drake's companionship. He invited Dr. Thomas Chaplin, who had tried but failed to save Drake, to travel with the survey party. Conder wanted company and a sense of safety. "The story of poor Drake's last days is a very troubling one," he writes Walter Besant, "and I feel his loss very much now that I realize it."

He was impatient to be joined by "old Kitchie." Much-loved Jonah had been left in Britain (though during Conder's absence the other men expanded the dog pack to fifteen, reduced by Conder on his return to four). Even without Kitchener, the party was mapping about eighty square miles a month. Conder attributed that fine rate of progress to good weather and countryside that was less trying than the valley. He was traveling with three British NCOs, eleven servants, two mule drivers, two elaborately costumed soldiers lent by the Ottomans, nine horses, seven mules, plus the dogs. The local sheikhs loaned guides for a fee and agreed to talk to the servants about the place-names.

Conder was also severely lovesick. In Britain he had fallen in love with a young woman, a true *coup de foudre:* seeing her for the first time some years before, as she came around the corner of a staircase, Conder felt he had been struck in the head. He was struck again by the warm comforting thought of her on that frightening day in Jericho when he was surrounded by his feverish comrades and praying for his life. He resolved in Jericho that if he could survive, he could summon the courage to woo her.

Because he was a gentleman, his letters are unfailingly, maddeningly discreet. In the first letters home the woman is nameless. Later she becomes "D." Finally "Miss Davis." He expresses more anxiety and a greater sense of risk about courting her than about the mapmaking in Palestine. "I have met my fate and must await the result as the most important crisis of my life," he writes home about his chances of persuading Miss Davis to marry him. "I did not believe myself capable of such feeling."

His are the consuming worries of someone lonely and obsessed by the conviction that he has a small, real chance for complete, perfect happiness—but only this one chance, once. For him she is "some silent temple or church," and he fears he would profane her. She is holy, his lowly self is as contemptible as gin. He sees no realistic hope of saving enough money to be able to satisfy the expectations of her family. Miss Davis' brother writes to ask that Conder not press at this time his wish to marry. Nothing is said to let him hope the family's opinion of him will change. Some of the correspondence has been lost, but from time to time Conder summarizes for his mother the view of each party. There are new calculations about his financial prospects and speculations about the strategy of the brother. In a letter home "D" becomes "my Darling"—a phrase that does more than the most dramatic of his reports about Palestine to make Claude Conder endearingly human. The terrible fright at Jericho had made him want something more than success. He is never more alive, vulnerable, or sympathetic than in the letters about "D."

Finally, he decided against making a formal proposal. His argument to himself was that he should protect Miss Davis' peace of mind; it seemed the gentlemanly thing to do. However, he lacked peace of mind himself. In letters home he regresses to sounding like a very young man unable to stop the excruciating self-torture. Then he reversed himself. He proposed marriage, and the all-important letter was sent from Jerusalem to one of his relatives with instructions to forward it to Miss Davis. He was telling her "that I loved her from the first day I saw her & shall till I die." He did not demand an immediate response, indeed did not want one. He liked having something important to hope for. "I am not anxious for a definite reply," he tells his mother, "unless it be entirely all I could wish." He steeled himself for the wait.

Herbert Kitchener had meanwhile received formal instructions from the Palestine Exploration Fund. He was told to consider no ruin too small or insignificant to be examined. As was now traditional, the PEF also requested that he do his utmost to hold down expenses. On the fourteenth of November 1874, Kitchener's boat reached Alexandria, giving him his first look at the Middle East, and he sailed onward to Jaffa, to arrive on the fifteenth at sunrise. In a letter to his sister, Millie, he sounds both entranced and determined not to let his feelings show. For most of his life he would cast himself as a person immune to surprise. "It was glorious more from associations than anything else[,] seeing for the first time that land which must be the most interesting for any Christian," he writes Millie about the approach to Jaffa. "The sun rose in a golden halo behind the hills and we rushed towards it through the deep blue sea."

He rode all night to Jerusalem and was welcomed by Conder, who declared himself "awfully thankful" to see his old classmate. Conder had been a year ahead at Woolwich, two years ahead in Palestine. He must have looked forward to resuming his role of learned elder. To avoid the previous winter's horrors, he had rented an airy, well-maintained house in Jerusalem a few steps from the Chaplin residence. Rain and cold forced the two officers to cancel a first working trip to the south, though neither of them was disappointed since they had gained more time to relax in each other's company. On Christmas Eve they attended midnight mass at the Church of the Nativity in Bethlehem, and what impressed Kitchener most at the church was the crowding, so severe that it caused people to faint. The ritual seemed secondary. When several women were in danger of being trampled, the Englishmen rescued them by directing their hunting crops against the mob. Dr. and Mrs. Chaplin invited the men for Christmas dinner in Jerusalem. And a few days later, Conder organized "a little visit" to Jericho.

Maybe Conder envisioned the Jericho trip as a way to show off his knowledge of the valley. Or to explain to the new man what the survey party had already accomplished and what Charles Warren had done at the great mound even earlier. Or to put to rest his fear and bad memories of that place. Maybe it was Kitchener who proposed the expedition, the better to satisfy a curiosity about the reality behind the famous place-name and to begin useful work. Whatever the case, it's striking that in his few notes made in advance of the trip, Conder regarded it as a jaunt to a place where nothing untoward had occurred, and where he could enjoy himself; and striking too is that he ignored his own advice that the valley was to be avoided at all costs until the rainy season ended, for important reasons of health. Ignoring the past, he and Kitchener spent New Year's Day 1875 at Ein es Sultan.

Compared to Jerusalem, it was warm, and dry of course, and the vegetation by the spring was high and thick enough to form a canopy over the water. Kitchener inherited Drake's responsibility for taking photographs and diligently practiced his picture taking. Claude Conder, explorer-traveler, posed for him at the spring. He half reclines on rocks in a jungly thicket of vegetation. The explorer-traveler wears a tweed jacket over two or more layers of silk and wool shirts, and hunting breeches and knee boots. One hand is clasped—lightly, delicately—by the other. His face is long and boyishly smooth with a mustache drooping to his chin. He modestly looks into the middle distance instead of into the camera; the slowness of the shutter freezes the flowing water to a milky blur.

Ten days later it was Conder's duty to inform the PEF that Lieutenant Kitchener was seriously ill. Conder wrote "Jericho fever" as the diagnosis, crossed that out, substituted "remittent fever"—probably malaria. Dr. Chaplin judged the case to be grave but predicted the patient would survive.

"If there is the smallest possible risk, I shall order him home," Conder told Walter Besant. "We must not kill another man if we can help it." Conder was torn between wanting to avoid another tragedy and desperately wanting Kitchener's company. He dreaded another bout of what he called the "Blue Devils," the dull awful loneliness that would surely infect him again if he did not have the companionship of someone he trusted. Someone as accommodating and forgiving as Drake had been.

Kitchener was resting comfortably in a room with a fire, now had little or no fever, and had someone watching over him every night. So he should stay for now, said Conder, since the new lieutenant seemed so well suited to his assignment. Plus well suited to Conder. "We are as opposite as possible in all opinions," Conder writes home, "yet have still the old sympathy which neither of us can give a reason for. His illness has bound us close together."

To give Kitchener more time to recover, Conder and the survey team left Jerusalem without him at the end of February, to map the territory between Hebron and the Dead Sea. In twelve days the party sketched the remains of Masada (the fortress known from Flavius Josephus), examined the oasis of En-Gedi on the shore of the Dead Sea, and mapped an impressive total of 330 square miles. There were the expected difficulties with the steep terrain and with weather. On the ride from Masada to Hebron, a storm blew the party's elderly guide off his pony, twice.

The Englishmen tied him onto the pony. Two of the mule drivers disappeared in the rain and wind, as did some of the dogs. Conder expressed relief dear Jonah was safe in England instead of exposed to the storm. What made Conder proudest was his economy: twelve days work for only seven pounds in baksheesh. In his report he congratulated himself for his management skills. Expenses were calculated to be one pence per acre; it was something everyone in London could appreciate. Most of the work was done, he assured his mother. He promised that the work to come would be easier, pleasant, smooth.

In mid-March Kitchener, tired of convalescence in Jerusalem, returned to the party's camp in company with a fox terrier named Looloo and the servant Habib. With his new reinforcements, Conder led everyone west from Hebron across Palestine's wide belly to the Mediterranean. When they reached the coast the Englishmen had the pleasure of daily baths in the sea. Lucky for Conder that Kitchener was now fully fit. He rescued Conder from a powerful undertow sweeping him out to sea, and Conder believed that if not for his old classmate, he would have drowned. Kitchener had rendered the first of two great services to Conder.

Even at this early stage of his career, Herbert Kitchener was distinctly cool. He was not easily liked. Conder attributed his friend's striking remoteness to his never having gotten over the death of his mother; ever since that tragedy Kitchener had wanted to shelter himself from strong feelings, so did his best to show none. He radiated calculation. He could sometimes appear unnaturally calm. Those were qualities a fighting army valued in an officer. He may have already made his decision to allow nothing that was merely friendship or loyalty to interfere with his career. While Conder spent the spring worrying over his chance of marrying Miss Davis, Kitchener told his friend he intended never to marry. His love was for advancement. Conder, in mid-June, was in any case still waiting for a response from "D."

On the tenth of July, the servants were erecting the tents near the town of Safed, in the Galilee. A few villagers arrived to watch the exotic foreigners. As usual, Conder dispatched a request to the local governor for soldiers to guard the camp and to ride with the party in the countryside. Half dressed, and resting on his bedroll, Conder heard the servants bargaining with the locals over this or that service—and this too was usual. Then the bargaining escalated into cursing.

The local sheikh had fingered a tent and called the servants "dogs." The servants were Christian, the villagers Muslim. One servant then claimed a revolver had disappeared from the tent. The servant insisted on searching the robes of the sheikh, and the curses became louder. When Conder approached, the sheikh grabbed him by the throat. Conder punched him, knocking him to the ground. He stood up. Conder punched him again. When the sheikh drew a knife, the servants grabbed it and tied his hands behind his back.

What the official reports of these events lack are the curses being spit out and the shouting, the confusion as people stumbled through an unmade camp, and the Englishmen's fright at seeing their worst fear being realized—a fight enlisting religious pride. The reports lack the sense of the events' terrific speed, as if a horse were rearing and left you only enough time to know—seeing sky, now ground very close—you were falling hard. Almost anyone would have preferred a serious case of fever to open conflict between Christians and Muslims. Not so many years earlier, in 1860, Christians had attacked Muslims in Beirut; Muslims in Damascus attacked Christians. More than twenty thousand people were slaughtered by the time the rioting ended.

Several hundred villagers answered the sheikh's cries for help. Stones hit Kitchener, hit two corporals, hit most of the servants. Conder was armed with a hunting crop, Kitchener with a walking stick. "I told them they were mad," Conder said, "and would be severely punished if they struck an Englishman." Someone with a nail-studded club struck Conder on the head, and the blood pouring from the wounds half blinded him. A blow to Conder's neck knocked him to the ground.

Kitchener fended off more attackers with his walking stick but then was wounded in one arm. But he had given Conder time to rouse himself. A scimitar missed a servant and sliced through the ropes of a tent. A stone struck Habib in the throat. The other servants were beaten and kicked. As commander, Conder gave the order to retreat. Kitchener heard a bullet whistle past, was chased by the villager waving the scimitar, but was the last to leave. He had rendered his second great service to his friend.

Conder saw within a few minutes the approach of their rescuers, after the survey party regrouped on a hill. They were the soldiers he had asked the local governor to send as guards. The stoning stopped; the villagers' clubs disappeared. He must have felt shame as well as relief—from the hill his enemies seemed to be young boys, harmless-looking against a group of well-equipped foreigners, and now he was being rescued by the Turks, whom he so disdained. Conder pridefully insisted the party keep watch from the hill throughout the night and did not lead them away until morning.

He was feverish. Kitchener sent to London Conder's report about the melee, and added alarming information about the injuries, and a doctor certified that the Englishmen were unfit for work. They left their camp and moved into a convent near Haifa. Conder informed the PEF that to continue the survey was impossible until the villagers were punished. Kitchener, too, wanted the party to go home, because of an epidemic of cholera that was emptying the countryside of people, and which seemed as dangerous as the recent events at Safed. The clearest signal that the expedition was at a temporary end was Conder's decision to send the party's mules back to their owner. All the survey equipment went into storage at the convent. Conder told his employers he would retrieve the equipment when he returned to Palestine, sometime in the spring.

There were alarming news accounts of the attack, letters of reassurance to the families of the men, contacts between the PEF and the Foreign Office, between the Foreign Office and the Sublime Porte. It was agreed there would be a trial. In Haifa, Conder rashly declared his unwillingness to resume command of the survey until justice was done. Perhaps his wounds affected his judgment. He assumed he was irreplaceable.

"My little army stuck to me to a man," he writes his mother. "The natives of course lost their heads but the coolness and steadiness of the English men and the way they obeyed my orders was beautiful. As for old K, nothing could be better than his coolness and courage. He saved my life and I hope you will write and thank him."

Conder said his feverishness was not just because of Safed. He had received a response from Miss Davis. He had ridden back to the convent after conferring with the Ottoman governor and felt so weak he could barely dismount, when he found her letter. Her answer to the proposal of marriage was no. She said she could never love him. His response will seem bizarre only to someone who has never been obsessed or never suffered from the wishful thought that the lover about to slip away is the one salve for all pain—and this is not to say Conder was wrong to believe she was his best chance for happiness. He decided he should not give up hope about her. He reasoned that she would think about him more, not less, because of the hurt she knew she had caused. Then he was angry. He was a freer thinker than Miss Davis; he had truer beliefs; her friends were snobs, and her Presbyterianism not fit for him. Then he was miserable. "I am going to sit down," he writes home from the convent, "and howl."

At the trial, the sheikh from Safed testified that on the tenth of July he had been taking an evening walk. Members of the survey party, he said, had then viciously attacked him. The court chose not to believe the sheikh. Conder and Kitchener sat in the courtroom but found it hard to identify the villagers who had been part of the mob. Sixteen men were eventually convicted of minor offenses and were sentenced, in most cases, to two to three months' imprisonment, and a modest fine was levied against the town of Safed. When the British protested the leniency of the court, the judges added a month to most of the sentences. The dispute over the fine lasted two years. The British demanded £600; the Sublime Porte ordered payment of £340. After many delays, the PEF received £262. Since any further wrangling seemed hopeless, and to hide its frustration, the PEF announced that as a show of goodwill toward the town it would forgo its claim to the rest of the money.

Claude Conder and Herbert Kitchener sailed home in October 1875. That winter, Conder continued to suffer from fever, from strange swellings, and because of his wounds, from sharp pains in his face. He and Kitchener were assigned offices in the Royal Albert Hall. The two lieutenants were to prepare for publication the maps of everything already surveyed and to begin assembling and translating the enormous list of Arabic place-names and to write descriptions of every natural feature and village and ruin and, in effect, to write the natural and archaeological history of Palestine. When his health allowed, Conder lectured to help drum up money for the PEF. His doctors then ordered him to rest at home. Arguing once again about expenses, he was just as cranky in Britain as in the field. He objected to every challenge to his way; when the PEF briefly considered letting go of Kitchener, to save the organization money, Conder sputtered that officers of the Royal Engineers would not accept shabby treatment and would think hard before recommending the PEF to other talented colleagues. It was Kitchener who apologized on Conder's behalf, asked the PEF to burn Conder's letter, suggesting an ill lieutenant should not be held responsible for having spoken his mind.

Everyone—especially Kitchener—was impatient for him to recover. Members of PEF's board knew contributors were more generous when the survey party was in the field and reporting new feats of discovery and courage. But there were more sick leaves, new reports from Palestine about outbreaks of cholera, the unresolved matter of the fine against Safed. The board worried about the loss of public interest and the potentially disastrous loss of money if there were not some clear sign of progress. Progress would be having the survey party back in Palestine. It would be announcing a firm publication date for the maps or for the written narrative. Only one person had the necessary knowledge and experience to describe what the party had done—Conder. Members of the board were unhappy about the pace of his work, furious he was also writing for magazines, furious the Fund was still paying him the handsome salary of an officer working abroad.

Conder intemperately complained again about money.

The member whose loans had kept the organization afloat lost his temper. Reduce Conder's pay, he told Walter Besant. Challenge his pride by taking away his command. "He might tender his resignation, and it would not be a bad thing to us to accept it, and complete the survey under Kitchener who has the spirit of an officer in him, and not of a bargain maker."

The PEF's letter, dated the twenty-ninth of December 1876, informed Lieutenant Conder that he would be remaining in Britain. Acknowledgment was made of the schedule he had submitted for returning to Palestine. But he was to continue his office work. Lieutenant Kitchener, the letter said, would take command of the survey party.

Conder's pay would be reduced since he would no longer be the officer in charge.

Herbert Kitchener reached Palestine in February 1877, without Claude Conder. Kitchener retrieved the survey equipment from the convent, and within a few weeks returned to Safed.

His visit there was timed to coincide with the arrival of a British warship on the coast. This time the village welcomed Kitchener as an honored guest and he spent much of his time receiving obeisant notables. The governor threatened to burn any village that impeded the survey party. So work went well almost everywhere. Kitchener sounded unfailingly able and confident in his dispatches, rarely complained, and lost his temper only once, when the PEF forgot to pay him. For the PEF, he was so much easier to work with than that man Conder. Kitchener made the survey and all success seem his own. He did not mind the limelight or the false impression that he had been present at every discovery.

He was able to give the PEF the news it desired. "I am sure you will be glad to hear that the map is an accomplished fact," he telegraphed on October 2 from Jerusalem, "and six years' work has been finished."

VIII

Dead Sea, Dead Land

The Dead Sea, depending on the light, was a polished sheet of silver or a molten sapphire. It was where in every century including this one people believed the true wilderness began, six hot miles south of Jericho. Gliding down the highway from Jerusalem, you saw the haze and blue. From Jericho, it was a mist. Jericho was the safe haven, the Dead Sea always beautiful, odorous, seemingly without life. After stopping at the shore, I would return to Jericho and find it worldly, wonderfully alive even as everyone slept through the afternoon, but nearly without grace, without beauty. But not threatening like the jeweled lake.

Claude Conder and Herbert Kitchener had been notably incurious about the water and maybe frightened of it. They made a thorough exploration of the shore only where it happened to be close to sites of obvious interest, like Jericho. Otherwise they seemed to regard it as only a dull, necessary border for the maps they would finish in London. In drawing the hilly landscape that was to the west, the survey party, oddly, slightly distorted it. It was a mistake a surveyor could make if he didn't trek through that territory all the way to the shore. With uncharacteristic terseness, the men reported finding "no place of interest in this desert." They were intimidated by the steepness of the hills. Or exhausted. Or put off by the reputation of the water.

What everyone noticed first was the sulfurous stench. It came from some of the nearby springs, which released water plus hydrogen sulfide. In the lake, small but extremely stable gradients of temperature and of salinity prevented the bottommost water from mixing with the topmost—kept them no less separate than if a sheet of steel were between them. The lower water had had no contact with the surface for at least three hundred years, perhaps for thousands. It trapped the sulfides. So the rotten-egg smell lingered.

A tenth-century geographer named the lake the Stinking Sea. The odor began to dissipate in 1979. The Dead Sea was by that time receiving substantially less freshwater than in previous centuries—because of the diversion of Jordan River water for agriculture, a long-lasting drought, the capture of other freshwater sources for drinking water. Surface water in the lake slowly became saltier, thus heavier. In February 1979, the "heavy" water descended. Lighter water rose from the bottom, and all the waters mixed. Hydrogen sulfide that had been more or less trapped under the surface was diluted or escaped. Thus the sulfurous odor was lessened, though it has not disappeared. Since 1979 the water has overturned, and repurged itself of hydrogen sulfide, ten times; if not for several winters with untypically heavy rains, the number of overturnings would be higher. The interruption is as temporary as the rains.

Travelers cataloged other unusual properties. Dead Sea water was greasy to the touch. It was not just salty but bitter. It supported no visible life. Having heard that people could float on the lake, the Roman emperor Vespasian sought proof by ordering men to be thrown in with their hands tied behind their backs. His experiment proved that one need not swim to remain afloat, and subsequent trials with camels produced the same result. In Genesis, the body of water was the Salt Sea. The Romans named it Lake Asphaltitis, for the large blocks of natural asphalt seen floating on the surface. It was Sea of Lot (its Arabic name), Sea of Sodom, Sea of Death, Sea of Devils, Sea of Hell.

It now is much favored as a winter resort. Freezing temperatures are almost unknown and sunlight has a reliable presence. Dermatologists prescribe the naturally filtered light to their patients, who come to a belt of hotels on the western, Israeli side of the shore, elevation minus 1,346 feet. The extra 1,346 feet of atmosphere filter enough of the sun's harmful rays to make it difficult (though not impossible) to become sunburned.

Neveh Zohar is the nearest real town. It has barracklike apartments, a small museum, a large police station, and a restaurant–grocery store from which emanates the heavy smell of grilled lamb. When the first of the hotels opened, at the end of the 1960s, the employees were given the choice of commuting across the highway from Neveh Zohar or fifteen miles from the town of Arad. Almost everyone chose Arad, including Yuval Shahaf. Shahaf was head of the local government for Neveh Zohar but preferred not to live there. "Arad is small," he said, "but this is smaller."

I asked about the museum, and Shahaf apologized for not having a key and muttered his frustration about the man in charge of the building. "He's convinced he has things of value in there." As we talked Shahaf scribbled on a sheet of paper. His pen was nearly out of ink and he scratched and pecked. Since museum visitors were rare, a notice posted on the door asked that they make arrangements in advance. We agreed I would have to return.

"At least you'll have this," Shahaf said, handing over the paper. Since he was also head of the local tourism council, he had signed it, to certify I had visited Neveh Zohar.

There is one hotel on the eastern, Jordanian side. It was strangely gloomy when I visited and did not seem a commercial success. But businesspeople in Jordan, in Israel, and in the West Bank insisted that the tourist market had barely been tapped. In a moment of optimism Israel and the PLO declared their intention to work as partners in creating a resort on the northern shore, a few minutes drive from Jericho. The project would demonstrate the financial rewards of peaceful coexistence, or so it was hoped; perhaps the resort will eventually be built.

On the western shore, where Conder and Kitchener had been reluctant to linger, were youth hostels, kibbutz-run campgrounds, an amusement park with water slides, in addition to the grand hotels. On sale in the shops was Dead Sea sulfur soap, Dead Sea black mud soap, foaming Dead Sea bath salts, Dead Sea facial cleanser, Dead Sea moisturizer. A consortium of kibbutzim, which marketed Dead Sea mud in fifty-kilogram barrels to health spas, operated a factory outlet store.

The store is on a hillside within sight of the water. Everyone working there and in the adjoining warehouse wore a doctor-style white coat to give the impression that you were amidst science as well as commerce. A poster showed a woman standing in shallow water, her back to the camera, and wearing nothing except theraputic mud. Copies of the poster were for sale in Tel Aviv, staid Jerusalem, everywhere.

Eighteen people disembarked from the first tourist bus of the morning. They were French. At their guide's behest, they seated themselves to watch a video promoting the full line of products, or inspected the sales counter. Everyone seemed attentive, as if a great healer were about to lecture.

"*Pour le corps!*" the guide said holding aloft a bar of black soap.

In the video, a woman in a revealing bathrobe was applying Dead Sea facial creams.

"*Pour le visage!*" the guide said, a different package in his hand.

"*Pour les mains!*" And white coated-clerks hurried to meet the sudden demand for mud.

Travelers saw the Dead Sea was without a visible outlet and debated why the lake did not flood all of Palestine. Water flowed in from the Jordan, the Arnon, the Zered—where did it go? In the fourteenth century an eminent geographer cataloged the explanations he had judged credible. Water from the lake traveled underground to a distant country and by the end of the journey was fresh instead of salty, he recounted; or the lake water made its way underground to the Red Sea; or sulfur burned deep under the surface of the lake and caused the water to evaporate; or the Dead Sea was bottomless. Felix Fabri, the fifteenth-century pilgrim from Ulm, said the sea drained into Hell. To discourage Fabri from venturing to the shore, his reluctant guides had warned him of the terrible stench. He was told a giant serpent lived there, a creature so venomous that if a horse were bitten both the horse and its rider would die. Fabri heard that a boat carrying passengers would float in the lake but that an empty boat would sink. An unlit lamp would sink; a burning lamp would float until the flame died. He noted the maxim that a false tale was true if it were about the Dead Sea. A sensible man would have to decide the truth of the maxim for himself.

The lake has greatly expanded and greatly contracted, more than once. Within the last thousand years it has been significantly longer north to south and also higher. Times of good harvests described by pilgrims match the datable physical evidence of a larger Dead Sea—both of which are evidence of plentiful rains. When more rainwater reached the lake, the lake's surface area expanded, increasing the area exposed to the sun. What was thought to be smoke from burning sulfur was the evaporative haze.

Depending on the water level, a peninsula between the lake's northern and southern basins shrank or lengthened. Travelers could ford the lake near that peninsula in the fourth century, the fourteenth century, and early in the nineteenth, because rainfall was unusually low, the lake exceptionally shallow. The twentieth-century geographer who more than any other has studied the variations in water level has found that when plotted on a graph, the changes form a staircase: an almost straight line, a steep step, another almost straight line, a second steep step, and so on. In the twentieth century, almost every step has been down. A steady water level, a drop, steady, another drop. When Israel began diverting most of the flow of the Jordan in 1964, the level of the Dead Sea dropped twenty-one feet. It dropped again when some of the remaining freshwater was diverted by the Hashemite Kingdom of Jordan. By the mid-1970s, the peninsula between the two basins was about to become an isthmus, the southern third of the lake a drying mudflat. To restore the southern basin, at least partially, Israeli installed pumps to lift water over the isthmus.

The saltiness is permanent and increasing. Some is due to the concentrating effects of evaporation, and some is a product of a salt stratum underground. Tectonic pressures cause the stratum to flow like a slow-moving river. Part of that deep river of salt—bent by the weight of the formations above it and torn by the movement of the African and Arabian plates—has leaked into the lake.

Those same forces are the most plausible explanation for the natural asphalt that occasionally bobs to the lake's surface. Seeing the water spit up asphalt, as has occurred from time to time, a person on shore could reasonably believe this was indeed the Sea of Devils. Or believe that a restless volcano underlay it. Dead Sea asphalt is much like the material used on roadways except the earth itself does the necessary heating and mixing. In the 1950s, winds swept to the western shore a block of asphalt weighing perhaps one ton. Arie Nissenbaum laments that no one thought to preserve it. A photo of the asphalt block hangs on the wall behind his desk at the Weizmann Institute of Science. Nissenbaum is a geochemist and an administrator at the institute, the most prestigious research center in Israel, and is also a devoted historian-archivist of the Dead Sea.

The block of asphalt was the size of a small car. Imagine an all-black car washing ashore at the beach and being so recently made it has a new-car smell. Nissenbaum has convincingly theorized that asphalt travels with the salt in the several large diapirs under the floor of the valley. One diapiric structure became Mount Sodom, the crystalline mountain at the southwest shore, and on a hot day asphalt oozes from this salt mountain, like viscous honey. Another diapir is thought to underlie the lake. The asphalt apparently leaks from time to time from the sides of that plug and seeps into the water. The leaks coincide with earthquakes. In any other natural body of water the asphalt would stay right there, at the bottom; in the Dead Sea are, roughly, forty-two billion tons of dissolved solids—water dense enough to allow asphalt to float.

Members of the PPNA culture at Jericho and other settlements, in about 8500 B.C., coated reed baskets with Dead Sea asphalt to make them waterproof. Asphalt was the glue that attached metal to wood; it was caulk for boats, an ingredient in medicines, was used in gardens as an insecticide. The historian Diodorus of Sicily tells of an unsuccessful attempt in 312 B.C. by the king of Syria to break the lucrative monopoly on asphalt held by the Nabateans, who lived east of the Jordan. (They defeated the king by building a fleet of reed rafts to carry six thousand archers.) Then the Nabateans profitably resumed exporting Dead Sea asphalt to Egypt for use in embalming. In the 1980s, Arie Nissenbaum, along with several colleagues, identified the asphalt's molecular signature. Signature in hand, they detected Dead Sea asphalt in mummies in the British Museum. In 1874, Charles Tyrwhitt Drake of the Palestine Exploration Fund survey party saw Bedouin bringing the asphalt to Jerusalem, for eventual transshipment to Austria for use in varnishes. But Drake said discovery of a deposit in Europe had caused the price to plummet.

Sodom and Gomorrah, famously iniquitous, stood in a valley with bitumen pits, according to Genesis. If the cities were more than metaphor, they were somewhere near what is now the lake. After they were destroyed and after Lot's wife was turned into salt, Abraham looked into the valley and saw smoke rising as if from a furnace. The smoky vapor rising from the lake was real, of course. The bitumen-asphalt was real. So was the salt. Anyone coming to the valley would want to know how those strange features came to exist. The explanations preserved in the Old Testament would also be incorporated into the Koran.

Mount Sodom is salt tinted gray by limestone. At the end of a winter day spent on the mountain, the geologist who was my guide picked up a fist-size rock of salt and made a present of it. Since then the rock has sat on a bookshelf and become noticeably smaller. Humidity has dissolved, so far, about half the salt. Groundwater is in the same way slowly dissolving Mount Sodom. It is in no danger of disappearing, though, since the salt diapir that created it is still rising.

You can see or think you see extended biblical families in the landscape. On Mount Sodom a formation called Lot's Daughters stands near Lot's wife. At the northern end of the lake, Bedouin pointed out stones they knew as Lot's Wife, Child, and Donkey.

You can see or think you see the lost cities. A twelfth-century pilgrim reported that stones and wood appeared on the surface of the lake on the anniversary of Sodom and Gomorrah's destruction. Another said the cities were visible in the water. Some travelers advocated the eastern shore as the cities' most likely site, others the western shore, the southern end, the northern end. Claude Conder cited the presumed great age of the cities and on that basis discouraged the PEF from expecting him to discover any rubble.

In 1924, William Foxwell Albright made the arduous trip to the southeastern shore to conduct the first modern, methodical survey of that part of the valley. He was at the beginning of a distinguished career as archaeologist, philologist, and polymath of the Old Testament. Except for the car used during the first leg of the trip, he could have been traveling in the days of Conder. On the eastern side of the river, the local governor assigned soldiers to escort the party down to the lake, since the region had retained its reputation for thievery. Mules, including three that tumbled off cliffs along the way, carried the survey equipment and several hundred pounds of canned food. After surveying the area for two weeks, Albright concluded the famous cities had stood somewhere in just that place—the southernmost part of the valley. He postulated that the cities were submerged in the southern basin of the Dead Sea since he saw no artificial mounds on the land. Even Albright, a figure of remarkable erudition, had gone where he believed the Bible led him, and saw what the Bible said ought to be present. The lake had expanded, he said, and, since the time of the cities' destruction, become deeper. That would account for the seeming impossibility of locating the cities more precisely. He went so far as to suggest a date (the eighteenth century B.C.) for the cities' destruction.

Albright believed the valley had sometime later undergone a large, lasting physical change. But it had not. The bathymetric history of the lake's southern basin precludes cities having been submerged in deep water there and in that way being entirely "lost." The geologic history of the valley rules out settlements being burned to ashes by an active volcano, despite the assumptions of early travelers, or being wholly wiped away by earthquakes.

Arie Nissenbaum rejects all the theories of cataclysm. "There is not even faint evidence," he said. "It is zero." As shorthand for the unknown, he spoke of "the Sodom and Gomorrah event." He did not reject the notion that the cities were real and for some reason failed and were lost. They could have stood, Nissenbaum said, near the northern end of the lake, near Hajla, the monastery of Gerasimus.

Then came, perhaps, a small, temporary change in climate, Nissenbaum said. At the northern shore of the Dead Sea, rainfall averages four inches a year. Imagine a long drought on the coastal plain and in the hills as well as the valley. Also imagine the turmoil as people saw food surpluses disappear when the rains failed. There would be disruptions in agricultural trade, the withering of trade causing the impoverishment of cities and eventually their abandonment. It is widely accepted that those conditions existed in Palestine in about 2000 B.C. and mark the end of the Early Bronze Age. Most of the buildings atop the mound that was Jericho were destroyed at about that time, though the reason is unknown. As happened repeatedly, the site was abandoned. Smaller communities closer to the Dead Sea would presumably have fared no better. When rains failed in a semiarid region, you moved, Nissenbaum said, or "you are dead."

He suggests drought was part of the history of Sodom and Gomorrah. "I think they were real places." You can almost see them, or almost think you do, somewhere on the white hot plain.

Elevation was a more subtle feature. One could not detect with the naked eye, no matter how sharp, that the valley and the Dead Sea were lower than the oceans. The topographic anomaly is invisible unless one makes a conscious effort to find it. The honor of its discovery belongs to two British travelers whom time has unfairly reduced to ciphers. They are G. H. Moore and W. G. Beek. What is known is that they traveled to Palestine in 1837, conscientiously surveyed part of the Dead Sea coast, and reported the lake to be less vast than its alarming reputation had caused people to assume. When they boiled water at the shore, the boiling point was observed to be higher than normal. If the boiling point was high, air pressure too was high—higher than at sea level. If air pressure was high, elevation was low. Moore estimated the elevation to be minus 500 feet.

His calculation was inaccurate but nevertheless the first. A German biologist equipped with a barometer advocated minus 600 feet; an Austrian naturalist said minus 1,400. Lieutenant J. F. A. Symonds of the Royal Navy settled the issue in 1841 by crossing from Jaffa to the lake with a theodolite. Symonds was one of several British officers just then charting the coast of Palestine in search of new routes to India, and the Royal Navy was always wanting to learn about a country in case of future opportunity to intervene. Symonds' side trip to the Dead Sea required ten weeks, during which he apparently worked alone. He found the elevation to be minus 1,311 feet.

He was correct or nearly so. The vagaries of precipitation and temperature that alter the water level season to season make the figure for 1841 hard to check. Evaporation can lower the level by an inch in one hot day. A wet winter can raise the level four feet. In the last decade, the staircaselike line on the graph has included a larger number of downward steps and shorter periods of stability: the reduction of freshwater reaching the lake is causing the "permanent" level to drop another thirty inches every year—but that too is an average embracing large variations. On a January day in 1994, the elevation was minus 1,346.47 feet. On a given day in 1841, the elevation may have been precisely minus 1,311.

An Irishman named Christopher Costigan was sufficiently ignorant and brave in 1835 to attempt to reach the lake via the Jordan. No one was known to have previously attempted the trip; every Western traveler assumed the famous river to be broad and straight.

Costigan chose to travel during the stifling month of August. With a hired servant, he spent three days capsizing a small boat on rocks and in rapids, then decided to travel the rest of the way to the Dead Sea by land, and employed guards to transport the boat by camel. It is hard to know why, in the heat and glare, he insisted on reaching the shore—everything overbright, the earth at the shore half salt and knee-deep with mud hot enough to blister the skin. Difficult too to know how he had survived that long. With the servant, he launched himself onto the water. On their sixth day on the lake, they exhausted their water. On the seventh they resorted to drinking the brine. Costigan collapsed in the mud when they returned to the shore, and soldiers half carried him to Jericho with the wooden boat, while at Costigan's order, the servant headed to Jerusalem to find help.

This is known because John Lloyd Stephens of New York City happened to stop in Jericho in 1836. Stephens was a thirty-one-year-old lawyer and an aspiring actor in New York politics. Perhaps no other traveler has been as gifted in rendering hardship as worthwhile experience. As far as is known, he had left New York because his physician had prescribed travel as a cure for a sore throat. Stephens began traveling as if his life depended on it. He reached Jericho after stops in Rome, Constantinople, Odessa, Warsaw, Paris, Alexandria, and Petra. He would later reach the Yucatán and Central America and become one of the discoverers of Mayan civilization. His observant, witty accounts of his travels, beginning with the visit to Egypt and Palestine, would be admired by a young Herman Melville and praised by Edgar Allan Poe, and make Stephens one of the most widely read authors of his time.

He arrived in Jericho wanting a place to sleep. Most of the huts had only three walls, barely the height of a New England fence. Stephens found a shack with the luxury of being more or less sheltered on all four sides, the front wall being a wooden boat. He learned the boat had belonged to a man named Costigan.

Stephens never lacked time or money to satisfy his curiosity. He found Costigan's former servant, by then in Beirut. "He was a little, dried-up Maltese sailor; he had rowed around that sea without knowing why, except that he was paid for it, and what he told me bore the stamp of truth, for he did not seem to think he had done anything extraordinary." The servant drew a map showing the lake's northern and southern basins and offered credible details about what he had seen. In that way he unknowingly established that he and Costigan were the first modern travelers to circumnavigate the lake.

In Jerusalem he had indeed found an Englishman willing to ride to Jericho to help Costigan, the servant said. For the whole of an unbearably hot day, the Englishman begged the villagers to help him build a litter so that Costigan could be carried to a doctor. But even an extravagant offer of baksheesh failed to interest the local sheikh. Three men finally bestirred themselves after dusk to lead Costigan's horse and its feverish rider to Jerusalem. Costigan died two days after he reached the city. No one could make sense of the notes he had scribbled about his explorations.

In 1847, Lieutenant Thomas Molyneux of the Royal Navy volunteered to undertake a more expert investigation of the Jordan. He was instructed that upon completing that task he should determine the depth of the Dead Sea. Thomas Molyneux in effect volunteered to retrace the route of Christopher Costigan. One measure of how little was known about the valley is that the Admiralty still hoped the Jordan could become a route to the East. Another is that Molyneux, like Costigan, chose to travel during August.

He served aboard HMS *Spartan,* commanded by Captain Thomas Symonds (as best as I can determine, no relation to the Symonds who had calculated the lake's elevation). Along with a hired guide and three other sailors from the *Spartan,* Molyneux took the ship's smallest lifeboat overland to the Sea of Galilee. He was unpleasantly surprised by the rocks in the Jordan, the constant turnings, and the pitifully small stream of water in late summer. "I am within the mark when I say that there are many hundreds of places where we might have walked across, without wetting our feet, on the large rocks and stones," he writes. "I never expected one tenth of the difficulties that we had already experienced." He unwisely objected to meeting demands for baksheesh from Bedouin along the route until the Bedouin robbed the three sailors, who fled into the countryside. Only the guide remained with Molyneux. They walked the last thirty or so miles to Jericho and after more misadventures, reached the northern end of the lake with the lifeboat. Along the way Molyneux managed to recruit a man from Jerusalem. There were two oars, three men. Molyneux was the only person who showed willingness to use the oars. He confessed to wondering just then if the expedition were "silly" or even dangerous. During the three days the party spent on the lake, he felt as if he were trapped in a well-heated oven. Lake water covered everyone with a prickly, greasy film and corroded all the iron fittings of the boat. He became interested less in making careful observations than in escaping the heat, the constant prickling of his skin, the terrible fatigue. When the little crew managed to return to the northern shore, he was almost giddy with pleasure. They dragged the boat with them to Jericho, and there were joined by the three sailors who had gone temporarily missing plus the British consul from Jerusalem. "We all dined in the tent and spent a most jolly evening," Molyneux said. After those seemingly endless days under the sun without shelter, every exposed part of him was sunburned—"scorched," the consul said.

Molyneux was looking forward to returning to the *Spartan.* He knew enough about his physical condition to say he also was expecting to die. Almost every traveler knew the grim stories about the great heat in the valley bringing fever.

"Yes, I am doing pretty well now—no fever yet," he said when about to leave, "but when I get on board and the excitement is over, then I shall catch it."

He became feverish a few days after returning to the ship. He died two months later.

I presumed nothing more was to be known of Thomas Molyneux. He was nearly as obscure as G. H. Moore and W. G. Beek, only less successful. As it happened, I did finally return to the village of Neveh Zohar, as the head of the local government had urged. I followed his advice this time by making arrangements in advance to visit the local museum.

Its main exhibit had been found during the early 1960s in Britain. An Israeli geographer attending a conference in London was told at that time of there being something worth traveling to see in the English countryside. He was directed to the estate of a family called Symonds. After a distinguished career, Thomas Symonds, captain of the *Spartan,* had retired from the Royal Navy with the rank of admiral of the fleet. The visitor to the estate examined Symonds' boathouse. Its wooden roof was attached to the walls only by vines. For a modest sum of money, the visitor purchased the roof and transported it to Israel.

What was the wooden roof rests in the center of the little museum. The roof has been turned right side up, has been heavily varnished, but the planks splintered by age were left much as they were found. Along one side is the long brass plaque that was noticed under the tangle of vines. Nearly half of the letters have fallen off, but they left shadows of themselves on the brass. It is not hard to fill in the gaps. The plaque, with one misspelling, originally proclaimed:

This Boat Was Built 1836 Visited Acre Cafr of Gallile
Lake of Tiberias Jordan Dead Sea Jerusalem Joppa 1847

Symonds had kept the lifeboat after Molyneux's death. I never learned when or exactly where the boat gained the metal plaque. The boat nearly broke apart during the necessary pushing and pulling to move it into the museum, and now looks to be held together by not much more than the layers of varnish. Three slender ribs brace its interior, and a small seat is at the stern. A high-waled canoe would be more comfortable and probably more stable. No one would want to row the boat across the Dead Sea, whatever the month.

William Francis Lynch arrived at the lake in 1848, a year after Molyneux. Given the difference in their approach, the gap might as well be a quarter century. Lynch was an American. Every nineteenth-century cliché about "American spirit," when applied to him, was appropriate and true. He was born in Norfolk, Virginia, in 1801; was optimistic, moralistic, improbably earnest, and believed American democracy was a close approximation of paradise. The royal families of Europe were regarded as a personal affront—"the whole worthless tribe of kings," he called them. His first cruise as a midshipman, at age sixteen, took him to Brazil, China, and the Philippines. He sailed to the west coast of Africa, fought pirates in the Caribbean, and saw action in the Gulf of Mexico during the Mexican-American War.

But when the fighting ended, he was becalmed. Writing the secretary of the navy, Lieutenant Lynch cited "there being nothing for the navy to perform" as his reason for proposing a special mission. Permission was requested "to circumnavigate and thoroughly explore the Lake Asphaltites or Dead Sea." Less than three months later, the secretary approved the mission.

Lynch drew inspiration from Edward Robinson. No finer role model could have been found: Robinson was American, already famous, the esteemed professor-geographer who had rediscovered hundreds of biblical sites during his travels in Palestine. Robinson's *Biblical Researches* had been acclaimed a scholarly masterpiece. Now, Robinson was urging that others undertake an expedition to determine, finally, the true course of the Jordan, and to examine the topography at the southern end of the Dead Sea; there were hopes of discovering the precise fate of Sodom and Gomorrah, at least of making more sense of the descriptions offered in Genesis. Contacted by Lynch, Robinson offered him the names of useful contacts.

The lieutenant learned as much as he could about Palestine. Based on his new knowledge he ordered the construction of two vessels unlike any others. The *Fanny Mason*—made of copper—and the *Fanny Skin-*

ner—made of iron—were the first metal boats designed to be repeatedly disassembled and reassembled. Broken down into their eight sections, the craft were easy to stow on a larger ship and, in theory, easier to transport across land. It was hoped they would stand up well to harsh treatment. In building the two ships, the Brooklyn Navy Yard pioneered modular construction. The Fannies, Lynch called them.

He chose the crew himself. He described its members as young, muscular, native-born Americans. One was his son, Francis; the second-in-command was Lieutenant John B. Dale. They all promised to abstain from alcohol. Everyone would travel across the Atlantic and Mediterranean on the *Supply*, a supply ship under Lynch's command. In the hold were dollies for the Fannies, fourteen carbines, fourteen pistols, a blunderbuss, swords for the officers, ammunition belts for everyone. There were water bags that, emptied, could serve as life preservers. For the American minister to the Sublime Porte, Lynch was bringing a case of books.

The *Supply* left New York in November 1847, reaching Smyrna in February 1848. Lynch disembarked to travel to Constantinople for the honor of an audience with Sultan Abdul Mejid. In a distinctly American reflex, the lieutenant asked for permission to be accompanied by all the officers from the *Supply*, and he refused to remove his sword before being ushered into the sultan's presence. Lynch's fellow officers were kept out. But the lieutenant retained his sword. He found the twenty-four-year-old sultan wearing a crimson fez, a black kerchief around his neck, a blue frock and blue trousers, and polished boots—"a grave, melancholy-looking man," Lynch said. In the name of President James Polk, he presented Abdul Mejid with books and prints depicting American Indians. To readers of his published report, Lynch apologized for accepting the imperial court's invitation to smoke tobacco. Somewhat to his shock, he found "the weed of royalty" much to his taste. The sultan promptly granted the American a firman for the expedition.

Lynch is worldly, parochial, innocent, impossible to startle. The democrat from Virginia finds it in no way intimidating to converse, albeit briefly, with the ruler of the Ottoman Empire. What Charles Warren would have given, twenty years later, for that audience! The immodest reaction of Claude Conder after meeting a sultan! Lynch brings the outlook of a Norfolk churchgoer, and he refuses to be awed by the temporal. Christianity is deemed by him an incontrovertible good, though Lynch grants that some of its rituals are as strange as those performed by the dervishes he watches in a mosque dancing themselves into exhaustion. The prophet Muhammad is dismissed as "the arch-imposter." Turks and Arabs are thought to be alarmingly sensuous. He cites licentiousness as the greatest of all evils, believing it the reason for the collapse of nations. If for no other reason than that, Lynch is certain the Ottoman Empire is destined to fall.

Compared to his contemporaries he is tolerant, even sophisticated. For he is willing to admire some of what he sees. He is favorably impressed by an Ottoman law that allows any slave to gain his freedom after seven years, and this causes him to reflect upon the slavery of Negroes in the United States. The practice is "deeply planted, it is a part of ourselves," he says. But he is unwilling to either praise or condemn it.

The *Supply* stopped next at Beirut. Having recently learned the sad fate of Thomas Molyneux, and knowing that of Costigan, Lynch recruited a Dr. Henry J. Anderson, of Beirut and New York, as physician for the party. He also presented to the pasha of Beirut the imperial firman granting the Americans permission to explore lands both east and west of the Jordan. What followed was a comedy of manners. To his considerable embarrassment, the pasha of Beirut was unsure whether the territory east of the river was his own or belonged to the pasha of Damascus. Not wanting to reveal his ignorance, the pasha of Beirut was reluctant to ask the pasha of Damascus. With help from Lynch, the pasha of Beirut consulted a map but found no answer. Later they determined the territory was the jurisdiction of the pasha of Damascus and sent a messenger to Damascus with the news.

At the end of March, the Americans finally reached Palestine—6,700 sailing miles from New York. The sailors brought the Fannies ashore through a dangerous surf near Haifa and then moved them closer to Acre. They pitched two tents and raised the American flag. The men also said their good-byes to the *Supply:* it had been decided the ship would busy itself with other duties and then sail to Beirut to wait for Lynch to complete his mission.

Even the local governor came to the beach to see the Fannies. The horses he provided were unable to pull the boats on their dollies. This brought about his offer to supply stronger horses, plus a retinue of guards, for eight hundred dollars—a stupendous sum. Lynch refused. He rented camels, after being encouraged to do so by a Bedouin sheikh who let it be known that he considered the governor a fool. Akil el Hasi was the sheikh.

"He was the handsomest, and I soon thought also, the most graceful being I had ever seen," Lynch writes of him. Akil el Hasi is "the bold warrior," "the admirable scout," "a magnificent savage," "brave," "generous." He was in fact brave, resourceful, and a law unto himself. In 1848, Akil el Hasi was de facto ruler of the Galilee and of lesser territories east of the Jordan, and leader of the small Hanadi tribe. He had inherited authority from his father, at the end of the 1820s, but then expanded it, and no other sheikh in Palestine would be as skilled at making and breaking alliances. He had a gifted dancer's sense of balance. Depending on circumstances, he was an ally of Ottoman authorities or their most dangerous rival. To Lynch, he was more magisterial than a sultan, for Akil was at home in the desert—in Lynch's eyes, the great frontier. He saw Akil as a liberator in the style of Washington, a born leader contemplating the overthrow of unworthies. Here, in American eyes, was a nobler Noble Savage.

Akil el Hasi agreed, for a price he left to the lieutenant's discretion, to provide protection.

Everyone reached Tiberias without serious incident, and once there, Lynch assigned duties for the trip down the Jordan. Lieutenant Dale was to lead three men to the Dead Sea by land, accompanied by Akil plus twenty of his horsemen. Lynch appointed himself commander of the *Fanny Mason* and leader of the river party. Another officer would be in charge of the *Fanny Skinner.* Before launching the Fannies into the Sea of Galilee, Lynch wanted to obtain another boat to carry some of the supplies. So for $21.25 he bought a wooden skiff. He christened it *Uncle Sam.*

Late in the afternoon of April 10, all the boats entered the river. On the eleventh, the party encountered rapids intimidating enough to persuade the men to unload all the cargo onto the riverbank, bring the boats unladen through the fast water, then reload them. It happened a second time, then a third. In that first day and a half, the Fannies had traveled south a distance the land party could have hiked in four hours. On the twelfth, the *Uncle Sam* broke apart on the rocks: Lynch had proof of the superior qualities of vessels with metal hulls.

Every few hours brought another small fright. Some of the men suffered from nausea, others from dysentery. One sailor went overboard in rapids but was rescued. Both of the Fannies hit submerged rocks broadside, took on water, rolled ominously in the current, but always stayed upright. A sketch by Lieutenant Dale shows the Fannies, innovative though they were, to be much like the rowboats one could now rent at an urban park for use on a placid lake.

Lynch recorded a vast number of details, not all of them terribly illuminating of anything except the passing moment. But he insisted on precision and, most important, because of his precision discerned the nature of the river. Neither Costigan nor Molyneux accomplished as much. Lynch was the first to arrive in the valley expecting hardship, and in a methodical way recorded everything he found of interest, in hopes of making sense of the landscape.

"2 P.M. Started again, the river becoming serpentine—course, all around the compass. A great many Arabs on the shore, who ran after us. . . . The river thirty-five yards wide, six feet deep, gravelly bottom; current, five knots. 2.18, four Arabs in sight; current strong but unobstructed. 2.39, remarkably smooth, but rapid descent. . . . 2.46, course S. W. to W. by N., thick canes and thistles; water appeared to have fallen two feet within the last day or two; steady descent." The Jordan was not straight, not deep, not constant, not to be relied upon as a highway. Lynch's observations brought the river out of the realm of legend.

After eight days, the boats and the land party reached the baptismal site near Jericho. Their arrival coincided with Easter week. At 3:00 A.M., the men were nearly trampled in their tents by thousands of pilgrims coming to the riverbank. Lynch ordered the boats a short distance downstream so the sailors could rescue anyone swept away by the current. For once, no such emergencies occurred.

Every sailor knew it was the last stop before the Dead Sea, and Jericho the last settlement. Walking there, some of the men hoped to buy fresh food. But like so many travelers before them, they found a crushingly poor hamlet surrounded by nearly impenetrable nubk. Nothing, not even bread, was for sale. Dr. Anderson was dispatched to Jerusalem to arrange for bread to be brought later to the shore of the lake. Lynch also handed him a letter to be sent to the secretary of the navy, a letter dutifully reporting the unplanned expenditure of $21.25 for the *Uncle Sam* and telling of the expedition's progress.

With no reason to linger at Jericho, Lynch had the water bags filled with river water and made arrangements with Lieutenant Dale, head of the land party, for the various groups to find each other later on the Dead Sea's western shore. It was April 18. At the end of the afternoon, the Fannies floated onto the lake.

And then were blown back to the mouth of the river. The wind was stronger than the sailors had expected. It thoroughly salted and exhausted them. They rowed for five hours before reaching the camp made by the land party. But because of the surf and the difficult terrain, the boats landed a mile from where Lynch had intended. During the long crossing of the Atlantic, months before, one of the sailors had dreamed he was riding horseback across the Dead Sea, the horse's hooves barely leaving an impression on the water, the lake thick like cream. No one in the dream was wet with spray or itched from salt.

Lynch devoted the nineteenth—the first full day on the shore—to rest. On the twentieth, the men took the Fannies onto the water for the first soundings. By the end of that day, Lynch knew the lake to be about ten miles wide at its hips and to have greatly varying depths. And every sailor must have felt relief at having reached their destination. But they also must have craved a respite from the brightness and heat. Over the next several days, Lynch led the expedition south by land to En-Gedi to establish a more comfortable camp. To honor "the greatest man the world has yet produced," he named the new headquarters Camp Washington.

This was a peculiarly accessible wilderness. Lynch was at the limit of the known world or that part of the world considered safe. The border was right there, at water's edge. "We had never before beheld such desolate hills, such calcined barrenness," he said, finding the scenery unrelievedly oppressive. Yet a day after Lynch chose the site for Camp Washington, Dr. Anderson, traveling from Jerusalem, reached it without difficulty and brought food. He was accompanied by four soldiers whose none-too-challenging duty was to guard the camp whenever the Americans were on the lake. A person could regard himself as being on the edge of recorded human experience. But with some effort he could hike in one day to the monastery called Mar Saba, and a six-hour ride from there would bring him within sight of Jerusalem.

The heat slowed every task. Sleep was a hardship because of mosquitoes. And the overbright water and white sky always surrounding the open, hot Fannies compounded the sense of being trapped and also adrift. "The mind cannot conceive a more dreary scene, or an atmosphere more stifling and oppressive," Lynch said. "The reverberation of heat and light from the chalk-like hills and the salt beach was almost insupportable." Camp Washington offered no relief: "Oppressively sultry. A foetid, sulphureous odour in the night; felt quite sick."

Worst of all was the blowing of the *khamsin,* the superheated wind that whipped the lake into foam, drying everyone like carrion left a long time in the sun; and some days it did not stop until after dusk. It made the men drowsy even as they rowed. They came to dread seeing large, glassy swells in the water—the warning of the wind's imminent arrival. At a camp on the eastern shore, Lynch recorded at 8:00 P.M. a temperature of 106 degrees. That night he dreamed of fresh cool water.

On the sixth day, the *Fanny Skinner* went south, beyond the peninsula separating the northern and southern basins. Lieutenant Dale was brought as close to Mount Sodom as the southern basin's shallow water allowed. Stepping from the boat, he sank through two feet of mud and a crust of salt, reached the shore to take measurements, then floundered back to the boat, an experience akin to walking on hot coals. Still in sight of the peninsula, Lynch named the northern point of it Point Costigan, the southern, Point Molyneux. The narrow channel connecting the two basins would be named—much later—the Lynch Strait.

He kept the men busy every day, except the early morning of the Sabbath, when they slept until awakened by the sun and the flies. The men established that a horse could, with great effort, stay afloat even in deep water, that a chicken egg too would float. On one Saturday, Lieutenant Dale climbed to the summit of a flat-topped mountain in company with several guides and satisfied himself that his illustrious countryman Edward Robinson had been correct, ten years earlier, in being the first to identify it as Masada. The crew of the *Fanny Skinner* took more soundings. Lynch, in Camp Washington, wrote a report for the navy.

He was admirably rational in his observations during even the worst of times. All theories claiming the existence of a pestilent atmosphere around the lake were discounted, even as his men became increasingly listless. Bedouin told him that three thousand Egyptians had been sent to the shore as colonizers not many years earlier; within two months, said the Bedouin, all of the Egyptians were dead. Lynch decided the story was exaggerated. And if not, then starvation would account for some of the deaths, he said. Not poison or a curse.

And he saw a frightening beauty in the stillness. The hills on the east and west are like curtains, each one flirtatiously lowering itself somewhere along the shore to show another drapery behind it. In late afternoon, when the air is clear, the mountains of Moab are reflected in the northern basin in pink. Sometimes, a pink, many-towered city deep in the water. In that landscape, Lynch expressed awe and a mature wonder. The lake changed color and character, often and suddenly, "as if we were in a world of enchantment." He admired the lake, did not regard it as something to be possessed, or subdued for his country, or made useful. He expressed more feelings, and feelings that were more generous and personal, than any of the men working for the Palestine Exploration Fund admitted to having until much later in life. The valley was dangerous, silent enough to be dead, "yet this is the most interesting country in the world."

The Americans rowed the entire coast and accurately sketched it. The men bottled lake water for analysis in the United States, collected plants, methodically recalculated the valley's elevation, and measured the water temperature at different depths. On the eastern shore, they recorded the first detailed descriptions of the canyonlike wadis. Lynch was naive about geology (he believed Mount Sodom was formed by a volcano), but his mistakes were consistent with what he wished to find. He convinced himself that the valley had sunk to its great depth because of some unknown catastrophe. He was certain too that what he saw confirmed the biblical story about the destruction of Sodom and

Gomorrah. For this conventionally pious man, such a finding was great relief. It justified every hardship by affirming his understanding of the world. Here was a weapon—the landscape itself—against doubters of Scripture.

Dr. Anderson inadvertently reached a different conclusion. For he judged every feature in the valley to be substantially older than the presumed era of the vanished cities. That is, the valley was much as it had been for a long time; no enormous catastrophe had occurred there during human history. But as if embarrassed by this train of thought, Anderson ignored it. He reported that nothing he had seen in the valley was irreconcilable with Scripture.

The soundings found depths exceeding a thousand feet in the northern basin. The southern basin was shallow—maximum depth, fifteen feet. Another expedition, 126 years later, duplicated the work using an echo sounder, seismic recorder, magnetometer, and hydrophones. Members of this later expedition placed the electronic gear on the afterdeck of a small barge. Salt from the lake quickly put the electronics into a profound sleep. The engine overheated; batteries drained by the heat were not much help in restarting it. The generator powering the magnetometer failed twice. When the researchers stopped for the night, a hot wind whipped up waves that nearly tore away the lifeboat from the barge. "We bedded down for the night on the beach near the boat," the project director reported in an echo of William Francis Lynch, "drenched in salt water and tormented by insects."

Lynch ordered the men to disassemble the Fannies after twenty-one days at the lake. From the shore, the party hiked to Mar Saba in one trying day but chose to spend the night outside the monastery rather than confront the fleas thriving indoors, then went to Jerusalem by mule, and then to Jaffa. All the way to the Mediterranean, Lieutenant Dale supervised a survey team. From Jaffa, he led it back to the Sea of Galilee, but upon arriving he was too exhausted to work. Dale and his compatriots were even weaker by the time they arrived in Damascus. Some of the men had to struggle to stay on their horses. To obtain medical care, Lynch hurried everyone to Beirut.

When they arrived on the twenty-ninth of June, the *Supply* was not in the harbor. The local doctors warned Lynch that cholera was sweeping through the region and advised he leave as soon as possible. Two weeks later, still no word of the ship.

Dale slipped into delirium. No one gave the affliction a name but the seriousness couldn't be doubted. "He laboured under a low, nervous fever," Lynch said, "the same which had carried off Costigan and Molyneux."

On July 24, Dale died.

Lynch hired a French brig within a few days to transport everyone to Malta. It could not have been a pleasant time, and what upset the lieutenant the most was the captain's refusal to take aboard Dale's body. One reason was the captain's superstitiousness, but a second reason obliquely cited by Lynch was some "unhappy accident," which had occurred when the coffin was being moved to the ship. Did the corpse tumble out? Lynch does not say. But against his wishes, he buried Dale in Beirut.

It was thirty-eight days to Malta, followed by a long quarantine that confined the Americans to one building on the island. The *Supply* arrived there, finally, in mid-September.

No organisms were seen, living or dead, when the water the expedition brought back was examined under a microscope. Whenever researchers subjected mud from the Dead Sea to a similar examination, they made the same negative finding. No life. This lack of life interested a biologist named M. L. Lortet at the University of Lille. He was searching in the 1880s for a naturally sterile water; and for his purposes, this lake water held obvious promise.

In his laboratory, Dead Sea mud was diluted with a solution that would promote the growth of bacteria in case any were actually present. Hundreds of flasks were filled with the mixture. After forty-eight hours, Lortet found bacteria associated with gangrene and tetanus alive in the mud. Injected with the solution, guinea pigs died from gangrene within three days.

However gruesome, his was an interesting discovery: there was life, of a sort, in the Dead Sea. It was less "life" than life-in-waiting, since those bacteria did not originate in the lake or multiply there, but were by chance washed into the water from some other, less saline, more hospitable environment. However, they survived. They could germinate if they reached a deep wound, a hospitable flask.

Discoveries of indigenous, "livelier" life came later, beginning in the 1930s. There are in the lake three indigenous species of bacteria. There is also an indigenous species of algae, the bacteria's main source of nutrients. In this marriage of bacteria and algae is a striking adaptation to long separations. The bacteria are tolerant of high salinity, the algae less so. When salinity rises, the algae disappear from the water column. But despite the lack of an obvious source of nutrients, the bacteria survive. When the algae are absent, the bacteria apparently derive energy directly from sunlight. If salinity drops, the algae reappear. Then the bacteria thrive. Their bloom produces a pigment that turns the lake a lovely purple-pink, but it is a rare flowering. Since 1964 the bloom has occurred three times. As the amount of freshwater reaching the lake declines, it is increasingly unlikely to be repeated.

The Palestine Exploration Fund restricted its curiosity to the changing water level, as if science could reach no farther than the lake's surface. After briefly camping at En-Gedi during the summer of 1867 with sixty Ghawarneh as guards against the Jehallin, Charles Warren had credited himself for proving that Europeans could survive the worst of the heat. Claude Conder and Charles Tyrwhitt Drake in 1874 had made the taxing effort to sink their specially marked iron poles into the lake bottom. Then, in 1900, the PEF called for establishing a truly permanent mark—a mark of an unknown kind to be established at some yet to be determined place—to permit precise, more regular measurement of the water.

Dr. Gurney Masterman accepted the challenge in October 1900 by riding to Jericho. From there, accompanied by a stonemason and an archaeologist in the employ of the PEF, he rode to one of the freshwater springs along the lake's western shore. When they could ride no farther, they hiked past a reedy marsh and jumped from boulder to boulder where the lake lapped directly against the cliffs, until reaching a rock that jutted over the water.

The mason carved a horizontal line on the rock. A tape measure showed the surface of the lake to lie, on October 9, 1900, precisely fourteen feet below the line. And beneath the line the mason added three letters.

$\overline{PEF}$

Twice a year for eleven of the next twelve years, Gurney Masterman or trusted friends went to the rock to determine the water level. For the PEF, the rock became a sort of godchild: "Our rock," Masterman called it. He observed the rising and falling of the lake to parallel (with a lag of several months) changes in rainfall measured in Jerusalem, and recognized the need for more data—accurate records of temperature, rainfall figures from more locations. He correctly discerned that the lake expanded or shrank depending on the amount of freshwater reaching it. If this seems obvious now, it was not in 1900; Masterman was the first to gather the evidence methodically and in useful form. The Sea of Devils, like any other bucket left in the sun, overflowed or emptied depending on how much liquid went into it.

World War I forced Gurney Masterman to leave Palestine. In the years that followed, the rock was rarely visited, and it was then forgotten, only to be rediscovered in the 1960s. A short time later it was slated to be bulldozed to make room for a highway. But the rock was preserved after a conservation group lobbied for the route to be altered—to save the PEF mark.

The stonemason's line and letters are painted bright red to make them clearly visible. They overlook the highway, built on dry, salty land that in 1900 was lake bottom. Some distance away is the present-day shore of the lake—smaller and fifty-eight feet lower than in Masterman's day and still dropping, becoming still smaller.

Explorers, and their financial backers, were tantalized by the idea of a canal that would connect the Dead Sea to the Mediterranean. At first, the interest was tied to the search for a shortcut to the East. Later, engineers began to give speculative thought to a canal that would carry enough water to operate a vast hydroelectric plant, to generate power for a no less vast or speculative industrial complex envisioned for the lakeshore. Seawater falling the many hundreds of feet in elevation between the Mediterranean and the Dead Sea could presumably be made to spin the turbine-generators—the source of electricity for a metropolis of factories, a forest of irrigation pumps, in a desert bursting with development. Theodor Herzl described the scheme in 1902 in his novel *Altneuland.* Proposing a canal and hydroelectric plant was at the time no more fantastical than his proposal for a Jewish state in Palestine. But by 1904, Herzl had decided industrialization at the lake, and the canal in particular, was *"eine technische Phantasie."*

Reading Herzl's novel, Mikhail Novomeyski, a mining engineer in Siberia, reached a different conclusion. In 1911 on a first trip to Palestine, Novomeyski visited Mount Sodom, took samples of the lake water, and, apparently by the time he left the shore, saw clearly that one could mine minerals from the lake. He roughed out a production method. After World War I, he moved to Palestine. His negotiations with the British for permission to begin the mining attracted rival claims and became the subject of considerable intrigue, so that Novomeyski's talks lasted nine years.

He opened the Palestine Potash Company in 1931 at the northern end of the lake. The products were potash and bromine, his techniques admirably logical. Lake water was evaporated from artificial ponds, and the solids left behind were harvested by hand and passed through a rudimentary refinery. A few years later the company took advantage of the higher mineral concentrations in the southern basin by adding evaporation ponds near Mount Sodom. The workforce commuted by boat. For its first trip south, the manifest, typed on company stationery, named the destination "Sodom-Gomorrah."

Only the small refinery near Mount Sodom survived the 1948 Arab-Israeli war, and just barely. What remained was rusted metal. Four years passed before the new state of Israel built a road to the shore and then nationalized the refinery. The Palestine Potash Company was renamed the Dead Sea Works. Its corporate headquarters building in Beersheba was named—in the British style—Potash House. At the Dead Sea, Potash House mines potash (for fertilizer), magnesium chloride (textiles, livestock feed), and bath salts. In the water is also the world's largest, most concentrated deposit of bromine (for flame retardants, soil fumigants, and a nearly endless chain of polymers)—enough bromine, at the current rate of consumption, to meet demand worldwide for the next millennium and a half.

Also sodium chloride—commercially insignificant, paradoxically, because the amount is so large. Mine all the salt in the Salt Sea, and the price of salt approaches zero. Ten million tons of sodium chloride precipitate every year onto the bottom of the southern basin. If spread evenly, a new seven-inch layer of salt year after year. Every twelve years, seven feet of salt. Because of plenitude, sodium chloride is a plague without end.

The Lynch Strait now is a concrete canal carrying water pumped twenty-four hours a day from the northern basin into the southern. Without the pumping, the southern basin would be dry. One's first impression when approaching the southernmost part of it is that a catastrophic train wreck has occurred, has exposed the mechanical works of the locomotives and of all the cars, and has knotted the rails. Steel tangled into ominously large forms extends for miles. It can be heard to whistle like a steam engine, and it sighs and exhales white smoke. Such is the Dead Sea Works refinery.

It overlooks a cascade of artificial ponds; guests at the resort hotels can mistakenly believe they are gazing at an entirely natural formation. There are the "preponds," for lack of a better name, which are warehouses for the water. Then a thirty-square-mile evaporation pond. Then the small working ponds from which concentrated brine is pumped to the refinery.

So large is the evaporation pond that all the hotels overlook it. Their guests wade not in the natural Dead Sea but in the artificial pond. It is enclosed by dikes that must be raised every four or so years because of the precipitating salt. The bottom, always coated with salt, is always rising. So trucks unload onto the dikes rock and sand scrapped from nearby wadis. The practice has not endeared Potash House to people who want the desert left undisturbed. But the dike raising will continue since the consequences of the alternatives are worse: Leave the dikes as they are, and allow the lake bottom to continue rising with salt, and the water to inundate the refinery and the hotels. Or dredge the salt from the pond, which unfortunately contains more salt than the world consumes in a year and if disposed of on land would cover a larger area, or need to be significantly higher, than Mount Sodom.

Dredges work in the preponds. And are much like monstrous insects: the horizontal augers giant mandibles, the winches and booms as active as feet sensing a safe path forward. Without the dredging, the quantity of salt reaching the evaporation pond and the refinery would be still larger. The dredges pump the salt through flexible pipes floated on the water to all-salt dikes—white and granular. With experience, the dredge operators learned that the augers and every other part exposed to the water should be made of steel, never aluminum. Magnesium bromide in the water renders aluminum into a fine dust. Not rust, dust. Until the mid-1980s, all went generally well with the dredging.

Something odd then began to happen underwater. Instead of lying in an even layer on the bottom, the precipitating salt collected into buttons. The salt buttons grew vertically, grew as fast as mushrooms, and grew into mushroom shapes. You went away for a week and when you returned could not help but see that the stems were higher, the caps wider. No one knew what caused the salt mushrooms to form, and no one knows now. They were extremely hard—harder than most types of concrete—and the average mushroom was somewhat more than six feet high and had a cap covering two hundred square yards. They threatened to turn the southern basin into a solid block of sodium chloride. If that happened, the Dead Sea Works would be forced to close.

In 1987, Yossi Kivshany suggested a solution. He was a former student of geology, geography, and economics at two universities, neither of which had granted him a degree; a former commander in the Israeli navy; one of the organizers of a special military unit that retrieves from the ocean what he blandly calls "lost objects"; and cofounder of Oceana Marine Research. As its corporate emblem, Oceana chose a shark with an open-mouthed wrench for its head.

Kivshany was about forty-five. A muscular man, attentive, efficient in a brisk military way, he channeled his swashbuckling through Oceana. He was intellectually restless, and the Dead Sea Works somewhat belatedly became alarmed about the mushrooms. Mushrooms made of salt seemed to him a worthy challenge. He considered trying to shatter the mushrooms with ultrasound, studied the effects of heating them, considered electrolyzing them. In his dreams, he would stand atop Mount Sodom, bring two huge electrodes into contact, and all the sodium would go to one side, the chloride to the other in a Mosaic parting of the pond. Kivshany said, "We have not skipped any crazy idea." He had seen in a trade journal an advertisement for an advanced dredge. This was a machine designed in the United States by Ellicott Machine, whose corporate lineage allowed the company to boast that its equipment had been used to dig the Panama Canal. A day after Kivshany called Ellicott, two of its representatives arrived at the Oceana office in Tel Aviv. Pooling ideas, Ellicott and Oceana built the dredge *Elliana.*

It was all straight lines—a flat steel platform, a small square bridge atop the platform, fuel tanks, and a square oily shed housing the engines. In front was a long steel boom supporting the cutting edge of the boat. The boom held two wheels onto which were welded sixteen buckets. On each bucket were steel incisors about three feet high. The trade name, appropriately, was Wheel Dragon. The dragon did not so much dredge as chew. Boom, wheels, and buckets, together, weighed twenty-seven tons. The wheels with toothed buckets were lowered into the water to tear and gnaw the mushrooms. When the buckets whirled, they splashed like paddle wheels and foamed the water white. The foam was chewed-up salt.

At first the work went more slowly than anyone had expected. Salt mushrooms covered about 5 percent of the pond's surface, according to the Dead Sea Works. Oceana commissioned aerial photos, overlaid a scaled grid to divide the lake into blocks of ten thousand square meters each, and recalculated the area covered by mushrooms. In the photos, the mushrooms were hazy white lights in a field of bright blue-green. Instead of 5 percent of the surface, they covered 25 percent. In some of the squares, the figure was above 60 percent. Thus, the slowness of the work. So *Elliana* was joined by *Victoria* and *Maria.*

Giora Nadav, admiral of the dredge fleet, was in command of the metal skiff delivering lunch and a visitor to *Elliana.* From the skiff, the mushrooms just under the water were milky clouds. The water was leaded glass that the boat barely scratched; we skimmed over it without leaving a wake. Every surface seemed to intensify heat and sunlight. Nadav wore a T-shirt emblazoned with the Oceana shark. With his weight lifter's arms and chest, he might have carried the boat.

The captain of the *Elliana* for this twelve-hour shift was Dro Brude. He was half again as big as Nadav. Every member of the crew was a former paratrooper or commando, or an explosives expert. Brude sat at the controls with a view of instruments and the bucket wheels. They never stopped chewing. The mushroom dredging continued every hour of every day, Yom Kippur included. When Brude stood to plug in a coffeepot, Nadav took Brude's place at the controls. The larger the area cleared of mushrooms each week, the higher the crew's pay.

"He makes the salary of a judge," Nadav said, jerking a thumb toward Brude. For the rest of the day Brude was known to everyone as His Honor.

The haze and the shimmering mirages made the pond horizonless. Crews became lost, in the sense that they couldn't judge how far a dredge had advanced. Everything was the same pale translucent blue. No one on the boats could confidently find the places that had been worked even an hour before. Then Oceana added a navigation system that told the crews their position in the pond to the nearest square foot. Every crazy idea was tried, again, to make the dredging go faster. The company settled on having divers place explosives at the base of each mushroom to fracture the cap. Weakened in this way, the mushrooms were more easily consumed by the dredge.

Brude maneuvered the boat with four anchors. Two were long metal shafts that moved hydraulically from the rear of the boat. When fully lowered, they planted their feet on the bottom of the pond. At the end of each shaft was a wedge-bottomed metal shoe, for firmer footing. When Brude wanted to move the boat, the feet were raised. The other two anchors were attached by cables and winches to the steel boom at the front.

The boat shuddered when the toothed buckets bit into salt mushrooms. It half reared like a beast restrained by a leash. Brude lifted one hydraulic foot, played out cable to one of the anchors in front, winched in cable from the other front anchor. He was swinging the boat from side to side—the front anchors the pivots—to get another bucketful of salt. Then reversed the winching and the playing out, and swung the boat again. The beast roared and tugged forward hard. Brude raised his other hydraulic foot, opened the throttle, and moved to the next mushroom. If His Honor wanted, he could make *Elliana* cha-cha. Repositioned in the pond, he lowered his hydraulic feet and resumed chewing.

The Dead Sea Works gave Oceana ten square miles to clear. That work may never be truly complete, since salt continues to precipitate. Mushrooms continue to form in the areas Oceana has not yet reached, and mushrooms reappear in areas already dredged. The mushrooms grow at an undiminished rate.

Giora Nadav, the de facto admiral, insisted on one more stop. He steered the skiff to one of the dikes made of salt. Everything digested by *Elliana* was pumped there. The dike appeared to be perfectly straight in length—perhaps five hundred feet. The base was the widest part, the sides convergent like those of a pyramid, but rising to a broad, flat top. The dike was untainted white, whiter than any cloud.

Nadav cut the motor at the base of the dike. He promised to wait.

The dike was twenty feet high and contained two hundred million cubic feet of salt. Halfway up, I began to lose my footing and looked back at Nadav. Lot's wife had done something similar.

"Go! Go! I wait!"

I climbed. On top, the dike was a hundred feet wide and crisscrossed with tracks from the tractors smoothing it. It was wide enough for six lanes of traffic. Impossible not to feel pure and lost and salt-blind. An all-white crystalline world. The Dead Sea Works planned to create twelve more dikes of the same composition and size.

"I was right to show you?" Nadav asked after I slid back to the boat.

The sloped white walls polished the sapphire lake into a square-cut gem.

Oh, he was very right.

IX
Last Rounds

In 1880, the Palestine Exploration Fund finally unveiled its map of western Palestine. It was twenty-six unbound sheets, each sheet nearly three square feet, dense with colors and hatchings and giving precise locations for about forty categories of built or natural features: dunes, scrub, vineyards, cisterns, mosques, and so on. Tyre, in present-day Lebanon, was the northernmost town, Beersheba the southernmost. Jericho was a small pink square. The Jordan snaked blue.

The PEF boasted that the survey party had discovered 172 sites named in the Bible. Claude Conder was credited for identifying the largest number of them, his finds ranging from Abel Meholah to Ziz. Walter Besant, the society's flinty administrator, hailed him for having recovered "more ancient names than all previous scholars and travellers put together." One copy of the map went to Queen Victoria. Another was sent to Sultan Abdul Hamid II in recognition that the territory was indeed his.

In the twenty-six sheets, the map preserves the country visited by

Conder and Herbert Kitchener, freezes it no less well than an airtight tomb. Their Palestine was an expanse of marsh in the north, was only sand dunes along the Mediterranean coast, was barely settled in the southern part of the Jordan Valley, and had fewer roads than aqueducts. In the valley the best roads were those dating to the Romans. The country still lacked its first mile of railroad track. Jericho seemed remote, was without prospects, seemed as cursed as when Joshua warned against it being rebuilt.

Conder and Kitchener regarded the land as a storage chest crammed with perishable treasures, and the Ottoman Turks as unworthy keepers who had carelessly left the chest unlocked. The surveyors had assumed Palestine would soon become available for the taking. The map is an artifact of those assumptions. And an artifact of a distinct religious outlook: supporters of the PEF believed that a close, careful examination of Palestine was the best way to illuminate the Bible and that this close, careful survey would confirm every detail of the biblical narrative. At the beginning, no one was more confident of such confirmation than the surveyors themselves.

I took pleasure in the map, was entertained by it, in the way I took pleasure from the old picture books that rendered Jericho a polished, densely settled place of gingerbread castles. Like the picture books, the map was a product of wishfulness. Its makers came to search for a Palestine already sketched in their minds. The surveyors found only parts of the wished-for country and, to their great credit, rendered the real instead of the imagined. Because of the map, the country gained a geographic reality. The giant serpents on the shore of the Dead Sea immediately died away; the river that had stopped flowing when the priests raised their hands became a muddy stream. In Jericho, Rahab's house disappeared forever.

Thanks to the map, everyone also gained a reliable measure of change. When the survey party arrived, Jericho was barely a village. It had been isolated by the topography, and the isolation made Jericho exotic to every traveler, until the traveler reached it. Conder found "mud hovels and black tents," the landscape "stony and unlovely." The Jericho that Conder saw has largely disappeared—for the better—and looking at his maps, I saw through the skin of the Jericho of my own time, and that town too was about to disappear. The map showed a lost country.

Writing the text that was intended to make sense of the map proved much more difficult. A publication date was announced but passed without any books. For the writing reopened every dispute the surveyors had suppressed during the fieldwork, and exacerbated every rivalry. Everyone wanted to have the last word in a work advertised as the definitive description of the country.

Conder complained that Kitchener's descriptions of the countryside were "vague and not accurate." Charles Warren, who had tunneled under Jerusalem, criticized sections by Conder as "too rough and meager," and mailed Conder "the sort of letter that will hurt him." Edward Palmer, the linguist who would be murdered a few years later in the Sinai, was dismayed by the Arabic place-names collected by, among others, poor Charles Tyrwhitt Drake. Palmer said everything about the Arabic names was "most misleading and inaccurate." One of the editors was Charles Wilson. It was Wilson who had led the first PEF survey in Palestine and had proposed the larger survey just completed. He too had complaints. Descriptions of the sites differed from his own recollections, and many of the identifications struck him as dubious. "Conder has not risen to the occasion," said Wilson.

The officers meanwhile resumed their careers. Herbert Kitchener was ordered to Cyprus to map the island. However, he encountered on Cyprus a commander interested neither in surveys nor in the lieutenant's way of conducting them. Charles Wilson rescued his young friend from frustration by steering him to a junior diplomatic post in Turkey. Wilson and his protégé were of like mind, since both believed that a well-drafted map was an outstanding investment in military preparedness. You surveyed little-known lands to be able sometime later to maneuver an army in them.

Service in Turkey completed, Kitchener returned to Cyprus. He was more polished and—if such a thing were possible—more determined to succeed. He did the survey *his* way. And for once, he seemed liberated from his own reserve, and a bear cub brought from Turkey became one of his housemates. Thirty-year-old Kitchener also grew and perfected a mustache. These many years later, one could mistakenly say that it was only a mustache. It was broad, thick, arched like a sea lion's whiskers, with the ends trimmed to points, and it gave Kitchener an advance on being memorable. It said, Here is a warrior. Later it would say, Here is Britain's best-known general. It was impeccably manicured, as august as the pediment of a temple, and came to seem as much a part of him as his eyes, rather than something he successfully cultivated for effect. To be noticed, to leap to the head of the queue, was of course what he had always wanted.

Claude Conder was assigned to build new defense works in Britain. At the same time he busied himself with writing. In 1878, the PEF published his own account of the survey in two volumes entitled *Tent Work in Palestine.* It was his first book and proved by far his best: part adventure story, part biblical history, and conveying his impressionability and excitement when his experiences were still fresh, and when the modern-day conditions in the country were still largely unknown to his readers. To a small degree, *Tent Work* made him a public figure. Serious magazines began to welcome his opinions about British interests in the Middle East and the future of Palestine.

Volume 1 of *The Survey of Western Palestine* was finally published in 1881. It appeared in an edition of five hundred copies to be sold by subscription. George Grove, founder of the PEF, reserved copy number thirty-five. Number forty-two was delivered to Charles Warren. Oxford and Harvard were among the early subscribers. Volume 1 devoted itself to the northernmost third of the country, named and briefly described every settlement there, every watercourse, all the other prominent natural features, and every discernible ruin, and when possible explained their link to the Bible and told the story of their discovery. It was not in any sense an easy book to read. The text was hopelessly arbitrary in organization, and the bound volume inconveniently heavy and large and not easily related to the twenty-six sheets of the map. A reader needed great dexterity and previous knowledge of the geography of Palestine.

Two more volumes appeared later in 1881, and the last four by the end of 1885. One consisted largely of articles that had appeared in the PEF's journal, another contained somewhat more than ten thousand place-names in Arabic and English, and one had the Reverend Henry Baker Tristram's admirable catalog of Palestine's flora and fauna: more than 3,000 plant species, and over 800 animals, including 348 of Tristram's beloved birds. These books, said the *Times,* were "the most important contribution to the study of the Bible which has been made in modern times."

Other reviewers compared the effort expended to the results and were less admiring. The great accuracy of the map and the thicket of details in the published books were indeed notable accomplishments, the *Edinburgh Review* mused in a lengthy essay. But the gain in historical knowledge seemed small. "We can almost count on our fingers what records and monuments of ancient life have been recovered." The anonymous essayist, like the public, was less impressed by a newly made map than he would have been by remains of an ancient temple displayed in a museum.

Commercially, *The Survey of Western Palestine* was a failure. Nine years after publishing volume 1, the PEF still had for sale fifteen of the original five hundred copies. That was in 1890. It was the year the PEF sent Flinders Petrie to Palestine and the year Petrie ordered his workmen to uncover part of the mound called Tell el-Hesi, one arbitrarily determined layer at a time. It was the first stratigraphic excavation in Palestine and ensured the obsolescence of *The Survey.* Compared to Petrie's excavation reports, the work done by theodolite was mere travelogue. Members of the survey team had in every sense limited themselves to describing the surface of things. It had been assumed, wrongly, that whatever lay underneath was of less importance.

Conder and Kitchener might have accomplished more had they taken time to explore some of the mounds and not just noted their location. But most of the second thoughts are unfair. No one in the region knew yet how to make clear sense of the contents of a mound like the one alongside Ein es Sultan; and perhaps it is everyone's good fortune that Charles Warren stopped digging in 1868 and that his successors made no attempt to emulate him, since their inaction preserved the contents.

The Survey offered a more accurate and more nearly exhaustive accounting of Palestine than anything published before it. It set a higher standard for the exploration and mapping of relatively primitive territories. And it endured. The map would not be improved upon until the 1930s, when the British commissioned a new topographic survey. Conder and Kitchener shouldn't be criticized for being only a half step ahead of their time.

Herbert Kitchener stayed abroad for most of the rest of his life. It was his good fortune that in 1882 Britain gained control of Egypt (one of the not clearly foreseen results of a British invasion). For an Arabic-speaking officer, the victory offered limitless opportunity.

Kitchener had an energetic patron—Charles Wilson—and luck. Claude Conder had neither. Kitchener was absent from most of the fighting in Egypt but was appointed second-in-command for training the Egyptian calvary. Conder, sent as a low-ranking intelligence officer, was present at the decisive battle but became ill with typhoid. He was sent home to Britain. Kitchener meanwhile went from strength to strength.

At Wilson's prompting, the PEF reemployed Kitchener to map the southernmost part of Palestine, the desert that lay between the Dead Sea and the Gulf of Aqaba. This time no one pretended the work was solely to further understanding of the Bible. Britain had a new, larger stake and wanted to know the neighborhood.

Walter Besant asked Conder to offer Kitchener advice before the new expedition began. Conder refused. He did not conceal his bitterness. Conder fumed that Kitchener was telling fellow officers he, not Conder, was the true explorer of Palestine and was claiming credit for Conder's discoveries. "He may now help himself."

Egypt and the Sudan would make Kitchener a British hero, owing largely to disaster befalling a British general. Charles Gordon was the general. In 1884, he was besieged in Khartoum by thirty thousand dervishes. Scouting the desert in advance of a rescue party, Kitchener was in occasional contact with him through scribbled messages carried by a network of spies. "Gordon" and "Kitchener" thereby became names familiar to every newspaper reader in Britain. Gordon, the brave hostage; Kitchener, the general's fearless link to civilization.

A disappointed Kitchener was not included in the rescue force, but that would be more good fortune. Charles Wilson was in charge after other officers died in a skirmish. However, he was wholly without experience in leading troops in the field. He reached Khartoum by steamer only after the besiegers had overrun the city and killed Gordon. Wilson showed great resourcefulness in organizing the retreat—his force of barely one thousand soldiers having been caught in a barrage from shore—but he was pilloried by the newspapers for having failed to save the general. Britain's government came to Wilson's defense by knighting him. During all the finger-pointing, Kitchener's reputation was only enhanced.

Kitchener became second-in-command of the army in Egypt, then commander-in-chief. In 1896 he began the slow reconquest of the Sudan. Not without forethought, he rode a white horse; for the popular press, Kitchener by then was akin to a cult. He had the now famous mustache and the famous unsmiling mouth and the famous cold blue eyes. "He has no age but the prime of life, no body but one to carry his mind," the war correspondent G. W. Steevens gushed in his book about the campaign. "His precision is so inhumanly unerring, he is more like a machine than a man." His forte in military strategy was perseverance, not imagination, and almost nothing was delegated because he trusted almost no one. He did not consult or confide.

The culminating battle took place in 1898 at Omdurman, across the Nile from Khartoum. Kitchener's use of overwhelming firepower worked devastatingly well against a dervish army that believed the best weapon was Allah. British casualties at Omdurman totaled forty-eight dead; the enemy lost more than ten thousand. The Sudan for at least a while would be British. When Kitchener came home, a grateful Parliament awarded him thirty thousand pounds.

For most of the rest of his life, he was regarded as the master of the empire's trouble spots. Kitchener was placed in charge of the war in southern Africa against the Boers, and he prevailed. Parliament this time gave him fifty thousand pounds. He was commander-in-chief in India, then British Agent in Egypt—in everything but name, ruler of the country. There was a life of ceremony, the sycophancy of others, a pasha's luxuries.

Then, in 1914, shortly before the outbreak of the Great War, he was persuaded to take charge of the War Office. The job was accepted only reluctantly: he was used to making decisions at a remove of several thousand miles from anyone who could overrule him. Not for him the asking and giving of advice. But he quickly immersed himself in his new duties, and he swore off alcohol for the duration of the war. The recruiting posters that soon blanketed the country relied on a likeness of the stern face with the famous mustache. Kitchener, like Nelson or Wellington, seemed to be part of the empire's fabric.

In London, he was the foreigner. For him, the cabinet room was the most arid of deserts. His lifelong habit of reserving most decisions for himself created impossible burdens in the job as War Minister. For the first time—the casualties at the front shockingly high, the war showing no sign of reaching an end—he was not a hero.

The painter James Guthrie included Kitchener in an imagined scene called *Some Statesmen of the Great War.* It hangs in the National Portrait Gallery in London. Seventeen dignitaries are crowded into the portrait. Kitchener, his face fleshy and tired looking, is placed to one side rather than at the center, a figure consigned as a relic of another era. He stands with one spurred boot on the neck of a tiger skin—Lord Kitchener the virile hunter. The other figures are bathed in brighter light, but none other is rendered as a symbol of courage. A second portrait shows him during the early, glory days in the Sudan. He is handsomely trim, unsmiling of course, and as ramrod straight as the minarets sketched in the background.

In 1916, it was decided Kitchener as War Minister should sail to Russia to confer with the Czar, Britain's ally. If nothing else, Kitchener could escape from squabbles in the cabinet. Other members of the cabinet were dissatisfied with him, in some cases envious, and were whittling away his authority.

I never found him truly likable. Until almost the very end, Kitchener was the master of infighting, defeating every rival as thoroughly as he had crushed the dervishes. Not even his friends could counter stories about his notorious coolness, and there were well-attested stories about his pocketing valuables from homes where he was a guest. How strange that a figure given literally a fortune by his government should covet and steal. The world, his behavior said, was his for the taking. But in his imperious way, he became, at least for the public, an emblem of all that was stoic. Even in the way he died.

He boarded the cruiser *Hampshire* late in the afternoon of June 5 on the northern coast of Scotland, bound for Russia. A gale forced the escort of destroyers to return to port, but the *Hampshire* steamed forward. Less than three hours after the voyage began, the cruiser struck a German mine. Intelligence reports warning of freshly laid mines had gone ignored, for reasons never determined. The vessel sank in fifteen minutes.

Of the 655 people on board, only 12 survived. The body of Herbert Kitchener was never found.

Charles Warren in 1876 was sent to Griqualand West, in southern Africa, to survey disputed borders. A short time later he commanded a regiment of soldiers in a dismally ugly war in the new diamond fields against the native tribes. In 1882 he went to the Sinai Desert to lead the grisly search for the murdered Edward Palmer. Then, he was ordered back to southern Africa—this time to Bechuanaland (the future Botswana)—to investigate land disputes between native tribes and the Boers. Warren decided—and this was something rarely done—in favor of the natives.

For two years he was in charge of Scotland Yard, a tenure made controversial by the murders attributed to Jack the Ripper and the failure by police to find the murderer. Warren was commander for five years at Singapore. He commanded all Royal Engineers in a large part of Britain. When the country went to war against the Boers, in 1899, Lieutenant-General Sir Charles Warren took command of an army division sent to Cape Town.

It was not his favorite war. Another officer publicly held Warren responsible for troops making an embarrassing, unauthorized retreat. Blamed him wrongly, Warren said. He became a victim of a tangled chain of command, messages that he received late or not at all from the men engaged in the fighting that day, and the iron determination of the other officer not to take responsibility for the debacle. Some of the battlefield messages that did get through were carried by a lieutenant named Winston Churchill. He was present as a junior army officer, member of Parliament, and newspaper correspondent. When the fighting was at its most confused, Lieutenant Winston Churchill impetuously offered General Charles Warren advice. Warren shouted for the lieutenant to be arrested. (The order was ignored.)

Warren did make mistakes but not the serious ones of which he was accused. Yet when he left Africa to return to Britain, his military career was over. He was a hearty sixty years old, headstrong and well-known to the public, though now not in the way he wished. He asked a friend what he should do next in public life. "Wait twenty years," he was told, "then do what you want."

He was not without quirks. He suggested that every community let loose wolves for the purpose of teaching children to be alert; later he judged that bicycles and automobiles admirably performed the same service. Much of his time was devoted to a troop of Boy Scouts and to teaching Sunday School, where he would bring rowdy classes to order by making loud animal noises. There were speeches on behalf of a temperance society and the PEF. In a book the PEF published, he attempted to trace the British system of weights and measures back to the biblical cubit. He was convinced too he had discovered a mathematical formula explaining the orbits of the planets. Eighty-five years old, he urged the PEF to be more spry and less dull.

"As for myself, I am ready to fight on any of the theories I uphold, but how can one enjoy shooting if one's antagonists lie low or hold up their hands?" He died in 1927 at age eighty-six.

Americans had begun group tours to Palestine in 1867, within six months of the first digging into the mound above Ein es Sultan. Samuel Clemens was a member of that first group. He was writing about his adventures under the name Mark Twain for a California newspaper, and the eight Americans who disembarked from a steamer in Beirut toured Palestine by mule for three weeks.

What distinguished the tourist from a pilgrim was the tourist's willingness to complain. A tourist could freely confess to disappointment, the lack of time for reflection. Twain found Jericho "not very picturesque as a ruin." The Dead Sea, "a scorching arid repulsive solitude. . . . It makes one think of funerals and death." All of Palestine was stony and unsightly: "It is a hopeless, dreary, heartbroken land."

Yet it was still exotic. Yet increasingly easy to reach. By the 1890s, the number of tourists traveling there first-class was more than a thousand a year.

Most were customers of Thomas Cook of Leicester, England. The idea of transporting ostensibly like-minded people from place to place as a group had occurred to him as he walked the fifteen miles from his home to a temperance meeting. He organized a first experiment: a chartered train carrying temperance supporters to another gathering. Several thousand spectators greeted the passengers. Cook expanded the new business by offering train excursions from Leicester to London and then from Britain to the continent. He invented the package tour in 1862 by including the cost of accommodations and meals in the price of the ticket.

In 1869 he offered his first tour to the Middle East. The forty-nine people who went chose either to spend seventy days in Palestine or to travel for somewhat longer to see Palestine as well as Egypt. The combined group made a three-day trek to the Dead Sea, was robbed of its baggage in Jerusalem, camped in carpeted tents, and both expected and received tea at the appropriate hour each day. Charles Warren had not yet finished tunneling under Jerusalem. Claude Conder would not arrive in the country for another three years.

Thomas Cook and Son became, like the pyramids, one of the expected monuments for English-speaking travelers. Entering the walled city of Jerusalem, the first thing the visitor saw beyond the sixteenth-century gate was a Thomas Cook billboard. Thomas Cook and Son provided Herbert Kitchener with tents, food, and camels when he surveyed the desert between the Dead Sea and the Gulf of Aqaba. The company operated the Nile steamers that took the British army partway to Khartoum. In Jaffa, the traveler looked for stevedores wearing red jerseys with the name Cook.

Arriving at Jaffa was usually the most stressful part of the trip. Seagoing vessels anchored a considerable distance from shore, and passengers were transferred into longboats to be rowed to land. Every passenger would be lowered by stevedores into the pitching boats. An early Cook customer named Edwin Hodder saw twenty to thirty row-boats race alongside his steamer. In each boat were four or five men shouting promises of exquisite service. "We were boarded by these natives," Hodder writes of his trip, "who seized us and our luggage indiscriminately until we were obliged to discuss the doctrine of free-will with our fists." The 1898 Baedeker for Palestine advised passengers to be certain that none of their luggage fell overboard in the confusion. Its list of useful Arabic phrases for the traveler at Jaffa included, "I do not care for you." Also, "Begone." The traveler was advised to wave a cane vigorously to make himself clear. Travelers were told to think of Arabs as children and thus worthy of a European's forgiveness. When beggars asked for a few coins, the tourist was to respond, "May God give thee," and continue walking. Baedeker reported Jericho, or Riha, was "squalid hovels." According to *Cook's Handbook*, "filthy and uninteresting." "Of all the horrible and disgusting spots in the Holy Land," said Edwin Hodder, "there is none worse than Riha."

Claude Conder credited himself with helping open Palestine to modernization. He had shown the true nature of the country by finishing the new map and the volumes of *The Survey* and, so he believed, alerted people to the land's great potential. His affection for the country was in any case unmistakably real. Of all the explorers sponsored by the PEF, only Conder adopted the country emotionally. It was the place, he believed, to which he had devoted his greatest affection and labor, and it became akin to a favorite charity. He wished the country good fortune, felt proud when generous attention was paid to it, took its neglect personally. But he always assumed that improvements would be the work of newcomers, not the Ottoman Turks or the Arabs.

In 1881 the PEF sent him back to the region to map the territory lying east of the Jordan. An American team had surveyed the area during the 1870s but produced a map the PEF found inaccurate. The Fund had recently canceled plans to publish it. Conder wanted to search for potential railroad routes as well as reexamine the coast of Lebanon, items always of military interest, so the Royal Engineers did not object to loaning a small number of men.

They traveled to Beirut and then to Jericho. It was always the logical last camp before a journey to the east bank of the river. Conder had the large handicap of being without the necessary firman; the Sublime Porte so far had refused to grant it. Also, the local governor had made it clearly known that British surveyors would not be welcomed east of the river.

Conder left most of his tents at Jericho and told the men to stay there. The more conspicuous the camp at Jericho, the better. It allowed Conder to cross the river without being detected. Later, the other men joined him. Conder bribed Bedouin to protect them, and Ottoman soldiers who found them were bribed to forget what they had seen. For eleven weeks the game of hide-and-seek continued. Then authorities firmly ordered the party back across the river. Conder had surveyed five hundred square miles—only one tenth the total area.

He stayed in Jerusalem to work on the new map. On hearing rumors of a new firman, he raced to Constantinople. He was told the firman had support from various ministries, that it needed only one more signature, that it would soon be waiting for the British ambassador—none of which helped him. Nine years would pass before the Sublime Porte granted the firman.

Having returned once again to Jerusalem, he served as a guide for Prince George (the future King George V) and Prince Albert Victor, grandsons of Queen Victoria. Conder and the princes became the first non-Muslims in twenty years to enter the Tomb of the Patriarchs in Hebron, held to be the burial place of Abraham. Presumably encouraged by Conder, the royal visitors examined the tombs with a tape measure. Conder also led them to Jericho and (with permission of the Porte) across the Jordan. Prince George, presiding many years later at a meeting of the PEF, described Conder as "my old friend."

As I retraced Conder's steps and read his articles and books, I slowly realized that he had been happiest and at his most productive during his first three years in Palestine. It was the period that ended with the party under his command being attacked at Safed. I was convinced he never regained all his physical strength after he was injured and never fully recovered his nerve. He found reasons month after month for delaying his return to Palestine to finish the survey, until the PEF appointed someone else to take charge—Kitchener, friend-turned-usurper. We know Conder did return to lead the newly commissioned work east of the Jordan. But the dangers reported to the PEF from there were, by his descriptions, never less than overwhelming. A half-dozen reasons were cited for stopping the work, and so the work ended; his colleagues in the field argued that they could have safely made more progress.

In 1877, Conder had married. His wife, Myra Foord, was the daughter of a general in the Royal Engineers in India. It is worth noting, given some of the groom's sharp opinions in the past, that Myra Foord was Jewish. In 1884, Conder was with Charles Warren in Bechuanaland as head of the mapping office. Offered another post in Africa, Conder, who had so craved travel, preferred to return to Britain. He was wedded to Palestine: Palestine tantalized him for the fame it seemed to offer, frightened him because of the unpredictable dangers and because of painful memories, yet it was where for a time he had risen to every challenge. His best writing, and perhaps his warmest thoughts, were all tied to that place. But he never recovered from Safed or from having received, a few days after the fighting there, the letter from Miss Davis—the woman he referred to as "D"—rejecting his proposal of marriage. Some of the intrepidness was lost.

Nothing in the rest of his career brought as much glory. After leaving Africa he commanded a company of Royal Engineers in Britain and directed the Royal Engineers department that engraved maps. He supervised disaster relief and construction projects. In 1904 he retired with the rank of colonel.

He never stopped writing about Palestine. There were magazine articles on an impressive variety of other subjects ("Public Works in Ireland," "The Canary Islanders," "Greek Art in Asia") but Palestine was his expertise, and the journal of the PEF the publication to which he contributed most often. He wrote seventeen more books—on Palestine, the Bible, and his earnest though unsuccessful attempt to translate inscriptions of the Hittites. Walter Besant generously praised him whenever the PEF celebrated its past and especially the glorious making of *The Survey.* Conder, said Walter Besant, "is *par excellence* the Surveyor of the Holy Land."

A now elderly grandson has a faint memory from the early 1900s of

Grandfather Conder. He was a mustachioed figure who, in the eyes of the child, carried a frightening, wonderful, enormous sword. He wore a colonel's impressive red uniform and a grand hat and played with his grandson and posed for a photograph that has faded into indistinct shadows.

He died February 16, 1901, when he was sixty-one. Claude Conder, Walter Besant said in the obituary he wrote, "has made a name which will last as long as there are found men and women to read and study the sacred book." How sad that Besant proved optimistic about the explorer's posthumous fame. The name has undeservedly faded.

I made my rounds again, my winter palace made of mud-brick and stucco to the great mound to the spring to the little downtown. Jericho was much busier now. People pointed out the place where a row of apartments was going to be built, or so everyone hoped, and examined the house where Yasser Arafat might or might not reside if he came to Jericho, and talked about the sudden race for office space, as if the town had anything other than a few storefronts. Israel and the PLO had agreed a few weeks before to have Palestinians, not Israelis, govern Jericho and the Gaza Strip. There would be Palestinian police, a Palestinian government, and eventually, money for development. If Israelis saw the change as an experiment, Palestinians regarded self-rule as an irreversible first step toward a state of their own. The first step—the experiment, if one wished—had not yet occurred, though other changes had.

Palestinian flags, previously banned, were everywhere. A last Israeli governor was about to abandon the stolid concrete fort. Khaled Amar was prospering. He was the young man temporarily denied a driver's license when Israeli authorities insisted his long dead father pay taxes, and Khaled Amar had been mostly idle. Now he worked for television crews. Israeli police at the fenced-in police station at the main square had packed files and emptied lockers. When the police drove away in a convoy, Palestinians threw stones at the cars. "Our little farewell," a doctor said.

The farmers were emboldened, and agitated for more water to be delivered from Ein es Sultan and the springs in the hills. Within a few months Jamil Khalif, the mayor, quarreled with Arafat over water as well as other matters; and after seventeen years in office, he said he was resigning.

People returned from abroad. Some were welcomed less than others. One middle-aged man—wearing a suit and tie, and in that way clearly marked as someone who had been living far away—arrived to be in charge of a plainclothes police force. He was the new governor in everything but title and established an office near the concrete fort.

There was also Rajai Abdo, moving back with his wife and their children from the United States to reinvigorate a family business on Jerusalem Road. It was the Hisham Palace Hotel. Its existence was a testimony to Rajai Abdo's late father-in-law, Salah Abdul. Salah Abdul, as the family tells the story, had owned large tracts of land in Jerusalem, was expelled from Palestine by the Ottomans (though no one remembers why), and returned during the British Mandate to settle in Jericho. The town was so remote his relatives were reluctant to visit. Salah Abdul established the bus line between Jericho and Jerusalem, built two movie theaters, and developed his properties in Jerusalem. In 1947 he opened the hotel.

It boasted Jericho's first swimming pool. King Abdullah of Transjordan was an occasional guest. "Jericho was the center of fun," said Rajai Abdo. To be sure of having accommodations Jerusalemites rented rooms for a year at a time. "If you wanted to gamble, enjoy good food, Jericho was the place."

A British resident of Palestine was one of the hotel's first guests, in January 1948. "Here I am in the new hotel at Jericho, since yesterday afternoon," he wrote to his wife, who had left the country to avoid the war everyone could see approaching. "It is a comical place, built with a great splash . . . and nothing works: no servants; windows won't open; no hot water jugs; no nothing, except the view out of my bedroom window, of which I send you a picture, drawn yesterday and this evening, standing at the door of a little balcony."

He sketched the mountains of Moab as the background. In the near distance was "a jolly group of mud-brick houses," and bananas were the foreground.

The hotel was in recent years perhaps the only place in Jericho where a man could arrive with a woman who was not his wife, leave after an hour or two, no questions asked. Rajai Abdo said he had cleaned the building "from a moral point of view as well as physical." But the floors were encrusted with dirt even after the cleaning; the kitchens remained unusable. Someone had long ago filled in the swimming pool.

The view from the little balconies was unchanged: mountains softened by haze, houses made of mud-brick, a jungle of bananas—majestic, poor, in places overwhelmingly lush, painfully overbright, like all the valley. Here was space for an elevator, Abdo said. This was the site for a new wing. He was meeting later in the day with architects. Thinking of the future, he pointed to the basement. "It could be a shelter," he said, "in case of a war."

I saw several artifacts on my way back to the mound—a bicycle rim, an empty can of cooking oil—but none of them old. Grass and mallow sprouted on the mound every winter, made a thick carpet of green at the bottom of the trenches Kathleen Kenyon had dug during her excavations in the 1950s, and always bloomed white and purple well before the first day of spring. I made a point once to visit on the anniversary of Charles Warren coming there. His first full day at the mound had been April 4 ("a delicious morning," said Warren) and by then most of the grass was already a crunchy brown. And then it became a summer-autumn crust, and everything looked dyed with henna. The mound changed color and the shape was never what I remembered but was steeper or smaller or undistinguishable from the natural landscape. Whatever one's expectations, the mound failed to meet them. It was older than the explorers had believed. One of the early cultures—the people of PPNA, ten thousand years ago—was unaccountably sophisticated; some of the later peoples were less, not more, advanced; the site was repeatedly deserted. The mound was gnawed, undressed, opened, the anatomy of ancient times exposed, the stones of twenty Jerichoes exhumed. Mud-brick and pottery were read for clues to personality like the palm of one's hand. Palestine was "overripe," said Richard Burton, the most adventuresome of the region's nineteenth-century explorers. "It is a luxuriance of ruin; and there is not a large ruin in the country which does not prove upon examination to be the composition of ruins more ancient still." The concrete fort on the edge of town was British, Jordanian, Israeli, now Palestinian. The little downtown slept, waked, slept another century, was waking. Another layer was nearly complete—being patted down. You become convinced this Jericho you see is the one that will last and that here—finally—is something permanent. Then another layer goes on top of it.

I trailed behind the first tour group of the morning at the mound, wanting to eavesdrop. I had done it many times. I would hear professional guides reading aloud from the Book of Joshua and a camel grunting in the parking lot and the honking of the buses and the desperate salesmanship of the men selling keffiyas. The small audiences usually wilted away in the heat. They stripped off as much clothing as decency allowed and swatted the flies. After reading a few verses most of the guides would point to the crumbly mud-brick and to the stones, and say something on the order of, You see, it is as I have just read.

The first guide of the day was far better. The audience emerging from the bus was French. He led everyone onto the well-maintained path overlooking Kathleen Kenyon's largest, deepest trench. From the path you look down upon the stone tower built by the people of PPNA, and ruins of walls atop walls atop walls.

"There was one people after another," the guide began. "*Voilà.* That is the story."

Notes

There is a vast literature at least tangentially about the exploration of Jericho and the Dead Sea—explorations undertaken to meet the needs of theology, imperialism, archaeology, or wanderlust. I have supplied notes citing the materials that were especially useful.

I relied heavily on the archives of the Palestine Exploration Fund (PEF) in London, especially the unpublished correspondence of Claude Conder, Charles Tyrwhitt Drake, Herbert Kitchener, and R. W. Stewart. Also important were the unpublished letters by Conder now in the collection of the Jewish National and University Library of Hebrew University in Jerusalem. In the case of letters quoted at length, I have supplied the date of the document.

Another essential source of information is the *Palestine Exploration Quarterly* (from 1869 to 1939, the *Palestine Exploration Fund Quarterly Statement*), an idiosyncratic record of the varying fortunes of the PEF and archaeological research. Most of the occasional field reports from the survey parties were first published in that journal, as were hundreds of articles at least touching on social conditions in the Middle East.

A work infrequently cited but to which I owe a large intellectual debt is Neil Asher Silberman's *Digging for God and Country* (New York: Knopf, 1982), which documents the links between archaeology and Western nationalism. I am indebted too to Yehoshua Ben-Arieh's encyclopedia of exploration, *The Rediscovery of the Holy Land in the Nineteenth Century* (Jerusalem: Magnes Press, 1983).

For the large supporting cast of Englishmen, biographical details from *The Dictionary of National Biography* and its supplements are not cited in the notes. Biblical quotations are from the Revised Standard Version (New York: Thomas Nelson, 1953). In transliterating Arabic names and phrases, I have used the spellings already familiar to me or those suggested by the individuals I interviewed.

Finally, a few words about geographical names.

I refer to Egypt and the eastern Mediterranean coast as the *Middle East,* a term coined in 1902. That was well after the work conducted by Charles Warren and the explorers who were his immediate descendants. But I find the term less musty, and perhaps less imperial, than the *Levant* or any other alternative.

Borders in the Middle East have changed more than once. For the sake of consistency, I have tried to use the place-names as they are applied today. (So Beirut, for example, is described as a port in Lebanon and not, as was the case until the 1920s, a city within Syria.) An unavoidable exception to the rule is *Palestine.* Here, the word refers to the territory between the Jordan River and the Mediterranean Sea—the area governed by the British as a single entity from the end of World War I until 1948. It is just that, and only that: a place-name. To interpret my use of it as commentary on the political fortunes of Israel or of Palestinians would be to mistake this book for something it does not attempt to be.

Abbreviations

AASOR	*Annual of the American Schools of Oriental Research*
BASOR	*Bulletin of the American Schools of Oriental Research*
PEQ	*Palestine Exploration Quarterly;* before 1939, *Palestine Exploration Fund Quarterly Statement*
SWP	*The Survey of Western Palestine*

I. Winter Castle

Charles Warren was new to Jericho and to Palestine; . . . : Warren's best account of his work in Palestine is *Underground Jerusalem* (London: Richard Bentley, 1876). I also relied on his dispatches to the PEF, collected as *The Warren Reports,* 1–47, 1867–70 (London: Wm. Dawson, reprinted 1968). See also Charles Wilson and Charles Warren, *The Recovery of Jerusalem* (London: Richard Bentley, 1871). Warren was bitter that the PEF withheld some of his reports to avoid offending financial contributors. Those reports were published as part of *SWP, Jerusalem* (London: Palestine Exploration Fund, 1884). A useful biography of Warren was written by a grandson, Watkin W. Williams, *The Life of General Sir Charles Warren* (Oxford: Basil Blackwell, 1941).

Royal Engineers mapped territory . . . : The Royal Engineers can trace their origins, albeit somewhat hazily, back to the engineer who built fortifications for William the Conqueror in 1066. See Whitworth Porter, *History of the Corps of Royal Engineers,* vol. 1 (London: Longmans, 1889). Warren's experiences at Woolwich are described by Williams, *The Life,* pp. 25–26. Mutinies by cadets are in Trevor Royle, *The Kitchener Enigma* (London: Michael Joseph, 1985), p. 19.

. . . an organization barely out of diapers . . . : V. D. Lipman, "The Origins of the Palestine Exploration Fund," *PEQ* (January–June 1988): 45–54. James Fergusson's role is described by George Grove in *PEQ* (July 1880): 197–98. The PEF offers a sanitized version of its infancy in *Our Work in Palestine* (London: Bentley, 1877).

Captain Charles Wilson was the officer . . . : Charles W. Wilson, *Ordnance Survey of Jerusalem* (London, 1865; facsimile edition, Jerusalem: Ariel, 1980). S. Anderson tells of the first PEF survey in Wilson and Warren's *Recovery of Jerusalem,* pp. 341–67. The early surveys are described by Jonathan N. Tubb and Rupert L. Chapman, *Archaeology and the Bible* (London: British Museum, 1990), pp. 15–20.

"To us of the Palestine Fund," . . . : Grove made his remarks in June 1871 at the PEF's annual meeting as reported in *PEQ* (August 1871): 146. For more on Jerusalem's centrality in Western thought, see Robert L. Wilken, *The Land Called Holy* (New Haven: Yale University Press, 1992), p. 11.

The Ottoman Empire was a Great Power . . . : Western artists' depictions of Islamic society are among the subjects of MaryAnne Stevens, ed., *The Orientalists: Delacroix to Matisse* (London: Royal Academy of Arts, 1984). See especially in that volume the essay by Malcolm Warner, "The Question of Faith: Orientalism, Christianity, and Islam," pp. 32–39.

So it was with Napoleon . . . : J. Christopher Herold, *Bonaparte in Egypt* (New York: Harper and Row, 1962).

Abd al-Rahman: Moshe Maoz, *Ottoman Reform in Syria and Palestine, 1840–1861* (Oxford: Clarendon Press, 1968), pp. 120–23, 132–34.

Muhammad Ali . . . Ibrahim Pasha: Maoz, *Ottoman Reform,* pp. 11–19, 70–71, 161–62. Ibrahim Pasha's downfall is described by Monk Neophitos of Cyprus, *Extracts from Annals of Palestine, 1821–1841,* trans. S. N. Spyridon (Jerusalem: Ariel, 1980), pp. 80–84. Details about the Ottoman taxation system are in Roger Owen, *The Middle East in the World Economy, 1800–1914* (London: Methuen, 1981), pp. 35–38, 81.

Felix Fabri: Felix Fabri, *The Book of the Wanderings of Brother Felix Fabri,* vol. 2 (London: Palestine Pilgrims' Text Society, 1893). The description of pilgrims visiting "with their eyes closed" is by Frederick Jones Bliss, *The Development of Palestine Exploration* (London: Hodder and Stoughton, 1906), p. 134.

"There was such a disturbance . . .": Fabri, *The Book of Wanderings,* vol. 2, pp. 42–43.

"I should never advise . . .": Fabri, *The Book of Wanderings,* vol. 2, p. 5. The warning from the Russian Orthodox priest is in Stephen Graham, *With the Russian Pilgrims to Jerusalem* (London: Macmillan, 1913), p. 6. Comments by François René de Chateaubriand are in his *Itineraire de Paris à Jerusalem,* vol. 2 (Baltimore: Johns Hopkins University Press, 1946), pp. 75–77.

Edward Robinson: Edward Robinson and Eli Smith, *Biblical Researches in Palestine, Mount Sinai, and Arabia Petraea,* vol. 2 (London: John Murray, 1841), pp. 267–85.

Something about the villagers . . . : Some women in Riha apparently were prostitutes who found customers among soldiers and other passersby. The expressions of disgust are from H. B. Tristram, *The Land of Israel* (London: Society for Promoting Christian Knowledge, 1866), pp. 209–10; and Edwin Hodder, *On Holy Ground* (New York: Whittaker, 1878), p. 122. John Lloyd Stephens, a young American lawyer who came to Riha in 1837, is seemingly the only nineteenth-century traveler to write favorably of the women: "It was a beautiful moonlight night, and all the women were out of doors singing and dancing. . . . I had never seen so gay and joyous a scene among the women in the East." This quote is from John Lloyd Stephens, *Incidents of Travel in Egypt, Arabia Petraea, and the Holy Land* (Norman: University of Oklahoma Press, 1970), p. 387.

Visitors found the heat intolerable: Lieutenant Van de Velde traveled through most of Palestine to map the country, only to have his work overshadowed by the much grander efforts of the PEF. C. W. M. Van de Velde, *Narrative of a Journey through Syria and Palestine in 1851 and 1852* (Edinburgh: William Blackwood, 1854), pp. 274–78.

Mr. and Mrs. Corsbie: Their story is told by Elizabeth Anne Finn, wife of the long-serving British consul in Jerusalem, James Finn. Elizabeth Anne Finn, *Reminiscences of Mrs. Finn* (London: Marshall, Morgan and Scott, [1929?]), pp. 229–30.

"We just pursued our own course; . . .": Edward Robinson's remarks are quoted by David H. Finnie, *Pioneers East, the Early American Experience in the Middle East* (Cambridge: Harvard University Press, 1967), p. 177. It was William Thomson who called Robinson "master of measuring tape," quoted by Finnie, p. 178.

"It may be said for a certainty . . .": Warren, *Underground Jerusalem,* pp. 196–97.

"Give us results . . . and you have the money": This unfriendly exchange between Grove and Warren is Warren's version of events and probably a paraphrase of the original correspondence, which has been lost. Warren, *Underground Jerusalem,* pp. 3–4.

. . . "or we shall be bankrupt": Charles Warren, *PEQ* (April 1925): 62.

Archbishop of York: The enthusiasm of members of the PEF is recorded in a report on the organization's annual meeting, held June 24, 1869. *PEQ* (July–September 1869): 90–103. A list of the PEF's first members is in *PEQ* (April 1869): unnumbered first page.

Grove already had a new project . . . : Grove made his optimistic forecasts at the PEF meeting held June 29, 1871. *PEQ* (August 1871): 145–49.

II. In a Postcard

The valley is an open-air theater . . . : Raphael Freund et al., "Age and Rate of the Sinistral Movement along the Dead Sea Rift," *Nature* 220, no. 6164 (1968): 253–55; Raphael Freund et al., "The Shear along the Dead Sea Rift," *Philosophical Transactions of the Royal Society of London, Series A* 267 (1970): 107–30; and Zvi Garfunkel, "The Geology of the Dead Sea Rift," *Rotem* (April 1986): 8–30.

Freund elevated one highly technical paper . . . : Freund, "The Shear along the Dead Sea Rift," p. 107.

. . . a British physician named Gurney Masterman . . . : Masterman, whose work is described in greater detail in chapter 8, regularly contributed reports to *PEQ* between 1902 and 1913. Mention of "unsettled conditions" is in *PEQ* (October 1910): 290–91. The warning that "no European would be safe" is in *PEQ* (January 1911): 59–61.

Kaiser Wilhelm's visit: Preparations for the kaiser's visit are described by Conrad Schick, *PEQ* (January 1899): 116–17.

It refers to events his generation . . . : The most scholarly account to date of the Palestinian exodus is in Benny Morris, *The Birth of the Palestinian Refugee Problem, 1947–1949* (Cambridge: Cambridge University Press, 1987). Danny Rubinstein, *The People of Nowhere* (New York: Times Books, 1991), adds useful details. Panic at the Jericho camps in 1967 is described by Peter Dodd and Halim Barakat, *River Without Bridges* (Beirut: Institute for Palestine Studies, 1969). For an account of Jordanian strategy, see Samir A. Mutawi, *Jordan in the 1967 War* (Cambridge: Cambridge University Press, 1987), pp. 117–46.

King Abdullah organized a political convention . . . : Moshe Maoz, *Palestinian Leadership in the West Bank* (London: Frank Cass, 1984), pp. 24–25; Mary C. Wilson, *King Abdullah, Britain, and the Making of Jordan* (Cambridge: Cambridge University Press, 1987), pp. 182–85.

"The system of government is simple," . . . : Claude Reignier Conder, *Tent Work in Palestine*, vol. 2 (London: Richard Bentley, 1878), pp. 265–66.

III. Downtown

Then they utterly destroyed . . . : Joshua 6:21, 24.

Joshua placed a curse . . . : Joshua 6:26; see Robert G. Boling and G. Ernest Wright, *Joshua,* vol. 6 of *The Anchor Bible* (Garden City, N.Y.: Doubleday, 1982), pp. 210, 214.

The story . . . was more than a tale of adventure: Boling and Wright, *Joshua,* p. 51; William G. Dever, *Recent Archaeological Discoveries and Biblical Research* (Seattle: University of Washington Press, 1990), pp. 32, 169–71; Roland de Vaux, "On the Right and Wrong Uses of Archaeology," in *Near Eastern Archaeology in the Twentieth Century,* ed. J. A. Sanders (Garden City, N.Y.: Doubleday, 1970), pp. 70–78.

In the second century B.C. . . . the Hasmoneans . . . : Anyone writing about the Hasmoneans, Herod, or the Jewish revolt against Rome is dependent on Flavius Josephus. The titles listed here are issued as part of the Loeb Classical Library. Josephus, *The Jewish War,* books 1–3, trans. H. Thackeray (Cambridge: Harvard University Press, 1989); *The Jewish War,* books 4–7, trans. H. Thackeray (Cambridge: Harvard University Press, 1990). Also, Josephus, *Jewish Antiquities,* books 12–14, trans. Ralph Marcus (Cambridge: Harvard University Press, 1986); *Jewish Antiquities,* books 15–17, trans. Ralph Marcus (Cambridge: Harvard University Press, 1990); *Jewish Antiquities,* books 18–19, trans. Louis H. Feldman (Cambridge: Harvard University Press, 1992); *Jewish Antiquities,* book 20, trans. Louis H. Feldman (Cambridge: Harvard University Press, 1993). For a scholarly though accessible biography, see Tessa Rajak, *Josephus* (London: Duckworth, 1983). A popularized account is by Mireille Hadas-Lebel, *Flavius Josephus* (New York: Macmillan, 1993).

In the imagined portraits . . . : An evil-faced Herod is in Matteo di Giovanni's *Massacre of the Innocents* in Siena, Italy. A no less intimidating rendering is in a mosaic in the Basilica of San Marco in Venice. They are reproduced in Michael Grant, *Herod the Great* (New York: American Heritage, 1971), pp. 225, 228.

. . . Jericho was meanwhile a private sunroom: Ehud Netzer is the area's latest excavator. The architecture of the Hasmonean and Herodian palaces and the probable uses of each building are described by him in "The Hasmonean Palaces in Eretz-Israel," *Biblical Archaeology Today, 1990* (Jerusalem: Israel Exploration Society, 1993), pp. 126–33; and "The Winter Palaces of the Judean Kings at Jericho at the End of the Second Temple Period," *BASOR,* no. 228 (December 1977): 1–13. See also Ehud Netzer and Eric M. Meyers, "Preliminary Report on the Joint Jericho Excavation Project," *BASOR,* no. 228 (December 1977): 15–27; and Ehud Netzer, "The Hasmonean and Herodian Winter Palaces at Jericho," *Israel Exploration Journal* 25, no. 2–3 (1975): 89–100. Excavations were also conducted at Wadi

Kelt during the early 1950s; see James L. Kelso and Dimitri C. Bramki, "Excavations at New Testament Jericho and Khirbet En-Nitla," *AASOR* 29–30 (1955). Plate 3 of the photographs clearly shows the remains of a trench dug by Charles Warren.

In old age he was in great misery: Grant, *Herod the Great,* pp. 210–11, offers speculations about Herod's illnesses. Other diagnoses are in "Notes and News," *PEQ* (July–December 1960): 77–83; and Stewart Perowne, *The Life and Times of Herod the Great* (London: Hodder and Stoughton, 1956), p. 186.

. . . Herman Melville traveled from Jerusalem . . . : Herman Melville, *Journals,* ed. Howard C. Horsford with Lynn Horth (Evanston: Northwestern University Press, 1989), p. 83.

From the palaces . . . Cypros: Its use as a monastic site is described by Yizhar Hirschfeld, "List of the Byzantine Monasteries in the Judean Desert," in *Christian Archaeology in the Holy Land* (Jerusalem: Franciscan Printing Press, 1990), p. 71.

Excavators found the Jewish burial ground . . . : Interview with Rachel Hachlili. See Hachlili, "A Second Temple Period Jewish Necropolis in Jericho," *Biblical Archaeologist* (Fall 1980): 235–40; "The Goliath Family in Jericho: Funerary Inscriptions from a First Century A.D. Jewish Monumental Tomb," *BASOR,* no. 235 (1979): 31–65.

"But as the place was naturally very hot . . .": Josephus, *Jewish Antiquities,* book 15, pp. 27–29.

An otherwise anonymous Christian traveler . . . : Details about the itinerary of the Bordeaux Pilgrim are from E. D. Hunt, *Holy Land Pilgrimage in the Later Roman Empire, A.D. 312–460* (Oxford: Clarendon Press, 1982), pp. 55–56; and John Wilkinson, *Jerusalem Pilgrims* (Warminster: Aris and Phillips, 1977), p. 18. For the Piacenza Pilgrim, see Wilkinson, *Jerusalem Pilgrims,* pp. 7, 79–82. Arculf's account is in Thomas Wright, *Early Travels in Palestine* (London: Henry G. Bohn, 1848), pp. 1–12.

Warren assigned some of his workmen . . . : Charles Warren, *Underground Jerusalem* (London: Richard Bentley, 1876), pp. 193–94; C. R. Conder and H. H. Kitchener, *SWP,* vol. 3, *Judea* (London: Palestine Exploration Fund, 1883), pp. 224–25.

Claude Conder retraced some of Warren's footsteps . . . : Claude Reignier Conder, *Tent Work in Palestine,* vol. 2 (London: Richard Bentley, 1878), pp. 6–7.

The flow is one thousand gallons . . . : Levy Kroitoru et al., "Hydrological Characteristics of the Wadi Kelt and Elisha Springs," proceedings of the symposium *Scientific Basis for Water Resources Management,* Jerusalem, 1985.

"Here we pitched our tents . . .": Captain William Allen, *The Dead Sea, a New Route to India,* vol. 1 (London: Longman, 1855), pp. 232–33.

The Reverend Henry Baker Tristram: H. B. Tristram, *The Land of Israel* (London: Society for Promoting Christian Knowledge, 1866), pp. 204–36. For the story of his discovering Tristram's grackle, see Rev. Canon Tristram, "The Natural History of Palestine," in *The City and the Land* (London: Macmillan, 1892), pp. 68–69. His accomplishments as a zoologist are cited by V. D. Lipman, "Origins of the Palestine Exploration Fund," *PEQ* (January–June 1988): 54.

Napoleon's brief occupation of Egypt . . . : A list of the savants is in Jean Tulard, "The Egyptian Campaign," in Jean Vercoutter, *The Search for Ancient Egypt,* trans. Ruth Sharman (New York: Abrams, 1992), pp. 130–43. Their work is described by Brian M. Fagan, *Rape of the Nile* (Wakefield: Moyer Bell, 1992), pp. 65–81. Also by J. Christopher Herold, *Bonaparte in Egypt* (New York: Harper and Row, 1962), pp. 30–32. A now classic discussion of Western fascination with the Orient is Edward Said's *Orientalism* (New York: Vintage, 1979).

George Grove convinced his friends . . . : The PEF's prospectus is reproduced in *PEQ* (April 1869): 1–3.

"The Scriptures of the Old and New Testament . . .": The Rev. Dr. S. Manning, at the PEF meeting held June 23, 1874. *PEQ* (July 1874): 229.

Every few years the PEF changed addresses . . . : Walter Besant, "The General Work of the Society," in *The City and the Land,* pp. 97–137.

An extra spur came from the United States: Warren J. Moulton, "The American Palestine Exploration Society," *AASOR* 8 (1928): 55–78.

"We should make a clean sweep . . .": "Annual General Meeting of the Palestine Exploration Fund," *PEQ* (August 1871): 139–56.

IV. DIGGING DOWN

Ofer Bar-Yosef was one of the excavators of Ubeidiya: Ofer Bar-Yosef and N. Goren-Inbar, *The Lithic Assemblages of 'Ubeidiya* (Jerusalem: Hebrew University, 1993), pp. 5–6, 21, 109, 199.

Sometimes the term is "tools"; . . . : Ofer Bar-Yosef et al., "The Excavations in Kebara Cave, Mt. Carmel," *Current Anthropology* 33 (December 1992): 497–550; Ofer Bar-Yosef, "The Pre-Pottery Neolithic Period in the Southern Levant," *Colloques Internationaux du C.N.R.S.* (Paris: Centre national de la recherche scientifique, 1981), pp. 389–408.

. . . serious-minded critic has pointed out . . . : Frank Hole, in Bar-Yosef et al., "The Excavations in Kebara Cave," pp. 536–38.

The Natufians . . . whose experiments succeeded: Anna Belfer-Cohen, "The Natufian Issue: A Suggestion," in *Investigations in South Levantine Prehistory,* ed. Ofer Bar-Yosef and B. Vandermeersch, BAR International Series 457 (Oxford: B.A.R., 1989), pp. 297–307; Ofer Bar-Yosef and Anna Belfer-Cohen, "The Origins of Sedentism and Farming Communities in the Levant," *Journal of World Prehistory* 3 (1989): 447–98.

... the Natufians had mice: Ofer Bar-Yosef and Anna Belfer-Cohen, "From Sedentary Hunter-Gatherers to Territorial Farmers in the Levant," in *Between Bands and States,* ed. Susan A. Gregg (Carbondale: Southern Illinois University Press, 1991), pp. 188–89; Bar-Yosef and Belfer-Cohen, "The Origins of Sedentism," pp. 453, 473; Ofer Bar-Yosef and F. Valla, "The Natufian Culture and the Origin of the Neolithic in the Levant," *Current Anthropology* 31, no. 4 (August–October 1990): 435.

Kathleen Mary Kenyon, the grande dame ... : Trude Dothan uses the term in a somewhat different context in an interview published as "An Archaeological Romance," *Biblical Archaeology Review* (July–August 1993): 27.

"Once man is settled in one spot ... the rest follows": Kathleen M. Kenyon, *Archaeology in the Holy Land,* 5th ed. (Nashville: Thomas Nelson, 1979), p. 7.

Sir William Matthew Flinders Petrie: Margaret S. Drower, *Flinders Petrie, A Life in Archaeology* (London: Victor Gollancz, 1985). Petrie's liking for sterling silver spoons is noted by Camden Cobern, "The Work at Tell El Hesy as Seen by an American Visitor," *PEQ* (July 1890): 166–70. Fagan, *Rape of the Nile,* pp. 326–58, offers an appreciation of Petrie's work in Egypt. His racial theories are explored by Neil Asher Silberman, "Petrie and the Founding Fathers," in *Biblical Archaeology Today, 1990* (Jerusalem: Israel Exploration Society, 1993), pp. 545–48. Silberman generously made a copy of his paper available before publication. For Petrie's work at Tell el-Hesi, see John M. Matthers, "Excavations by the Palestine Exploration Fund at Tell el-Hesi, 1890–1892," in *Tell el-Hesi: The Site and the Expedition,* ed. Bruce T. Dahlberg and Kevin G. O'Connell (Winona Lake, Ind.: Eisenbrauns, 1989), pp. 37–67; and W. M. Flinders Petrie, "Exploration in Palestine," *PEQ* (July 1890): 159–66.

The archaeologists fought a war of labels: For comparisons of systems of periodization, see William G. Dever, "The Chronology of Syria-Palestine in the Second Millennium B.C.E.: A Review of Current Issues," *BASOR,* no. 228 (November 1992): 1–25; and Rupert L. Chapman, "The Three Ages Revisited: A Critical Study of Levantine Usage," *PEQ* (July–December 1989): 89–111.

Ernst Sellin thus came to stand ... : Ernst Sellin and Carl Watzinger, *Jericho Die Ergebnisse der Ausgrabungen* (Leipzig, 1913; reprinted Osnabruck: Otto Zeller Verlag, 1973). An intellectual profile of Sellin is in Silberman, "Petrie and the Founding Fathers," pp. 548–49.

In 1926 Watzinger conscientiously reviewed the archaeological finds ... : His revised conclusions about ancient Jericho were published in *Zeitschrift der deutschen morgenländischen Gesellschaft,* 1926, pp. 131–36. For an unfavorable commentary, see W. J. Phythian-Adams, "Israelite Tradition and the Date of Joshua," *PEQ* (January 1927): 34–47. William Foxwell Albright had already noted problems with the dates first assigned to the ruins; see his "Excavations and Results at Tell el-Ful," *AASOR* 4 (1924): 147–49; and "The Jordan Valley in the Bronze Age," *AASOR* 6 (1926): 49–53.

"The trouble is . . . brick looks . . . like any other sort of earth": All the comments by Thomas Hodgkin are from E. C. Hodgkin, ed., *Thomas Hodgkin Letters from Palestine,* 1932–36 (London: Quartet, 1986), pp. 7–21.

Garstang's first impression . . . : John Garstang and J. B. E. Garstang, *The Story of Jericho,* 2nd ed. (London: Hodder and Stoughton, 1947), pp. 43–44. Garstang's preliminary reports on the excavations at the mound appeared in *PEQ* from 1930 to 1936; more detailed reports, entitled "Jericho: City and Necropolis," appeared in *Liverpool Annals of Archaeology and Anthropology,* 1932–36.

She was in every sense a large, domineering figure: For a portrait of Kenyon's upbringing and character, see P. R. S. Moorey, "British Women in Near Eastern Archaeology: Kathleen Kenyon and the Pioneers," *PEQ* (July–December 1992): 96–99; P. R. S. Moorey, "Kathleen Kenyon and Palestinian Archaeology," *PEQ* (January–June 1979): 7; and Jacquetta Hawkes, *Adventurer in Archaeology, the Biography of Sir Mortimer Wheeler* (New York: St. Martin's Press, 1982), p. 132. A posthumous evaluation of her career was written by one of her closest collaborators, A. D. Tushingham, "Kathleen Mary Kenyon," *Proceedings of the British Academy* 71 (1985): 555–82.

She was refining techniques . . . : Concise descriptions of the Wheeler-Kenyon method are in William G. Dever, "Archaeological Method in Israel: A Continuing Revolution," *Biblical Archaeologist* 43, no. 1 (Winter 1980): 44; and Amihai Mazar, *Archaeology in the Land of the Bible, 10,000–586 B.C.E.* (New York: Doubleday, 1990), pp. 23–25. Kenyon herself wrote two archaeological handbooks, "Excavation Methods in Palestine," *PEQ* (January 1939): 29–37; and *Beginning in Archaeology* (London: Phoenix House, 1952). She had in fact independently reintroduced methods used earlier in the region by George A. Reisner. See John E. Worrell, "The Evolution of a Holistic Investigation: Phase One of the Joint Expedition to Tell el-Hesi," in *Tell el-Hesi: The Site and the Expedition,* pp. 74–78.

Kenyon had some twenty assistants . . . : Daily routines among the excavators are described by Margaret Wheeler, *Walls of Jericho* (London: Readers Union, 1958); P. R. S. Moorey and P. J. Parr, *Archaeology in the Levant* (Warminister: Aris and Phillips, 1978), p. ix; and Kay Prag, "Kathleen Kenyon and Archaeology in the Holy Land," *PEQ* (July–December 1992): 113.

By the end of the first season . . . : Kenyon describes her work in Kathleen M. Kenyon, *Digging Up Jericho* (London: Ernest Benn, 1957); and in her *Archaeology in the Holy Land.* The preliminary excavation reports appeared in *PEQ,* 1951–57, 1960. As described later in this chapter, the subsequent final reports are in some senses incomplete. The five volumes, plus one volume of plates, were published from 1960 to 1983, beginning with Kathleen M. Kenyon, *Excavations at Jericho,* vol. 1, *The Tombs Excavated in 1952–4* (Jerusalem: British School of Archaeology in Jerusalem, 1960). A detailed summary that adds more recent findings is T. A. Holland, "Jericho," in *The Anchor Bible Dictionary,* vol. 3 (New York: Doubleday, 1992), pp. 723–37.

No matter what technology was applied . . . : A provocative discussion of the limits of pottery typology is in D. Glenn Rose, "The Methodology of the New Archaeology and Its Influence on the Joint Expedition to Tell el-Hesi," *Tell el-Hesi: The Site and the Expedition,* pp. 72–87. See also G. Ernest Wright, "The Phenomenon of American Archaeology in the Near East," in *Near Eastern Archaeology in the Twentieth Century,* ed. J. A. Sanders (Garden City, N.Y.: Doubleday, 1970), pp. 26–28; and Donald Kuspit, "A Mighty Metaphor: The Analogy of Archaeology and Psychoanalysis," in *Sigmund Freud and Art,* ed. Lynn Gamwell and Richard Wells (New York: State University of New York Press, 1989), pp. 146–50.

The hill was called Amarna . . . : The discovery of the Amarna letters is described in A. H. Sayce, *Reminiscences* (London: Macmillan, 1923), pp. 251–61; A. H. Sayce, "The Discovery of the Tel El-Amarna Tablets," *American Journal of Semitic Languages* 33 (1916–17): 89–90; and E. A. Wallis Budge, *A History of Egypt,* vol. 4 (London, 1902), p. 185. Quotations from the Amarna letters are taken from William L. Moran, *The Amarna Letters* (Baltimore: Johns Hopkins University Press, 1992).

"Desolate is Tehenu; . . .": James B. Pritchard, *Ancient Near Eastern Texts,* 3rd ed. (Princeton: Princeton University Press, 1969), pp. 376–78.

"That we miscalculated," . . . : Tushingham, *Proceedings of the British Academy,* p. 567.

Bar-Yosef concluded that water and mud . . . : Ofer Bar-Yosef, "The Walls of Jericho: An Alternative Interpretation," *Current Anthropology* (April 1986): 157–62.

The archaeologist Peter Dorrell: Moorey and Parr, *Archaeology in the Levant,* p. 15.

A year later, she began excavating in Jerusalem: An evaluation of the work is in the final excavation report, H. J. Franken and M. L. Steiner, *Excavations in Jerusalem, 1961–1967,* vol. 2 (Oxford: Oxford University Press, 1990), p. 1. See also A. D. Tushingham, *Excavations in Jerusalem, 1961–1967,* vol. 1 (Toronto: Royal Ontario Museum, 1985).

My summary . . . is William Dever's: Interview with Dever. Also, William G. Dever, *Recent Archaeological Discoveries and Biblical Research* (Seattle: University of Washington Press, 1990), esp. pp. 56–64.; and William G. Dever, "Archaeology and the Israelite 'Conquest,'" *Anchor Bible Dictionary,* vol. 3, pp. 545–58.

. . . an alternative process is Israel Finklestein's: Interview with Finklestein. Also, Israel Finklestein, *The Archaeology of the Israelite Settlement* (Jerusalem: Israel Exploration Society, 1988), esp. pp. 295–302, 336–48.

V. SHEEP TRAILS

Herders were an offspring of early farmers . . . : Ofer Bar-Yosef and Anatoly Khazanov, *Pastoralism in the Levant* (Madison: Prehistory Press, 1992), pp. 1–9. In the same volume, Eran Ovadia, "The Domestication of the Ass and Pack Transport by Animals: A Case of Technological Change," pp. 19–28.

Rabbinic sages were intrigued by the story: Nogah Hareuveni, *Desert and Shepherd in Our Biblical Heritage*, trans. Helen Frenkley (Lod, Israel: Neot Kedumin, 1991), pp. 17–22.

Hisham Abed al-Malilkh: Laura Veccia Vaglieri, "The Patriarchal and Umayyad Caliphates," in *The Cambridge History of Islam*, ed. P. M. Holt et al., vol. 1a (Cambridge: Cambridge University Press, 1970), pp. 57–96; Albert Hourani, *A History of the Arab Peoples* (London: Faber and Faber, 1991), pp. 22–31.

"Of him it was said," . . . : Vaglieri, "The Patriarchal and Umayyad Caliphates," p. 80.

The Umayyad architects chose . . . an area: R. W. Hamilton, "The Baths at Khirbat Mafjar," *PEQ* (January–April 1949): 40–51; *Khirbat al Mafjar* (Oxford: Clarendon Press, 1959); and "Who Built Khirbat al Mafjar?" *Levant* 1 (1969): 61–67.

The palace ruins became one of the oddly shaped mounds . . . : F. J. Bliss, "Notes on the Plain of Jericho," *PEQ* (July 1894): 175–83. Conder wrote of the ruins in C. R. Conder and H. H. Kitchener, *SWP*, vol. 3, *Judea* (London: Palestine Exploration Fund, 1883), pp. 211–12.

Drake was always unlike the others: An account of his early years is in Walter Besant, ed., *The Literary Remains of the Late Charles F. Tyrwhitt Drake* (London: Richard Bentley, 1877), pp. 1–6.

Edward Henry Palmer: Walter Besant, *The Life and Achievements of Edward Henry Palmer* (New York: Dutton, 1883); Walter Besant, "Edward Henry Palmer," *PEQ* (January 1883): 4–7; and Watkin W. Williams, *The Life of General Sir Charles Warren* (Oxford: Basil Blackwell, 1941), p. 126.

As a reward for the work in the Sinai . . . : Palmer's account of the work in the Negev is E. H. Palmer, *The Desert of the Exodus* (New York: Harper and Brothers, 1872).

No portrait of Burton could be too bright . . . : Of the many biographies devoted to Burton, the two relied on here are Edward Rice, *Captain Sir Richard Francis Burton* (New York: HarperPerennial, 1991); and Georgiana M. Stisted, *The True Life of Capt. Sir Richard F. Burton* (New York: D. Appleton, 1897). Other details are from Richard F. Burton and Charles F. Tyrwhitt Drake, *Unexplored Syria*, 2 vols. (London: Tinsley Brothers, 1872).

Life with the Burtons could surpass . . . : Rice, *Burton*, pp. 523–24.

Burton was fired . . . as consul . . . : Rice, *Burton,* pp. 529–33; Stisted, *The True Life,* p. 361. Burton describes the events in Burton and Drake, *Unexplored Syria,* vol. 1, pp. 21–22.

"I am sorry I am not in a position . . .": Letter of September 30, 1871, Drake to PEF.

Edward Palmer in the years ahead . . . : Besant, *Life and Achievements,* pp. 120–26, 219–28, describes Palmer's rejection by Cambridge and his series of odd jobs. For an account of his disappearance in the Sinai and the search for him, see Alfred E. Haynes, *Man-Hunting in the Desert* (London: Horace Cox, 1894). A day-by-day record of various missteps by the military is contained in a submission to the Houses of Parliament, *Correspondence Respecting the Murder of Professor E. H. Palmer, Captain Wm. Gill, R. E., and Lieutenant Harold Charrington, R.N.,* London, 1883. Charles Warren prepared his own report, *Colonel Warren's Proceedings, Report to Admiral Alcester,* February 15, 1883. The PEF archives contain a small part of Palmer's diary as well as items recovered near the bodies.

Dr. Thomas Chaplin . . . was one of the animating figures: His remarks on Jerusalem's unhealthfulness are quoted in Yehoshua Ben-Arieh, *Jerusalem in the 19th Century, the Old City* (New York: St. Martin's Press, 1984), p. 90.

"I ride up to a man ploughing . . .": Letter of February 1, 1872, Drake to PEF. The letter was published in *PEQ* (April 1872): 36–47.

VI. "Working Like Smoke"

In 1805, Ulrich Seetzen . . . : [Ulrich J.] Seetzen, *A Brief Account of the Countries Adjoining the Lake of Tiberias, the Jordan, and the Dead Sea* (Bath: Palestine Association of London, 1810), pp. 41–42.

Jean-Louis Burckhardt: John Lewis Burckhardt, *Travels in Syria and the Holy Land* (London: John Murray, 1822).

"In England," he writes Besant . . . : Quotations from Conder, Drake, and other members of the survey team are, as noted above, from letters now in the archives of the PEF and the Jewish National and University Library of Hebrew University; from Claude Reignier Conder, *Tent Work in Palestine,* vols. 1 and 2 (London: Richard Bentley, 1878); and from the field reports published in *PEQ.* Conder's complaint to Besant, and the list of supplies to be sent from Britain, are in a letter written in Nablus, dated July 18, 1872.

For glory, Conder in the autumn of 1872 . . . : Conder and Drake's sketches of the figurines are in the PEF archives. Clermont-Ganneau and Drake offer details about these sculptures in letters appearing under the title "The Shapira Collection," *PEQ* (April 1874): 114–24. Some aspects of the controversy are described in Neil Asher Silberman, *Digging for God and Country* (New York: Knopf, 1982), pp. 32–34; and Naomi Shepherd, *The Zealous Intruders, The Western Rediscovery of Palestine* (San Francisco: Harper and Row, 1987), pp. 210–13.

Two feet wide, about three feet high . . . : The story of the Moabite Stone, from the point of view of Prussia, is reprinted from the *Zeitschrift der deutschen morgenländischen Gesellschaft* in H. Petermann, "The Moabite Stone," *PEQ* (August 1871): 135–39. For Warren's version, see Charles Warren, "The Moabite Stone," *SWP, Special Papers* (London: Palestine Exploration Fund, 1881), pp. 123–25. Helpful reconstructions of events were in Siegfried H. Horn, "The Discovery of the Moabite Stone," in *The Word of the Lord Shall Go Forth,* ed. Carol L. Meyers and M. O'Connor (Winona Lake, Ind.: Eisenbrauns, 1983), pp. 497–505; and Silberman, *Digging for God and Country,* pp. 100–112. A useful account, including a new translation of the Moabite inscription, is André Lemaire, "House of David Restored in Moabite Inscription," *Biblical Archaeology Review* (May–June 1994): 30–37.

"Like a lucky actress or singer," . . . : G. Rawlinson, "The Moabite Stone," *The Contemporary Review* (November 1870): 97.

The hero is Charles Drake: Drake restates his opinions about the figurines in a letter sent to Walter Besant and dated November 11, 1873.

Evidence has been found to support him: The excavations, and the recently discovered sculptures, are described in Itzhak Ben-Arieh, *The New Encyclopedia of Archaeological Excavations in the Holy Land,* ed. Ephraim Stern, vol. 2 (New York: Simon and Schuster, 1993), pp. 1230–33. Mention of the sculptures is made in Shepherd, *Zealous Intruders,* pp. 214, 221.

After touring North Africa, the painter Eugène Fromentin . . . : Cited in Malcolm Warner, "The Question of Faith: Orientalism, Christianity, and Islam," in *The Orientalists: Delacroix to Matisse,* ed. MaryAnne Stevens (London: Royal Academy of Arts, 1984), p. 34. Artists' false realism is among the subjects of Linda Nochlin, "The Imaginary Orient," *Art in America* (May 1983): 118–31, 187–91.

Thanks to diplomacy of Charles Warren . . . : Warren's good relations with the Jewish community are mentioned during one of the PEF's annual meetings, in *PEQ* (July–September 1869): 347. Also, Watkin W. Williams, *The Life of General Sir Charles Warren* (Oxford: Basil Blackwell, 1941), pp. 423–24.

Conder's ultimate prescription . . . : Conder's changing opinions about Jews and their role in Palestine are found in the following publications of his: "The Present Condition in Palestine," *PEQ* (January 1879): 6–15; "The Colonisation of Palestine," *PEQ* (April 1880): 116–18; "The Future of Palestine," in *The City and the Land* (London: Macmillan, 1892), pp. 46–54; "Jewish Colonies in Palestine," *Blackwood's Magazine* (June 1891): 856–70; and "The Zionists," *Blackwood's Magazine* (May 1898): 598–609.

In the year 478 . . . : For the history of Mar Saba, see Yizhar Hirschfeld, "List of the Byzantine Monasteries in the Judean Desert," in *Christian Archaeology in the Holy Land* (Jerusalem: Franciscan Printing Press, 1990), pp. 31–32.

In the few photographs from that time . . . : The photographs are reproduced by Peter G. Dorrell, "The Spring at Jericho from Early Photographs," *PEQ* (July–December 1993): 95–114.

Common wisdom . . . : *The Theological and Literary Journal* (New York, July 1849–April 1850): 300.

To their great credit, Conder and Drake . . . : Drake suggests that Palestine has not changed radically since Bible times in *PEQ* (April 1874): 75. Borrowing heavily from his colleague, Conder makes the same argument in *PEQ* (July 1876): 126–32; and later in *Tent Work,* vol. 2, pp. 26–27.

He had provided services in the 1860s . . . : H. B. Tristram, *The Land of Israel* (London: Society for Promoting Christian Knowledge, 1866), pp. 220–21.

"They were kindly, good-natured, and obliging fellows . . .": Tristram, *The Land of Israel,* p. 268.

Even the name was inauspicious: Tristram, *The Land of Israel,* pp. 350–53, 372.

A telephone crew . . . : Hananya Hizmi, "The Byzantine Church at Khirbet El-Beiyudat: Preliminary Report," in *Christian Archaeology,* pp. 245–63.

A few of the tribes prospered . . . : Changes in Bedouin society, and especially of the Bani Sakhr, are described in Norman N. Lewis, *Nomads and Settlers in Syria and Jordan, 1800–1980* (Cambridge: Cambridge University Press, 1987), esp. pp. 135–37. See also Mary C. Wilson, *King Abdullah, Britain, and the Making of Jordan* (Cambridge: Cambridge University Press, 1987), pp. 98–99.

Conder knew them as "hating . . .": Claude Reignier Conder, *Heth and Moab* (London: Macmillan, 1892), pp. 326–27.

For part of the way, the governor himself . . . : E. W. G. Masterman and R. A. S. MacAlister, "Occasional Papers on the Modern Inhabitants of Palestine," *PEQ* (October 1915): 176–78; Harry Charles Luke and Edward Keith-Roach, *The Handbook of Palestine and Trans-Jordan,* 2nd ed. (London: Macmillan, 1930), p. 201; E. C. Hodgkin, ed., *Thomas Hodgkin Letters from Palestine, 1932–36* (London: Quartet, 1986), pp. 125–26.

After World War I . . . : Yehoshua Porath, *The Emergence of the Palestinian-Arab National Movement, 1918–1929* (London: Frank Cass, 1974), pp. 98–99, 202–6; Ronald Sanders, *The High Walls of Jerusalem* (New York: Holt, Rinehart and Winston, 1983), p. 653; and Conor Cruise O'Brien, *The Siege* (New York: Simon and Schuster, 1986), p. 146.

At Ein es Sultan, the Frenchman ordered the workmen . . . : Charles Clermont-Ganneau, *Archaeological Researches in Palestine,* vol. 2 (London: Harrison and Sons, 1896), pp. 27, 32–33, 39.

Clermont-Ganneau spent a day with Charles Drake . . . : Charles Clermont-Ganneau, "Letters from M. Clermont-Ganneau," *PEQ* (April 1874): 83; C. R. Conder and H. H. Kitchener, *SWP,* vol. 3, *Judea* (London: Palestine Exploration Fund, 1883), p. 210.

Louis-Félicien de Saulcy: F. de Saulcy, *Voyage autour de la Mer Morte,* vol. 2 (Paris: Gide et J. Baudry, 1853), pp. 159–67. His tumultuous career is described in Fernande Bassan, *Carnets de Voyage en Orient (1845–1869)* (Paris: Presses Universitaires de France, 1955), pp. 2–5, 20.

In 1902, Gurney Masterman . . . : E. W. G. Masterman, "Ain el-Feshkah, El-Hajar, El-Asbarh, and Khurbet Kumran," *PEQ* (April 1902): 161–62; and his "Notes on Some Ruins and a Rock-Cut Aqueduct in the Wady Kumran," *PEQ* (July 1903): 267.

Discovery of the first Dead Sea Scrolls . . . : Philip R. Davies, *Qumran* (Guildford: Lutterworth Press, 1982), pp. 30–36. For a concise account of the significance of Qumran, see J. Murphy-O'Connor, "Khirbet Qumran," in *The Anchor Bible Dictionary,* vol. 5 (New York: Doubleday, 1992), pp. 590–94.

Flavius Josephus placed it ten stadia . . . : Locations proposed for biblical Gilgal are listed in C. Umhau Wolf, "Khirbet en-Nitla not the Byzantine Gilgal," in Kelso and Bramki, *AASOR* 29–30, pp. 58–59; and Boyce M. Bennett, Jr., "The Search for Israelite Gilgal," *PEQ* (July–December 1972): 111–22.

What had excited Conder . . . : Conder, Drake, and Clermont-Ganneau sent the PEF separate reports on Gilgal. They appeared in *PEQ* and were reprinted in *SWP,* vol. 3, *Judea,* pp. 174–84.

What had he found?: For the modern excavation report, see Dimitri C. Bramki, "The Excavations at Khirbet en-Nitla," in Kelso and Bramki, *AASOR* 29–30, pp. 50–52. See also Hirschfeld, "List of Byzantine Monasteries," pp. 50–52.

. . . a later survey found *fourteen* sites . . . : Study by G. Dalman, "Der Gilgal der Bibel und die Steinkreise Palastinas," published in 1920, cited by Bennett, "The Search for Israelite Gilgal," p. 115.

"If Drake's health does not get better . . ." Conder's letter of December 12, 1873, to the PEF.

Jericho fever: Details about the symptoms, identification, and transmission of cutaneous leishmaniasis are drawn from Gerald L. Mabell et al., eds., *Principles and Practice of Infectious Diseases* (New York: Churchill Livingstone, 1990), pp. 2067–77; Paul D. Hoeprich and M. Colin Jordan, *Infectious Diseases* (Philadelphia: Lippincott, 1989), pp. 1341–52. Biographical information about Dr. William

Boog Leishman is from Robert S. Desowitz, *The Malaria Capers* (New York: Norton, 1993), pp. 44–46; and M. Walker, *Pioneers of Public Health* (New York: Macmillan, 1930), pp. 252–63. Leishman's major success was discovering that the parasite *Leishmania* was responsible for kala-azar.

In 1918, Gurney Masterman . . . : E. W. G. Masterman, "Hygiene and Disease in Palestine in Modern and in Biblical Times," *PEQ* (April 1918): 61–69.

People knew it as swamp fever: This account relies heavily on Desowitz, *The Malaria Capers,* esp. pp. 149–51, 199–206. See also Marc Kusinitz, *Tropical Medicine* (New York: Chelsea House, 1990), pp. 71–72.

Charles Warren had attributed his own case . . . : Charles Warren, *Underground Jerusalem* (London: Richard Bentley, 1876), pp. 164, 203.

Yet he sounded cheerful enough . . . : Drake's last report was found among his papers after his death and was published in *PEQ* (January 1875): 27–34.

In mid-June, Dr. Chaplin wrote to inform him . . . : Chaplin's letter to Conder dated June 11, 1874.

One of the guests at the PEF's annual meeting . . . : Besant's comments about finances are in Besant, *The City and the Land,* pp. 107–8. Conder's speech and the comments of others at the annual meeting are in *PEQ* (July 1874): 221–40.

VII. Pious Ambition

A monk named Gerasimus . . . : This account of Byzantine monasticism in the Judean desert, and the story of Gerasimus and the monasteries built at Hajla, is drawn mainly from interviews with Yizhar Hirschfeld and his published writings. See Yizhar Hirschfeld, "List of the Byzantine Monasteries in the Judean Desert," in *Christian Archaeology in the Holy Land* (Jerusalem: Franciscan Printing Press, 1990), pp. 1–89; *The Judean Monasteries in the Byzantine Period* (New Haven: Yale University Press, 1992); and "Gerasimus and His Laura in the Jordan Valley," *Revue Biblique* 98 (1991): 419–30.

The Jews in the valley . . . : For the story of Na'aran, see the entry by Michael Avi-Yonah in *The New Encyclopedia of Archaeological Excavations in the Holy Land,* ed. Ephraim Stern, vol. 3 (New York: Simon and Schuster, 1993), pp. 1075–76.

Felix Fabri: Felix Fabri, *The Book of the Wanderings of Brother Felix Fabri,* vol. 2 (London: Palestine Pilgrims' Text Society, 1893), pp. 175–77.

Claude Conder, in the 1870s, knew the name Hajla . . . : C. R. Conder and H. H. Kitchener, *SWP,* vol. 3, *Judea* (London: Palestine Exploration Fund, 1883), pp. 178, 213–19.

. . . an insightful scholar named Jean Louis Féderlin . . . : Yizhar Hirschfeld drew my attention to the work of Jean Louis Féderlin and cites his "Recherches sur les laures et monastères de la plaine du Jourdain et du désert de Jérusalem," *La Terre Sainte* 20 (1903).

The river of pilgrims . . . : The log of accident and crime is from W. M. Thomson, *The Land and the Book* (London: T. Nelson and Sons, 1873; originally published 1859), p. 615.

. . . a British journalist named Stephen Graham . . . : Stephen Graham, *With the Russian Pilgrims to Jerusalem* (London: Macmillan, 1913). Russian pilgrimage is one of the subjects of Derek Hopwood, *The Russian Presence in Syria and Palestine, 1843–1914* (Oxford: Clarendon Press, 1969), esp. pp. 144–46.

Great friends, those two: Material about Kitchener's early years and personality is from Trevor Royle, *The Kitchener Enigma* (London: Michael Joseph, 1985); and Philip Magnus, *Kitchener* (London: John Murray, 1958).

"It was glorious more from associations . . .": Kitchener's letter to his sister, Millie, is quoted in Royle, *The Kitchener Enigma,* p. 30.

On Christmas Eve they attended midnight mass . . . : Kitchener's account of events in Bethlehem was found among his personal papers after his death. Kitchener said the events occurred in 1875, but he was mistaken, since in December 1875 he was in Britain. The more likely date is Christmas 1874—a few weeks after he arrived in Palestine. H. H. Kitchener, "Christmas at Bethlehem," *PEQ* (January 1917): 36–39.

"He might tender his resignation . . .": Letter of William Morrison, to Walter Besant, December 11, 1876.

The PEF's letter, dated the twenty-ninth of December 1876 . . . : Letter to Conder from W. H. Dixon, chairman of the PEF.

VIII. Dead Sea, Dead Land

Claude Conder and Herbert Kitchener had been notably incurious . . . : C. R. Conder and H. H. Kitchener, *SWP,* vol. 3, *Judea* (London: Palestine Exploration Fund, 1883), p. 386. Distortions in the map are noted by Ian Blake, "El Kuseir: A Hermitage in the Wilderness of Judaea," *PEQ* (July–December 1969): 91.

What everyone noticed first was the sulfurous stench: Interviews with Aharon Oren and Arie Nissenbaum. Aharon Oren, "The Microbial Ecology of the Dead Sea," in *Advances in Microbial Ecology,* vol. 10, ed. K. C. Marshall (New York: Plenum Press, 1988), pp. 195–96; Arie Nissenbaum, "Chemical Analysis of Dead Sea Water in the 18th Century," *Journal of Chemical Education* (April 1986): 297–99.

A tenth-century geographer . . . : This is Istakhri, the first of the great Arab geographers, "a native of Persepolis . . . [who] states that he wrote his book to explain the maps which had been drawn up by a certain Baljkhi, about the year 921." Guy Le Strange, *Palestine Under the Moslems* (London: Alexander P. Watt, 1890), pp. 5, 31.

In the fourteenth century an eminent geographer . . . : Dimashki (1256–1327) was the geographer. Le Strange, *Palestine Under the Moslems,* pp. 66–67.

Felix Fabri: Felix Fabri, *The Book of the Wanderings of Brother Felix Fabri,* vol. 2 (London: Palestine Pilgrims' Text Society, 1893), pp. 150–53, 164–65, 169. Tales of the giant serpent are explained by Arie Nissenbaum, "The Dead Sea Monster," *International Journal of Salt Lake Research* 1 (1992): 1–8.

The twentieth-century geographer . . . : Changes in the water level of the Dead Sea are documented by Cippora Klein in "Morphological Evidence of Lake Level Changes, Western Shore of the Dead Sea," *Israel Journal of Earth Sciences* 31 (1982): 67–94; and in "Fluctuations of the Level of the Dead Sea," paper delivered at *International Symposium on Scientific Basis for Water-Resources Management,* Jerusalem, 1985.

Dead Sea asphalt . . . : Jacques Connan et al., "Molecular Archaeology: Export of Dead Sea Asphalt to Canaan and Egypt in the Chalcolithic-Early Bronze Age," *Geochimica et Cosmochimica Acta* 56 (1992): 2743–59; J. Rullkötter and A. Nissenbaum, "Dead Sea Asphalt in Egyptian Mummies: Molecular Evidence," *Naturwissenschaften* 75 (1988): 618–21. The eleventh-century Persian traveler Nasir-i-Khusrau spoke of the asphalt's use as an insecticide, in Le Strange, *Palestine Under the Moslems,* p. 65.

Bedouin pointed out stones . . . : E. W. G. Masterman, "Dead Sea Observations," *PEQ* (April 1902): 161.

In 1924, William Foxwell Albright . . . : W. F. Albright, "The Archaeological Results of an Expedition to Moab and the Dead Sea," *BASOR,* no. 14 (April 1924): 2–12; and "The Jordan Valley in the Bronze Age," *AASOR* 6 (1926): 57–68. A concise history of exploration of the southeastern shore is in R. Thomas Schaub and Walter E. Rast, *Bad edh-Dhra: Excavations in the Cemetery Directed by Paul W. Lapp (1965–67)* (Winona Lake, Ind.: Eisenbrauns, 1989), pp. 15–18.

They are G. H. Moore and W. G. Beek: "On the Dead Sea and Some Positions in Syria," *Journal of the Royal Geographical Society* 7 (1837): 456; "Mr. W. R. Hamilton's Anniversary Address," *Journal of the Royal Geographical Society* 9 (1839): lxiv.

Lieutenant J. F. A. Symonds . . . : J. Vardi, *Mediterranean-Dead Sea Project Historical Review* (Jerusalem: Geological Survey of Israel, 1990), p. 34.

An Irishman named Christopher Costigan . . . : John Lloyd Stephens, *Incidents of Travel in Egypt, Arabia Petraea, and the Holy Land* (Norman: University of Oklahoma Press, 1970), pp. 385–98. The story is retold by E. W. G. Masterman, "Three Early Explorers in the Dead Sea Valley," *PEQ* (January 1911): 14–19.

In 1847, Thomas Molyneux . . . : Lieut. [William] Molyneux, "Expedition to the Jordan and the Dead Sea," *Journal of the Royal Geographical Society of London* 18 (1848): 104–30. The British counsel who joined Molyneux in Jericho was the long-serving James Finn, who had also watched the boat's launching onto the lake. Finn's comments and Molyneux's prediction of ill health are in Masterman, "Three Early Explorers," pp. 25–26.

William Francis Lynch: The lieutenant wrote one account for a popular audience, a second as the official report to the navy: *Narrative of the United States' Expedition to the River Jordan and the Dead Sea* (Philadelphia: Blanchard and Lea, 1849); and *Official Report of the United States Expedition to Explore the Dead Sea and the River Jordan* (Baltimore: John Murphy, 1852). Another account was prepared by a member of the crew, Edward P. Montague, ed., *Narrative of the Late Expedition to the Dead Sea* (Philadelphia: Carey and Hart, 1849).

Akil el Hasi was the sheikh: Moshe Maoz, *Ottoman Reform in Syria and Palestine, 1840–1861* (London: Clarendon Press, 1968), pp. 138–40. Lynch believed that Akil secretly wanted the Americans to help him overthrow Turkish authorities in the territory east of the Jordan and presumably make him the new ruler. Lynch, *Narrative*, p. 369.

Another expedition, 126 years later . . . : John K. Hall and David Neev, *Final Report No. 1 on the Dead Sea Geophysical Survey* (Jerusalem: Geological Survey of Israel, 1975), pp. 6–8.

. . . a biologist named M. L. Lortet . . . : M. L. Lortet, "Researches on the Pathogenic Microbes of the Mud of the Dead Sea," *PEQ* (January 1892): 48–49. Aharon Oren, "Bacterial Activities in the Dead Sea, 1980–1991," *International Journal of Salt Lake Research* 1 (1992): 7–20.

Dr. Gurney Masterman accepted the challenge . . . : Masterman was a worthy successor to the illustrious Dr. Thomas Chaplin as a physician and a figure interested in the PEF. Like Chaplin, he worked at the Jerusalem hospital run by the London Society for the Propagation of Christianity. His reports about the Dead Sea appeared regularly in *PEQ* and were summarized by him in *PEQ* (October 1913): 192–97. On the "rediscovery" of the PEF rock, see H. W. Underhill, "Dead Sea Levels and the P. E. F. Mark," *PEQ* (January–June 1967): 46.

. . . *"eine technische Phantasie"*: Vardi, *Mediterranean-Dead Sea Project*, pp. 38–39.

IX. Last Rounds

These books, said the *Times* . . . : Issue of January 27, 1882.

"We can almost count on our fingers . . .": *The Edinburgh Review* 159 (January–April 1884): 461–62.

. . . the PEF reemployed Kitchener . . . : For this expedition, Kitchener was accompanied by geologist Edward Hull, who wrote the final report: *Mount Seir, Sinai, and Western Palestine* (London: Richard Bentley, 1885).

"He may now help himself": Quoted in Philip Magnus, *Kitchener* (London: John Murray, 1958), p. 38.

"He has no age but the prime of life . . .": G. W. Steevens, *With Kitchener to Khartum* (Edinburgh: Wm. Blackwood, 1900), pp. 45–46. This book by Steevens, a correspondent for the *Daily Mail,* went through at least twenty-two editions.

In 1916, it was decided Kitchener . . . should sail to Russia . . . : The description of his last years is drawn from Trevor Royle, *The Kitchener Enigma* (London: Michael Joseph, 1985), pp. 369–75; and David Fromkin, *A Peace to End All Peace* (New York: Avon, 1990), pp. 79–87, 216–17.

It was not his favorite war: Sir Redvers Buller was the officer with whom Warren disputed responsibility for the British retreat from the site called Spion Kop, in January 1900. Watkin W. Williams, *The Life of General Sir Charles Warren* (Oxford: Basil Blackwell, 1941), pp. 283–332. For a generally favorable evaluation of Buller, see Thomas Pakenham, *The Scramble for Africa, 1876–1912* (New York: Random House, 1991), pp. 568–75.

"As for myself, I am ready . . .": Charles Warren, "The Diamond Jubilee of the Palestine Exploration Fund," *PEQ* (April 1925): 61–65.

Samuel Clemens was a member . . . : Mark Twain, *The Innocents Abroad* (New York: New American Library, 1966), pp. 429–41; Franklin Walker, *Irreverent Pilgrims, Melville, Browne, and Mark Twain in the Holy Land* (Seattle: University of Washington Press, 1974), pp. 163–69.

Most were customers of Thomas Cook . . . : Robert Ingle, *Thomas Cook of Leicester* (Gwynedd, Wales: Headstart History, 1991).

An early Cook customer named Edwin Hodder . . . : Edwin Hodder, *On Holy Ground* (New York: Whittaker, 1878), pp. 5–6.

The 1898 Baedeker . . . : Karl Baedeker, ed., *Palestine and Syria* (Leipzig: Karl Baedeker, 1898), pp. xxxiii, xliii, 6–7. J. E. Hanauer and E. G. Masterman, *Cook's Handbook for Palestine and Syria* (London: Thos. Cook and Son, 1907), pp. 86, 96; Hodder, *On Holy Ground,* p. 122.

"Here I am in the new hotel in Jericho . . .": The letter writer was R. W. Hamilton, excavator of Hisham's Palace and head of the Palestine Department of Antiquities. See his *Letters from the Middle East by an Occasional Archaeologist* (Durham: Pentland Press, 1992), pp. 42–43.

"It is a luxuriance of ruin; . . .": Richard F. Burton and Charles F. Tyrwhitt Drake, *Unexplored Syria,* vol. 1 (London: Tinsley Brothers, 1872), p. 4.

Selected Bibliography

Books

Allen, William. *The Dead Sea, a New Route to India.* 2 vols. London: Longman, 1855.

Baedeker, Karl, ed. *Palestine and Syria.* Leipzig: Karl Baedeker, 1898.

Bartlett, John R. *Jericho.* Guildford, England: Lutterworth Press, 1982.

Bar-Yosef, Ofer. "The Last Glacial Maximum in the Mediterranean Levant." In *The World at 18,000 B.P.,* ed. C. Gamble and O. Soffer, vol. 2, pp. 58–77. London: Unwin Hyman, 1990.

———. "The Neolithic Period." In *The Archaeology of Ancient Israel,* ed. Amnon Ben-Tor, pp. 10–39. New Haven: Yale University Press, 1992.

———. "Archaeology of Palestine (Prehistoric)." In *The Anchor Bible Dictionary,* vol. 5, pp. 99–109. New York: Doubleday, 1992.

Bar-Yosef, Ofer, and Anna Belfer-Cohen, "From Sedentary Hunter-Gatherers to

Territorial Farmers in the Levant." In *Between Bands and States,* ed. Susan A. Gregg, pp. 181–202. Carbondale: Southern Illinois University Press, 1991.

Bar-Yosef, Ofer, and N. Goren-Inbar. *The Lithic Assemblages of 'Ubeidiya.* Jerusalem: Hebrew University, 1993.

Bassan, Fernande. *Carnets de Voyage en Orient (1845–1869).* Paris: Presses Universitaires de France, 1955.

Belfer-Cohen, Anna. "The Natufian Issue: A Suggestion." In *Investigations in South Levantine Prehistory, BAR International Series 457,* ed. Ofer Bar-Yosef and B. Vandermeersch (Oxford: B.A.R., 1989).

Ben-Arieh, Yehoshua. *The Rediscovery of the Holy Land in the Nineteenth Century.* Jerusalem: Magnes Press, 1983.

———. *Jerusalem in the 19th Century, the Old City.* New York: St. Martin's Press, 1984.

———. *Jerusalem in the 19th Century, Emergence of the New City.* New York: St. Martin's Press, 1986.

Besant, Walter. *The Life and Achievements of Edward Henry Palmer.* New York: Dutton, 1883.

———. *Thirty Years' Work in the Holy Land.* London: A. P. Watt and Son, 1895.

———, ed. *The Literary Remains of the Late Charles F. Tyrwhitt Drake.* London: Richard Bentley, 1877.

Bienkowski, Piotr. *Jericho in the Late Bronze Age.* Warminster, England: Aris and Phillips, 1986.

Bliss, Frederick Jones. *The Development of Palestine Exploration.* London: Hodder and Stoughton, 1906.

Boling, Robert G., and G. Ernest Wright. *Joshua.* Vol. 6 of *The Anchor Bible.* Garden City, N.Y.: Doubleday, 1982.

Burckhardt, John Lewis. *Travels in Syria and the Holy Land.* London: John Murray, 1822.

Burton, Richard F., and Charles F. Tyrwhitt Drake. *Unexplored Syria.* 2 vols. London: Tinsley Brothers, 1872.

Chateaubriand, François-René de. *Itinéraire de Paris à Jérusalem.* 2 vols. Baltimore: Johns Hopkins University Press, 1946.

Clermont-Ganneau, Charles. *Archaeological Researches in Palestine.* Vol. 2. London: Harrison and Sons, 1896.

———. *Archaeological Researches in Palestine.* Vol. 1. London: Harrison and Sons, 1899.

Conder, Claude Reignier. *Tent Work in Palestine.* 2 vols. London: Richard Bentley, 1878.

———. *A Primer of Bible Geography.* London: Sunday School Union, 1884.

———. *Syrian Stone-Lore.* London: Richard Bentley, 1886.

———. *The Survey of Eastern Palestine.* London: Palestine Exploration Fund, 1889.

———. *Palestine.* London: George Phillip, 1891.

———. *Heth and Moab.* London: Macmillan, 1892.

Conder, Claude Reignier, and H. H. Kitchener. *The Survey of Western Palestine.* Vols. 1–3. London: Palestine Exploration Fund, 1881–83.

Davies, Philip R. *Qumran.* Guildford, England: Lutterworth Press, 1982.

Davis, Moshe, and Yehoshua Ben-Arieh, eds. *With Eyes Toward Zion: Western Societies and the Holy Land.* New York: Praeger, 1991.

Desowitz, Robert S. *The Malaria Capers.* New York: Norton, 1993.

Dever, William G. "From the End of the Early Bronze Age to the Beginning of the Middle Bronze." In *Biblical Archaeology Today,* pp. 113–35. Jerusalem: Israel Exploration Society, 1985.

———. *Recent Archaeological Discoveries and Biblical Research.* Seattle: University of Washington Press, 1990.

———. "Archaeology of Palestine (Bronze-Iron Ages)." In *The Anchor Bible Dictionary,* vol. 5, pp. 109–14. New York: Doubleday, 1992.

———. "Pastoralism and the End of the Urban Early Bronze Age in Palestine." In *Pastoralism in the Levant,* ed. Ofer Bar-Yosef and Anatoly Khazanov, pp. 83–92. Madison: Prehistory Press, 1992.

Dodd, Peter, and Halim Barakat. *River Without Bridges.* Beirut: Institute for Palestine Studies, 1969.

Drower, Margaret S. *Flinders Petrie, A Life in Archaeology.* London: Victor Gollancz, 1985.

Faban, Brian M. *Rape of the Nile.* Wakefield, R.I.: Moyer Bell, 1992.

Fabri, Felix. *The Book of the Wanderings of Brother Felix Fabri.* Vol. 2. London: Palestine Pilgrims' Text Society, 1893.

Finkelstein, Israel. *The Archaeology of the Israelite Settlement.* Jerusalem: Israel Exploration Society, 1988.

Finn, Elizabeth Anne. *Reminiscences of Mrs. Finn.* London: Marshall, Morgan and Scott, (1929?).

Finnie, David H. *Pioneers East, the Early American Experience in the Middle East.* Cambridge: Harvard University Press, 1967.

Fischer, Yona, Vincent Ducourau, and Isabele Julia. *Album de Voyage, Des artistes en expedition au pays du Levant.* Paris: Seuil, 1993.

Franken, H. J., and M. L. Steiner. *Excavations in Jerusalem, 1961–1967.* Vol. 2. Oxford: Oxford University Press, 1990.

Garstang, John. *Joshua, Judges.* London: Constable, 1931.

Garstang, John, and J. B. E. Garstang. *The Story of Jericho.* 2nd ed. London: Hodder and Stoughton, 1947.

Glueck, Nelson. *The River Jordan.* Philadelphia: Jewish Publication Society, 1946.

———. *Rivers in the Desert.* Philadelphia: Jewish Publication Society, 1959.

Gottwald, Norman K. "The Israelite Settlement as a Social Revolutionary Movement." In *Biblical Archaeology Today,* pp. 34–46. Jerusalem: Israel Exploration Society, 1985.

Graham, Stephen. *With the Russian Pilgrims to Jerusalem.* London: Macmillan, 1913.

Grant, Michael. *Herod the Great.* New York: American Heritage, 1971.

Guérin, M. V. *Description géographique, historique, et archéologique de la Palestine—Samarie.* Vol. 1. Paris, 1874.

Hamilton, R. W. *Khirbat al Mafjar.* Oxford: Clarendon Press, 1959.

Hanauer, J. E., and E. G. Masterman. *Cook's Handbook for Palestine and Syria.* London: Thomas Cook and Son, 1907.

Hareuveni, Nogah. *Desert and Shepherd in Our Biblical Heritage.* Trans. Helen Frenkley. Lod, Israel: Neot Kedumin, 1991.

Hawkes, Jacquetta. *Adventurer in Archaeology, The Biography of Sir Mortimer Wheeler.* New York: St. Martin's Press, 1982.

Haynes, Alfred E. *Man-Hunting in the Desert.* London: Horace Cox, 1894.

Herold, J. Christopher. *Bonaparte in Egypt.* New York: Harper and Row, 1962.

Hirschfeld, Yizhar. "List of the Byzantine Monasteries in the Judean Desert." In *Christian Archaeology in the Holy Land,* pp. 1–89. Jerusalem: Franciscan Printing Press, 1990.

———. *The Judean Monasteries in the Byzantine Period.* New Haven: Yale University Press, 1992.

Hizmi, Hananya. "The Byzantine Church at Khirbet El-Beiyudat: Preliminary Report." In *Christian Archaeology in the Holy Land*, pp. 245–63. Jerusalem: Franciscan Printing Press, 1990.

Hoade, Eugene. *Western Pilgrims*. Jerusalem: Franciscan Printing Press, 1952.

Hobbs, Joseph J. *Bedouin Life in the Egyptian Wilderness*. Austin: University of Texas Press, 1989.

Hodder, Edwin. *On Holy Ground*. New York: Whittaker, 1878.

Hodgkin, E. C., ed. *Thomas Hodgkin Letters from Palestine, 1932–36*. London: Quartet, 1986.

Hoehner, Harold W. *Herod Antipas*. Cambridge: Cambridge University Press, 1972.

Hoeprich, Paul D., and M. Colin Jordan. *Infectious Diseases*. 4th ed. Philadelphia: Lippincott, 1989.

Holland, T. A. "Jericho." In *The Anchor Bible Dictionary*, vol. 3, pp. 723–37. New York: Doubleday, 1992.

Hopwood, Derek. *The Russian Presence in Syria and Palestine, 1843–1914*. Oxford: Clarendon Press, 1969.

Horn, Siegfried H. "The Discovery of the Moabite Stone." In *The Word of the Lord Shall Go Forth*, ed. Carol L. Meyers and M. O'Connor, pp. 497–505. Winona Lake, Ind.: Eisenbrauns, 1983.

Hourani, Albert. *A History of the Arab Peoples*. London: Faber and Faber, 1991.

Hull, Edward. *Mount Seir, Sinai, and Western Palestine*. London: Richard Bentley, 1885.

Hunt, E. D. *Holy Land Pilgrimage in the Later Roman Empire, A.D. 312–460*. Oxford: Clarendon Press, 1982.

Ingle, Robert. *Thomas Cook of Leicester*. Gwynedd, Wales: Headstart History, 1991.

Irwin, Robert. "The Orient and the West from Bonaparte to T. E. Lawrence." In *The Orientalists: Delacroix to Matisse*, ed. MaryAnne Stevens, pp. 24–26. London: Royal Academy of Arts, 1984.

Kenyon, Kathleen M. *Beginning in Archaeology*. London: Phoenix House, 1952.

———. *Digging Up Jericho*. London: Ernest Benn, 1957.

———. *Excavations at Jericho*. Vol. 1, *The Tombs Excavated in 1952–4*. Jerusalem: British School of Archaeology in Jerusalem, 1960.

———. *Excavations at Jericho*. Vol. 2, *The Tombs Excavated in 1955–8*. London: British School of Archaeology in Jerusalem, 1964.

———. *Amorites and Canaanites.* London: Oxford University Press, 1966.

———. *Archaeology in the Holy Land.* 5th ed. Nashville: Thomas Nelson, 1979.

———. *Excavations at Jericho.* Vol. 3, *The Architecture and Stratigraphy of the Tell, Text,* ed. Thomas A. Holland. London: British School of Archaeology in Jerusalem, 1981.

———. *Excavations at Jericho.* Vol. 3, *Plates.* London: British School of Archaeology in Jerusalem, 1981.

Kenyon, Kathleen M., and T. A. Holland. *Excavations at Jericho.* Vol. 4, *The Pottery Types Series and Other Finds.* London: British School of Archaeology in Jerusalem, 1982.

———. *Excavations at Jericho.* Vol. 5, *The Pottery Phases of the Tell and Other Finds.* London: British School of Archaeology in Jerusalem, 1983.

King, Peter. *The Viceroy's Fall.* London: Sidgwick and Jackson, 1986.

Kreiger, Barbara. *Living Waters.* New York: Continuum, 1988.

Kuspit, Donald. "A Mighty Metaphor: The Analogy of Archaeology and Psychoanalysis." In *Sigmund Freud and Art,* ed. Lynn Gamwell and Richard Wells, pp. 133–51. New York: State University of New York, 1989.

Landau, Jacob M. *Abdul-Hamid's Palestine.* Jerusalem: Carta, 1979.

Lewis, Norman N. *Nomads and Settlers in Syria and Jordan, 1800–1980.* Cambridge: Cambridge University Press, 1987.

Luke, Harry Charles, and Edward Keith-Roach. *The Handbook of Palestine and Trans-Jordan.* 2nd ed. London: Macmillan, 1930.

Lynch, W. F. *Narrative of the United States' Expedition to the River Jordan and the Dead Sea.* Philadelphia: Blanchard and Lea, 1849.

———. *Naval Life; or, the Midshipman.* New York: Charles Scribner, 1851.

———. *Official Report of the United States Expedition to Explore the Dead Sea and the River Jordan.* Baltimore: John Murphy, 1852.

Magnus, Philip. *Kitchener.* London: John Murray, 1958.

Maoz, Moshe. *Ottoman Reform in Syria and Palestine, 1840–1861.* Oxford: Clarendon Press, 1968.

———. *Palestinian Leadership in the West Bank.* London: Frank Cass, 1984.

Matthers, John M. "Excavations by the Palestine Exploration Fund at Tell el-Hesi, 1890–1892." In *Tell el-Hesi: The Site and the Expedition,* ed. Bruce T. Dahlberg and Kevin G. O'Connell, pp. 37–67. Winona Lake, Ind.: Eisenbrauns, 1989.

Mazar, Amihai. *Archaeology of the Land of the Bible, 10,000–586 B.C.E.* New York: Doubleday, 1990.

Melville, Herman. *Journals.* Ed. Howard C. Horsford with Lynn Horth. Evanston: Northwestern University Press, 1989.

Montague, Edward P., ed. *Narrative of the Late Expedition to the Dead Sea.* Philadelphia: Carey and Hart, 1849.

Moorey, P. R. S. *A Century of Biblical Archaeology.* Louisville: Westminster/John Knox, 1991.

Moorey, P. R. S., and P. J. Parr. *Archaeology in the Levant.* Warminster, England: Aris and Phillips, 1978.

Moran, William L. *The Amarna Letters.* Baltimore: Johns Hopkins University Press, 1992.

Morris, Benny. *The Birth of the Palestinian Refugee Problem, 1947–1949.* Cambridge: Cambridge University Press, 1987.

Mutawi, Samir A. *Jordan in the 1967 War.* Cambridge: Cambridge University Press, 1987.

Neophitos of Cyprus. *Extracts from Annals of Palestine, 1821–1841* (reprinted from *Journal of the Palestine Oriental Society,* 1938). Trans. S. N. Spyridon. Jerusalem: Ariel, 1979.

Netzer, Ehud. "A Byzantine Monastery at Nuseib 'Uweishira, West of Jericho." In *Christian Archaeology in the Holy Land New Discoveries,* pp. 191–200. Jerusalem: Franciscan Printing Press, 1990.

———. "The Hasmonean Palaces in Eretz-Israel." In *Biblical Archaeology Today, 1990,* pp. 126–36. Jerusalem: Israel Exploration Society, 1993.

Oren, Aharon. "Microbiological Studies in the Dead Sea: 1892–1992." In *The Dead Sea.* Forthcoming.

Owen, Roger. *The Middle East in the World Economy, 1800–1914.* London: Methuen, 1981.

Pakenham, Thomas. *The Scramble for Africa, 1876–1912.* New York: Random House, 1991.

Palestine Exploration Fund. *Our Work in Palestine.* London: Bentley and Son, 1877.

———. *The City and the Land.* London: Macmillan, 1892.

Palmer, E. H. *The Desert of the Exodus.* New York: Harper and Brothers, 1872.

Perez, Nissan N. *Focus East, Early Photography in the Near East (1839–1885).* New York: Abrams, 1988.

Perowne, Stewart. *The Life and Times of Herod the Great.* London: Hodder and Stoughton, 1956.

Porath, Yehoshua. *The Emergence of the Palestinian-Arab National Movement, 1918–1929.* London: Frank Cass, 1974.

Porter, Whitworth. *History of the Corps of Royal Engineers.* 2 vols. London: Longmans, Green, 1889.

Pritchard, James B. *Ancient Near Eastern Texts.* 3rd ed. Princeton: Princeton University Press, 1969.

Rajak, Tessa. *Josephus.* London: Gerald Duckworth, 1983.

Rice, Edward. *Captain Sir Richard Francis Burton.* New York: HarperPerennial, 1991.

Robinson, Edward, and Eli Smith. *Biblical Researches in Palestine, Mount Sinai, and Arabia Petraea.* London: John Murray, 1841.

Royle, Trevor. *The Kitchener Enigma.* London: Michael Joseph, 1985.

Rubinstein, Danny. *The People of Nowhere.* New York: Times Books, 1991.

Said, Edward W. *Orientalism.* New York: Vintage, 1979.

Saulcy, F. de. *Voyage autour de la Mer Morte.* Vol. 2. Paris: Gide et J. Baudry, 1853.

———. *Voyage en Terre Sainte.* Vol. 1. Paris, 1865.

Sayce, A. H. *Reminiscences.* London: Macmillan, 1923.

Schaub, R. Thomas, and Walter E. Rast. *Bad edh-Dhra: Excavations in the Cemetery Directed by Paul W. Lapp (1965–67).* Winona Lake, Ind.: Eisenbrauns, 1989.

Seetzen, [Ulrich J.]. *A Brief Account of the Countries Adjoining the Lake of Tiberias, the Jordan, and the Dead Sea.* Bath: Palestine Association of London, 1810.

Sellin, Ernst, and Carl Watzinger. *Jericho Die Ergebnisse der Ausgrabungen.* Leipzig, 1913. Reprinted, Osnabruck: Otto Zeller Verlag, 1973.

Shaw, Stanford J., and Ezel Kural Shaw. *History of the Ottoman Empire and Modern Turkey.* Vol. 2. Cambridge: Cambridge University Press, 1977.

Shepherd, Naomi. *The Zealous Intruders, The Western Rediscovery of Palestine.* San Francisco: Harper and Row, 1987.

Silberman, Neil Asher. *Digging for God and Country.* New York: Knopf, 1982.

———. *Between Past and Present.* New York: Henry Holt, 1989.

Steevens, G. W. *With Kitchener to Khartum.* London: Wm. Blackwood, 1900.

Stephens, John Lloyd. *Incidents of Travel in Egypt, Arabia Petraea, and the Holy Land.* Ed. Victor Wolfgang von Hagen. Norman: University of Oklahoma Press, 1970.

Stern, Ephraim, ed. *The New Encyclopedia of Archaeological Excavations in the Holy Land.* New York: Simon and Schuster, 1993.

Stevens, MaryAnne. *The Orientalists: Delacroix to Matisse, European Painters in North Africa and the North East.* London: Royal Academy of Arts, 1984.

Stisted, Georgiana M. *The True Life of Capt. Sir Richard F. Burton.* New York: D. Appleton, 1897.

Le Strange, Guy. *Palestine Under the Moslems.* London: Alexander P. Watt, 1890.

Theoderich. *Guide to the Holy Land.* Trans. Aubrey Stewart. New York: Ithaca Press, 1986.

Thomson, W. M. *The Land and the Book.* London: T. Nelson and Sons, 1873. (Originally published 1859.)

Tibawi, A. L. *British Interests in Palestine, 1800–1901.* Oxford: Oxford University Press, 1961.

Tristram, H. B. *The Land of Israel; a Journal of Travels in Palestine.* London: Society for Promoting Christian Knowledge, 1866.

———. *The Survey of Western Palestine, The Fauna and Flora of Palestine.* London: Palestine Exploration Fund, 1885.

Tubb, Jonathan, and Rupert L. Chapman. *Archaeology and the Bible.* London: British Museum Publications, 1990.

Vaglieri, Laura Veccia. "The Patriarchal and Umayyad Caliphates." In *The Cambridge History of Islam,* ed. P. M. Holt et al., vol. 1a, pp. 57–103. Cambridge: Cambridge University Press, 1970.

Van de Velde, C. W. M. *Narrative of a Journey through Syria and Palestine in 1851 and 1852.* Edinburgh: Wm. Blackwood, 1854.

de Vaux, Roland. "On the Right and Wrong Uses of Archaeology." In *Near Eastern Archaeology in the Twentieth Century,* ed. J. A. Sanders. Garden City, N.Y.: Doubleday, 1970.

Vercoutter, Jean. *The Search for Ancient Egypt.* Trans. Ruth Sharman. New York: Abrams, 1992.

Vikan, Gary. *Byzantine Pilgrimage Art.* Washington: Dumbarton Oaks, 1982.

Volney, C. F. *Voyage en Syrie et en Egypte.* Paris, 1787.

Walker, Franklin. *Irreverent Pilgrims, Melville, Browne, and Mark Twain in the Holy Land.* Seattle: University of Washington Press, 1974.

Walker, M. *Pioneers of Public Health.* New York: Macmillan, 1930.

Warren, Charles. *Underground Jerusalem.* London: Richard Bentley, 1876.

Warren, Charles, and Claude Conder. *The Survey of Western Palestine, Jerusalem.* London: Palestine Exploration Fund, 1884.

Wheeler, Margaret. *Walls of Jericho.* London: Readers Union, 1958.

Wilken, Robert L. *The Land Called Holy, Palestine in Christian History and Thought.* New Haven: Yale University Press, 1992.

Wilkinson, John. *Jerusalem Pilgrims.* Warminster, England: Aris and Phillips, 1977.

Williams, Watkin W. *The Life of General Sir Charles Warren.* Oxford: Basil Blackwell, 1941.

Wilson, Charles W. *Ordnance Survey of Jerusalem.* London, 1865. Reprinted, Jerusalem: Ariel, 1980.

———. *Picturesque Palestine.* 2 vols. New York: Appleton, 1881.

Wilson, Charles W., and Charles Warren. *The Recovery of Jerusalem.* London: Richard Bentley, 1871.

Wilson, Mary C. *King Abdullah, Britain, and the Making of Jordan.* Cambridge: Cambridge University Press, 1987.

Wright, G. Ernest. "The Phenomenon of American Archaeology in the Near East." In *Near Eastern Archaeology in the Twentieth Century,* ed. J. A. Sanders, pp. 3–41. Garden City, N.Y.: Doubleday, 1970.

Wright, Thomas, ed. *Early Travels in Palestine.* London: Henry G. Bohn, 1848.

Ziegler, Philip. *Omburman.* London: Collins, 1973.

Periodicals

Aharoni, Yohanan. "Nothing Early and Nothing Late: Re-Writing Israel's Conquest." *Biblical Archaeologist* (May 1976): 55–76.

Albright, W. F. "The Archaeological Results of an Expedition to Moab and the Dead Sea." *Bulletin of the American Schools of Oriental Research,* no. 14 (April 1924): 2–12.

Anati, Emmanuel. "Prehistoric Trade and the Puzzle of Jericho." *Bulletin of the American Schools of Oriental Research,* no. 167 (October 1962): 25–31.

Bar-Yosef, Ofer. "The Walls of Jericho: An Alternative Interpretation." *Current Anthropology* 27, no. 2 (April 1986): 157–62.

———. "Prehistory of the Jordan Rift." *Israel Journal of Earth Sciences* 36 (1987): 107–19.

———. "The PPNA in the Levant—an Overview." *Paléorient* 15, no. 1 (1989): 57–63.

Bar-Yosef, Ofer, and Anna-Belfer-Cohen. "The Origins of Sedentism and Farming Communities in the Levant." *Journal of World Prehistory* 3 (1989): 447–98.

Bar-Yosef, Ofer, and F. Valla. "The Natufian Culture and the Origin of the Neolithic in the Levant." *Current Anthropology* 31, no. 4 (August–October 1990): 433–36.

Bar-Yosef, Ofer, et al. "The Excavations in Kebara Cave, Mt. Carmel." *Current Anthropology* 33, no. 5 (December 1992): 497–550.

Bar-Yosef, Ofer, and Bernard Vandermeersch. "Modern Humans in the Levant." *Scientific American* (April 1993): 94–100.

Bennett, Boyce M., Jr. "The Search for Israelite Gilgal." *Palestine Exploration Quarterly* (July–December 1972): 111–22.

Cauvin, Marie-Claire, and Jacques Cauvin. "La Séquence Néolithique PPNB au Levant Nord." *Paléorient* 19, no. 1 (1993): 23–28.

Clutton-Brock, Juliet. "The Primary Food Animals of the Jericho Tell from the Proto-Neolithic to the Byzantine Period." *Levant* 3 (1971): 41–55.

Conder, Claude Reignier. "In Memoriam, Charles F. Tyrwhitt Drake." *Palestine Exploration Quarterly* (July 1874): 131–34.

———. "Tour of Their Royal Highnesses Princes Albert Victor and George of Wales in Palestine." *Palestine Exploration Quarterly* (July 1882): 214–34.

———. "The Exodus." *Palestine Exploration Quarterly* (April 1883): 79–90.

Connan, Jacques, Arie Nissenbaum, and Daniel Dessort. "Molecular Archaeology: Export of Dead Sea Asphalt to Canaan and Egypt in the Chalcolithic-Early Bronze Age." *Geochimica et Cosmochimica Acta* 56 (1992): 2743–59.

Cook, Stanley A. "The German Excavations at Jericho." *Palestine Exploration Quarterly* (January 1910): 54–79.

Danin, Avinoam. "Palaeoclimates in Israel: Evidence from Weathering Patterns of Stones in and near Archaeological Sites." *Bulletin of the American Schools of Oriental Research,* no. 259 (August 1985): 33–41.

Dever, William G. "Kathleen Kenyon (1906–1978): A Tribute." *Bulletin of the American Schools of Oriental Research,* no. 232 (Fall 1978): 3–4.

———. "The Impact of the 'New Archaeology' on Syro-Palestinian Archaeology."

Bulletin of the American Schools of Oriental Research, no. 242 (Spring 1981): 15–29.

———. "The Middle Bronze Age, The Zenith of the Urban Canaanite Era." *Biblical Archaeologist* (September 1987): 148–77.

———. "Archaeology and Israelite Origins." *Bulletin of the American Schools of Oriental Research,* no. 279 (August 1990): 89–95.

———. "The Chronology of Syria-Palestine in the Second Millennium B.C.E.: A Review of Current Issues." *Bulletin of the American Schools of Oriental Research,* no. 288 (November 1992): 1–25.

———. "What Remains of the House that Albright Built?" *Biblical Archaeologist* (March 1993): 25–35.

Dorrell, Peter G. "The Spring at Jericho from Early Photographs." *Palestine Exploration Quarterly* (July–December 1993): 95–114.

Drower, Margaret S. "W. M. Flinders Petrie, the Palestine Exploration Fund, and Tell El-Hesi." *Palestine Exploration Quarterly* (July–December 1990): 87–95.

Elath, Eliahu. "Claude Reignier Conder." *Palestine Exploration Quarterly* (January–June 1965): 21–41.

Franken, H. J. "The Problem of Identification in Biblical Archaeology." *Palestine Exploration Quarterly* (January–June 1976): 3–11.

Freund, Raphael, et al. "Age and Rate of the Sinistral Movement along the Dead Sea Rift." *Nature* 220, no. 6164 (1968): 253–55.

Freund, Raphael, et al. "The Shear along the Dead Sea Rift." *Philosophical Transactions of the Royal Society of London, Series A* 267 (1970): 107–30.

Fritz, Volkmar. "Conquest or Settlement? The Early Iron Age in Palestine." *Biblical Archaeologist* (June 1987): 84–100.

Garstang, John. "The Date of the Destruction of Jericho." *Palestine Exploration Quarterly* (April 1927): 96–100.

Gibson, Shimon. "The Holy Land in the Sights of the Explorer's Camera: The Photographs of the Palestine Exploration Fund." *Palestine Exploration Quarterly.* Forthcoming.

Hachlili, Rachel. "The Goliath Family in Jericho: Funerary Inscriptions from a First Century A.D. Jewish Monumental Tomb." *Bulletin of the American Schools of Oriental Research,* no. 235 (Summer 1979): 31–65.

———. "A Second Temple Period Jewish Necropolis in Jericho." *Biblical Archaeologist* (Fall 1980): 235–40.

Hadas, Gideon. "Where was the Harbour of En-Gedi Situated?" *Israel Exploration Journal* 43 (1993): 45–49.

Hirschfeld, Yizhar. "Gerasimus and His Laura in the Jordan Valley." *Revue Biblique* 98 (1991): 419–30.

Ingholt, Harold. "Charles Clermont-Ganneau." *Revue Archéologique* (May–June 1923): 342–45.

———. "Bibliographie de Charles Clermont-Ganneau." *Revue Archéologique* (July–December 1923): 139–58.

Kirkbride, Diana. "Five Seasons at the Pre-Pottery Neolithic Village of Beidha in Jordan." *Palestine Exploration Quarterly* (January–June 1966): 8–88.

———. "Beidha 1965: An Interim Report." *Palestine Exploration Quarterly* (January–June 1967): 5–13.

Kislev, Mordechai E., and Ofer Bar-Yosef. "The Legumes: the Earliest Domesticated Plants in the Near East?" *Current Anthropology* 29, no. 1 (February 1988): 175–79.

Kislev, Mordechai E., Ofer Bar-Yosef, and Avi Gopher. "Early Neolithic Domesticated and Wild Barley from the Netiv Hagdud Region in the Jordan Valley." *Israel Journal of Botany* 35 (1986): 197–201.

Klein, Cippora. "Morphological Evidence of Lake Level Changes, Western Shore of the Dead Sea." *Israel Journal of Earth Sciences* 31 (1982): 67–94.

Lipman, V. D. "The Origins of the Palestine Exploration Fund." *Palestine Exploration Quarterly* (January–June 1988): 45–54.

Molyneux, Lieut. [William]. "Expedition to the Jordan and the Dead Sea." *The Journal of the Royal Geographical Society of London* 18 (1848): 104–30.

Moorey, P. R. S. "Kathleen Kenyon and Palestinian Archaeology." *Palestine Exploration Quarterly* (January–June 1979): 3–10.

———. "British Women in Near Eastern Archaeology: Kathleen Kenyon and the Pioneers." *Palestine Exploration Quarterly* (July–December 1992): 91–100.

Muilenburg, James. "The Site of Ancient Gilgal." *Bulletin of the American Schools of Oriental Research,* no. 140 (December 1955): pp. 11–27.

Netzer, Ehud. "The Hasmonean and Herodian Winter Palaces at Jericho." *Israel Exploration Journal* 25 (1975): 89–100.

———. "The Winter Palaces of the Judean Kings at Jericho at the End of the Second Temple Period." *Bulletin of the American Schools of Oriental Research,* no. 228 (December 1977): 1–13.

Netzer, Ehud, and Eric M. Meyers. "Preliminary Report on the Joint Jericho Excavation Project." *Bulletin of the American Schools of Oriental Research,* no. 228 (December 1977): 15–27.

Nissenbaum, Arie. "The Dead Sea—A Gate to Hell?" *Salinet* (March 1993): 53–54.

Nochlin, Linda. "The Imaginary Orient." *Art in America* (May 1983): 118–31, 187–91.

Noy, Tamar, et al. "Gilgal, A Pre-Pottery Neolithic A Site in the Lower Jordan Valley." *Israel Exploration Journal* 30 (1980): 63–82.

Prag, Kay. "The Intermediate Early Bronze-Middle Bronze Age Sequences at Jericho and Tell Iktanu Reviewed." *Bulletin of the American Schools of Oriental Research*, no. 264 (November 1986): 61–72.

Richard, Suzanne. "The Early Bronze Age, The Rise and Collapse of Urbanism." *Biblical Archaeologist* (March 1987): 22–43.

Rullkötter, J., and A. Nissenbaum. "Dead Sea Asphalt in Egyptian Mummies: Molecular Evidence." *Naturwissenschaften* 75 (1988): 618–21.

Russell, Kenneth W. "The Earthquake Chronology of Palestine and Northwest Arabia from the 2nd through the Mid-8th Century A.D." *Bulletin of the American Schools of Oriental Research*, no. 260 (Fall 1985): 37–59.

Shanks, Hershel. "Kenyon Report." *Biblical Archaeology Review* (July–August 1991): 4–10.

Silberman, Neil A. "Visions of the Future: Albright in Jerusalem, 1919–1929." *Biblical Archaeologist* (March 1993): 8–16.

Ussishkin, David. "Notes on the Fortifications of the Middle Bronze II Period at Jericho and Shechem." *Bulletin of the American Schools of Oriental Research*, no. 276 (November 1989): 29–53.

Vincent, H. "Les fouilles allemandes à Jericho." *Revue Biblique* 6 (1909): 270–79.

Wilkes, John. "Kathleen Kenyon in Roman Britain." *Palestine Exploration Quarterly* (July–December 1992): 101–8.

Wood, Bryant G. "Did the Israelites Conquer Jericho? A New Look at the Archaeological Evidence." *Biblical Archaeology Review* (March–April 1990): 44–57.

Zertal, Adam. "Israel Enters Canaan—Following the Pottery Trail." *Biblical Archaeology Review* (September–October 1991): 28–47.

Zeuner, F. E. "The Goats of Early Jericho." *Palestine Exploration Quarterly* (January–April 1955): 70–75.

———. "Dog and Cat in the Neolithic of Jericho." *Palestine Exploration Quarterly* (January–June 1958): 52–55.

Acknowledgments

If not for the support of friends, I might not have begun the writing of this book and surely would not have finished it. If not for Holly Selby, my wife, the project would have been even more difficult. She, more than anyone else, shared the travails and the pleasures; she has made generous gifts of patience, enthusiasm, and love.

Marian Wood, executive editor at Henry Holt and Company, was willing to share my risks. Deborah Harris, my literary agent, offered her confidence and encouragement. I owe much to David Brown for his insights about biography, adventure, and the art of writing.

During my stays in London, Patricia Allemonière, Sheila MacVicar, and Richard and Susana O'Mara were generous hosts. Dr. Rupert Chapman and Shimon Gibson unlocked every door for me at the Palestine Exploration Fund, opened every box, and exhumed every photograph. The late John Brinton gave me free reign in his remarkable private library and home.

I want also to thank Mary Curtius, Steve Luxenberg, George Moffett,

Carol Morello, Mark Reutter, Carol Rosenberg, and Douglas Struck. They offered support in the Middle East, on the road, in the United States, or by long-distance telephone. Help also came from Peter Bowe, Saeb Erakat, Sir Anthony Lousada, and Dr. Aharon Oren. Dr. Hans Goedicke has for many years offered provocative conversation about the Middle East, ancient and modern.

Yael Ashkenazi, Danna Bethlehem, and Julie Blum were assistants in the Jerusalem bureau of the *Baltimore Sun* and worked as researchers for me in the West Bank and Israel, even before I knew what I was researching. Sue Trowbridge provided valuable help in the United States. The maps were the expert work of Ann Rebecca Feild.

I am especially grateful to the editors of the *Baltimore Sun* for sending me to the Middle East and, then, for allowing me to stay and stay. I also thank them for their granting me a generous leave of absence that allowed me to complete this book.

Thanks, too, to Jeff and Anne Price for suggesting I make a first visit to Jerusalem.

I made the trip. Then we went to Jericho.

Index